BIGGER THAN LIFE AT THE EDGE OF THE CITY

A NOVEL

by
GENE GREGORITS

End of 2014 I'm abducted by men with shotguns and slung in jail with a small army of child molesters. Following year and the year after that, I'm still in there, awaiting trial, while my family and friends get to work dissolving any possibility of a future that I would ever have. I grew my hair down past my shoulders and wrote a book, *Bigger Than Life At the Edge of the City*, which did not contain the remorse that a team of probing state prosecutors and defense attorneys were demanding. Both sides had the same idea: to get me the maximum sentence allowed by Florida law, which was 20 years. *No remorse* made that goal completely possible.

I gave them some 400 handwritten pages of *no remorse*.

Bigger was a book which appeared to them, as it appeared to all thoughtless readers (the only kind it's ever had) to be about degeneracy and meanness and failure. The book was actually about *Time*. It was about death and mostly it was about oblivion: the passage of *Time*.

(Nothing, if you stop to consider it, nothing so remorseless as Time.)

Time, in my story, was the Atlantic ocean, and the Gulf of Mexico, in the year of 2012. *Time* was Tropical Storm Debbie rising out of the Gulf to baptize me in the excreta of the most wretched people on earth, as I swam above the wretched land where I had fallen.

Time was Hurricane Sandy rising up out of the Atlantic to drag New York City into its darkest hours since 9/11, amputating the island City and its outer boroughs from the outside world, and eventually from much of its own history.

I'd been stranded there -ostensibly as a Floridian - at the very end of it, during the cleanup process, and a few years later, when I was in the process of capitalizing so icily on the New York storm in yet another gory novel of warts-and-all street picaresque, I was powerless to ignore the rapidly amassing truth, the assault of all erosion. I knew I'd be turning 40 in captivity. Then 43, 45, 48, etc. If I was released at all. Time washes away everything.

Everywhere I turned I was confronted by the demoralizing realities of Time, by crudest and most denuded existence. I was experiencing a flood of this, and this, and this. Upon finishing the novel, I felt I'd hit It back square in Its face.

My first good novel.

A right proper novel.

It was more than good: it was actually kinda great. Because it was *about* something.

Something universal.

So the world might finally *know* me.

(The universality of *Dog Days* proves elusive for most, particularly women but most men, also. It is there, nonetheless, revealed in clever, well-timed bursts which lend that book, my only financially significant publication, whatever lasting appeal it can be said to have.)

(And after 40 or 50 thousand copies have entered circulation, yes, yes it can be said.)

"*Time!* Hear it for yourself!" James Leo Herlihy wrote in 1965's *Midnight Cowboy*. "Time is a Colossus, and he's marching up Broadway! Can't you hear him coming?"

Bigger Than Life was a violent New York street hustle psychodrama that riffed on the universe, death, Time. It was cosmic sleaze, like a more pop-culturally-fixated *Tropic of Cancer*, with some semblance of a plot: the fight to get back to Florida, and to my cat.

Time! Time! Time! I couldn't wait to read the word over and over again, finally vindicated! In one orgasmically grateful book review after another! Reviewers left *fuckstunned* by my hyper-visceral prose uprising! To view in all that celebration real B&W evidence of my vision, to experience my most fevered paroxysms to date through the eyes and in the examinations of the smartest, hippest literary critics in the world. My worst enemies would be swept away in my flood of Death and Time, infected by my river of blood, left swooning, ultimately, in the foamy salinity of *Bigger's* high tides.

Of course, the book alienated even my dearest sympathizers, while richly satisfying a necrophiliac, dandified horde of enemies. And as for the critics: it didn't reach a single one: hip, great, or otherwise. It was an expensive silence which greeted me, after two solid years of smuggling it in small portions out of Apalachee Prison, and exhausting the patience of its faithful publisher, Edward Sullivan-Honauer of the Providence noiserock band Finished. (Ed later absconded with my sweetheart Annapurna, the only *civilized* woman I'd known in a decade -meaning that she'd read Céline- and also with my publishing outfit Monastrell Books; he buried both of them.)

I remember waiting... waiting for years... *to hear it coming!*

The spot-on observations and uncanny deconstructions of my Time/Tide/Death masterpiece!

A few amateur reviews surfaced on the Internet, on "blogs".

None of them used the word *time* once.

Some people liked the book, among the very few able to purchase it before it was mysteriously yanked from the Amazon website. A free electronic version was offered some months afterward, circumventing the yank. *Bigger* continues to circulate, but it doesn't matter. No one sees it. No *hearts* for its horrors; no *eyes* for its terrible beauty.

All you see is the splatter.
And now you can not see *Bigger* again.

Gene Gregorits
St. Petersburg, FL
1/3/2025

INTRODUCTION

The bigger picture: it was as much the cursed ground I'd landed on as the domestic massacres I'd fled that forced me to seek out the intracoastal fantasia. And it was effortless, immediate, this transition from brutal excremental to pure permanent hallucination; I simply went to sleep and remained there, establishing a kind of beachhead of the mind, submitting fully to what I can only describe as a *psychedelic* despair, and for all my tragedy – or rather, *because* of my tragedy – the St. Pete Beach deathtrip was *the* big haunt, it was *the* end of the road, and if I'd overdosed, if I'd been murdered, if I'd drowned, the truth remains that I could not possibly have asked for a finer climax to 20 years lived in service of divine escape at any mortal price. When I hit St. Pete Beach, when I hit my nocturnal stride in the brokedown hurricane *streets* of St. Pete Beach, I understood that it was indeed the *exact* moment I'd sought from the very beginning... the moment captured, sustained, a living Polaroid of the perfect afterlife, and I learned how to swim in it, I could coast in it, float in it, dissolve in it to the point of expiration, or pull back at the last second if I so chose. It was a place, a time, a way, to drift from concrete to cloudstuff, uninhibited, unassisted, and completely without pretense.

It began as a ghoulish experiment set to Big Star's *Third* – lost and toxic – and ended in hyper-violent disgrace, a scourging in broad daylight, but a SMALL price for all my psychedelic tropical wasteland. March April May June July August of 2012 when the black surf met the black sand met the black sky and all the rolling black did whisper soothing demon gibberish to me, with or without sex/dope/drink, with or without the heartsick vacant morbidity of Alex Chilton, with or without the conscious thought or spiritual presence of Kerouac / Lovecraft / Melville: the edge is the edge, it will not be denied and the sensible know to stop at flirting, while I was pregnant with it in my bones.

Contrary to popular belief, you *can* fall off the sand, and knowing that cosmic dread placed me both in orbit and in handcuffs. More'n once. More'n I can even remember. And inside, the whole time, *inside* I was singing my own horrible music, more'n halfway expecting the earth to split open beneath me, and *wanting it to.*

Bigger Than Life at the Edge of the City is about what happened the day it finally did. This is what came *after* the storm.

After ALL the storms.

- Gene Gregorits

(FADE IN)

September - October 2012

When the shining city is at hand, a special slum will be built for me and my meanness. I will be the person, if that's what I am, in the slum; there will be one of everything; one rat, one tin can. The shining city will beckon in the distance. The shadow of the Bakunin monument will not quite stretch to my door. In the evening, the sound of happy syndicalist badminton finals will be borne to me on a sweet wind that sours as it enters my slum. I will behave poorly.
Thomas McGuane, *92 in the Shade*

I'd been to Australia.
Melbourne.
Two weeks.
Methamphetamine.

A scene at the airport with the girl: Rebecca. Dead ringer for Sofia Coppola, didn't everyone say?

But fat. Quite: I'd been lonely back on the beach, hadn't I? And it seemed we made a nice couple. I'm not so hard to please.

Am I?

And so, at customs, a well-to-do man, a birdlike man in a faun colored sports jacket, did collapse and split his head open.

The epileptic seizing, the blood all over the lacquered floor, Rebecca waving to me at the end of the long corridor, crying.

I did nothing to assist the fallen man; what's more, I stepped *over* him to prolong the moment with poor Bec.

She couldn't see the crisis.

I remember wanting to tell her, or maybe wanting to NOT tell her but for her to simply know, *without being told*. I remember having only the faintest awareness of my being petulant, silently petulant at having been abandoned: "Look, Bec! Look at the LATEST thing! We can't even say goodbye, can we? Get used to it! That's our future, a lifetime of talking monkeys, and defective ones at that, so that we can't have a civilized fucking moment! I'll think of something!"

I'd been *abandoned* to all the blood, I felt that way when I realized what it all meant, what it meant that she could not see the crisis. The man grunted and pissed and belched. Bec stood safely at the edge of the food court, tormented by my promises and crying the way you're supposed to at an airport: a normal goodbye, as far as appearances went.

But mine, blood soaked, now smelling of fresh shit, was mine.

I bought three pints of Jack Daniels at the duty-free with my last Australian bills. The flight was long, 15 hours or so, and then I was in LA, trying to call Bec from a phone at the boarding gate: another 6 to Tampa.

I stayed drunk, fleeing the torrents of guilt for having abandoned Sam to a person I knew well to be unfit as a cat-sitter: a juvenile delinquent, and more importantly, a schizophrenic, the SPC Christopher Cope.

I wrote (badly) in a small Chinese notebook, a parting gift from Bec.

It was handmade.

At Tampa International I begged cab fare - $30 - from a pair of traveling businessmen. (You can make a small fortune, begging in airports, if you care to develop a bit as an actor. I observed then, in a manic state, that you can enjoy great success in any endeavor which you attack completely, which you approach with an irrational edge, the true edge, the passion, which is so rare in today's karaoke culture, will create illusions which are as enduring as they must be, invisible lines of opportunity which can necessarily exist for that most aberrant man, that throwback *"sincerist."* In essence, I sensed that my business had failed, and my only hope was in brutal hustling.)

The cabs wanted $45 for the long ride, which led to my placement in a "shuttle bus," which was neither a cab nor a bus, but a minivan already populated by a pair of young women, Irish girls, bound also for St. Pete Beach.

STINK: that's what sums up the entire experience for me, of ARRIVAL...the freak place in the morning, making a bid on some kind of recognizable normalcy, but this is not possible - the reclaimed lawn water, the palpable malevolence of rotting vegetation clinging to your skin, the threat of a good time... a clammy morning, early September, early Gulf Coast morning stink.

The threat of a good time: we sped across the first blaze of blue water, Tampa Bay, like a theme park ride. The girls squealed and whispered and snapped photos, and then we were within St. Pete city limits, St. Pete just as naked in the morning as Waukesha or Williamette or Baltimore, hot but "naked" in a dangerous manner, "naked" meaning the heavy salination of alien waters, and hangover, and a new ennui. This is nothing to do with the rugged utilitarianism, the organized primality, of the Northern states, the cold and banal landlocked states I knew so well.

I was wearing a black suit and biker boots: I smelled like a toxic chemical spill. The girls spoke of their lodgings, and I volunteered the following: "The Postcard's really fucking swanky. Try to get the Jack Kerouac room." Even in their fear, the bristling young cunts could not withhold eye rolling and lip-making, but such impudent expressions are typical of European vacationers (and besides, I must now correct myself here and properly identify them as the cunting young *Scottish* girls they certainly were).

The squalid residential depravity on display through the van windows included old women in flower printed mumus drinking beer out of plastic tumblers, fat young men standing half-naked in carports with cigarettes and killer dogs on leather straps, one retrograde Caucasoid cliche after another stretching on forever like to outlast this warped tropical sun-up into a lovely post-coital nonchalant noon but the faces of Apollo and Sharon roused me from my sickly trance just as we pulled onto the zombie wonderland, Corey Avenue: I'd convinced myself it would no longer exist if I fucked off to "the Antipodes" without a dollar to my name and my cock hanging out but the neighborhood hadn't changed in two weeks and a misting rain now, a light misting rain which I found incredibly depressing, even insulting, but I'm getting used to dismal homecomings, middle age and failure, you know, all that, getting used to "nobody on the road/nobody on the beach," etc.

It didn't matter: my $200 a week scum-jake beach hut was still standing. I wished the girls well, such pretty, well-to-do young girls on vacation from one of the most godless places on earth, as the driver asked me starkly for a tip.

What gall. What an ugly morning.

But I am so, so happy to be home again.

Breaking in through my bathroom window requires a chair, a shovel, and a screwdriver, but that's all easily arranged. I melt into relief and wonderment with the bobcat -SAM- in my arms, but the place smells like death alright, and the front door is immediately opened, my little Chelsea Hotel room in heaven coming back to life as a high fever continues cooking my brain. What little sun there is tries to penetrate the dank portal, its walls draped with ragged movie posters, photos of Charlotte Rampling half-naked in a Nazi hat, photos of John Lydon, photos of the dreaded bull shark in action and at rest.

I feed Sam a tilapia filet.

I shower.

I sleep a few days: the ocean will bring me back.

Prehistoric algae and unnamable gases: the primordial stew.

"Let love in" is the overall gist of my return, now that Bec and I have deigned to work on a relationship-type thing.

And so it is: Skype video calls, all hours of the day and night. She's 14 hours ahead of me, something like that, I can never quite keep it straight, but we manage it. We manage meals together, movies together, it's international long distance love, it's the whole wide world, it's all the butter cream bullshit anyone ever wanted, and I celebrate it profusely, back on the piss.

A man dies on my doorstep.

A dead girl turns up in the intra-coastal waterway.

My neighbors won't leave me alone.

Bec has to explain video-call etiquette to me; I have to explain my Gulf Coast death trip to her. I curse myself for frightening her, but this is my life now and I've never been happier.

An overdose down the street.

A suicide next door.

I suppose she's sensible, to be frightened. But preciousness and fear summon infernal contempt in me.

People, nearly all of them it seems, have unlimited luxury: they produce nothing.

I have unlimited grief, interference, harassment. I have destitution. I have produced 12 books this way, in as many months.

One grows tired of spoiled brats.

One grows tired of slobs, and cripples.

Then I'm getting crazy again: around Halloween I chase my landlady down the street with a machete. I threaten to butcher Suzanne "like a hog."

Bec threatens to cancel her visit.

That's when the homicide cops start parking and staring.

Staring at me in my swim trunks and baseball cap, seated at my big desk with my skull and bones paperweights and my dolphin lamp and my fucking crack pipe.

They circle, they creep. They follow me to Sunshine Liquors. They even wave hello. And after parking and staring, on the third day, they approach:

"Looks like you've got yourself a nice little business."

"Yeah."

"You know your door's been wide open for 3 days?"

"A.C.'s busted."

The homicide cops are in nice suits, of course. One of them leans across my mattress, opposite the desk and hits the POWER button on my window unit. It groans to life. He holds his hand there.

He gives me a look of unrestrained contempt.

Tells me to get out of town, and "we're not buying it."

"Get off the beach or go to jail," the other one intones. "We investigate murders, and we're good at it. If anything happens to that woman, you know we'll be coming directly for you, Mr. Grahgortis. Don't even think about playing fucking games with us. It's time to find somewhere else to live."

Homicide: like she was already dead.

That awful bitch, Suzanne: demon blood, true blue Florida wicked, a slavic ghoul with a phony identity, a curious brand of karmic damage after 25 years in the St. Pete criminal underworld.

They said she was losing it all, losing mansions, losing strip clubs, losing Rolls Royces, losing $200 a week scum-jake bungalows.

She had pissed off the lowest and loathsomest of the old gods, in the antechambers and penthouses of the occult Florida: harelipped Hassids breaking bread with Birmingham jungle bunnies and refugee Balkan war criminals, the jail-educated cracker swamp rat waiting his turn too, of course.

Suzanne swam with sharks, but I'd gotten to her.

I'd gotten to the cops.

Dirty cops.

Dirty fucking Suzanne.

It was an entire city of MYTHIC SCUM, and I couldn't see them getting me. I was so proud of myself, my books, my alcoholism, my ten dollar machete: who would dare? Who was smart enough? Who was dirtier than GENE FUCKING GREGORITS?

As they had fed – were feeding – on the poor and pathetic junkies of St. Pete, so would I nosh a bit on HER ruined flanks.

The old gods had given her a few pieces, tolerated her, but Suzanne must have forgotten her place.

She must have learned a few terrible lessons.

There's always something more to learn, about the animal world, about natural laws, and local manners.

Because you can always go soft for a minute.

You can always slip. You can always lose your rhythm.

You can always lose everything, again.

And the hardest part of all is living like that.

Like you're already dead.

SHIPWRECK

(PART ONE)

When a ship founders, it settles slowly; the spars, the masts, the rigging float away. On the ocean floor of death the bleeding hull bedecks itself with jewels; remorselessly the anatomic life begins. What was ship becomes nameless indestructible.

Henry Miller, *Sexus*

The shack has an aluminum door.

An unsettling hollow sound, a sub-aquatic pop when the street trash comes begging in the paranoid early evening... new arrivals, the regulars, it doesn't matter at all... they knock the same way... no manners... toxically insane like that, motherfuckers'll walk right on in.

Man draws you out of a DEEP drowning sleep, a subconscious romp, soaring over Mediterranean sand: a detox coma.

POOMP POOMPPOOMP

<fuckhead murmurs>

DURMP DURMPDURMP

The shack only has one window: on the side. Its one room is a perfect deprivation tank. You wake up after sweating yourself half to death, solid black innerspace so perfect and dense that there were times I could have given up the ghost but for the twinkling little Christmas lights stapled up along the edges of that one window which itself is sealed up tight with a blackout sheet. I'd drifted from and returned to those lights for days on end during and after the night sweats that were really day sweats, thinking I was in heaven, really BELIEVING I'd passed away, DIED, and woken up, skin tender, in fucking HEAVEN. Ain't that wild? Afterlife Christmas lights, green and red! They SANG to me! Not like nightbirds or desert winds or police sirens: they sang like beautiful hallucinations, a blow job on the high seas of schizophrenia, like detox clinic hallway lights, or sex in a hospital room.

It's my birthday and I'm due for eviction. I know who's out there now. My stomach tightens: "Hold on."

I pad – wearily and bones popping – into my bathroom and lift up the tutu: a warble of orange piss.

PARMP PARMP PARMP

"Mr. Grah-tortis! County Sheriff's Office!"

November 5, 2012

"Awww, that really sucks, Gene!"

Apollo is half-Apache and looks at me with a child's approximation of brotherly sorrow, but there's a hidden glee in his eyes, misery seeking its own level.

I'm morose, but I lift my head, grin: "You gonna show me the ropes, papa?"

"Hey, you got another beer?"

I reach into the crumpled black plastic and snap off a can of Hurricane from the plastic 4-ring, hand it over to Apollo as the clouds roll, a block over and a block up from my little shack, Fisherman's Park, where we can enjoy the Gulf of Mexico from a handsomely constructed but now fairly disintegrating sea wall. Fisherman's Park is Town Square for the Corey Avenue coke and dope brigade, and Apollo's wife Sharon grins her metallic grin at me. A decade in the streets does worse to most.

"We're gonna set up behind the dentist's office tonight. You know the place over there by -"

"No."

"The fucking... what is that, Sharon... 75th, by..."

Apollo squints, permanent conjunctivitis, and behind us the clank and boom of prep workers as they lunge about in the prep rooms of The Sloppy Pelican, Dakiri Dek, Willy's Burgers and Booze, Woody's Waterfront, The Oyster Shucker. (These are all fine places to go broke on a Friday night, except Woody's which is owned by high-ranking members of the Ku Klux Klan.)

It's mid-day. A crowd of 9 discusses Jackie's split with Jerry Taco, a shy old lush who has taken to sleeping in a box behind Beach Laundry on 70th and Gulf since The Wharf in Pass-A-Grille fired him. Jerry is too old for dishwashing: he can handle the alcohol, but his body has broken down, like an old mule, from the *WORK*. We all realize that Jackie is on her way out, without old Jerry to keep her.

And it's been established that Crazy Carla, a 40 year old crackhead and junkie, was tracked down once again by her rich family and placed in a mental hospital, "Baker Act'd" as it's called here. (Gulf coast misery addicts, such as my present company, mythologize every aspect of themselves, each other, and the beach life, up to and including the feared and reviled "Baker Act" whereupon a single anonymous phone call can lead to the swift seizing and involuntary committal of any individual at any time.) It's another day in my tutu, boots, and baseball cap, except a dourness which may or may not be detectable to a stranger; certainly noticeable though is the irregular sized eviction notice safety-pinned to my right nipple. Blood trickles straight down my chest until my raised rib cage catches the stream and channels it into my navel where it pools and darkens. It's quiet. The lull of hangover and the melancholy of dull weather. The Gulf stares away from us somehow.

I find myself next to a troubled young missionary named Erin, who clutches a green backpack upon the lone bench at the edge of our outdoor living room. Fisherman's Park would be brighter and cleaner with a normal family, but we do not pick up our cigarette butts and maybe it's true that plants respond to human energy. There's no denying we're pitch black, psychic tar babies the way I'm saying.

Erin's having a crisis, and it's of a religious nature: every member of this loose-knit street gang, which I became the unofficial leader of last May, can see that as plainly as I can. It's a boring observation, so pedestrian to us that when she's gone we won't even discuss it. The beach is like a drain-catch overflowing with the Erins of the nation. Of the world.

Apollo and Sharon smoke their one dollar packs of "little cigars" and we swing our legs off the cement wall, six feet above the water. Even in my dingy, lurid Michael Alig getup, I stand out from the *truly* battle-torn Corey Crew, especially to Erin who is a mousey girl and is also a hedonist just underneath the missionary guise. I ask her if she knows who Annabeth Gish is. I compare Apollo and Sharon to Mad Max characters but she doesn't know Mad Max either.

I leave her side to sit with the Gruesome Twosome, because the three of us together are classics, post-nuke B-movie icons, all keloid scars, jail tattoos, homemade jewelry, all rough grooming: thick hair, dirty manes that suggest military knocks, tactical reserve, forced readiness, all manner of special training, but 20 years ago. It's an act, of course.

The Gulf sparkles off to the southwest, maybe 100 yards out. The body of water directly below is an inlet, a turbulent channel which runs the length of Sunset Beach on the other side.

The channel doesn't have a name but is very much its own creature: a wide mouth invites scores of predators from the Gulf. Above it, Fisherman's Park, and Sunset Park just a few dozen yards down, are hangouts for all manner of lost folk: drunks, tourists, refugees, photographers, cabbies, dog walkers, bird watchers, widows, retirees. Fishermen are there as much for the view as for the sport. Their ever-present chum buckets and live bait buckets summon super birds: five foot tall cranes, great blue herons and pelicans. The pelicans are imposing and aggressive. Wood storks quickly became my favorites, but they're rare. It's a lot to take in, a lot to let go of.

David Wells, a/k/a Homer Simpson, has been babbling to himself in the grass behind Apollo and Sharon, pulling Natural Ice cans from an improvised cooler: 5 or 6 layers of plastic shopping bags, a dirty t-shirt, and a half bag of ice. He's a diminutive nuisance, harmless, thick as shit. Cirrhosis at 27. Dave gets drunk quickly and tries out his new "raps" on whoever's around. It's like watching a dog with a broken back drown in an inch of water.

My own efforts have also been in vain: the book business, the touring, the gang of degenerate beach scum. Everything is ending, and my eviction is only the tip of the iceberg. What's happening around me in the little park is the closest thing to a going away party I'm going to get.

Erin wants me to stop harming myself, that's what she says after Apollo convinces her to try marijuana for the first time. I pull the pin from my nipple and hand her the eviction notice. "Keep that, " I say. "It's important history. I'm a great writer."

"Then why haven't I heard of you?" she says playfully.

"Because we are living in a post-literary age," I reply.

Erin says, "Huh?"

She's stoned. I'm grateful for that. Soon after our exchange (she dutifully places the eviction notice in her bag, as if she'd not understood my sarcasm, or seen through it), Erin from wherever is asking questions and smiling like a familiar. The god stuff, when it emerges, offends no one.

I take a running jump off the wall to clear my head. Sharks and stingrays scatter below me as I fall, I can see them for just a second and I have no fear. In my experience, dolphins and jellyfish are far more aggressive animals.

A ruthless current will drag me two miles up the coast if I want to "ride," but instead I angle back to the rocks, balancing myself with expert precision, for the bacteria upon the razor sharp coral can be lethal when it hits your bloodstream. And the healing process is protracted by the slime, turning a 4 day scrape into a 4 week infection. I observe often that it is the same with us street trash: PERMANENT character.

Topside, I find Erin drinking one of Dave's Natty Ice beers.

The blue cans, blue and black design, my summer memories painted in those colors, knocking back the putrid ale, pissing it all away. There's already been a disconnect. I can't chase that blue and black feeling anymore.

Erin begins removing her shoes. I'm ready to leave.

"Is it okay if I take some photos?"

And there goes her mystique, flung out into the channel like a struck match. There's nothing romantic about a thousand dollar camera. And no one exploits these dying people but me.

Goodbye Sylvia Plath. I've got to go.

I've got to die a *man's* death.

That's when Jackie arrives: What Heroin Does on two legs.

Erin raises her camera: Apollo and I lock eyes.

Last month it would have been fine

Last week we'd have loved it.

I say, "Are you fucking kidding?"

Erin freezes, sobering in a flash: "I...I thought..."

Maybe even yesterday...

But Jackie doesn't see Erin OR her device. Jackie is a monster, done like this dirty Gulf does the most vulnerable, the faltering, the doubtful, the WEAK: MRSA sores and tracks and blisters, an expression like she just took a heavy board to the beak. But it's not an expression.

It's just how her face is now.

Erin's on the verge of tears.

"I'm sorry," I tell her. "Look, Herbie's here. He won't mind."

The bird approaches. Herbie is a Great Blue Heron, the largest of all the park birds. Apollo's buddy.

Erin snaps Apollo throwing Herbie a bait fish from an abandoned bucket. The bird gets close. The girl oooohs and awwwwws.

"The birds eat better than we do," I say on auto-pilot.

"Fuckin beach life," Apollo tells her.

Erin studies me, Apollo, then ugly Jackie, smoking a joint on the bench with two black eyes, bleak and blotto.

"Where are all the cats?" Erin asks.

"Cats don't come up here. The beach cats, they all have homes kind of."

"More stray HUMAN FUCKERS in St. Pete than stray anything else," Apollo snarls. "Fuckin Homer Simpson back there, fuckin... GENE, the non-famous writer, he's homeless, everyone's homeless. We're all... what we ARE, is like... modern day PIRATES."

Apollo makes his best ham actor face, his eyes narrowed to slits, a James Dean sulk which he holds and pretends to be lost in. Then, he pretends to be startled out of it. It's delightful.

"Hey ah...hey, SHARON," a VICIOUS snarl: "GET THE FUCK OVER HERE."

T-Fly, Danny, Irish, and Zeke wander into the park, but hang back to steal the last of Dave's beer.

"Listen," Apollo continues, "They found a fuckin...DEAD GIRL in the... SHARON! Where was that, down by –"

Sharon, finally disentangled, rolls her eyes. "It was in the intracoastal somewheres, I don't know, under the Pasadena Bridge, probably."

"Me and Gene talked that shit to death once. Remember? How easy it is to drop a body out here? Fishing line and a few blocks, shit... you get the teeth and fingers, that whole RUSSIAN thing, remember, Gene-O? That whole Russian-style..." The pontificating Apollo returns. "Yeah you'd get away with it, no PROBLEM."

Erin shoots a pleading look to Sharon, who has been shaking her head: "You guys are sick."

"It's time," I say. "Gotta go."

A wink to Apollo and then glancing down at Erin, "Let's get a drink sometime."

She blushes, digging through her backpack. She produces a black and white flyer.

"You guys need to eat. None of you are. Come here on Sunday and we'll feed you. It's a huge dinner, just over on –"

"Today's my last day."

I smile.

Leaving Fisherman's Park, the horror dawns on me all over again: I'm going to have to say goodbye to Sam. The skeleton of a plan, assembled over the last several days: I'd reserved a storage unit and arranged for Sam's care with Wendy and Jarrod, a couple staying in the small unit behind mine. I gave Wendy sixty dollars, the last of my cash, and instructions, all the graceless imploring that accompanies such an unpleasant action.

Zeke, the junkie patriarch of the Ragno clan, whose children I'd so often watched while he and his wife made their runs, had volunteered to help with the move: we would load up the contents of my beloved publishing office into his 30 year old Subaru hatchback with Little Mermaid decals stuck over all the bullet holes.

Beach Storage is only two blocks over on Coquina Way, but I'm in no shape for something like that.

Zeke emerges shirtless, his fat-free junkie frame hunched forward and his head down, as if stepping into a monsoon. He has a shit-cigarette in his clenched jaw, an elfin Keith Richard with Iraq War PTSD. I'm either too crazy, too stupid, or too sweet to fear him. In fact, Zeke is the closest thing I have to a best friend.

The Ragnos occupy the "deluxe" unit at the center of Suzanne's sprawling, ill-maintained complex. The center unit is cavernous, cramped, and airless exactly like the smaller units. They have all been constructed more like bunkers than bungalows.

In six months, Monastrell Books had taken on a lot of weight. Now, with the minutes ticking off towards doomsday, a dozen large boxes of my second book (a 900 page collection of old fanzine detritus called *Hatchet Job*) block the door, and then there is the equipment I'd used to produce it: a scanner, a laser printer, 2 giant cork boards, a metal filing cabinet, two digital cameras, and so on. Much of this would have to be scrapped, I reasoned. (In fact, I had plenty of space in the locker, but didn't care to be burdened any longer because I had failed.)

A half-dozen trips, Zeke silent and tense from oncoming withdrawal, is what it takes. I am practical about everything. I have to be. The last round is mostly the high backed leather swivel chair with 400 pound power-lift. Locker 37 isn't even half-full at that point but I've made a major step toward recovery. It's a gesture.

Pulling back into Zeke's spot on 73rd, where Sam lounges in my wide-open doorway, we encounter Suzanne. The witch is making her way across the vacant lot opposite the complex, returning from the rental office on Corey Avenue, where her second complex also rots.

Suzanne and Zeke were on the best of terms until very recently. The two of us had been installing air conditioners in her Tierra

Verde mansion for $10 an hour, a temporary solution to our mounting back-rent. "You are my only decent tenants, boys. The rest are SCUM, NO GOOD! Foo!"

And now, we have joined the ranks of Suzanne's Zombie Squad.

I watch her long, proud strides, her sundress and sun hat rippling in the sea breeze, I say, "FUCK YOU SUZANNE YOU RAGGEDY ASS BITCH!"

"I call POLICE, GENE!" No more of you, you crazy person! You must get help, the police take you back to crazy house!"

"You call, you CALL 'EM! GOD DAMN YOUR ROTTEN OLD ASS! THIEF! FILTHY NO GOOD CUNT!"

"I'm outta here," Zeke says. "Good luck."

Back in my gutted unit, I lay upon the bedbug-infested mattress with Sam, waiting for the cops to arrive, but they never do. I ponder my prized possession: the Ambassador IV. The pristine cherry wood executive office desk is a platform of superior function and efficiency, which, after my decade of impoverishment all across the United States, had served my art and my publishing for less than six months. But these had been my happiest months: I'd endured that decade of brutality and hunger simply to have those days and nights with my business and my cat on the beach: the Ambassador IV was my yacht, and together, we'd broken through in profound and surreal ways, necessary ways, often at a breakneck pace. I would sit at my station for days on end, not sleeping, my dignity restored, rescued from the icy depths. The Ambassador IV allowed me to leave my shell once and for all, to shed my last layer of skin, ever the more grimly determined to locate the most difficult and arcane recesses of myself, black AND white, as I set traps and laid down gauntlets, I had be PUSHING, I had been STEALING WITH BOTH HANDS, hacking at any and all resistance, a perverse self-sabotage, a Satanic amusement, and somehow it was all about WRITING. (Of course I'd written nothing.)

Feeling panic rising, I feed the bobcat a quarter pound of raw salmon, fix him a bed out of stray laundry, and head for the bar. Cutting across the vacant lot on Coquina, the sky loses its light and static electricity fills the air. I double back to my room and find it haunted, no longer mine. My machete is still duct-taped to the back of the door: I tear it down and hack off the kitchen cupboards leaving a few thousand German cockroaches homeless. Sam, I realize, will be loitering there for days or even weeks, until he accepts my absence.

I raise the blade and, without unplugging it, chop off the refrigerator's thick black power cord. A ferocious wallop of electricity sends me sprawling and I lay there, watching the cat watching me. I put him outside with a kiss, and rip the toilet bowl out of the floor in the bathroom; it gets hurled against the far wall where it connects with the blacked out window.

My right hand is now laid open, from the wrist down to the tip of the thumb. A cloudburst begins outside, and Sam bounds into our empty home with fresh droplets on his brow.

I peel off my St. Pete Beach t-shirt, wrap the hand, standing where I once stood, splashing new blood on all that old blood.

It'd been a hell of a summer.

It'd been a hell of a fall.

-4-

"Are you ever NOT bleeding profusely?"

"It's under control."

"Can't have it, Gene. I can't have this in my bar. OUT."

Ammo pulls back my pint of watery Busch.

I hold up a brown roll of gaffer tape: "Watch this."

She scowls as I tape up my hand: "I thought you got kicked off the beach."

"I'm being evicted. Hey, they can't kick me off the beach. You can't kick a person off a public beach."

"Oh man. You - ALL you guys, are about to get a rude fucking awakening."

"Yeah."

"Gene! The fucking POLICE DEPARTMENT is shutting down! That entire BUILDING is about to be empty! If they can 86 THE COPS, I think they can handle YOU, Gene. When was the last time you ate?"

"That's a bunch of bullshit."

"Hey, that's my tape. How did you get my tape?"

"It was sitting on the-"

"Give it here. It's not BULLSHIT. It was - don't you watch the news? What do you crackheads talk about all day?"

"No more cops, then."

"Yeah, Gene. They're gonna leave a whole town without cops."

"Sheriff's Department."

"Sheriff's OFFICE, dumbass. Yeah. So you need to take Sammy, get a place downtown, clean yourself up for a few weeks. You smell like a bowl of shit."

I take two steps back.

"Listen, the beach cops think you guys are real cute. The Sheriffs'll give y'all a year in county. YOU will end up with a sex charge for indecent exposure. You're half the fucking reason this is happening. You're all they talk about anymore. Gene, please listen to me."

I shimmy my hips, causing my swim trunks to drop: "Drinking is the most fun you can have with your clothes off." I take back my pint and drain it.

"The crack DEFINITELY shrunk your penis, Gene. I thought only steroids did that."

"From an acorn grows a mighty oak."

"You poor baby. You know I'm getting married, right? Just clear out for a while. After the sheriff moves in, you might be able to rent a room from Gordy at the Hideaway. But he's probably already heard all about you and Suzanne."

"Seeya."

"Hey. You owe me two bucks. What is that behind your head? Is that... goddamnit, Gene, I told you not to bring that machete in here."

"Whoops."

"Give it to me. You're gonna get yourself shot."

"No."

"GIVE IT TO ME."

"NO."

(Ammo and I never slept together but she's my only genuine crush. She's Florida white trash with a brain. Ammo, like every one of my young, attractive female bartenders, was offended by my originality, angry that I couldn't be more of a gangster. Sex, with us, never would have worked. She'd accuse me of homosexuality when I couldn't or wouldn't subdue and subjugate her like the roid-raging Harley-Davidson skip-tracer of her dreams. She'd call me a sissy bitch when I didn't yank her down by the hair to suck me off hard enough. And I'm really NOT half-a-fag. I don't wear cologne. I enjoy physical violence most of the time, particularly upon a smaller man who hasn't a chance of overcoming me. I don't listen to Death Cab for Cutie or the White Stripes. What it is, is that I can't help but be aware of things, most of the time, things like the REALITY of the sex act, which means that I need to be extremely drunk, mean-ass drunk, to be interested in it. There's always so many other things to busy myself with, life-affirming things, things to delay once again becoming *aware* that pussy could *never* be the be-all end-all unless one is mentally ill and that's all love is anyway. And the perfume is always revolting and the pubic hair must always be shaved in some tacky, trashy manner, and there are contraceptive devices and politics and the ugliest tattoos, occasionally one finds a piercing, or a tampon, and then you have all that porcine squealing. So I'm worried half to death about being the last of the sophisticated barbarians, about the utter dearth of an essential old school degenerate film noir nihilism in our culture, about why someone isn't bombing shopping malls or assassinating Oprah Winfrey. I'm AWARE that ALL DAY/EVERYDAY, right NOW, cats are being tortured by spics, by niggers, by cokehead Crowleyites, by Kim Kardashian and her film crew, I'm AWARE that the hypersexual squealing and grunting of grown women sounds uncannily close to "JERRY! JERRY! JERRY!" and all the chanting of crowds in coliseums which should be targeted first and foremost, I'm AWARE that it's a lot of horror to wrap one's head around but in the END it is better than having to produce the epithets and the expletives and the PRIMATE MISOGYNY which she all but defecates at the mere thought of, what would turn a naturally occurring fiend-fuck into a WWF monster truck fuck, a METH-MATCH, it would be like throwing gasoline on a fire, and that if a gang of young niggers DID bust in and toss me into a corner, then proceed to "FUCK the bitch all three holes" as such monkey shining lads are WONT TO DO, the pure SATANIC LOGIC of the scene would shimmer in the dark of me forever, because of course that's all I need, a red string on my finger to remind me I ain't missing much, and a man ought not have anything he's afraid to leave anyway but AH! I HAVE known a good woman and she DID fuck like a beast DID go for the dark stuff and the weird stuff we WERE *innocent* and *literary* in our coprophagia and violence, and she didn't have to ask twice for a hard slap with a few drinks in her, NEVER, and I remember how safe we both were from the vulgarian legion, the feral patriotism and canine cunt-lust, like my family and her family and ALL families because she'd come from the most vile cretin hicks and I never understood HOW, for she was so beyond lovely my Kate and it was something we laughed about, her backwards kinfolk, my own misanthropic head case Hungarians, but she was a decade older and vanished with such an appalling violence it was as if she'd never existed at all, none of it, all that laughing and her teaching me to cook and renting lousy movies from the mountaintop gas station in 1996, ALL OF IT a morbid pantomime ever since as I steer clear of gladiators and laugh with broken old addicts about places that exist and places that don't, my Kate like the seashore neither land nor sea, laughing all night long.)

"FUCKING GIVE IT TO ME, GENE!"

"NO."

-5-

Coquina and 73rd: the concrete jungle. The door of my home hangs open as twilight descends, and a man emerges: Danny. The paunchy, hirsute cretin bares his rotten, broken orange teeth at me when he says, "You tore that bitch UP, boy!"

"I guess I did."

Danny scratches his groin, sucking loudly at his teeth. "That shit ain't right. YOU ain't right. You ain't wrapped too tight, Gene-O!"

"Spread the word that Suzanne's turning her own tenants into the Sheriff's Office. She's doing background checks and everything."

"Who told you that?"

"A cop."

"You full of shit. A cop?"

"You don't have to believe it."

"Where's Sammy?"

"A friend's."

"Aintchoo moving to AWL-stralia or some craziness?"

"I don't know. Listen, Suzanne lied about the back rent I owed, she told a judge it was double what I really owed so she could get me out."

"Took her long enough. You broke the record, boy."

"And she stole my TV while I was in the nuthouse."

"You got my brass knuckles, I need-"

"They're in my desk! Just shut up a second. Do you think you can get everyone to come in here tonight and destroy the place?"

"Yeah, I might could. Gimme my nucks."

Brass in pocket, Danny mounts his Huffy and coasts off in search of companionship. A sour feeling overtakes me as I enter the bacterial netherworld of the concrete jungle, and knock softly upon the first door: brmp, brmp.

Pop of a deadbolt, whine of dry hinges. No lights.

"Hey Gene," Wendy whispers.

"Did you-"

"We grabbed Sammy, he's sleeping. We thought you got picked up by the cops. Suzanne's been marching around, screaming. You messed the place up pretty good she says."

"Yeah. I'll check back tomorrow."

"We've got Fancy Feast for Sam. Don't worry, just take care of you, ok?"

"Thanks, Wendy."

Another squeal. Another pop. I collect my machete and its shoulder holster. I unchain my bicycle from the light pole beside my room, and speed to Beach Storage: Unit 37.

Pop the lock/wrench open the roll door:

Crash one.

Fumble in the dark through piles of things: glassware, beach gear, bottles of shampoo, bottles of bathroom cleaner, jars of dry spice.

Glass shatters, my fingers touch cloth, the box revealed: my fingers fish out a t-shirt, a brown bomber jacket made of good European leather.

I toss the machete inside. Fumbling in the dark, on the ground. I fumble in the gravel for the lock. I fumble for the keys.

A blaze of sweat. Groping through all that twilight soup.

Crash two.

And from Corey to Gulf, past the Waffle House and Twistee Treat, I let the black and white fixed gear toss me off at the entrance to

Sunshine Liquors. Apollo and Sharon kick it old school down along the side of the little strip mall. Present also are the cross-dressing black skate punk named Xavier, and the Moroccan giant known only as "Mo." The former is an eerily taciturn 22 year old virgin for all intents and purposes - for the time being - happily lost in paradise. Mo is a ticking time bomb, a 7-foot-tall onetime soldier of fortune now gone to alcoholic impotence and amateur cocaine slinging. His jumbo-sized German Shepherd, also called "Mo," has been investigated twice for assaults on small dogs and their elderly owners. That both of them are still free to endanger the public is a very curious thing indeed. I assume that the bribe money is running out, or has already. Mo's drinking will cost him his dog, and probably everything else. He's halfway to being one of us.

Sharon's familiar whine, "HEEEY, honey!" is what I'm considering when Mo knocks me off my bike, blindsiding me, and I hit the asphalt trapped in a vice of metal and rubber. I smell and feel dog hair, and Mo has my calf then, blood popping through the spokes, white foam and dark blood, a tussle between the two Mo's, Sharon's voice returning, and Apollo untangling me from it all.

"I'm okay," I say, but a section of my lower left leg is gone. It's ugly. A mess. Mo, apparently not too far gone to realize his dog has attacked someone again is punching Mo in the face and in a blink they've moved off the boulevard.

Sharon is hysterical ("oh my GAWD that's a chunk he gawt") and Apollo is making an Apollo face, like he's straining at stool ("daaaaamn, Gene!") when a strange man emerges from a parked car with a beach towel and a cell phone, one in each hand, outstretched, like each is the answer to everything.

"Hey man, I fucking saw that entire thing! You need a witness!"

The man is beach-tanned, young and wealthy. Ray-Ban aviators are hanging from the neck of his football jersey, indicating tribal tattoos and Axe deodorant beneath it. Apollo lights into the creep before I can,

"Look here, uh, Justin Bieber. We're fucking VETS, okay? This motherfucker picked up two purple hearts out there in fucking....FALLUJAH, okay? He just needs a fuckin BEER. Gene, you ok buddy?"

Axe cringes in horror, either at the old Apache, or my leg, or both. I take his towel and begin wrapping it around my calf, the oval shaped pit having already overflowed with gore, which alternates from a strawberry red to maroon in the blinking liquor store neon.

"You need to call the cops, " Axe says.

"Awww, that NIGGER's going to prison anyhow," Apollo sneers. "U.S. FUCKIN MARSHALLS are ON his nigger ass! THAT mother-fucker burned his LAST fuckin-"

"Listen," Axe implores, ignoring Apollo and looking chain-whipped, "I'm bar certified. Take my card, ok? You need to follow up on this."

"I'm fine," I protest very weakly. "Apollo, here's ten bucks. I don't want to mess up the guy's floor. Get me a big Mickey's."

Still holding the phone up like a dog biscuit, Axe is trying to channel The Little Saint, his mother's nickname for him ever since 9-year-old Axe cried at the end of Good Will Hunting. Axe's good Christian fiancée, Jen, will listen to his Sunshine Liquors story and remind him that he is still his mother's Little Saint, who always has the less fortunate at the back of his mind, who suffers all the suffering of the world, when Axe returns home with a case of Bud Light and a fifth of Absolut Citron: "Honey, why don't we volunteer at the homeless shelter this Thanksgiving?"

Axe says, "Think about it, man. You give the cops a statement, make a report tonight, and you'll end up with a respectable settlement. This is what I *DO*, okay? Don't you want to get off the street, maybe quit the drugs? You seem a little smarter than your friend, and I'm sure that -"

"Listen," I wheeze, coughing and scratching my beard stoically. I stare Axe in the eye and instruct him, gently but flatly:

"It is only when you possess nothing that you may appreciate everything."

Axe freezes, then nods. A sickening solemnity spreads across his gorilla jock mug. "I understand. I really do. I... envy you, in a way. Be careful out here. Get that leg seen to."

"Your towel," I say.

"Keep it."

"Thanks," I smile. "It's my birthday."

Moments later, Apollo returns with a plastic bag full of beer. I wring a half-pint of blood out of the towel by the ice machine. I dial 9-1-1 and prepare to tell them everything.

Apollo extracts my quart of Mickey's and snarls, "I hope that nigger bitch gets AIDS in prison."

-6-

The Ambassador IV retails for $2,599.00. I paid a little less than half that for mine the previous May. Measuring 8 x 4 x 3, and weighing nearly 400 pounds, it's a King Hell Mother of a piece, a leviathanic marvel of contemporary office furniture which more than made up for all the desks I never had, for every makeshift writing table, every hijacked kitchen counter and ironing board, every nightstand and egg crate. When I arrive back at Suzanne's jungle, it occurs to me that the only man crazy enough to surrender his home to it is Alabama.

I find his door in the dark, pomp-pomp-poomp, instigating his unmistakable bark: "GIT DUH FUCK OFF MAH PORCH GOT DAMMIT."

"Alabama, it's Gene."

I know that Suzanne, now forced to occupy one of her own hovels, could emerge from the passageway at any moment. When Alabama and I begin our work, we're as mindful of the noise as we are of our own bare feet. A security light in the seething dark corner, next to the slumlord's door, clicks on and off (randomly?) as a billion little lizards sleep underneath and behind all still objects. Pebbles from the cigarette butt-infested rock gardens which line the narrow sidewalks find their way between our toes. It's a painful ordeal, with us having to rest every fourth or fifth step. We need a third man. A fourth man. Even a fifth man. We need a heavy-duty dolly cart. Bruised fingertips and baby steps, we make it the thirty feet back into the concrete jungle. There's barely enough room to swing the thing around so as to begin feeding it into Alabama's living room.

"It won't fit," he says.

"It *will*. We've almost got it. Just keep it a few days and I'll buy you two fifths of Crystal Palace."

"Fuck Gene," he whines. "I got *A INTERVIEW* in the morning."

My Edmund Fitzgerald is halfway into the filthy efficiency when Suzanne explodes upon the scene like a one-woman SWAT team:

"YOU CAN'T PUT THAT IN THERE! TAKE IT OUT, GENE! YOU CAN'T DO THIS! Jeremy, I am throwing you out! I'm calling the police, Gene! You're going to jail! I saw what you've done! I will show you boys how we do things down HERE!"

The rain begins again. Alabama scatters.

I am slumped down against the desk, a whipped dog, when the miniature fleet of St. Pete Beach police vans arrive with their tasteful dolphin emblem, and their pleasant white finish, and the flashing lights which drive a wedge into the civilized melancholy of the uncivilized beach night.

Suzanne, gone completely to gravity and bad nerves during recent times now struts to and fro in her red sundress, without makeup, like an aggravated hen, like ZsaZsa Gabor. She babbles uncontrollably at the police who are not happy to be back at the jungle for the fourth or eighth time that day.

"Where's the body, Suzanne? Where's the dead body? Should we get you an ambulance, I don't see any blood..."

"He is OUT, offy-SAR! I ee-veek heem! I TELL HIM, he must be GONE by 9am, Sheriff's Office TELLS HEEM this this, and he vandalize the ha-PARTMENT with an AXE! He cost me -"

"Suzanne," a large, bearded cop begins -

"NO! NO! NO! For THREE MONTHS, he pays me NOTHING, and now he destroy my PROPERTY! YOU MUST-"

"Gene, what did you do, trash the place?"

"I moved out THIS MORNING, officer. I left the door open because I don't have the keys anymore. If anything was damaged, it happened after I left. And the place oughta be condemned anyhow."

"THESE ARE LIES, OFFEE-SAHRS! You all know he is CRAZY! He must be in JAIL! He THREATENS MY LIFE and police department does NAH-THING! SHAME ON ALL OF YOU! He wants to KILL ME, you must understand this!"

"Suzanne, you know how this works. We've been through it all a hundred times. Gene, you can't be here. You're trespassing. You can't keep your things in the other units. She doesn't want the desk in her unit, in ANY of her places, ok? Aren't you supposed to be in Australia?"

"Sir, its a $3,000 desk. Isn't there -"

"C'mon man. You're smarter than that. Don't waste my time. You have 5 minutes to get rid of it. Suzanne, we're gonna leave a patrol unit here till he and the desk are gone."

"I WANT HIM ARRESTED! YOU DO YOUR JOB AND ARREST THIS MAN!"

The old bag has gone beet red there in the black rain. She storms off like a funhouse mirror version of Blanche DuBois. "I KNOW THE MAYOR OF ST. PETERSBURG!"

The beach cops have all returned to their vehicles after much head-shaking and quiet laughter. Every one of them has been tolerant of me and the others. Their humanity has cost them their jobs. The sheriffs, and the city police, are known to razor the tents of homeless families, to plant evidence, to mistreat animals: "How we do things down HERE."

Zeke appears in his fatigue trousers and Army Poncho and desert hat, a cheap smoke in his teeth. He tells me that, only a few hours ago, he'd ran into Suzanne at 7-11, after a week of meticulous avoidance (there can be no other kind when your landlady lives right behind you). He had no choice then but to inform her that he'd be moving out, as opposed to paying her the 6 weeks she'd had coming.

Suzanne had *liked* Zeke. "Zeke," she'd tell me, "ZEKE is a good friend for you, Gene. He is a HARD WORKER, he has a GOOD family and a GOOD heart." She would tell Zeke, "You are not LIKE all these trashy people out HERE, Mr. Ragno."

"Hey, uh... like whenevah ya fuckin ready theyah, Gene," Zeke says.

And my heart sinks.

There's no picking the behemoth up this time.

We grind it across 73rd, to the field, and leave it there.

Leave it in the fucking rain.

Like that.

Apollo and Sharon walking south in the rain, south on Gulf Boulevard when I spot them in front of the Pineapple Arms, which everyone calls the Pincushion Arms. I hop off my bike, walk with them to Walgreens where we beg enough money for a fifth of Popov: about 7 bucks. My legs ache. The town doesn't want me anymore. It's a slick of oil. Winter's coming. My feathers stink.

A young man with dreadlocks and a steel-framed ALICE pack like mine joins our party as we trudge off towards the bus stop in front of the Sweet Bay supermarket. We occupy that cigarette-blasted enclosure and watch the cars, mixing the vodka with Faygo orange soda until the rain stops. The kid is Alex, from Greensboro, an average-looking junkie whose "epiphany" at a Phish concert a year ago led him to... etc. Alex would very much like to find his ex-girlfriend in Austin but the motherfuckers back at the tent village got his phone and his welfare card and of course his heroin use has nothing to do with any of it. He won't stop quoting Dylan Thomas and I can't get drunk this way, with the rain and the anger and the heartache. THE GUILT. The guilt and the worry which have won, like my enemies have all won. I find footholds, lose them: a putrid airless freefall. We stare out at the night, at the patio of Riptides Bar and Grill, dim wonder about the action at Mermaids tonight.

The kid is fried beans, shot out, won't shut up. Apollo resorts to baiting Sharon: she slaps him across the face so fucking hard he looks dead for a split second. The rain stops. It's time to bed down for the night. We climb to our feet and shove off, leaving the hippie shithead lost in dope sickness. But once we make it across Blind Pass, he's yelling for us to wait.

A flash of lightning.

"You gotta be QUIET, Gene! Don't fuckin ruin this for us man. It's a good little spot. We might could keep this for a year."

An uncomfortably tight corridor between an out-of-business insurance office and a dentist's office leads to a pitch black backyard, exactly the type of little yard that you see swarming with police and police lights on television. It's lined with medium-sized palm trees and a chain-link fence. It most certainly has never been made use of by the dentist or his staff, not as an outdoor dog pen and not as a smoking area. At the back, a row of bushes conceals us from a residential home's back porch where a couple of idiotic old men are popping cans of beer and murmuring, low and lifeless.

The building itself is industrial no-frills, cinderblock, with a flat roof providing just enough overhang to keep us dry should the rain return. Apollo says it will.

We line up against the office, along the walkway, foot to head: no hope of partaking in that giggly summer camp thing, swapping jokes, whispers, passing the vodka back and forth. Only this: "Don't fuck around Gene, the sensors are on. Go to sleep. And Alvin -"

"Alex."

"- you shut the fuck up, too."

And there are shapes in the purple dark, movements like small breaths being taken, delicate movements, terrible shapes inching towards and away in the cruel fog reminding me that a pressure is being increased, stretching me, I cannot let go of my business, my Sam, my Bec, but holding on will tear me open. I'll *split*. I *am* splitting. It cannot be both things, the bottom and the fight AGAINST the bottom.

The bottom and the fight cannot co-exist.

A miserable night but a temporary night, lost in space.

A drop zone.

I light a cigarette, afraid to move. (The old men have gone inside.)

My bleeding leg thumps, thumps, thumps.

"Apollo, give me the vodka."

"Man, get the fuck outta here," he hisses.

Sorrow grips me.

Everything's going to come together. Think!

I'm exhausted.

THINK!

The rain returns: drift/wake.

The kid murmurs: drift/wake/drift.

The dream: my last morning with Sarah, the last chance, a sweltering heat in the airless room, before I lit the fuse. I wake to her blonde hair spilled over my chest and then it clicks, a few seconds too late: "You always SAY you want me to suck you while you're passed out..."

WAKE: the kid has one arm over my chest, the rest of him concealed by my bomber jacket, working at my cock.

I leap to my feet, howling and cursing.

It's cold: first light. An unnatural phosphorescence, a gaseous gash in the sky.

Damp set into my bones: corpse rot. Rigor. Something...

Apollo farts, curses.

"I gotta go."

The kid is off pacing in the wet grass, humiliated, babbling. I haul my pack off the ground, now covered in thousands of tiny, sticky little burrs. I freeze then, flush with dread at the realization that my precious bike has been stolen.

Limp the blocks back to Blind Pass, find the bike u-locked to a stop sign: sag from the shock.

Hop on, ride. A good feeling in that.

Coffee and toast at Waffle House.

Sleep-ride to Sunset Park, watching the morning spread across a black and white Gulf, a nuclear dawn, a vertical ballet of black and white pelicans plunging from heaven into the sea.

I don't know what to do.

-9-

The Gulf neither notices me nor ignores me.

At 7 A.M. I cycle the half block over to the shack: 10 years adrift, with only 6 months of dock-time. The idea of it taking another decade to fight my way out of the abyss. Another 10 year pummeling.

The air is heavy with nightmare now. Nightmare is my skin, and the blood under my skin. My breaths are wild, lethal things called nightmares. An icy sweat when my bowels drop: I scan the neighborhood for a public toilet I know isn't there, then drop into the channel with only seconds to spare.

Soaked and miserable, I coast off sleepy Sunset Drive onto old 73rd, my 60% eyes straining for signs of Suzanne, but perhaps baiting her too because I find myself circling the entire block. Where the condo towers loom over the rocky tip of Sunset Beach, above the secret garden, above Upham Beach to the south and ALL of Corey Avenue to the north, this nightmare remains a free flowing thing, a liquid substance, it is a color and an odor and a place. The Sundial Motel is still, and Mo stands in a ridiculous Superman pose on the balcony of his own rundown apartment house, one of dozens lining the neighborhood's narrow avenues. Mo drinks his coffee, ignoring me. The dog howls from somewhere behind him.

And I approach it there in the vacant lot, its cherrywood going strong against the rain, like a performance art stage, a living installation, like one of Marcel Duchamp's readymades, like time-lapse photography of CBGBs' bathroom or a secret history of South American murder films.

I grapple with possible escapes, with practicalities, too, as the sky darkens and a monsoon begins:

November 6, 2012.

The shack's doorway fills with the shape of a human being. I stiffen against the meaning, and the implication, against the fear: only a few years ago, Suzanne could have simply had me killed.

"Who's that?" I say, too sodden, too sick, to experience normal fear, and as much as I want to lose the attraction, to lose sight of what the place was to me, I can't and I suppose it's true we did too much beachcombing. Maybe we got too much sun.

36

The shape is a woman, a disheveled woman who, having wobbled and limped outside, releases her long red hair from a banded ponytail. She adjusts her baggy skirt, turning onto the walk leading back to the rear of the bunker jungle. She is barefoot. She's scowling like a barn whose fire has just been put out.

"That's my fucking house," I can't help whining. And it is, for another 90 minutes or so. The street shows no other signs of life. I hide my bike underneath the Ambassador and approach the shack. The smell reaches me as I cross 73rd, and I flinch from it: a diagrammed police evidence photo of feces, rubble, horror quickly develops in my mind. At the door, I hold my breath. At the door, the angry scrawl of my 8.5x11 sign reads, "YOU ARE BEING VIDEOTAPED." I tear it down, unamused that the packing tape, and the sign itself, have withstood so many weeks of rain.

Below that sign, another: "GONE BUFFALO HUNTING."

And another: "IF YOU DO NOT HAVE HALF A DUB, DO NOT KNOCK ON THIS DOOR."

I smile. Weakly.

I tell myself the tale, it comes at me like a kind of fit, and I am not prepared: a boy and his cat. Williams Park. Central Station US19. Pasadena Causeway and Pasadena Lanes and the Palms of Pasadena Treasure Island and Madeira Beach, and Apollo DeLeon, King of ALL the beaches. Crack cocaine mornings and Waffle House mornings. The Old Northeast and Lealman and Paterra Park, the south side and the Baywalk 20, the Emerald Bar and Mastry's Bar, Detroit Liquors, and ABC Liquors, Norm's Liquors and Sunshine Liquors, Renee and Sloan who are mother and son, and Jim Lopez the whispering faggot, swimming in the dark and diving for sand dollars, sand crabs and sea turtles, stingrays and sharks, the Hideaway Lounge and Smiley's Lounge, Riptides and the Undertow, the 27 bus and the 18 bus and the Beach Trolley, and shooting drugs in my arms with dying strippers, George with no nose and Ozzy with no liver, stink of charred skin and disused tire gauges, clumps of barbequed Chore-Boy and eyes rolling back, black coffee and brass knuckles, robbed tourists crying for help in the dark, the laughter, the laughter, the laughter and the knowing, the awareness we all had – being sensible men and women – that it was ending quickly, but laughing and shouting and talking all night.

I take a step back because I can't breathe, because I don't need to see any more death and destruction.

I tear down the other two signs: Keepsakes. Mementos of Tropical Storm Debbie and Monastrell Books and everything else.

A surreptitious dash back to Wendy's place: brmpbrmp?

Murmurs. "Fucking Gene."

Hacking, cursing.

Wounded murmurs: "Sammy's fine, Gene. We're SLEEPING..."

But it's late evening in Australia.

I observe several cars swerving suspiciously off a deadened Gulf Boulevard where the monsoon hits blackout status, saturating the torpid airspace above St. Pete Beach and I make it 25 blocks down to Dolphin Village through the cold wall: 2 feet at Howard Johnson, 3 feet at the Mariott, above my rib cage at the Tradewinds Island Grand. We – the Giordano fixed gear death machine and I – are swimming above the parked cars, the ocean and the sky intertwining, an apocalyptic tongue-fuck is going strong beneath my paddling feet at the Sirata Hotel Resort and I lose my flip flops in a tidal wave pregnant with palm branches and newspaper boxes. The sandals were 35 dollar Reef Phantoms and that's how I get the idea (rage) to infiltrate the Sirata whose rear patio may be above water and I have one hand clutching a parking meter in guest parking – we robbed a drunk family of 5 there (2k cash) – and the other hand on my bike when a sneaky son of a bitch guster tears through slamming me into a wide, jagged section of cheap bamboo latticework from Dockside Dave's Tiki Hut and under the deluge I go as a reverse wave slams in from 59th Avenue, the traffic lights blinking yellow are among the only still operational and I discover that I am no longer in guest parking but the middle of Gulf Boulevard with my face badly creased by the spokes of the bike and a few takeaway swaths of bamboo, lost now, the water obviously a biohazard with residential and business sewers running over, a region-wide sewer overflow crisis in full swing and I think of my dog bitten calf – so many factors – and the opportunities for looting unless the drain-off is a rapid and well planned affair. (I saw a DEPARTMENT OF CITY SEWERS official descend into the manhole at 73rd and Coquina one morning with several gadgets including a 2 way radio and a pressure gauge of some kind, or maybe a methane detector...she seemed on top of everything) (and foxy). The universe above explodes with and end of the world thunderclap. You do not impress me, Nothingness.

So I have two choices: another attempt at the Sirata, or a block further down to Beach Internet Cafe on the ground floor of Surf Inn where I won't have to worry about ejection because they are open to the public... the water keeps rising. Could Beach Internet be wiped out? I return underwater, locate a NO PARKING sign holding the bike keys in my teeth. It takes several passes but I secure the machine with a U-lock and commence breast stroking my way towards the blighted beach, the raging surf. A Coleman cooler floats by, it is red and white like my own back home (I found Sammy asleep in it once), it catches my eye and I pop the lid with a petulant fist to find two 24 ounce Corona Extra cans and secure them down my trunks, but one wiggles through the sour netting and that's another $2.99 I'll never enjoy.

The beach patio is submerged of course but the pool area, perhaps two feet above, has been fortified with sandbags; hotel guests mill about with generic disaster giddiness playing with their smart phones, the fat men playing stoic and their soulless wives playing rattled in their plastic hotel ponchos and plastic hotel hats taking banal photos of the torn aluminum, planks of wood, slabs of hairy brown palm husk bobbing and listing from side to side in the defeated wading pool. Twisted black nails like bared teeth serve to remind all admirers of the flood that this is not a theme park ride. The sea itself can only be heard, all theoretical absolute. Broken glass tables huddled together upon the Karaoke stage.

I stagger inside and find a seat at one of the Sirata's guest computers – nobody talks to me. I pop my Corona, good memories of those colors, blue and gold, while the Sirata employees push hot chocolate on everyone. I take a cup of that too, indignant, excessive: "Thank GOD the Internet's up. I lost track of everyone! My phone's ruined!" The doe-like girl forms an expression of mute horror: "Let me know if you need anything."

I log on to Skype, find a message from Bec: "There's no coming back from this one, Gene. My father is an alcoholic and I lived with that abuse –"

"Oh fuck me in the ass," I mutter. A scan of our last exchange (or was it a call - don't I record my calls?) might explain it but it's an old story, an old plot, 200 years running in place; crashing rushing running. And a police helicopter is on the beach with these dramatic floodlights, search and destroy high beams the cafe clears out leaving me to my Bec - misery. Everyone wants a photo of the helicopter, and there's an electronically amplified voice. A flash of light.

From behind the Sirata bar I swipe two bottles of some obscenely mediocre California Zinfandel, the kind of plonk that fat old whores who smoke Virginia Slims and haven't been fucked in 5 years like to "stock up on" (three lousy bottles) when it's on sale at fucking Safeway. I spend an hour and a half knocking back the wine in a warm, silent toilet stall. I emerge euphoric and the storm has relented, all anyone can hear is water, water dripping, water draining, water flowing, water splashing, until the sirens begin. I make my way to the drowned bicycle and the drowned road, the stoplights no longer flashing but fully dead.

I slice my way north up to Beach Lounge before the winter water rises again. It's 10 A.M.

The morning was only a storm, like Bec was only... whatever Bec was.

It doesn't matter now. Both are fading.

-11-

"My cigarettes got ruined. You need anything?"

Tough old Maggie says, as always, "No thank you, Mr. Gene."

At Walgreen's, Apollo is begging with Mark, who tells me, "I'm dyin, bro."

"I'm sorry," I drone.

Inside I shoplift a handful of "St. Pete Beach" t-shirts, buy a pack of Marlboro Blacks, make an unsuccessful go at engaging the counterman. It was he who stood exactly there, as now, the night I came inside the Russian lesbian, Leissane Kazan, who dragged me by the ear to buy her a morning after pill. Until last week, Walgreens at Blind Pass and 75th was a 24-hour location.

I say, "I can't make my late night runs anymore! I'm very upset."

"Yeah," he mumbles.

The counterman is a handsome young non-entity with a bull neck and a neatly trimmed goatee and he REALLY doesn't care for me. But he's right: that scene with Leisanne was horrid. Was there another one? *TWO* morning-after pill scenes? Certainly not with Leisanne: once was enough for her. (We'd fucked on Sunset Beach, then drank too much wine, talking about Dostoevsky and why I'm so inarticulate. A wonderful experience, naked in the surf making the best of our mid 30s at the edge of the universe.)

In the oily air, Apollo is giddy, the way he tends to get when someone is suffering, when there is a scene, when damage is being done, when the shit hits the fan.

Mark says, "I'm fuckin DYIN, bro! I got 200k coming from malpractice, but I'll never live to see it. After 50 fuckin years broke as a joke."

I say, "Where's Roxy?"

"Back at my place."

(Roxy is a sweet old Rottweiler. Mark has a "service dog" certification for her, acquired phonily. That's a common practice among beach losers who are not handicapped at all, but nearly insane with loneliness.)

Fire trucks now. Storm images and post-storm sounds: "Roxy don't like all this chaos." Mark says, trailing off, stomping out a little cigar.

And then there's a howling, rippling explosion in the distance, the stoplights flickering.

Apollo says, "Hehhehheh. Oh, you fucking *wait*. They had a BUDGET, fucking... new signs, new sidewalks, new jobs, the whole

40

fucking BAG, and now they ain't gonna have *shit.* Millions of dollars, man those fuckin assholes are FUCKED."

"Where's Sharon?"

"I don't *know*, Gene, guess she had to go change her fuckin TAMPON."

Apollo squints his runny eyes, another stoic pose, another brooding fit. I smile. He doesn't try so hard for anyone else. It's flattering.

"Yeah, where the fuck IS Sharon? Takin a fuckin shit I guess. You're gonna LOSE that fuckin leg, Gene-O."

I pull the bundle of shirts out of my crotch, peel off my present rag for a change-up, hand the rest to Apollo.

"I don't want your dirty shit, motherfucker!"

"They're brand new, suit yourself."

"No shit. Well GIMME the fuckers, then."

"You got a hooch for the night?"

"Maaaan, I don't *know*! This here's some heavy SHIT. Motherfucker, you better get that leg wrapped up. Ya got raw sewage out there! That dookie bacteria gets in your fuckin blood you're gonna be *fucked*, Gene!"

"Fellas, I gotta go."

"Where ya goin?" Mark says, a plea in his voice.

"Beach Lounge. I gotta call Maggie somehow."

"Call Maggie?" Apollo fairly roars. "Maggie's WORKING!"

"Bec! I meant Bec!"

"BECK? What kinda fuckin name is BECK?"

"Rebecca, fuckhead. She thinks I want to be homeless. She dumped me."

"WANT TO BE HOMELESS? Listen, Gene, fuck that whore. She's in fuckin AUSTRALIA you moron! What're you fuckin STUPID?"

"What happened to the kid?"

"The dying of the light? You broke his HEART! He went back downtown, I guess. How the fuck should I know? If I tried to keep track of every-"

"Yeah, alright."

"Hey, if you see my stupid wife -"

"Alright."

Palm branches block my exit. Mark looks terrible. Chapped lips from the obvious: "hard." And the smell of high gravity ale.

A swamp ride to the curb: unsettled streets. Uncertain streets.

Plumes of brown water, the storm streets.

Sepsis.

-12-

The St. Pete Beach public library isn't half bad for a beach library.

I log on to Facebook. I am one of 9 homeless men logged into Facebook. One of 7 billion devolving electro-perk junkies logged into Facebook, logged *out* of everything else. Forever.

There are more sirens outside. I'm in a movie. I'm always in a MOVIE like this. I can't SEE myself anymore, blinded by action. Different landscapes. High adventure. Skin of my teeth exits.

But there are no rich friends offering to bail me out *this* time.

All I can think of is oblivion. I wouldn't even know how to begin.

All I see on the computer screen is 4 or 5 dozen "happy birthday" messages, they are identical, and a migraine begins punching the backs of my eyes.

Instead of growing concern for the work, for the work's production office, or Sam, it's THIS and I understand what I'm facing: "There's no coming back from this one, Gene."

I write a crazed e-mail to Bec, and another, and another, alternately desperate and smug. Groveling to peel paint.

It's the fight that kills you.

A message appears as the library's fluorescent lights begin flickering, a 10 minute warning. Or maybe the end of the world. The message is from Cynthia Mariano, a *fan* I suppose you'd call her but I'm not convinced. Cynthia is a dumpy aficionado of New Jersey bar bands who put up the $2,500 I needed to pay off Suzanne and publish *Hatchet Job* last August. I hadn't counted on going to war with anyone. I hadn't counted on homicide cops.

Cynthia and I have the same birthday. Her message reads: "Happy birthday to US, Tiger. Are you on the street? Do you need help? Sent 300 to Paypal. Let me know you're alive. 201-600-5665."

The woman is mentally ill, I can see that plainly enough. Slicing off my earlobe, then eating it, was the best publicity "gag" I could muster during one of the summer's many rent crises, and that was the beginning of the end. There were 6 or 7 Cynthia's, and I didn't NEED a better plan. I'd always landed on my feet.

The mutilation video went viral, and the door opened to me. For the first time in my 20 years as an independent publisher, I was receiving legitimate media attention, most significantly from VICE Magazine. Their feature on me, largely an interview by that notorious nitwit, Lisa Carver, hadn't been published yet, but the word was out and sales were up. I quit my telemarketing job, which was devouring me at an accelerated pace, and assumed my worries were over.

It was FEAR, and my autocannibal cash flow, after two months living at night, was long gone, one wet crocodile snap: I woke up one morning and I couldn't buy beer. I had the shakes, I was withered and whimpering and it would have been catastrophe THEN were it not for THE CYNTHIAS, mainly Cynthia herself, and it was to be paid back, THE MONEY IS ALWAYS TO BE PAID BACK but it was as if no one had read the book, the book was called *Dog Days* and its words, I'd believed, would REDEEM me and more importantly FINANCE ME, but no one read the book, and I was told that the REAL problem was my ATTITUDE, and my pages were NOT BLANK ENOUGH, I could sell a billion blank pages with a blank smile and a PROPER SENSE OF COMMUNITY.

For me, there was only one truth and it consisted of WORDS.

I told myself, "Shit on every single one of them. You can't translate the truth for these people."

Were it not for my ten loyal readers, perhaps I'd still be stranded in Detroit with a zombie skank and her gaggle of retarded children. Now, I'd lost far more than I'd even had enough strength to recognize, and my ten loyal readers were gone.

When I approach the Wells Fargo ATM with a can of Hurricane and a limp, there is only one truth and it is SERVITUDE.

-13-

Blind Pass Road would be Gulf Boulevard were it not for Sunset Beach. It's all one coast, yes, but there are small breaks: when the land separates at the south end of Treasure Island, the beach road narrows and retreats into the soft folds and geriatric stillness of Sunset Beach.

This is one mile or so of mid-range vacation homes, condo complexes, and nearly invisible bungalows, and its rocky southern end tapers off into the slack mouth of the same nameless inlet we crackhead Corey boys call "the channel." At that point, one Gulf Boulevard has ended, and another, across the channel and two blocks east at 75th Avenue, has begun. In between, people like myself, Zeke Ragno, Crazy Carla, and Apollo DeLeon engage in high risk sex and dream of murdering the bitch Suzanne. That's the best I'm able to explain it.

There is no bridge from one to the other: the residents of the slender but overbuilt Key prefer quiet and they demand privacy. I've often mused on the irresistible depravity of standing on the intracoastal tip of Sunset Beach, where its charmless ultra-modern condos gape like autistic children at that ravaged (non) mainland, when the putrid felons of Corey Avenue are at play on a sweltering Friday night, at the height of the tourist season, to stand there as a survivor and fully protected by that treacherous tributary, from the rapes and the fights and the arrests, the Southern Lights (blue and red) on a clear, hot night and the splashing of sharks feeding is closer than the dope action, to have ALL of it so very nearly within arm's reach because UNCOUNTABLE are the memories of caged animal fear and murderous intent POWMP-POWMP-POWMP-POWMP-POWMP-POWMP-POWMP-POWMP POWMP following a botched drug sale or unsuccessful delivery of stolen guns or wake one morning to the voice of a LIVID man saying YOU HIT ME WITH A FISH, A, A, MOTHERFUCKA DID YOU JUST HIT ME WITH, WITH, WITH A **FISH** and when I flung open the hollow dented aluminum door to disperse the men from my porch these LOUD men who could not POSSIBLY be the architects of a street melee in which a red snapper or GOD forbid a baby shark was being used as a bludgeon, THEN as I entered the wild ass morning ready to begin my groggy reprimand it was none other than a STILL LIVING SEA BASS which caught me full in the mouth leaving me very much at a loss for words until this very day and a thousand other memories of those perfect moments when I walked into perfect darkness knowing how well and truly REAL it all was and how REDEMPTIVE it was in itself to love a delirium so fully a sickness so wildly to love all that is finite BECAUSE it is finite to raise my machete and walk these streets so ALIVE WITH ESCAPE AND SO HIGH ON ESCAPE and so FUCKING BEAUTIFULLY GOD DAMN DRUNK THAT NOTHING AND NO ONE COULD TAKE THAT BLADE FROM ME so please understand now the sad wonderment, the questioning of a VANTAGE POINT of a PROTECTION now when I am weak when I want to BE across those black waters which no one ever swam at night (not even me) (oh fuck) to be atop the Sunset Beach Watchtowers to have a Coquina Way experience from THE SKY or from one of those hundreds of balconies that KEPT US LOW or for no other reason the listless reappraisals of our station, the bored behemoth hypothesis, the many lazy day angles of a single thing the juicehead occultism of a Corey Avenue lifer alone in Fisherman's Park on a moonless night while the tourist joints hum and whine, the scattered evidence of microwaved tourist clip joint junk food when there's nowhere left to go but further up the coast because the wild harelipped boys are taking a breather, the mile it is, onto Blind Pass Road the long ride on the Suncoast trolley bus nipping a half pint and ride all night for 5, all the way to Clearwater and in the morning wake in wretched stiffness among Busch cans behind the 7-11: ride all day in the rain.

-14-

I watch two police cruisers glide past through the branches, behind the library shrubs which are decorated with King Cobra cans and Hurricane cans I pretend are a cluster of microphones at a press conference where I announce my dying plans.

It's an entirely sovereign galaxy back there when the day gets away. The last car pulls out of the library parking lot jogging my memory and I emerge like an albino grizzly bear or a child killer like Peter Kürten the Vampire of Düsseldorf, to see the sun has only just set. That's a melancholy time, but an exciting time because the nights last longer and the nights allow reflection.

Apollo and Sharon turn up on the next block homesteading a public bench next to Beach Theatre which is showing a gritty cop drama with Jake Gyllenhaal. Also present are Robbie and Amber, a combustible pair on their best day and for that reason alone, two of the area's most dangerous habitués. Whispers persist about alleged double-dealings and police informing (but I'm a gun runner and a hitman, if you believe the dopes).

Robbie's got "Running with the Devil" tattooed on his left bicep, and indeed the young man is moved to unmistakable innocence by Van Halen played very loud, but Robbie already has liver disease and will tell you also that in prison he'd "hit ya in the haid, bout...eight, nine time, then fuckin...have sex with you." (He looks innocent then, too. Just not innocent of violent rape.)

Amber's a half-Mexican kleptomaniac with perfect tits. She is frequently beaten into emergency rooms for behavior that would bring any ANY saint to arms. We head north on Blind Pass beyond the Spanish churches and the lonely laundromats and the dreariest two-story apartment complexes I've seen outside of Detroit.

One block at a time.

LONG blocks.

Washout blocks. The warm tingle of a drug buy in the air, throwaway lines like "I hope they have clean needles" that replace dread with the reflexology of by-proxy drug sex. We FORGOT that we were brothers and sisters while I was gone and they were forced to move three fucking times but we REMEMBER now so there is that collective hope for us AMONG us vile human forfeitures walking in the rain in the storm-lashed 4-lane road which is forced and weighted down like a child's single-parent Sunday after the matinee.

Robbie wears jail-issued rubber sandals, "shower slides," and Amber's in pink Reeboks. Amber can be cute but dorky, damaged-cute with her big fat broken nose and Kathleen Turner laugh. She's known far and wide as "Scamber" for a reason. Arm's length, friend, and be mindful of your good shit.

Sun Island Motel is the halfway point of that ugly interstitial stretch, that inert intracoastal run between Treasure Island and St. Pete Beach. Sun Island is the ledge beyond the edge, where you go when Suzanne Ferry has you permanently shit-listed. I'm thinking of Sam's breath in my face, my perfect morning, letting the locker room air and Port-Au-Prince visions of Blind Pass carry me past the Sun Island parking lot and the tall electric Sun Island sign and *into* the last-chance outpost SUN ISLAND where too many of the rodent people lay in wait, driven into intermission by the rain.

Overflowing ashtrays: cigarette soup.

Overflowing pool in the courtyard.

A sagging moment in a sagging place.

And Miss Tang is a Vietnamese Suzanne, no less and no more, elegant and ruthless at the age of 68. She shakes her porcelain doll head, watching our approach. She smokes and watches the rain.

-15-

Two knocks on the green door of room 11 - pop pop! - reveals six yapping Chihuahuas and the heroin party. A Chinese takeout bowl filled with bleach water and rigs. There are little amoebic spots of oil floating on top, residue from won-ton soup. One of the *The Fast and the Furious* movies on the TV. Everyone's chatty and welcoming and worthless. We cop, shoot, play with the dogs. Shoot again, with the same needles.

-16-

The ruined beach.A plastic fifth of vodka.The heroin arrogance.Robbie and me in the black surf.A police searchlight.

Lying on the cool sand, we evade Florida conflicts, future conflicts, smoking good Marlboro cigarettes.

"When's the book coming out Gene?"

"Yes."

"NO, WHEN."

"It takes many years to write a good novel."

"Gene, man, you really doing the book?"

"Yeah."

"Corey Avenue Boys?"

"Oh yeah."

"We really in it?"

"Yes."

Amber: "He's full of SHIT, Robbie."

A flash of light. Ocean sounds. The vodka jug groans and pops in Robbie's massive hands. Everything is illicit and arcane tonight.

"Electrical storm. Safe to swim with all that going on up there?"

"I don't know. Why don't you go give it a try?"

"Amber's got great tits, Rob."

"Better watch your mouth, Gene Gene Jellybean."

"Robbie, g'wan beat his faggot ass."

"I'm going swimming."

"Nice knowing you."

"That's the smallest dick I've seen in a long time, Gene. Holy shit."

"It gets really big, no one believes me."

"Yeah."

Little fires in the rolling black clouds, the whole Gulf coast, you can see all the way to

Sunshine Liquors is managed by Nadeem, a handsome and peculiar Arab with thick black hair he styles in a kind of 1980s bouffant, like James Spader in *Less Than Zero*. Nadeem is a novelist and uses Amazon's digital print-on-demand platform like me. His first book, *The Wooden Children of Saba*, is 550 pages of young adult fantasy fiction inspired by the loss of his beloved handcrafted furniture during a turbulent divorce. (You learn this in the author bio at the back of the book.)

He's never sold a copy. But it's on sale there along with the joke lighters, phone chargers, and plastic flowers.

"Nadeem, have you considered -"

"I'm not cutting off my ear, Gene."

The rain is back, a cold snap. Robbie and Amber are banned for stealing. Nadeem bags my 12 pack of Yuengling, and Amber's 6 of Mike's Hard Raspberry Lemonade. Robbie holds the door for me, sneering at Nadeem.

Outside, there is talk of the grieving widower, John: "Don't be weird, Gene-O, maybe he'll let you stay."

Amber forces her hand into the bag, takes a bottle, and doesn't say thank you.

Robbie opens his phone, winking at me, and there is a moment of stillness, just long enough to realize -

"Yup. We're gonna bring the writer, okay?"

- that my blood is still splattered across the front of the ice machine and the pay phone.

I pick up the phone and dial: "Did you arrest that nigger and his wolf?"

"Mr. Gregorits, we need to speak to you immediately."

What song? Which dream?

And I see Dave Waverly rolling around on the grass at Twistee Treat, blood falling out of a gash in his brow, brass knuckles. And more lights in the sky. Suzanne's Rolls slows to a stop at the corner: 4-way's on.

"Hey Robbie, you talked to your mom in a while?"

"My mama dern warsh'd 'er hainds since ahr robbed mah grammama. Ain't nern uh us any damn good."

Amber: "My family thinks I got the devil in me."

"You sher doo, thes mah SON, thes mah lil' baby."

We approach the Tropical Cove Apartments on 71st and Sunset. Four little bungalows.

Rafts and chairs left out in the rain. Hand painted greetings on coral and conch. Range Rover in the drive, Harley on the porch. Toys.

Music from the inside: Stones. Eighties Stones. Lousy Stones.

"Be cool, Gene."

The family scene: ex-Marine John, a double for that actor Robert Patrick, the macho B-movie guy. Buzz cut and Eastwood squint.

He's truly gone on something. He begins talking over or through what has been explained to me, cursorily: grief.

It's a widower's grief. Two couches and a chair, all rotten with grief.

But no one mentioned the kids. Aged 10 and 15, John's daughters like to fuss over their visitors and the beach is that way naturally: permissive. It's a sad scene, the Stones fade out and somehow I DON'T have permission. John and I are at a wordless standstill. I can't even scope the room, except peripherally, which I'd better stop doing before... something...

Now it's Aerosmith. I say, "This is *Pump*! That's the only record of theirs I like."

"Why?"

"Because it has "What It Takes", which is the only SONG by Aerosmith that I like."

The gaze deepens. John's grip tightens. I know I'm in.

John: "Sara? Play track 10."

-19-

"The writer, the writer, the writer. You're the writer."

"Yessir."

"What are you, 40? You don't have to call me sir. *I'm* 40. Why you call me sir?"

I point to the photo of a man with a large woman, a fat woman. The man is in uniform. There are two little girls. I say, "You're military."

"I *was*. I WAS a Marine."

"Did you part ways amicably?"

"AMICABLY. Hmm. YEAH, I ... don't see how THAT is ANY of your fucking BUSINESS, friend."

I shift the carryout bag in my hands, its handles pinching me numb. I flash on the coming 86 but Amber is very wise to relieve me of the bags two minutes later when Steven Tyler steps in with that slicing wail of pain, "and I don't want to BURN in PARADISE," John and I are *IN* the song which *IS* about this moment tonight on St. Pete Beach and the alcohol sympathy wins out, the insane brutality of love and defeat and retreat and regret and surely we just got off on the -

48

"Look man I think we got off on the wrong - hey, what kinda guy just stands there all night? I ain't gonna bite ya. Now... I APOLOGIZE, these are my DAUGHTERS, SARA say hello, ANNA say HELLO to the WRITER, writer sit DOWN, have a beer, and LET'S GET ON THE RIGHT FOOT."

"Oh Daddy," Sara says. That's when I really SEE her, and the tragedy.

Amber hands me a bottle of beer, unopened.

I say, "I'm Gene."

-20-

"My wife died. My girls don't have a mother. Ain't nobody can change that. I'm gonna drink another few days, then...life goes on. We're a family."

"You're fine, daddy," Sara says. I can't - won't - lay eyes on her. Sara is a whir of pastel in the corner. "Mom is proud of us. We're all so strong."

A cat drops in Sara's lap. Another bounds across the throw rug between the large sofa (Robbie and Amber, legs crossed, grinning) and the glass coffee table. Sara is packing a pipe with the notorious "synthetic marijuana" known as "spice."

I say, "I'm so sorry, John."

He mumbles something about God, last amid the agonizing final chants of "What It Takes" and the melodrama is transcended. But the pain in the room is suffocating, regardless-

John takes the pipe from Sara. "Don't you girls ever touch this crap."

"Hush, daddy."

Robbie and Amber sit as if invisible. Mesmerized. Couchbound.

My heroin cruise has run aground and when John offers me the black ceramic, I accept. I've seen spice turn the whole neighborhood from dopes into outright zombies, people say they make the crap out of fluorescent lighting chemicals. But this is a night for bonding.

John takes a pull on a longneck Budweiser, patting Sara, who has joined us on the couch, lightly on her left arm: "I got my girls. See, I loved her, she had the best heart of any woman I was ever with, anyone I served with, or my family, I mean...she was an ANGEL, that's what I called her. Everyone else she was Angie, but I called her my angel. I can't even listen to that song, you know, 'Angel' by Aerosmith?"

"Oh yeah."

"You don't like 'Angel'?"

"No, I do. I didn't mean what I said."

"How do you not fucking mean what you SAID."

"I was over simplifying. Making a long story short."

"Uh huh. I got my eye on you. So this is good for us. It's gonna be good. We're gonna live on the beach."

"A lot of people do that."

"Live on the beach? Yeah, we ain't exactly alone out here."

"No, a lot of people come here for a fresh start. I did."

"Where'd you come from?"

"Baltimore. Fucking cops were after me."

"Oh yeah?"

"My girlfriend was nuts. Her brother was a murder police."

"Murder? What'd you do, kill her?"

"No, no... it was... it's a long story."

"Well, suppose you TELL it."

"There was a stabbing, and-"

"So you stabbed her."

"No! She stabbed ME!"

"Looks like you get stabbed a lot. I got my eye on you. So, I got my girls. I loved Angie more than anything, but my girls, they lost their only mom. You only ever have but one mom. You better do right by your mom, always, even if she ain't... see, I cursed my mom, and told her off, and she died before I could TELL her, cuz you know you don't mean things, how they come out."

John hits the pipe: "We're gonna get through this. I feel bad, I mean, it's... I know how it looks, but these girls are so goddamn STRONG, that's their MOTH -"

"Hush, daddy."

Sara is impossibly dead center.

I ask, cautiously, "How long you guys been here?"

"Couple weeks. Been gettin our feet wet. Come down from North Carolina. I thought it would be good for the girls."

"It's beautiful, daddy."

The *Pump* CD begins repeating. Little Anna sits cross-legged on the dirty floor watching Animal Planet on mute: big cats tearing the ass out of a zebra.

Sara brings a round of beers.

John hits the pipe. I raise my beer. The room comes alive a little.

"To survival," I say.

"To the beach," John says.

"To the beach," I say.

"Sara, put on that Van Morrison. So you cut off - hey Robbie!"

Robbie and Amber are asleep.

"So you cut off your EAR?"

Now he appears not to have had a drop, or a toke, of anything.

"It was for money," I begin.

Digging my hole.

"Did it hurt?" Sara's gone nuts for the ear thing. She is at my side, inches from my face. She pinches the ragged stump and squeals.

"Sara, for CHRIST'S SAKE."

John hands me the pipe.

"It didn't hurt too bad," I say.

"He's punk rock, daddy!"

I notice Sara's little toe-rings. Sara's cuffed cut-offs. She's ridiculously, dangerously beautiful.

"Punk," John says. "Huh. Buddy I served with lost an ear in Baghdad. He didn't get shit for it. Cuz he could still hear out of it, they said. S'called a 'cosmetic injury,'"

The girls begin dancing. Van Morrison. "Wild Night."

I say, "Do they really LIKE our shit?"

"They kinda like everything. I play 70s shit. 60s shit, but mostly 70s. Sara's into all that hardcore shit. I don't pay attention to the new shit, tell you the truth. All it is, is drugs. Nothing else. That shit ain't music."

"Yeah. When punk went to the suburbs, it was all over."

"Punk? I'm talking, like, fucking Neil YOUNG, dude."

Sara says, "You guys should hear yourselves."

I cycle to the store for another 12 pack, fully expecting to be out or ditched when I return, but the door is open, and I end up going one on one with John in the kitchen. I try to explain Celine and Burroughs to him. He's enjoying my monologue. I let him pick my head. The spice gets us on the same wavelength even as I introduce the subjects of Nazism and wife-killing. The link is pain. I talk of nothing but pain, but we're nodding our heads and smiling. It's healing.

John leaves at midnight. "Rocket Man" playing low on a boombox in the tiny kitchen when he walks out the door. He hops into his Range Rover. He drives away. I find a copy of *Exile on Main Street* in John's CD cabinet. *Good* Stones. *Final* Stones.

I'm happy to drink all night long. I fix a bowl of spice. My center shifts which is fine until it isn't. I think I might die. Sara catches my waving hands and I hear her say, "I'll call you later." She hangs up to talk me down. I let her pick my head once I'm sure I'm not dying. She is a young Ammo; she's an Elisha Cuthbert double, that's both of them. Sara moves like something that is neither girl nor woman, for she *is* neither, she is exactly that nameless creature, exactly that phenomenal energy, made all the lovelier, made devastating – if one is to be truthful – for the *near* seamlessness of adult transition, and it's the pure misogynist id which Sara's counterfeited perversion of maternal instinct speaks so purely and directly to... something you know to avoid with a defeated shake of the head that men use to skirt the edge of the abyss without speaking, really, and I say, "You're terrific. Download everything by The Velvet Underground."

I drink two beers just watching her do the fucking dishes.

Anna is a nervous child with long brown hair like her mother, held by a blue plastic headband. She turns the music off in the middle of "Ventilator Blues." I can hear the voices from Family Guy.

Robbie and Amber are bickering. It's a lot to understand.

-22-

I wake in darkness to a shout: "Sara!"

I say, "Hello?"

Panic.

I feel a table, a chair – it's a kitchen. I probe along a countertop, the fridge, the faces and the scene return to me.

"You're awake?" It's Sara.

"What's going on?"

"Blackout. Anna, give me the lantern. The light thing, with the radio on it. Where are y-"

She flicks the switch, re-appearing to me in the tight kitchen: bikini-cut Levi's again, the white tank top. She leans across me to bend a venetian blade with one finger; I see water hitting black glass, and the most beautiful woman in the -

- house FLOODS with white light and engine howl.

Car door slams.

John barrels in, soaked, his arms lined with plastic sacks. A human pack mule.

"How long," he says. "Sara?"

"A while, maybe a half hour? TV went out, cable, and then everything."

"Fuck. I'll call 'em. You alright?"

"I'm fine. Everybody was sleepin."

A pillar of light pounds the beach, shaking it and us, and we can all see each other. I feel like a cockroach. There's a full beer in front of me.

And thunder pounds the house. Everyone says, "holy shit" and "fuck" except Robbie and Amber. They've vanished.

"Put everything away girls. I'll get my tent, and we'll go watch the storm on the beach. Power oughta be fixed in a few hours."

So that's what we do.

-23-

You feel naked at the edge of the world when it's getting shot to pieces.

One block to Sunset, two down to Upham Beach, established by the Upham family in 1961: the whole town was a raw swamp. In 2012, the resorts are gray shapes sulking back at the light show down the coast, no rain, the Rossmoyne Building and its balconies forming a wall, NORTH Upham and out in the surf are the mobile-home sized sandbags called "t-groins" which preserve it all, HISTORIC Upham: the racist butchers who invented St. Pete Beach. We lay a bedsheet down on the Upham sand.

"Tell me a story, daddy," says Anna. "I don't like it out here."

The lightning explodes every Upham house and beyond: THERE, you can't miss the gothic *castillo* DON CESAR! Owned by the Loews Corporation! It's PINK!

I re-submerge – for the leg – and when the warm blackness hits my waist I can hear Robbie and Amber behind me. I say, "This ain't no good." A hard scab has formed. It needs a blade. The light show is the ghost of a tormented child, still acting out, jagged white lines that freeze frame the cottony black void.

Back on land, I immediately smell crack. I think, "Oh that's ABSOLUTELY crack cocaine," and begin grinding my crack-withered choppers.

"Gene Gene Jellybean," Robbie says. Mushmouthed.

"Where did you guys go?"

"Guess," he grins.

"STORYTELLER," John booms. "Tell us a story."

"Aww, I can't do that. My head's all messed up."

Robbie hands me a crack pipe, his finger pressed to his lips.

John motions "go ahead" and I don't know if he means the crack or the story. I fish a longneck Icehouse out of the cooler and hit the pipe.

John says, "Sara, I thought you wanted a story."

He hits her with the Coleman lantern's bright yellow beam. She picks an ear bud out of her ear.

"What?"

"This is family time. Get over here."

The girl plants herself between John and I. It's a tight squeeze, and the crack has summoned it in me: I'm a werewolf.

"Anna? Where are you?"

"I'm here," she says, gobbling Doritos in the dark.

A flash-expands-holds-freeze frame on Sara's silver toe rings.

OH SWEET CHRIST.

"Once upon a time," John begins, "there was a family on the beach."

"But it wasn't a normal family," Sara says.

"It was a broken family," I say, feeling embarrassed to be human, like when someone makes you do the high 5 thing.

"But they pulled together, like sailors in the middle of a storm..." (It's John vs. Crack: crack's winning.)

53

"And just when the boat was about to snap in half, getting tossed all over the ocean..." (Sara's tired of cheap poignancy, I don't blame her.)

"They reached an undiscovered island..." (John's phoning it in.)

"Populated by cannibals," I say, crack-crazed, a *shrinking* werewolf.

"No, dumbass," Sara snaps. "By a tribe of FISHERMEN, a peaceful tribe, like potheads, and they brought the sailors to their village and they put spells on them to fix their broken bones and hearts and their druggy HEADS..."

Sara smacks John in the ear.

John hits the pipe.

John agrees, casually: "They're ALL fucked up."

"And they healed for many, many weeks," I continue, "being fed by the villagers. The ship was gone..."

"But it went down slow enough," Sara chirps, "that they could grab bits and pieces, like their GPS, some oars, rope, their *hats*..."

"Hats?" John says. "What hats?"

"They gotta have their white sailor hats so people know they're not pirates. The villagers are gonna build 'em a new ship."

"But they don't have to leave..."

John laughs. He hands me the pipe. I pass it on to Robbie.

An end to penance?

The lantern has a radio on it. We look for music. We look for things on the beach. The night is alive. Sara wants to hear hip hop. Anna laughs.

-24-

MAYDAY: the sky is a sucker punch of vertigo, euphoria's part of it but first the mortal confusion, the cosmic fear.

Sunlight. Bird sounds. I can move my fingers: FUCK.

The world exists, and I'm spinning with it, or maybe on it *and* with it?

Should I hold on to something?

ON THE BEACH: gravity is a mule kick that explains everything back again, until I trust that I'm alive.

Hunger and thirst, the water and the land, my feet and my hands.

Nothing to hold on to?

FEAR: nothing was done about me THIS time...maybe the next? Cops, or will I float into the cosmos one way or another, from Mother Earth?

Try it sometime.

Screw your brain up real good and fall asleep out there.

It's a pure man's finest decadence, to wake like that, scrambling for your corporeal self through open sky, like your ribcage and kneecaps were your wallet, or keys, your very own infant son.

Two seagulls approach my gangrenous calf:

"Don't even think about it, assholes."

-25-

A solid wood door, the sick early morning: meck-meck-meck.

Hydraulic whine of a beach bus, and then the plock/flock of the deadbolt.

John, bleary: "Nooooo, man. Nooo."

"I'm sorry, but... I need my stuff."

"Nah, don't try that, don't pull that shit man. You didn't leave anything."

"Wallet? Keys? Beer?"

"Nannn... ehh... fuck..."

"I'll settle for the wallet and keys." I smile.

"Fuck... yeah... just be quiet. Girls... girls are sleeping."

I swipe two Yuenglings from the fridge, leave two. The rest is on the coffee table. Robbie and Amber are curled up like a pair of stinking ferrets, on the couch. John stands at the door, rubbing his temples.

"Thanks, John. I left you some beers."

"Alright."

I steady myself to take on the overbearing vitality of the morning.

Stand a moment, plotting: Waffle House?

I check my wallet. $220. I flip through the bills three, four times. There are never enough twenties. Twenties go fast.

As I'm unlocking the bike the door opens once again. John and his pipe.

He extends it.

I pop a beer, shaking my head.

"Listen, the cable's still out. You said you had a DVD collection?"

"Got a whole library, yeah. Over at Beach Storage."

"The girls are all pissy about the cable, so -"

A cat whips around John's ankles and slinks into the shrubbery lining the clammy porch.

"Goddammit. Look, why don't you just bring everything over man?"

"It's heavy, like 50 pounds."

"Oh Jesus. I'll drive you over, but... and we should get some beer, I guess. Help me find that fuckin cat."

I finish my beer.

"You got any Roxy Music?"

-26-

Sara rubs her puffy eyes. Her red sweatpants are folded down in the front and when I look up from a copy of Tampa Bay Times, my nose almost lands in her pubic hair. She scratches at a black sports bra and mumbles, "I should make you guys an omelet."

"Put some goddamn clothes on Sara! We got people over."

"Gene, would you like an omelet?"

"Just a beer, sweetie."

"Get me one, Sara. Please."

John and I moan like shot dogs. The ferrets join in, an escalating horror soundscape.

"Better bring four, baby."

"What?"

"Bring four. Four beers, sweetie."

Sara drops a complete four pack of Colt 45 on the table: "Y'all gonna kill yourselves."

-27-

The atrocity exhibition:

"Oh my god. Daddy..."

"God damn friend. You need to go to the hospital."

"It'll be oh -"

"Ok my ass. You're gonna lose that fuckin leg, Gene."

Sara pops to her feet and bounds over the couch into the bathroom.

I don't want to ruin the party, and I'm ashamed of my bad leg, of having repulsed the girl when she returns with a laundry basket full of towels and first aid.

-28-

She whispers in my ear: "Don't worry, I got this."

John returns with a four pack of Yuengling and his pipe.

Amber's husky whine: "I've got R.N. training"

Sara snarls back, "SO DO I."

John: "Hell you do."

Sara: "Mom took me in, like, a hundred times. I'm treating it."

John: "Anna baby, you hungry?"

Anna, sitting in a pile of dolls facing the front door, simply lifts her Pop-Tart in the air and continues playing, without a word.

Sara: "Lift your leg up."

She drapes a stained beach towel with Garfield the cat on it across the coffee table, clicking on the Coleman lantern to illuminate a muscular calf swollen to bursting with infection.

John hits his pipe.

Rain taps on the windows.

Anna says, "That TV ain't comin back on, I know it."

Sara prods at a puncture, just below the primary wound, a gash, and I wail...

"Look," I announce to all, "we're gonna need beer. I'll buy some beer, and then we can swing by Beach Storage for-"

"Fuck! We forgot the fuckin movies."

"Daddy, don't curse so much."

"Sorry honey."

"We'll get my movie box, alright? And I'll fix up the-"

My face goes white, my head implodes and my vision blurs.

"THERE," Sara exhales exhilarated, ecstatic, as she retracts a five inch steak knife from my calf.

Amber flaps her hands and runs out the front door.

Robbie smiles.

Sara collects herself: "Everybody BACK OFF. I need LIGHT."

"Okay Sarah, we're done playing fucking EMERGENCY ROOM for -"

"Daddy, hush. Just watch. Gene, hold still. You're doing good."

Anna stands over all of us, atop an easy chair, still nibbling at her Pop Tart. John sees her and smiles.

"This better than TV, honey?"

"I don't know" she says. "I guess."

Sara tells me, "This will hurt. A LOT, okay?"

"Jesus."

"But then it'll feel better. You ready?"

I wonder if she's a virgin. And I know what's about to happen.

She's leaned in close, both hands in latex gloves, thumbs and forefingers upon my tree trunk calf, framing a weeping black tri-cornered center.

"How'd you get legs like that? Biking?"

"Fixed gear biking, yeah."

"What's that?'

"Uh - OW - it's... gearless riding, uh... you can't shift, it's... just..."

"Easy."

"High gear, permanently, like..."

"Breathe."

"Stuck in one direction-"

"Shhh. Don't look."

"Can't STOP -"

"Oh KAY!"

E-X-P-L-O-S-I-O-N

The room is silent. I feel the warmth of it, then I can hear the screams. And the laughter.

Amber: "I'm gonna throw up. Robbie, I'm gonna be sick."

Beside my leg, on the towel, is a mound of bright purple substance like plum pudding. True to her word, the thumping pain is gone. I wiggle my toes and smile. It's just then, while everyone's mouth remains agape and I am rendered complacent by endorphins, that the little scamp makes her boldest move, gripping my leg and twisting with both hands in opposite direction, as if wringing the neck of a crazed animal; this releases the lion's share of sick, the diamond-shaped puncture enlarged to a kind of crude fistula, vomiting and defecating grape-sized blood clots in a rushing tide of that creamy raspberry filling.

This time, the room *stays* quiet. Until Sara breaks it.

"Fuck," she says, collapsing back on the couch with a sheen of sweat on her brow.

Amber has fled. Robbie, also, is no longer with us.

"I'll get some paper towels," says Anna, her mouth full.

"Beer," says John, shaking his head.

The leg glistens in the blank blue glare of the TV screen.

-29-

Sunshine Liquors and high beams and more fucking rain. We are cruising past Suzanne's Rolls which is now sitting on cinderblocks, the back wheels gone.

Past Suzanne's cinderblock bungalows. Suzanne's pool and Suzanne's rental office.

"Stop," I say.

"Come on, man."

"A quick dip in the pool, clean the damn thing out. Chlorine's what it needs."

"I've had just about enough of your nasty ass dogbitten leg for one day, that okay with you?"

"Sorry."

"Where's the place?"

"Block up. Here. HERE. Go left here."

We roll into the snuff film tableau of Beach Storage, aisle one, opposite the blacked out rear windows of a dozen Suzanne bungalows hiding there in the rain, mounds of dogshit and a few thousand beer cans below them. ("OFFY-SAR, these TRASH is not from my places, it was DUMPED here, you have NO RIGHT to ACCUSE me, OFFY-SAR, what is your badge number?")

On the right side, the ancient white washed roll doors, cinderblock limbo, invoking every kind of psychic exhaustion. I hop out, pop the lock in the wet dark. The chrome-plated metal burns ice-cold and brutal in my hands.

John backs up a bit giving me more high beam there in the godless rows. Things could be worse: I could be out here with Sam.

The dim sodium lamps at each corner of Beach Storage are said to be equipped with cameras. If you are caught living in one of the crude units, you AND your possessions are tossed. It says so right in the contract, I'm told.

To keep control, I disengage. There are rough patches. There are ALWAYS rough patches. Sam and I freezing in Pittsburgh.Sam and I freezing in Manhattan. Sam and I freezing in Baltimore. I do as well for the beast as I can do for myself. It's temporary. It's ALWAYS temporary.

Yank the roll gate: Crash one.

The unit: a dumpy, damp mausoleum.

"Here lies Gene Gregorits, and Monastrell Books."

Removal: three copies of Dog Days.

Removal: an aluminum case containing 30 years of subnormal film obsession.

Removal: the expensive black suit given to me by Richard Wellington at the Melbourne Underground Film Festival last September. I am plotting the suit's ruin. It reminds me of Bec, who is currently snorting drugs with Eurotrash film producers, who are always also drug dealers.

She gets glamorously numb.

I get Beach Storage in the rain.

Yank the roll gate: crash two.

-30-

Evan Williams with big cans of beer set John and I to babbling. We're getting too honest. It's dangerous, and we both understand that completely.

Little Anna has gutted the metal box: the room has become a lake of black Mylar DVD sleeves. Leone, Lynch, Fuller, Buñuel, Tavernier, Blier, the Maysles, Andrei Fucking Tarkovsky: all rejects!

But there's hope: she's found Ren & Stimpy Volume Three, The Pretenders Video Anthology, John Lydon's Megabugs, The Dark Knight, Spider-Man, and the Best Of When Animals Attack.

"That's pretty excellent for a kid," I tell John.

"Yeah. Hey, I think you ought to take a fucking shower, Gene."

"Yeah, alright."

John gets cozy as Sara packs him a pipe of spice. I grab my suit, and head for the bathroom.

Under the sink, I locate a gallon of bleach, which, once under the hot water, I begin dousing my calf with. I scrub my filthy hair with Hannah Montana shampoo. Chunks of b-movie gore spurt onto the shower curtain when I flex the wound with my hands. Water rolls off my rail thin frame in brown sheets.

I dry quickly and make faces in the mirror... shave carefully with a pink safety razor which I wrap in toilet paper and toss. I decide I look sharp, but I'm drunk, and I always think I look sharp when I'm drunk. Doesn't everyone? Fuck everyone. I look 25, and feel even younger than that.

On goes the suit, and that's how I return: shirtless, suited up, and slicked back.

"Oh la la," Sara taunts. "Now you need a haircut."

"Man, DON'T let her cut your goddamn hair."

"Hush, daddy."

On the TV, Johnny Rotten is covered in leeches. Anna is hypnotized.

"Sara, no fuckin haircuts."

He's getting surly. Next, he'll be sentimental.

I pour myself a coffee cup full of whiskey, reconsider my predicament. A developing drift into worry, sadness, is broken when Sara guides my limp right hand under her Slipknot t-shirt, pressing it firmly into her left breast.

It's a jolt that freezes my blood, attacks my entire nervous system.

"Shhh," she whispers. "He's asleep."

A chance glance at John confirms this. Both of his hands are flat, palms down on the arms of the plush chair next to the couch. It's a stoic position, as if he's meditating.

I try to retract my hand when the little beast grinds it into her right breast and leans in to pierce the skin of my girder-stiff neck with her teeth.

And, as if she was never there, Sara departs. I stare into the center of my palm where it seems perfectly logical that one or both of her erect nipples would have left a scar.

Whiskey lulls me into artificial confidence, false comfort. My swollen balls encourage persuasively heroic fictions of their own.

Sara re-appears at my feet, and begins rolling the sleek Aussie cloth over my calf up to my knee: "Your poor leg. The swelling's gone, for now. It'll have to be re-drained." And what a fucking scene as she wraps me once again in clean, white gauze with her little hands.

"Sara's gonna be a hair stylist AND a nurse," Anna says.

John stirs. His eyes register the situation to his right and a scowl forms.

"Pal," he intones flatly, "I think it's time you hit the road."

"Daddy!" Sara towers over her father, a pair of black eyes accompanied by a dagger of admonishment: "APOLOGIZE! YOU APOLOGIZE TO HIM RIGHT NOW!"

She owns the room. John gazes at his hung-over, wet-brained reflection in the window beside him, pockmarked by droplets of new rain. He sighs.

"I'll head out. I don't want you guys fighting."

"No man, she's right. You ain't done nothing but respect me and my girls. I apologize. Sara, get me a beer. Please?"

"Me too, Sara," I say. Too quickly. John stiffens. John hits the pipe. And, exhaling, begins examining one of the paperbacks I'd left on the floor several hours back: "Dog... Days. A FUCK... of a RIDE. Vice Magazine. Hmmm. There's a magazine called VICE?"

"Yeah. It's popular with kids, I guess."

Sara places 2 cans of High Life on the table. "Y'all never drink the same thing twice. It's called 'continuity,' Gene."

"Now, let me ask you something... GENE... who the fuck puts the word 'FUCK' on the front cover of a book? Cuz I read, you know, probably not the arty farty shit you read, but I ain't ever seen a book with the word 'fuck' right there on the front like that."

I stare straight ahead, a queer in the headlights.

"He's punk rock, daddy. I wanna give 'im a mohawk."

'What's this thing *about* man? Come on...'

"It's about grief."

"Excuse me? *Grief?*"

"Grieving, yeah. A guy's son is killed by pit bulls and he..."

"That happen to you?"

"Yeah."

"I'm real fuckin sorry man. I didn't... I'm an asshole..."

"No you're not! I don't mind talking about the book."

"I keep snappin at ya, and it's... it's just... I got kids here, you know and-"

"Daddy, hush."

"Sara, SHUT YOUR MOUTH!"

"Drunk asshole! Have another DRINK!"

She storms off.

"Aw, Sara honey..."

We sit in silence a moment. I'm about to leave when the girl returns, in tears. There's no point pretending I'm not in love with her.

"Gene, you bring a few of them books for the girls?"

"All three of you, sure."

Sara squeals, rubbing her sad, smart face into a t-shirt sleeve and sniffing: "Sign it, I'll only read it if you *sign* it, Gene!"

Anna finally turns away from Spider-Man with a look of sincere contempt: "You guys are all NUTS."

John has already flipped to the first page.

"'It was a straight-up rape.'"

I shrug my shoulders with a weak smile, and try to look as baffled as him. Sara shoves a black Sharpie marker at me, with a book, and that's enough to convince Anna, too. She crawls under the coffee table with the last copy in her mouth, forcing herself between Sara and I.

I wink at Sara and hold up a finger, as Anna shakes my wrist crying, "ME FIRST!"

I find the title page: "A MONASTRELL BOOK 2012."

(It lasted only a year?)

(Waking up with Sam in my own beach pad, signing books to little dolls. It wouldn't have been a bad life.)

"For... ANNA..."

Squeals! All around!

John can't resist a grin, but there's something in it. A threat: "Watch it motherfucker." There's also a compliment, somehow. "Well done, motherfucker."

"Stay... in... school... watch... for... stingrays..."

Little Anna now lit up like a Christmas tree, scampers off with her prize. I don't worry about the book's evil, and it *is* evil: she'll read it if and when she's ready for it. And besides, it has redeeming qualities. A cautionary tale?

Moving right along then:

"Sara...with an H?"

"No, stupid."

"SARA!" John barks.

"For... Sara... make it... a mohawk... sister."

"OH! OH DADDY! Let me cut his hair please let me cut his hair!"

"A... blue... mohawk."

I close the book and give it to her. I don't know why it matters to me, but I already have decided that Sara will never read the book. Anna would, in a few years, but hers will be long gone by then. Odds are, all three books will be in the next trash pick-up.

Sara whispers to me, "I have the stuff."

"Huh?"

"The blue stuff, I can DO that."

I reach for John's pipe, and pause for his okay.

He scratches his head, opens his left hand palm up.

"Help yourself, man."

Robbie and Amber, the hillbilly Sid and Nancy, appear in the front window, grinning, grinning, grinning.

-31-

Taste of cinder.

Pain.

Fear, and pain, and cinder.

Taste of blood.

I don't want to open my eyes.

I have to open my eyes, because there's a chance I may not be too late.

I see:

Black macadam.

Chain link.

Keys, a padlock.

BEACH STORAGE.

I don't want to try my extremities.

I MUST MOVE: my legs won't bend.

I roll onto my back, a stomped sardine, and THERE IT IS.

The whole wide world -BLUE- and I find my strength in the bird calls, in the salt winds, in this voice which tells me I've got two days to live.

The morning air is cold, an arctic cold, sharp upon my head.

But if there *is* a way out... bike gone... whatever the damage... blood on my hands... smashed kneecaps... broken ribs?

Crash one.

Pull on my boots. Beach Lounge is a block away.

Crash two.

-32-

"Hey Maggie."

"What the... HELL?"

"Gimme a pitcher."

"Rolling Rock."

"Sure. Whatever."

Baby steps. Door halfway off its hinges, at the end of the bar...

An awful smell.

I flip the lights on; THERE IT IS:

Blue mohawk.

Two black eyes.

Broken nose.

I light a cigarette, try to smile: goddamn.

At the bar, I try not to move at all, ordering: Pepsi. Whiskey. Aspirin. Orange juice. Potato chips.

Anything I can think of.

"Don't you think you should go get looked at?"

"That's what I'm doing here, heh-heh... -ow. Aw. Fuck."

"I'm not your *mother*, Gene! Your buddy Dave Waverly came in all tore up yesterday." Maggie turns her back to me, flipping through TV stations with a remote. "Don't know what the hell's the matter with you guys."

-33-

PARMP PARMPPARMP

Wendy's ashen face, shower-raw, can't open her eyes: bunker life.

"Sammy's sleeping, Gene. You figure something out?"

"I'm leaving today."

"The police are looking for you. You gotta get out of here. Sammy's fine. You got my number?"

"Yeah."

"Well, bye. Be safe."

Leaving the jungle, I run into Dave Waverly.

Two black eyes: "Hey Geeeeeeeene!"

I stand over my dismantled desk in the field, across 73rd.

A stack of cherrywood.

And that's that.

-34-

Dave is buying $5 20-ounce rumrunners at The Sloppy Pelican. First floor patio, in the back: the channel's edge.

A Jamaican man is singing "Cheeseburger In Paradise" on acoustic at the end of the bar. The sky goes overcast, comes back, a spooky languor.

Dave smiling through his bruises and cuts: "I bet you $20 you can't do 3 shots of tequila and swim the channel."

"I don't have $20 to wager, Dave."

"I'll PAY you, hah-hah! HAH-HAH! THE SWIMMING OF THE CHANNEL," he begins chanting, his voice like a sick child's, like Michael Pollard, all *hardcore* wet-brain. "THE SWIMMING OF THE CHANNEL!" Dave pounds on the bar with both fists, his bloodshot Irish blues flushing with idiot fury. "THE SWIMMING OF THE CHANNEL!"

The barmaids at Sloppy's are all young and foxy and witless. Except ours: "DAVE! SIMMER DOWN!"

"THREE SHOTS FOR THIS MAN! GEEEEEENE's gonna SWIM THE CHANNEL!"

"Not now he's not," the displeased young grandmother says. She places a hand on my wrist. "Gene, look at that riptide. You'll drown."

"Gimme the shots, Melanie."

"GIVE HIM THREE STIFFIES, MELANIE! THE SWIMMING OF THE CHANNEL! THE SWIMMING OF THE CHANNEL!"

"Oh, shut the fuck UP, already. JESUS, Dave."

But she pours them, and I drink them. I strip down to my suit pants and nothing else.

"Gene, don't die," Melanie whines.

And then I'm off, a full running leap on broken legs, with a standing O from a dozen women - and Dave - roaring behind me. I meet the rushing water like a daydream; as I return to the surface, I catch a glimpse of them, at the edge of the bar's disused pier, soundless, and begin.

The crossing takes me nearly 20 minutes, as my strength is lost almost immediately against the insidious current.

When I reach Sunset Beach, I crawl to my feet and take a bow.

A distant chorus of catcalls.
Pelicans dropping from the sky in slow motion.

-35-

Drunk, incapably drunk at Fisherman's Park, I take the fifth of Gordon's gin from Mark, whose eyes are black from cancer. Romance-proof reek of hundred-proof railyard, turn your fucking stomach.

"You know I got your movies, Gene," he wheezes all hangdog, patting his Rottweiler bitch on her haunches. He leans back into the park bench. He stretches his legs.

"Which movies?"

"You come by with the whole CASE, dude! All of 'em. You were dragging the fucker, you was ALL fucked up. You don't remember?"

"You have my bike, too?"

"No bike, just the DVDs. You know, you probably have internal bleeding, the fuss you were making... your RIBS, your RIBS, and the fucking *angel* shit... you *saw* an angel, *saw* an angel... hehhehheh."

Then the manatees come. I take off my jacket and dive back into the channel. Most of the small pod glides away from me, six or seven of them, but I find myself facing one, and there just isn't enough space between us or enough time for the slow-witted creature to escape me.

One hand on his back, the other at his side, I let him tow me halfway back to Sunset Beach before I drop off, for fear I may be molesting him (I only want to TOUCH the fucking thing) and I'm not in any pain then, the sun setting and alcohol bringing all manner of pleasing thoughts, the sharks minding their own and keeping a distance, when I hear the 2 way radio sounds, the white noise...

A flash of light...

"Come on out, Gene."

-36-

I backstroke in circles, twenty feet out. The police are speaking delicately in hushed tones, and I imagine them as Roswell scientists, myself a stranded spaceman. But their conversation ends, and it's back to: "Come on OUT, Gratortis."

"I HEREBY INVOKE *MARITIME LAW!*"

One of the women steps forward, and I make an effort to study her, my chin on my chest. I return to a sprawled state, thinking of Amy Ryan in The Wire. I study the jet streams and the colors.

"Maritime Law is for BOATS, dumbass," she declares.

(chuckles, murmurs, beeps and pops)

(boots crushing the gravel)

One of the men: "Get out or you're going to jail. Party's over."

I right myself in the water, breast-stroking lazily:

"HIS ROYAL HIGHNESS THE KING OF ACHEM SEIZES ALL VESSELS THAT RUN AGROUND ON THE REEFS OF HIS COASTAL WAH-TAHS!"

(giggles, curses, shaking heads)

(it's getting dark now)

"Gene, we're gonna give you a break if you come up here and talk to us nicely."

"UNSOCIALBLENESS TOUGHENS A MAN'S HEART AND THEREBY RENDERS HIM FITTER FOR GREAT DEEDS!"

The man again: "I'm going to put my hand out. Do you promise not to pull me in?"

I turn and face the sunset. I won't see it again for a long, long, time. I climb onto and over the razor-sharp rocks.

I take the officer's hand.

He pulls me up with one hard yank. "Now, take a seat," he says, with a note of relief.

I reach for my bottle underneath the bench once I'm collapsed on it, heaving. The same officer kicks it over.

"Keep it up, fucknuts. You are now trespassed from -"

He puts up his hands, fingers extended for maximum emphasis: "NINE addresses now. NINE. I'm not reading you the list. I'm gonna tell you for the last time to clear off or catch a charge."

"I'm TRYING."

(whispers, laughter, shaking heads)

A female cop with red hair, a smirking mouth which attempts to diffuse her astonishment, hands on her hips.... I decide I like her best. She says: "You ain't tryin shit, getting butt nasty drunk and floating around out there with your pants on -"

She shakes her head, pointing at the water -

"... right when the fucking BULL SHARKS come in to FEED. You're gonna get yourself KILLED."

"I was planning on-"

"No plans," another male cop says, stepping close, and poking a finger in my eye. "You can make plans somewhere else. You're GONE TONIGHT. Do you understand? Tell me we have a deal."

"I'll go."

"You have an hour, sir."

He puts a bus pass in my hand. Ride all day for 5.

"Good luck to you. Take better care of yourself."

Crash one: typewriter. Dry socks.
Crash two.

St. Pete Beach library. 7:45 PM.
I log onto Facebook.
"You have a new message from Cynthia Maviano."
An address: 17300 Kennedy Boulevard. West Palm Beach.
The Bon Ton Hotel.

Sunshine Liquors: Nadeem quit.
Waffle House: Renee and Sloan, the mother and son who have sex, are back.
Beach Cinema: "Goodbye BEACH FRIENDS - THANKS FOR THE MEMORIES! 1992 - 2012."

I wake up under a moldy quilt.
I am under the bridge, under the Pasadena Causeway: an abandoned fisherman's shack shellacked in satanic graffiti.
This is the east end of Corey Avenue, on the intracoastal waterway where the road simply ends, where the strangest ones sit in parked cars because there's a death vibe here which calls to them, the hopeless ones from Iowa and Montana, and Utah and New Hampshire, disgraced businessmen and mentally collapsed housewives and heartbroken dykes and all serious-minded individuals seeking a reprieve, weighing the options, leaning towards weightlessness.
I have decided to hide *here* to risk it *here* for a few days living in my own little movie as we all do I suppose. I don't ponder very much, extracting cigarettes with my swollen DT fingers, watching the headlights of passing cars on the black intracoastal, and listening to the wet slapping hum of their wheels, Goodyear on grid iron, rrrrrrrrmp, rrrrrrrmp, rrrrrrmp, they'll be ON THE LOOKOUT FOR A MAN ON A BICYCLE, they'll have issued a B.O.L.O. WARNING FOR A MAN WITH A BLUE MOHAWK so I make up songs and sing them there in the putrid shack and at some point the thrashing gets the best of me and I brave the streets for a case of Colt 45, knocking them back and taking dips in the intracoastal, I need a hat, and I'm supposed to be in... Miami? November 12? 22? Time to think, a

week, tomorrow.... too narrow? Whatever it takes to GET IT STRAIGHT, to THINK, a little nightswimming, to sing the way you NEED to sing, COOL to the TOUCH and KILL a week, calling all cars, calling all cars, they smell FEAR so I cool it DOWN in the coastal waters of Queen Suzanne where they found that dead girl floating - I probably could have saved her - cool in my walk my boardwalk walk is like my sidewalk walk cool operating under the volcano as the sun rises blowing smoke and singing songs announcing a clean BREAK with Corey Avenue - hit the road, Jack - when life gets too hot ya got to COOL IT DOWN goddamn I'M BURNING ALIVE and the cool dips ain't helping so I wonder if I ought to thought I ought to thought I should CALL SOMEBODY and the ocean's waiting then but REAL sharks don't read panic signals at night at the east end of Corey Avenue where the weirdos sit in their parked cars at night wanting to die: "I'm not playing these games anymore" -

-41-

What colossal fuck-up *now* bathed in white and non-stop drone of PA speakers that designates hospital? In the movies I yank out my IV limp pitifully into the embrace of a wealthy film producer's bored wife, who actually READS my books since I began writing movie-bait like the rest of them and who has secured me a cozy basement writer's pad in Santa Monica.

In the movies I look for a call button when I wake from a vision, eyes sunken swollen shut and the feeling that I'm very much in the dark even now – the movie involves a woman, my skin cools at the sight of a small Indian woman in white pants, a white jacket bathed in hard white light but hard to imagine she sees me as a sexual possibility -

"Mr.... Justin? Has Dr. Ross been in to see you, Mr. Justin?"

"Gene... Gregorits... Gene Greg-Or-ITS."

"Mr. Gray-gortless, have you seen the doctor?"

"No. I don't know."

"He wants to talk to you. Do you remember coming in?"

In the movies, I am handcuffed to the bed.

"Was it the police? Am I under arrest?"

"You come here very late, after midnight. You are drunk, you have high fever, you are carrying a backpack, you are very, very sick. You don't remember."

"No. I was living in a shack. By the water."

"Dr. Ross wants to talk to you. He should come soon to see you. I want you to rest, okay? You almost died. So rest, and he come in to see you. How do you feel?"

"I hurt."

"We'll get you another round of meds shortly."

68

In the movies, I imagine ice cream, in a plastic cup. I'm supposed to have ice cream.

And there is a wind chime tinkling down the hall.

All the doctors smoke cigarettes.

-42-

"Mr. Greg...grottis? How ya feeling?"

"Weak. Hungry."

"You're probably wanting a drink. You remember coming in?"

"No. I was -"

I glance around: some relief comes to me with the discovery of a white plastic property bag placed next to my boots on the floor by a red vinyl chair.

"You have an infection... well, your immune system has collapsed and that infection has set into the bone of your left leg. So, obviously-"

"THAT's a hell of a..." I chuckle, begin kicking the air with my toes. "Life with one leg."

"Doesn't seem to bother you."

"It doesn't. I'll qualify for disability then."

"Well don't get your hopes up."

I look at him for the first time. He's one of those young TV doctors.

"I have some concerns. We gave you a strong anti-biotic, which ought to... Justin, we basically saved your leg. And your life. Do you understand that even another 12 hours without treatment... forget the leg... you would have died. Legs, arms, everything. Rest in peace."

"The nurse said I came in at midnight. What time is it now?"

"Midnight on Thursday. It's Saturday."

"Erm."

"I have serious concerns. Would you care to hear them?"

"Do I have a disease?"

Dr. Ross takes a deep breath and holds up a finger.

"We haven't got the bloodwork back yet but you show the signs, you... have all the symptoms of someone who is HIV positive. But you, I'm *assuming* you don't get tested regularly."

"No."

"You have a collapsed immune system. You have needle marks, fresh tracks on both arms. You were sweating so profusely that we had to get fluids in you."

"I know how it looks."

"You are also severely underweight for a man your size."

"I'm having a bad week."

"Justin, I..."

"GENE. GENE. GENE."

"You've been hospitalized before. You know the routine. You're uninsured and we can NOT keep you whether you want our help or not. What *I* would like to do-"

"I'm leaving town, you know. I have family in Savannah. They're waiting. I appreciate what you're saying."

"Gene, you're going to collapse sooner or later, the way you're going. Permanently. Ok? You're close."

"I gotta straighten out. I know. I know what I've gotta do."

"And the self mutilation concerns me. It's Florida law that you be involuntarily committed if I think you're a threat to yourself or others, but I already know... and to be back out on the street in your condition, well... you could still lose your leg, for one thing."

"I have family in Tampa."

"You were talking about pit bulls when you came in. We treated your wounds as dog bites."

"It's a German Shepherd bite." I notice the bandages on my hand. "And the hand. That's from coral. In the ocean."

Ross flips through a little notepad.

"Who is Amanda...Hokestein?"

"Hockstein. She killed my... she's a former neighbor, up... up north."

"In Baltimore."

"Hey man, that's not something I talk about with strangers."

"And you ARE the book writer who - one of the staff said you... *ate* your earlobe, cut it off and... I noticed it's missing, the right one."

"Yeah. That's old news."

"Well... someone will be in to take out your I.V. You'll be discharged. If you want the results of your blood work, you can-"

"No thank you."

"Very well. I hope you'll-"

"I don't have a phone anyway."

"Now THAT's a shocker. You guys always seem to keep a working phone. You're totally on top of your phones."

He shakes his head, turning towards the door.

My ears burn. My teeth clench.

"Cell phones are why this entire country is now mentally retarded. I don't know which GUYS you're talking about, all due respect. *Thank* you for saving my leg. I'm from New York fucking City and I don't HAVE a CELL phone."

"Take care, Gene."

I wait until Dr. Ross is gone and yank out my I.V.

Just like in the movies.

Coming over the Pasadena Causeway back into St. Pete Beach in the late afternoon wearing a blood stained golf cap picked up from the room opposite mine a million dollar view of the glittering evening coast including this very bridge I cross on the westbound side pedestrian walkway catching a chill when I see two cruiser cars parked down below at my derelict Satan shack wondering now if I left anything but with my boots my typewriter my ALICE pack I'm a motherfucker alright Mad fucking Max feeling all the world like Richard Gere in *American Gigolo* and I imagine lovely Ammo in the Lauren Hutton role – a sun-baked crackhead remake – and how do you like that, a perfectly good pair of Reef sandals there in the Exxon's alleyway at Corey and Blind Pass, they're almost my size, and give my skinless heels a break already.

Side streets to Sunshine Liquors for a case of High Life, under the Upham Beach boardwalk, I retire there (in truth a small access bridge but a boardwalk all the same) and what I busy myself with is delirium (delirium TREMENS) it's just self-pity fear cigarette smoking till dawn.

Junkie couple stiff with cold, white power tattoos on both necks, bun in the oven, they come sniffing around at first light.

"You get a voucher, man?"

"Pardon?"

"They givin out vouchers, the church."

"Vouchers for what?"

"Motel rooms. For thanksgiving."

"Giving out bus tickets, anywhere in the whole country," says the female.

"They're cleaning house," I say.

"S'cold."

"Yeah."

I open my typewriter. Re-spool it to look busy.

"Haven't seen one of those in a while."

"Oh yeah."

"You're that crazy fucker cut his ear off!"

"Yeah."

"Hey baby, check it out! Remember that guy they was talking about on the Bubba the Love Sponge?"

The unlovely young woman hugs herself, irritable with dope sickness, her skin putrid with acne. "You got a cigarette?"

"No."

I can't sit still. It must be 50 degrees. Lower. And I don't even *see* the ocean anymore.

A constipated acidic walk, shivering, to Beach Storage.

Crash one: ditch the typewriter. Ditch the suit. Ditch the boots. Swim trunks and blankets, down on the cold concrete floor of Unit 37 for rest, *good* rest but there is a mass exodus of cockroaches, who have run out of food. Seeya next summer, gang! Hah-hah. Hah!

Sit and type a poem about blowing my head off.

Another about blades. Spiteful. Methodical.

A post-literary age. Hah-hah.

Hah!

-45-

I am hiding in the bathroom of the AIDS family, with Suzanne's rental office at 550 Corey Avenue right next door.

She's on top of me. Around me. In my blood.

She knocks on the front door, demanding rent money and I hide from the beast cunt in the shower with the AIDS soap and the AIDS shampoo and the AIDS conditioner. Alone in the apartment, I look out the peephole straight into the rental office where Suzanne waves her saggy arms around and screams at her 98 year old mother while stomping back and forth with her hands on her fat hips. A blonde cat lands on my chest as I pour sweat and thrash and giggle and I cry out SAM but it's not Sam at all, "*that's* not Sammy," says the AIDS child, and the entire AIDS family tries to make me eat so I have an AIDS sandwich with Miracle Whip and mustard. I drink a cup of AIDS Kool-Aid. I wash a week's worth of dirty AIDS dishes. I observe 100 hours of our empire's collapse as bright pounding AIDS tabloid television on mute. I sweat out a lake of cheap yeast and 5,000 unpronounceable Philip Morris neurotoxins upon the dirty AIDS couch. The blonde AIDS cat looks and smells and behaves exactly like Sam, although it is so much smaller, and I realize that I have shrunken also.

When it is time to find another foxhole, I stand at the door and I say, "I'm watching you Suzanne. It would be like this, with me watching you, dirty cuntbitchwhore Suzanne."

-46-

"From: Cynthia Maviano (18 hours ago) Where are you?"

-47-

"From: Gene Gregorits (0 minutes ago) Bad Shape. Cops. Need bus ticket. Help."

Beach lounge, Ammo mouths the word GO and points to the bathroom and I understand that she is telling me to go wash up turn toward bathroom Ammo grab me hard by my ear from behind the bar Ammo say it's a cop get the FUCK out Gene

Crash one. Typewriter. Crash two.

THANK YOU for riding the PSTA! Central STATION. Central STATION. Next STOP Central AVENUE, AND... twenty seventh STREET.

Even undone I am sure to choke up, to choke ON, the memories of my first Gulf coast explorations: they remain new, they do not feel borrowed.

There I am, only one year ago, cashing my weekly bonus check, lost in the FLA sunshine, scum wilderness and fighting for a beach existence as I'd never fought for anything. And I ran it dry. I'm 200 pounds of consummate non-partisan East Coast *survivor-type*, but the flight path is obstructed, unsustainable, fossil fuels, Kerouac and Celine, the secret hopes of the world sticking to my filthy skin tonight in the final beach trolley ride liquidation express never had money for anything but booze

Sundown I deboard at Central and MLK downtown St. Petersburg with my typewriter and my ALICE pack, feel an evil chill, it's a cold spot in the middle of a vacant lot, the city that never wakes, little portals opening and closing in the deadness. You can find them when you are near death. Not good for much, the cold spots in dead areas, but they exist. I enter Kerouac's old Greyhound depot and "Not today man, I can smell you from here. You gonna have to sober up first, I'm sorry. Change your clothes."

The only Greyhound ticketing agent in America with standards.

First time in 25 years.

By 2030, there will be no Greyhound at all.

No bookstores.

No United States Postal Service. My holy trinity: future secret history.

But every second of every porno movie ever made, for free. Future freedom.

Little portals opening and closing in the deadness.

-53-

Open season on me declared, I sit in Williams Park and watch the birds all day, another day, maybe three? South Side alley near the bay I wake to find myself following an old queer man to Publix fancy a bottle of Chilean Sauvignon Blanc only six dollars and then another we watch the birds forever in a day until I depart for the Emerald Bar rich hipster children make me their mascot for a 2 day spree a girl all legs and eyes like a young deer a doe-like girl who sparkles and is all mouth and soft brown ponytail when she laughs and she laughs a lot gives me twenty dollars for a copy of Hatchet Job promising me 200 more I'm an old man in ratty trunks filthy sandals that don't fit a suit jacket and a brown bomber jacket covered in sticky burrs lugging that goddamn typewriter don't think Jack done it this way "you should keep the mohawk it's you" and "why Fort Lauderdale?" and "I'll give you the money gigolo be safe in West Palm BEACH, don't cry it's the BEACH, dear."

That's right, little girl, little 6'1" forest creature, it's got to be the beach I mean, you can't fall off the SAND... Right?

-54-

It's dark in the suburb tonight. It's dark in this room. The doe sleeps.

I'm inclined to set the strange house on fire but she's been generous and while I regret being so much older the heart wants what the heart wants walk 50 blocks south to the park to Williams Park to Mirror Lake "interesting places to urinate unable to communicate" I type amid a flurry of egrets chuckling repulsively on a bench then later find human shit everywhere behind Janus Landing only the fakes survive but I enjoy the weather and sun and limbo, the limbo moan limbo moon limbo rain limbo cigarettes end up taunting an old man in a doorway until he draws a knife chases me three blocks coming to rest Colt 45 limbo and Budweiser limbo behind a church yard in the ratty pine bushes to kick it old school to wake up rolled with wallet gone typewriter gone and then I rise with two cops staring directly at me from a parked cruiser shaking their heads, the curled finger the insults C'MERE and GET THE FUCK OUT OF DOWNTOWN DIRTBAG but they don't know who I am hah-hah! hah-hah! and under my Aussie jacket you could call me thin alright on a warm afternoon a lovely afternoon a desperate afternoon to walk it all off all things put together a time to put all things back together like the logistics of escape the legislature of prophecy the procedure of the end times all the way to THE NORTHEAST SECTOR John Hawkins' delightful home at 635 8th Avenue NE my former home my homeless home where I had SUMMONED THE TROOPS (come back from the dead) straight up the porch steps past the mounted American Flag at half mast find the door unlocked and each room empty smells of dog piss Italian leather cigarettes smells of cheap cologne find a Blu-ray player a laptop two laptops find a large black garbage bag find a prescription bottle of amphetamine tablets and take the red brick alleyways down to the pawnshop on 4th so smooth with 75 in cash and the speed going to my groin when the Beach Trolley-Bus collects me and the steel framed ALICE pack on Central Ave ride all day for 5 I say to the driver who is Pam my girl so ashamed of me because I told her I'd save her (romance) and now you see me yes you certainly do all the way west 30 minutes along Central Avenue and hang a hard LEFT onto Pasadena thinking thank GOD I didn't lose my keys lose my pack 75th AVENUE please WATCH YOUR STEP and THANK YOU FOR RIDING the Paterra SUNCOAST Transit Authority life is cruel I say oh fuck off Gene and a beer at Beach Lounge Oh NO Mr. Gene but the plan EMERGES when I see THE BOX under the pool table, the BOX just large enough for THE MONASTRELL BRAIN small enough for the ALICE pack so crash one deposit the box stash the pack withdrawing from my cinderblock memory bank a laundry basket clothes stiff with blood stiff with shit stiff with mold withdrawing the box of LATE BOOK ORDERS more crucifixion there but we're in DEF CON 4 withdraw the handwritten 200 page manuscript of *DOG DAYS 2* finally the MONASTRELL BRAIN an ACER 2 TERABYTE PC ain't BUILT TO LAST build a BED for the BRAIN in the BOX the padded envelopes of twenty late orders and the vile washing to keep my soul safe the box in the bag snug as a bug on drugs dragging it ALL into the dark with me crash two to pound my pud and level off the speed rush a blind demon in a black box, crash one and crash two spat back heart attack in the godless rows entirely certain it'll be hell on my nerves but I'll get back *after* because the sun is setting, with just enough time to say goodbye, Fisherman's Park one last time so beautiful at sunset and the fellas the *FEDDOWS* on the lonely ridge below the Sunset Condos see me as I pass Willy's Burgers and Booze and the Oyster Shocker my friends wave and there is laughter there is unspoken memories THIS IS NOT AN OFFICIAL VISIT MY DISTINGUISHED SIRS and the smiles are gone two steps back too late to change my mind knowing what I've done when Danny with the inbred smile takes a shot quick brass connecting perfect with my left eye fuckin pervert with my left temple with my nose I *GOT* kids

Gene with my right eye SPARKS and I fall onto the cement and Herbie the Heron takes flight blood between my fingers the mess the mess another mess "Danny, enough" I say "Danny I've already SAID my goodbyes" the crowd all telling me to shut up the crowd now including Zeke and J-Fly and J-Bird and Robbie and Amber, the crowd at Fisherman's Park telling me shut the fuck up telling me I'm sick with more blows connecting the crowd getting its sneaky shots in you pervert piece of shit but I've already SAID my goodbyes shots to my back and balls to my ribs my mouth the mob the knocks the new cuts the birds still scattering into the sunset I'm SAYING my goodbyes each goodbye hurting my eyes and my lips so bad copper in the salt winds and I should have lost consciousness but the speed won't let me with kicks coming to my head to my eyes blood there upon the beach and the bare feet and the sneakered feet of the mob blood pooling among the beer cans I spit and curse and if I see you again you'll get the same Gene: it's over.

Almost dark and nothing to do but laugh with blood falling being lifted to my feet by Apollo and Sharon being dragged off past the Sloppy Pelican down 75th Avenue with blood dripping with a righteous Vietnam smile with a Serbian sense of the absurd veering onto Coquina Way to Beach Storage we kick it old school with Hurricane high gravity cutting my shock babble down to size making me intelligible down to earth *black to comm* in my unit the belly of sin the lay of the land "you're a tough son of a bitch Gene-O" as Sharon treats my cuts with a first aid kit borrowed from Sloppy's even though they're banned we kill a few hours bleeding (SAMMY!) in the cool dark when we look at Sharon's little phone it is time to go and Sharon's little tears tempt mine and then we're both making fools of ourselves making Apollo jealous good BYE, GENE he says and the Honeymoochers are off to Beach Lounge as I sit in the dark tomb seeing finally that I'd only flickered around the edges of it all and no one can say I haven't taken my licks and been back been really BACK a heavy duty homecoming with blood in my teeth blood in my nose blood in my ears blood in my hair I'd SAID my goodbyes and it wasn't an official visit perhaps not astral projecting out over the channel over Sunset Beach the Pasadena Causeway the Tradewinds Island Grand very much a part of the circumscription of The Dream, Corey Ave's cut-rate Casablanca, the Redneck Riviera they always did say but when the night found me I was always already gone in spirit leaving only my body in the dark always unsure of the dark not knowing whether this was a benevolent lift or a malevolent lift only knowing that it was a necessary lift only knowing that whatever kind of dark I swam in was, it was real, and I would honor my home in darkness with my life.

Sam's name is at the tip of my tongue which I use to probe the lacerations of my lips my gums my inner cheeks feeling my eyes swelling shut the parting shots of my dearest chums and when the morning finds me I am unable to move but I call and call until Suzanne's handyman finds me, Keith always liked me and I'm standing with a crowbar for a cane, but ya can't take my crowbar Gene he says lemme think and Keith is gone I have a cigarette to mask the blood I check my cash I practice a walk but the pack weighs 50 pounds, "fuck," I spit blood and Keith jogs back to me at 65 years of age perhaps feeling younger to look at me and I take what he has brought with unforced gratitude: a wooden bed slat.

Keith loads me up, all Mad fucking Max and THANK YOU FOR RIDING THE P.S.T.A that violent right onto Central Avenue has me crying out drawing stares but it's the black coffee and Jim Beam a going-away present from Maggie that has me dragging the Monastrell brain across that lot on MLK (I don't look for the cold spot) to the Greyhound when my passport gets my boarding pass but not my approval: look man I told you once and I'm tellin ya yeah yeah yeah and ya got jumped AGAIN I see I don't want nobody dyin' on my fuckin bus now jesus christ alright ya got three hours go clean up somewheres.

-55-

"Wel-come ah-BOARD, my name is DARNELL I'll be your DRIVER today for West Palm BEACH we have stops in Sara-SOTA, Port CHAR-lotte, Ar-CADIA, we will be stopping in Fort LAUDER-dale. Please re-FRAIN from loud conversations, keep your music DOWN, if I can hear it it is FAR too loud, and your conversations are to be PRIVATE conversations, I do not want to hear your CELL phone con-ver-sations, and I know you KNOW better than to have AL-cohol there is no AL-cohol on this COACH. Uh, we are running ON time, our next stop is Sara-SOTA, I will let you know when we ar-RIVE. There will be a ten minute REST STOP, for SMOKERS. If I catch you smoking in the restroom, you will be taken off the bus, so don't smoke in there, you should be used to that by now, ladies and gentlemen, it's banned everywhere else TOO. Thank you for choosing GREYHOUND."

-56-

Black out there. Rolling.
Lost in space. Rolling.
No grand adventure. Rolling.
A dull, slow plunge. Rolling.
A bacterial jam in a wound. Rolling.
A chunk of shit in a broken pipe (but once you hit the highway you might get a little woozy - let the wheels hum a long-delayed

voice of reason). Rolling.

You might skip an hour or two, rolling
You might dodge the evil of it.
Rolling all night long.

My shoes are not shoes, but another man's sandals, and I sip a pint of Canadian Mist, reading from a water-damaged copy of my novel *Dog Days*, and I drift off, I fantasize a bit, I sigh my hundredth "my millionth fucking Greyhound" sigh the romance of it died in my 20s and the waste of it was incalculable in my 30s a tragedy I could only observe or conceive of in mythic terms biblical terms Greyhound buses piled sky high the unrequited lust thick as diesel exhaust my mythic biblical goddamn misery but pain is the only teacher and the woman's love is to be had the lesson learned in the wee hours in the occult spaces in the cold dark dawn that love is to be HAD I hit it HARD not chasing the dollar or the fellowship not even liking my brother quite possibly detesting him and I suppose I TOOK a FEW LOVERS in all these years gone by perhaps a few too many perhaps it was simply not DECENT when I lost my head from time to time in all that taking that clumsy begging that ghoulish integrity I called it PASSION no denying I was crazy then and I'm crazy *now* in this type of rolling nearly 40 still rolling nevermind my lowlife limits BECAUSE my lowlife limits impose aberrant wisdom: CRIMINALITY upon the noble impulse to surrender to withdraw to atone BECAUSE I'm pitch black with it now gone mercenary with it now and I *took* my love again, and again, and again, the Satanic logic of the act made real which now shimmers in the dark of me forever that love always being such a liability that there was simply no way I wasn't going to HIT IT HARD and that's an enterprising young man for you without pretense making for the toilet (wanna fuck?) making for the hall (let's fuck) making for the street (miles in the rain) and it never lasting never working never straying too far from ROLLING and I shiver soaking wet with the ache the pulsing ache that's got me so hooked I'm HOOKED so goddamn BAD ma I got it BAD because of evil pride of hideous arrogance of Pain so you see I had to TAKE IT – no way in Hell I wasn't going to HIT IT HARD – and is it romantic tell me to wake in fear to hurt to hate every day to sob and shake to beg for cocksucking MERCY in the rooms full of Hell the apartments and basements and bathrooms and hallways of the animal KINGDOM ma YES IT IS ROMANTIC MA just a jolt of whiskey and I am a mist settling across all of outlaw Florida and all its demonic secret, flutter their dirty eyelashes at me on my romantic tropical run, another Fugitive Florida run after the town has HIT ME PRETTY FUCKING GOOD if I live long enough to write the book to sell the book to sell a few hundred books but for now the Monastrell brain is safe is lost in space but safe in this hard rain *saved* by the neverending rolling.

GIGOLO

(PART TWO)

I take it anywhere / anytime that I can / I am the fucking son / of a superman
Germs, "Sex Boy"

Florida, coast to coast.

It's a three hour journey by car, or you could walk. Take you around three weeks.

Greyhound-style, with the detours, the layovers, you're talking 14 hours. A whole day or a whole night of road sickness.

I watch for cast-off items in empty seats, eating cold french fries off an armrest in the early evening. My absent chewing, set to thoughts of violent outbursts. It's always someone else who explodes, but when they do, it's because there's so few people capable of any grace, or wit, or warmth.

And simple generosity is always a ruse.

I drink the dregs of a Diet Pepsi left by the gum popping, dreadlocked girlfriend of a lethal young hoodrat in the late blue evening.

Someone has magic markered the word "killuminati" on the bathroom door. I don't know what that means.

Do you?

Fort Lauderdale is all cops.

West Palm by night: Spanish buildings, dead train yards, and I inch along with smashed kneecaps and swollen ankles after leaving the ALICE pack and the Monastrell brain with a semi-cognizant ticketing agent:

"I can't carry it with me."

Low altitude/high humidity. I crawl north a mile, sweating myself to death, out of money, parched.

No lights, and back past the train yard, corrugated orange steel canopies and mock-adobe roofs, the palms I found so mysterious and enchanting last year make me miss Detroit in these barren streets now. The chorus of tree frogs can only summon rage.

The stretches of flat industrial give way to cliché outskirts: idling taxis and railyards and darkened gas stations. A cabbie tells me where Kennedy Boulevard is: through downtown, around downtown, below downtown, it's not clear, too much and too muddy for my mind in that heat. So I make wrong turns. I penetrate golf courses, used car lots, overpasses, a post office, a masonry, a lumber yard, museum grounds, I get dug in tight with a residential district, swipe a warm bottle of Orangina from a darkened and sullen carport with "BEWARE OF DOG" signs propped up against the filthy windows, dead spider plants swinging on wires, aural phantoms. I glide across a man-made lake, risking alligators, cursing the walk back for my sandals, cursing the chickenshit gators.

The outskirts of the outskirts is a humming power station, more dead tracks, the Mutual Benefit Life Building announcing a return to downtown, and the Hyatt, a convention center, and universities glitter behind me, I emerge as an athlete of the netherworld experience, the flying trapeze with an aerial perspective of ALL wastelands: West Palm is small game showing me its small dull ass while its poor residents and wealthy residents sleep, the Mariott like a sterile battle station but were there anything worth protecting: just a few dozen sushi joints and Ponce de Leon's sword. Three miles, four miles, early Sunday morning, cracktown, the blowing garbage district... the Bon Ton Hotel.

-59-

It's a postmodern, real Eurotrash shithole. Hideous, desperate, expensive white walls and waxed hardwood floors, an aggressive barrenness at work and worst of all is the child-size chairs only swarthy Dutch cocaine dealers with names like Nico and Rene would be able to relax in.

I hit the bell, and wait. I hit the bell again, wait some more.

My reflection explains the quiet (I am El Pulpo). Then my first break – "I HAVE A RESERVATION," I scream.

And a doughy Eurotrash faggot in Roy Orbison glasses and greasy six-inch bangs emerges slowly from behind a frosted glass sliding door, a look of disgust not hiding his fright, itemizing my facial injuries.

"GREGORITS," I say.

"I have...called zee POLICE you KNOW? Just *leeeef*, please?"

He tries to look angry while sweeping his dyed black bangs out of his eyes with two fingers and tucking the hair behind an ear.

"I HAVE... LOOK, THIS IS A PASS-PORT, OKAY? PASS... PORT. I HAVE A RESERVATION HERE."

He draws closer.

I hold my hands up, my passport still in my left.

"I was robbed. I need my room now, please."

He pops the deadbolt: SHIK-SHIK.

"Oh my."

-60-

Hunger consumes me. The room isn't ready, and I'm two days early, but I talk the Kraut cunt into charging Cynthia anyway. I can't sleep. Hunger ridicules me. The sun rises: continental breakfast. My mind is made up that I'm wanted by everyone, vulnerable to anyone, and I have tried washing my putrid clothing in the sink but it's no use and the pool is a bust waiting to happen: I won't even check it out. In the tiny, impractical breakfast room the cocaine crowd ridicules me but there is vitamin C which I remind myself is the secret to a long, healthy life once declared by Dr. Linus Pauling to be a miracle element both under-consumed and under-researched. Pauling was a highly honored MENSA affiliate and he lived to be 103. Something like that.

Day 2 I brave the predawn streets to infiltrate a Taco Bell dumpster but a patrol car spooks me right back to DTs in bed and the Discovery Channel. A paranoid late night dip in the pool to clean my clothes and stimulate the purification process ends badly when I am admonished by a similar hotel employee for multiple violations and threatened with the police yet again. "I AM NOT A CRIMINAL! STOP TALKING ABOUT COPS!" The man repeats "I do not like" several times.

Back in the room, which has taken a dislike to me also, I cannot focus on any one image or theme or sound coming from the television. I am only aware of the tints on the wall, and the way the shadows move on the wall, as if laying in this bed, in THIS condition and between THESE walls, is all I can expect, all there will ever be. Because it's entirely possible that the woman will cancel, or overdose on pills before arrival (she appears mentally ill, she has textbook crazy eyes, and what other kind of 50 year old still does drugs?). I can smell the Burger King 3 blocks away when I snap a disposable razor in half and lance my swollen eyes with the tiny blade.

Day three I return from the shrinkwrapped croissants and powdered orange juice to find the room door ajar.

FROWMP! Pheeeeeert! Prap-rap-rap-rap-rap!

My blood freezes: "With the front *DOOR* wide open?"

My skin ices over: "It was horrible *WITHOUT* a shitting scene."

PHA-RERMP! Flump Flump Flump, prap-shrap-BROWMP!

And my instincts, so rarely wrong, paint a picture in my mind which dominates violently from any angle, my *life* having come to this, because I am thoroughly FINISHED as a man. It's a picture of me having to sleep with the old bag, the crazy old bag currently shitting herself to death scant inches from my mangled nose with only thin art deco frosted glass to shield me from a furious gastrointestinal squall, the shitstorm of my own egotistical creation.

I can FEEL the old woman's spasms and oafish fatperson self-pity from where I stand at the end of the walk by the parking lot where I fume and curse in the wet air where I stand flattened against the outer wall behind an aloe bush where I smell the woman's shit in waves and like blasts of sour ozone as if I am the toilet itself and despite all of this freakshow indoctrination I remain steadfastly protein-crazed, my appetite undiminished, beyond debased, beyond broken, glutting on my own rage at having LEFT MYSELF WIDE OPEN for the universe to FUCK ME IN SUCH A WAY... it IS too late.

The room (HER room) (oh sweet christ OUR room) has gone silent there behind the aloe and the palms. The room, I consider, is a sanctuary, and I might have seized up its peacefulness, set myself to capitalizing fully on its healing power but I need energy before I can rest because the kind of rest I am facing is a grueling, exhausting rest, a rest of knitting tissue and of ALL rest, a rest which requires NUTRITION for my mutant healing factor to run on when I am otherwise *in the red*, in the shadows of a blazing South Florida day sweating out my sickly sugarsweet toxins cruelly stricken with hunger pangs, a limp pallid ghoul contemplating drastic measures to procure a taco, a shrimp cocktail, a tray of chicken livers, and tequila shots, tequila margaritas, tequila daiquiris when it is some kind of dry outside, a nice day perhaps but not for neverending DT jitters and getting gawked at with broken/gashed/black/purple/yellow everything, walk a step and a half at a time to the pool hidden out back where a lunatic optimism is summoned ("maybe she'll suggest a steak AND a bottle") because couldn't it be possible that the schizophrenic beast shitting itself to death in room 19 is NOT predaceous is NOT expectant is NOT the most nauseating error of my entire career as a taking-no-giving kind of guy, as a suicide monkey, as human anti-matter, and *OH* how I want to flee.

I'm the last freak on Earth and I don't even know where the fucking beach is from here.

-62-

"Hello?"
"Hel-LOH!"
Cynthia: disheveled, obese, bucktoothed. In a shapeless frock, hair dyed brown from gray, hair that is frazzled and tied into garishly girly pigtails and a round batshit crazy face slathered with makeup, she is equal parts Tammy Faye Baker, Holly Woodlawn, and Gena Rowlands. I consider running. Right then and there, God help me, I want to run and not look back. But it's hard to run on two cracked kneecaps.

"It's not so bad, the bruises," she says, rapidly, self-consciously playing up her New Jersey accent, that *clipped* thing. "The guy up front wasn't sure... I had to satisfy his curiosity. I think he's afraid of you."

I shrug my shoulders.

An uncomfortable hug.

The smell in the air.

The brown elephant in the room: I imagine the situation as a trite, shallow, road movie, one of those mismatched buddy movies they made so many of in the 70s.

Cynthia has a makeup bag in her fat little hands, fidgeting in a hypersexual panic. Her luggage and a few plastic shopping bags are strewn across the unmade bed. She paces back and forth, rummaging through it all in disoriented swipes, as the bathroom continues to leak stench.

She says, "let me think for a sec-" and "oh shit" and "there's got to be-" and "do you know if-" and finally collapses into the little chair by the door as I pretend to watch television on my feet. I pray that the chair will take her weight.

"I need a nap," she says.

"Listen," I half-whisper, "I'm sorry to ask but..." (I'm thinking of the woman lying prostrate and snoring upon the bed, and another minute, interminable wait, another soul-killing bout with hunger)

"You're *HUNGRY*, shit. Yeah. Let's go out. I need to eat too."

"I'm sorry..."

"What? Stop. You ready?"

The rental car smells like bubblegum, and we hit the main drag, a dismal hispanic ghetto which looks and feels like the worst of LA where I was stranded for three years.

I recognize the strip malls and vacant lots and vacant buildings from my pre-dawn hotel hunt, and imagine myself stranded within or among THEM for 3 long years, Cynthia and I pretending, as Lydia and I had pretended, to be lovers or somesuch. As it is, Cynthia's body language is appalling: the fidgeting and twitching is making me suicidal, because her agonizing insecurity is malicious, it is utilized by the fat little troll from *Don't Look Now* as a passive-aggressive weapon. She is authentically soulless however, that much I can plainly see when she is nodding to herself; she involuntarily reinforces her own statements with these terrified little fits of nodding, her own convictions eluding her like a rigged game of whack-a-mole.

Cynthia's fan letters gave her away from the very start: she'd not *READ* the books, but merely flipped through them. After 20 years, I can tell who's read me and who hasn't. But this is predation and this is the law of the jungle, a substance abuse panic, maybe it's a pre-menopausal panic, it's general female rottenness, and on a Sunday in West Palm's browntown, the desolation of it all is overpowering.

-63-

We pull into the desolate parking lot of a desolate restaurant.

"Aww, poor baby – you're shaking."

She pets my head. It's all I can do not to smack her.

Inside, a skeleton crew seems astonished (or offended) by our arrival. The food is mediocre, fried fare, tourist trash, but the protein count and grease and six Heinekens have my body – the most complicated machine ever created, I'm told – humming and zipping and throwing electricity like a Harley Davidson turning over for the first time in six months.

We have our first real conversation, about the band X, and Exene Cervenka.

Me (mouthful of deep fried clams, cole slaw, potato salad): "Yeah my ex waz old pals with'r, I 'member she useta call alla time, seemed like ahr real nice lady. But I only like the first two albums. Fake Americana. She's from St. Pete."

Afterwards, we pull into a strip mall for alcohol and Cynthia hands me a wad of bills – "will this be enough?" – and I notice that my salvaged sandals are softer now under my feet, my feet have taken to trusting the ground beneath them, balance has returned, my legs and arms and eyes all in sync and I'm happy to have them back. Mass isn't a problem so much as weight. So once the beer is sorted out – it's Sunday and we have to wait five minutes for the old man to unlock the coolers – it's right back to the pursuit of weightlessness and we drink poolside, mocking one another's selections (hers is an apricot flavored microbrew, while my Colt 45 pint cans are coherent enough declarations of my frugality when spending someone else's money). She has also bought my favorite cigarettes, and I smoke, smoke, smoke long drags, thoughtful and appreciative drags, my enjoyment compromised only by the butts which are piling up, poolside, because of the way people are about cigarettes these days.

"I quit. You make me want one," she says, like she hasn't seen anyone smoke in all the years since. "It was a birthday present to myself," she says, reminding me that we *share* a birthday. I am resentful of the implication and pretend to be hearing this for the first time, in the pitiful hope that she'll never bring it up again. She's probably lying anyway.

And we babble out there, happily drunk and dramatic, all afternoon. We babble about Tom Petty and Lucinda Williams and Steve Wynn and Paul Westerberg and Townes Van Zandt and Alejandro Escovedo, particularly Escovedo whose latest album, *Big Station*, quickly became something very dear to me last July and about which Cynthia says, "There's something missing there. I don't know what it is but that record comes *so* close," which sounds like such as general criticism, the type of thing which could be said of any record ever made. She's making shit up to impress me and a feeling of grimness washes over the euphoria. It's quickly forgotten when she begins telling me about the cocaine party.

"I can't touch it. Really. I'm sick, I'm tore up, and besides that, cocaine makes me very dark. I ought to stay here and rest."

"Why don't you just see how you feel once we get there? No one's pushy. And Mimi's fantastic, she knows who you are and she's all excited to meet you. I think you should come."

Cynthia nods her head rapidly, eyes narrowed as if straining at stool, agreeing with herself intensely after every sentence. Moron.

I say, "Fuck. I almost forgot about the brain."

"Huh?"

"My computer. I left it at the bus station."

-64-

It looks the same in the sunlight: cruel and necessary. I think of Jim Thompson and smile. Did I abandon the north for this? I call Wendy on Cynthia's phone as she parks. No answer.

The day is hot. Loud, also, with a train pulling in. I grew up using a conjoined station: Amtrak and Greyhound, both. Amtrak was cheap back then. Walking into the ticketing office, it occurs to me that I've been imagining a southwest vibe, or even imagining the southwest *completely*. I reminded myself that Florida can't be dismissed yet. (Sam)

I retrieve the Monastrell brain.

I retrieve the late orders and the nuthouse manuscript.

I'm drunk. Cynthia's drunk. The sun has set, and we drive drunk through a lifeless West Palm Beach. Still no beach. The roads narrow. We stop so I can piss. I purchase two large cans of Budweiser. Everyone drives drunk, it seems. I've never known anyone to get caught. I've never been in a car accident. Mine are not everyday terrors.

Elevated highway views of the entire city: where's the ocean? High speed turns in the mall sports car, smoking Marlboros as the sky darkens: Cynthia loses her way, makes calls, I enjoy the ride.

In the soft light Cynthia negotiates the serpentine driveway of a menacing 70 story condo tower: Elysian Heights. Hunter Thompson wrote a story about these people: the drug sniffing idle rich of West Palm Beach. "I've been everywhere," I think to myself.

As we park, I ask Cynthia if I stink. I know I do, but it's too late now. She says, "I haven't noticed anything." My mohawk has turned from blue to green and the facial swelling hasn't gone just yet. We stop there on the walkway, as Cynthia scrambles for something in her purse, and I can't resist leaning backwards to stare straight UP at the monolith directly at its base. I collapse.

"Oh." Cynthia says. "Gene."

"Goddamn," I say. "That's awful."

"You don't have, what do they say, uh, vertigo."

"I don't even like being this tall."

"Come on, we still gotta get through security."

Cynthia waddles. She's a fat old duck. In Florida, you see these fat old ducks after there's been a good rain, crossing residential streets with a dozen ducklings. Where are the fathers?

She speaks into a box and a guard approaches the door.

"Penthouse. Mimi Edelstein."

The guard opens up, leading us to his control station in the middle of the imperial lobby. We surrender our ID's, and then he leads us to the elevator.

"Going up: PENTHOUSE," he says.

The doors close. The elevator says, "GOING UP. PENTHOUSE."

"I despise anyone with money," I tell Cynthia. "I've never met a single person with money who I could respect or even appreciate. No decent human being has any fucking money." The guard grins surreptitiously.

"That's ignorant," Cynthia says, pouring sweat from her 15 yard waddle. "Mimi's cool. She doesn't *act* rich. Give her a chance."

Cynthia tells me that Mimi has a perfect body. ("I've fucked her.") She brags that fucking MIMI is selling this three million dollar condo for a move to ASPEN.

I roll my eyes.

Wretched old cunts.

"PENTHOUSE," the elevator says.

We are greeted by a hyperkinetic dwarf in leotards. "MIMI" is morbidly healthy, all arrested development and New Age arrogance, a Sephardic Jewess with hairy arms, and the demeanor of a gossip show host. "GENE, the WRITER, you're CRAZY, man!" she says, and I'm a pillar of frozen repugnance in her patchouli cloud.

A sharp young real estate agent named Harrison asks me if I'd like a drink and when that's presented (a yellow thing, passion fruit and vodka) I take to the couch and busy myself with a Taschen coffee table hardback of fetish porn.

Mimi motormouths about her bowel movements and her inheritance. I let myself out on the balcony to look for the ocean, where I get the jump anxiety. There's nothing but the little lights, sparkling urban sprawl.

THE FRIENDS ARRIVE. I shake hands and communicate my displeasure as delicately as possible. They are stockbrokers and drug dealers. No one asks questions about my appearance or odor. Mimi twirls and laughs very, very, very loudly. She closes the Taschen book to make room for a large cocaine tray, glancing back at me with her spandex ass in my face as she does so: "Great stuff, huh?"

"Yeah, it really is," I say. "My ex used to have that book."

I realize that I'll be fabricating every statement I utter, for as long as this situation drags on, and as they're sitting down, I excuse myself to the bathroom. Providentially, it is located just to the left of the kitchen, so I am able to palm a beer and take my time on the commode. I'm experienced enough to find amusement in the ritualistic cocaine behavior, the poorly disguised junkie restlessness in the forced conversation, or maybe it just sounds that way to me because it's so fucking dull. Regardless, I'm able to hear everything.

When I return, the party has moved behind closed doors, except for Cynthia, and one of the men, a Rolex and Khaki'd fellow who nods nervously at my return and slinks off to the bedroom.

"How ya feeling?" Cynthia asks, trying to look and sound sexy behind cocaine and booze. It reminds me of too many other old, boring, superficial women. At some point, I stopped caring, I guess.

"I feel lousy," I say. "I'd like to go, but I can wait in the car."

"Well, they're gonna be indisposed," she says, pointing at the large wooden door. "Gimme a few minutes, we'll go. I haven't seen Mimi in years."

I look at all the cocaine. She sees me look, and offers me a metal straw. Up the snoot snout goes 20-30-40 dollars.

Kissing Cynthia is like bobbing for meatballs in mashed potatoes. I have her tits out, a fully replenished glass of Grey Goose, and an encyclopedia of base possibilities squirming to life in my coca-contorted cranium.

"So are you, like, menopausal yet?" I say.

Cynthia erupts in tears. But I take her out to the balcony and began apologizing fitfully, blaming it on the coke. The people in the other room are moaning and grunting. This terrorizes me. I can't get it up, although it's in Cynthia's mouth.

"When we get back," I whisper, turning the tables on her, all the way around.

The debutante and her minions return, and we find ourselves waylaid in the kitchen where the oversexed coke fiends have gotten into a frenzied gab-session about their favorite movies. I can't resist setting them straight on a few things regarding *Goodfellas*, and then *Blade Runner*. The real sour note comes when Mimi's tallest, tannest friend, Johann, begins to disparage the recently released *Prometheus*.

"That film was very misunderstood. First of all, no one has the balls to admit that it's only the third legitimate Alien film."

"*Alien 3* has its good points," he says.

Another of the men shakes his head. "*Alien Resurrection* was a good sequel."

"It's not a - wait, it's a, what? A good -"

"It's a good sequel, yeah."

"It's not a sequel at ALL. Neither of those movies will ever *exist* in any intelligent conversation about *Alien* or *Aliens.*"

"Uh... I don't follow."

"Yeah," says a grinning howdy boy in Birkenstocks. "It's ... those movies are part 3 and part 4 in the series. How can you say...?"

"They're insults. Those movies are beneath contempt."

Then someone, rightfully sensing trouble, changes the subject to Stanley Kubrick, who I loathe.

The cocaine comes out again. I whisper to Cynthia that I am leaving.

We make an uncomfortable goodbye.

In the elevator, I ask her: "Did you get a to-go bag?"

Cynthia sighs. "I got some, a little, but we can't do it all. I wanna save some for the wedding reception tomorrow."

"Who's getting married?"

Cynthia sighs, "Forget it."

-65-

In the room, we lay out the lines and I am left cowering in the shadow naked and strangled tip-toeing along the ledge of a heart attack. Cynthia gives me head for an hour and passes out. How is it that people pass out on coke while I haunt myself to death?

After draining a dozen beers, I watch, horrified, as shapes twist in the shadows outside.

Nothing will put this fire out.

On the way to the pool, shadows lunge and hiss at me. Hard knots of fear attack my muscles.

I smoke out of nerves. A whole pack disappears. The shadows laugh and curse: next it'll be the cops. Dawn arrives. And eight o'clock. Nine o'clock.

I brave the streets in search of a bar for whiskey shots.

My legs ache and it could be another stroke and shop owners are only just raising their gates.

Twenty used furniture shops in a row, and not-one-single-bar.

The sun is rising in the sky.

The sun slices through my clothing like boiling water.

The fear is rising in the street.

The self-loathing-the panic-only alcohol can neutralize me.

I'm going to die out here: 25 blocks.

I'm out of water, out of gas out here: 30 blocks.

Can't produce spittle/can't swallow. And the attempts to swallow (diffuse the fear) keep failing (magnifying the fear) and then a panic attack, a hyperventilation episode (deathly fear) so it's too late to turn back.

It's too late NOT to turn back.

An egg on a grill: miles of this/going to die/longest walk of my life, it is: the lesson I cannot and will not learn.

-66-

I wake in the evening. Cynthia is packing her things around me: it would be laughable, if only...

"Aren't you late for the party?"

"I just got back. You didn't miss much."

"I snorted all the coke. I'm sorry."

"I knew you would. It's okay."

"I can't do drugs anymore. My circuitry's fried. I nearly died out there trying to find a bar to calm down in."

"You need to rest. You're fine. I got you a seat on my flight to Jersey, in the morning. We have to leave at 8. Do you want some beer?"

"Yeah."

"You told me my dress was ugly."

"Jesus. What an asshole. I'm really... so sorry."

"Yeah, but you know, you meant it. Like, I knew you were being honest. It wasn't to be mean. You just always say what you think. It's okay."

"Erm."

"I picked up more coke at the party," she says, trying to appear distracted, or random, or casual. "I guess you don't want any."

And as if yanked by a length of barbed wire, I'm out of bed and you don't need to be a fucking seer. I'm pounding into her, standing up, when I notice that she's left the dress draped fully out upon one of the nightstands and that's no accident either.

-67-

West Palm's airport is small, and it's early, so very late for us, because indeed we are, the two of us, walking billboards for cocaine possession.

Waiting in line is horrific. Cynthia whispers to me, "There's no such thing as 'internal possession' so just try to relax," but I can't, and somehow the legal specificity isn't the issue, and I'm thinking *that's kind of not the point, Cynthia*, finding her and her brazen New York attitude increasing repellant. Legally sound or not, I am aghast at the very prospect of hiding in plain sight for it conjures the sensibility of attorneys and pornographers and other cannibals, and it is my inherent decency that is hounding me to death – the cops can only do so much. They are victims. I fear myself. I fear the waiting jet plane. I fear the vile sex orgy raging unabated in my putrid sex beast brain.

"They can't touch us," Cynthia whispers. She sounds like – looks

AND sounds like – a complete fucking psycho, a lather of sweat and misery right there at the security gate. Fifty year old cokehead Cynthia, who prides herself on skillful drunk driving and drug smuggling expertise, doesn't seem to notice or care how hugely powerful – indomitable – my cocaine terror really is. She watches, pathetically aloof, as two security guards take my entire pack apart and pat me down SLOWLY. Not without a crippling resentment, they clear me for boarding. I dare not lift my head for the entire room is complicit in this judgment, this unifying contempt. It's almost as if my satanic drug onanism hit such a peak intensity that an osmotic metabolic reversal began occurring, at a cellular level, whereupon the room would erupt in a new form of sexual panic manifesting itself primarily in acts of homicidal rage, the entire room, now nude and spontaneously ejaculating while tearing me – the obvious culprit – limb from limb. I feel all the world like a smear of shit on a marble floor.

Cynthia's two bags are both black, and one of them contains a large glassine bag of high-class coke. She's doing her best to play it cool, but it's an arrogant performance, bursting with the clichés (all New Yorkers secretly believe that someHOW the entire fucking CITY must rightfully belong to them) but she runs out of steam when her bags begin passing through the x-ray box, resorting instead to a kind of chuffed helplessness, all ducky and SUBNORMAL helpless as if it's just now occurring to the old duck that she and I were red-flagged as a pair of idiots the very second we walked in and what the arrogant hog fails to understand, even now, is that she's about to be arrested.

The passengers behind Cynthia continue to stare me down as she is searched, as I slip my sandals back on and fight the drug rigidity which mimics cerebral palsy. I'm feeling the onset of a surefire aneurysm when an old man loses his balance, sending half of the conveyor ramp's contents – including Cynthia's coke bag – onto the floor. The sight of her switching bags with the person behind her during the commotion is a real life movie experience wherein I am able to transport from the hellish meltdown event of two seconds prior into the relative safety of a heartless Hollywood suspense film and when we huddle around the dirty bag as they're opening the clean one, perhaps they suspect something but we ride our instincts clean through to the other side of that mine field and it was all natural born lowlife street sense or maybe just dumb luck: the standstill must be seen to, and we, Cynthia and I, are sure to spend the next hour getting fucked up on ten dollar sea breezes at the airport Applebee's with hushed whispers of jubilance and degenerate in-flight behavior.

But when I wake to her snoring snout I'm in New Jersey.

This is the tracking shot: a sea of designer winter wear and Christmas hats, Chanel and DKNY and Drakkar Noir ads, display cases full of smart phones and Dolce Gabbana purses, a wall of money, a wall of Revlon revelers, a stampede of brown leather riding boots and flannel scarves with not a single fat person or old person or ugly person or poor person in sight, and then it's CYNTHIA AND GENE crumpled in the corner of an airport "Irish Pub" called McSorley's sipping 24 ounce glasses of Sam Adams now pale, toxic, destroyed, in sandals.

Don't fuck that up in the movie.

-69-

The car's windows are filthy with road salt after three days in guest parking.

It is a tiny gray Honda, one of those new things that look like a bubblecraft, whatever a bubblecraft is. And through the windows: brutal, vulgar, toxic New Jersey.

Cynthia talks and talks, an inexhaustible main artery of unimpeachable hometown pride: in the aftermath of Hurricane Sandy, the worst storm ever to hit the NYC/NJ megalopolis, I am essentially guaranteed an overdose of sentimental chatter; which I do my very best to politely indulge while otherwise engaged in mental jujitsu with all the barbaric nuclear winter scenery, and craving a drink.

"The whole fucking CITY was underwater," she wails for the third or fifth time, and it's unclear whether she's referring to Jersey City, or Hoboken, or Newark – I don't give a fuck and it's all going by in a blur. For me, it's a changed city anyway, they're ALL changed cities and I'm too old for the reptile zoo, under the water or above. The anecdotes and factoids flow freely and I don't want to dampen her enthusiasm, borrowed and desperate and dull as it may be, but New York City is all bad memories for me, Jersey City and Hoboken too, memories of being too young and too soft and too damaged and too naked, memories of too many rich old women playing too many nasty games, too many people with too many demands, all that shady business, all that sex and drug and art hustle, the childishness of it all, it all seeming so unnecessary now, so all of a sudden seeming so much worse than my recent troubles, perhaps only because so much more was possible in those days. I could have been kinder. But the New York romance I'd coveted was for so many reasons impossible for me then, and now I just don't care.

Why had I forced myself upon it nearly 20 years ago? I'd been married to a 16-year-old Jehovah's Witness who became intent on

95

upstaging and outperforming me, or so my 19-year-old self believed. I took to drinking cough syrup and antagonizing my mother-in-law, as well as the late night DJ at the most popular radio station in Harrisburg. I imploded as stylishly as I knew how, taking a graveyard shift approach to the whole teenage misanthrope divorce scenario. I conned my way to New York after a year or so of proto-sleazoid hard times, lycanthropic living. But can I bear admitting to myself that it was really only having to do with a pissing contest between my teenage ex-wife and I? A pissing contest which Lydia Lunch had unwittingly been roped into, and several others, was that all it was? I could reach back further, to my trailer park hillbilly adolescence during which I'd read too many CBGB's stories, and seen too many Abel Ferrara movies.

It's 2012 and I no longer bruise, so the scenery whips past uninvolvingly. I've got no use or time or taste for what I took with me, for what I left behind. I cannot recall my Times Square stories, my Hell's Kitchen stories, my South Street Seaport stories, my Rockaway Beach stories, not without unleashing all my bleakest curiosities about the evil of me/them/it, not without wanting it all over again, not without astonishment of never having picked up AIDS, not without feeling like any other ex-New Yorker.

I was always cold and hungry in New York, except during the rancid hungry summers roaming Coney Island and Red Hook and Greenpoint stark and raging thin the way only very young men can be. For the hundred or so women I so briefly hid within (up), a hundred thousand others saw clearly what I was and caught a terrible shiver. All the little sewing kits in all the handbags in all the bars from University Place down to Battery Park could not have closed my wound.

I've always regretted my relationship with New York, because the hurt, and the hurting of so many others at my hand, at whoever's hand for there was no end to it, was by the end of my third year beginning to seem quite irremovable from the beauty of New York, and it's possible that I had acquired just enough wisdom at 23 to insist, if only for the sake of self-preservation, that beauty did not HAVE to be barbaric, that love was NOT impossible without trauma, and where I went does not matter, and what NEW violence was visited upon me in the new place does not matter, because I'd seen the beast alive, seen it for what it was, and turned my back on it. I left wisely, with my pride, with my love tangled and putrid, but intact. I left New York unresolved because New York, in the end, was about masochism. It was about suffering:

The Brooklyn suffering.

The Jersey suffering.

The suffering south of Houston Street, and 14th Street and Rivington Street and Metropolitan Avenue, noise and panic and fury and suffering, each tip of each nightmare, each drug dream splintering off into the apartments the faces the heat of all that tawdry gluttonous opportunistic sex mania every other night those years when I took on the city and the self and the woman simultaneously like it was life and fucking death while insisting each and every live-long day that I could exist in a world of PEOPLE to digest the tin and iron and plastic of PEOPLE and in the end the city was the city and I stood quite clearly a casualty, back now, so much older in Florida alcoholic swim trunks and Florida alcoholic sandals, surrounded by terrible black snow, in a no-fucking-around blizzard, the aftermath of it all...

"Are you getting out?"

The city that never weeps.

-70-

It's cold in the bar, a charmless 1950s theme bar which I recall as a videotape rental shop in 2002 when I was fleetingly entangled with the P.R. manager of Penthouse Magazine. Lainie was a super-hip mid-30s Jewess in black NY hipster leather who lived one block off Hoboken's quaint main drag, in a cavernous little ground floor apartment. The place had been nicely converted from an old two-story house, which gave it considerable more character than your average city rattrap. Alex Trocchi had lived there in the early 1960s, or maybe it was the late 50s, I found that out later. He was already a full-fledged junkie by then, with a pretty, young American wife who he'd put the heroin bite on also. In that exact same front room, the afro'd little black leather sexpot and I would snort coke and smoke dope, talking about Charles Bukowski and John Lennon and Al Goldstein and GG Allin. We did our fair share of screwing. It was nice.

(Cynthia has to park directly in front of the fucking place, of course. Maybe I should have stuck around.)

In the bar, she notices my shivering: "We're going to find you some clothes today."

"All I need is a little corner to write in. I'll type up *Dog Days 2*, and turn that into some quick cash. A few hundred overnight, and after that-"

"You need shoes. You need pants and a coat. Just let me buy you a fucking winter coat. And you'll need a phone."

"Where do you live?"

"Oh come on. You can't be that... are you fucking kidding?"

I contemplate the woman's old country Italian features: the hook nose, the kind of anti-forehead, with a widow's peaked hairline all but making contact with her thick eyebrows... but Gena Rowlands figuring most prominently, and... no. Just, NO.

"Gene..."

"What's wrong? What did I do?"

She closes her eyes. Hard. I see her hands on the table, stretching, then snapping back into tight fists.

"What!"

"I'm just... I feel very foolish."

"Why?"

"You didn't read ANY of my emails did you?"

"Well, *yeah*!"

"The long ones you didn't read."

"Like, the one about going to see Springsteen?"

And that's how she becomes a blubbering disaster. I'm aloof, or maintaining my IDEA of aloofness, as a means of protecting myself, because I've got no interest in heroics, especially when that type of covert narcissism is in no sense required, like in the absence – total and utter absence – of romance which turns heroics into something else entirely anyway... but Cynthia has other ideas. I won't give an inch. (Well, maybe a better and more honest way to explain myself is to say that I won't give her another inch, because that would be *seven* inches after all, however crude or cruel that sounds, and if one allows such psychotic sexual possessiveness to go unpruned, one runs the very real risk of waking up one morning with *NO* inches.)

"Oh, Cynthia," I say. Blankly.

"Goddammit, you..." Snot and all. Jesus. "Gene, my husband threw me out. I have to get a new place. So, for now, I'm staying in hotels. WE are staying in hotels."

"Jesus, THAT'S got to be expensive."

"I use the discount websites," she says, wiping away mucous with her napkin. Her eyes dart around the empty bar, and she's bawling again. I can't stand it. I take one of her little fat hands, squeeze it, thinking NO, NO, NO.

"Gene, I'm working today. We're gonna check in down the street, and I need to get over to the shop. Just... hang out in the room till I'm done."

I can't resist: "Where do you work?"

"ASSHOLE!"

She throws a twenty and two fives across the table.

-71-

The Holland is a sooty flop at the Jersey end of the Holland Tunnel, and it says everything there is to be said about Christmastime in NYC. It's a loud, filthy, expensive slap in the face.

In the lobby, we distract ourselves from the soul-killing frivolity of check-in and check-out with a short exchange about Lucinda

98

Williams.

Cynthia: "She's a big phony." I don't agree, but I know what she means – daughter of musicians, all that. But Lucinda can really write. Cynthia, like almost everyone in America, has no respect whatsoever for language. FOR WORDS. Cynthia is a big phony. Far worse than Lucinda.

There are half a dozen Japanese girls at the counter; the lobby is tiny and we are getting claustrophobic but the girls appear unaffected. Cynthia begins staring at my bare feet: "Why don't you have any toenails?"

"I have a few."

"What happened?"

"Horses."

"What?"

"Horses stomped my toenails off. It's true. My first job was getting bitten and stomped by horses all day and night for $1.00 an hour."

"Get the fuck outta here."

"Pennsylvania. I've had that kind of life. I'll go grab the bags."

"Do you have clothes?"

"Not really. Just the brain."

"The what?"

"My computer. The Monastrell computer."

"Oh. Yeah, wow. You'd better-"

"I'm going to set up a temporary office, pull myself out of the mud. A lot of people are angry with me. A lot of people -"

"-never got their books?"

"Exactly."

"Hey grab my phone, and get... hold on... shit..."

Cynthia's frantic digging summons violence in me. I have a very light trigger when it comes to women rummaging in their fucking handbags. Get it together, you stupid fucking -

Cynthia, now sweating from the strain of it all, says, "Ah shit."

Fifty years on Earth and she still can't get it right.

"The Holland Tunnel," I think... which one is that? Am I across the river from Hell's Kitchen, or Tribeca? How many years? Why does the city feel so impenetrable now? I drank a lot of whiskey in those days. It got me into a lot of trouble. I can taste the same whiskey, the same way. I am in the same place, but I can't remember where I left the remote control. Where are my keys? It's like that.

It's our turn. An Indian woman smiles at me from behind the counter. The Japanese girls giggle down the hall.

-72-

The room is drab, but it's alright. Alright is fancy for me. It's the

99

cold that offends me. I'm vulnerable without shoes or a hat or a coat. That's my idea of a joke.

Cynthia is putting on makeup. She emerges from the bathroom – we're on the fourth floor with a view of the Holland Tunnel – and she's tying up her hair into a second ridiculous pigtail with a business card in her mouth. She completes the twist-tie and hands me the card: "Another Man's Treasure." Ridiculous 70s style lettering, psychedelic lettering, an ugly card. A stupid name. It's in Jersey City.

"Grove Street," I say.

"We're *ON* Grove Street. Just go out the way we came in and turn left. It's about 10 blocks if you want to come by. I'm closing up at 11 or so."

"You'll be busy, right?"

"It's that time of year, yeah. Here's some money. Get some food."

I dread the slap of the door. Cynthia's a MOTHER now, a protector, and I can't get snagged on my own ego. The cold, the chaos, and the sobriety will kill my life.

The door SLAMS.

A knife at my throat. Down the hall I follow her far enough behind to avoid notice. The Holland is only six stories but there is an elevator. She takes it. I take the stairs. I watch her getting into her car from the lobby, while fumbling for a cup at the self-serve coffee station.

"No coffee, sir. Seven A.M."

The Honda's tail lights fade out into gunmetal Tuesday evening and all its traffic.

-73-

On a bench, my mangled toes bare against black snow, a black plastic bag of Heineken at my bare ankles, I stare out across the Hudson at the great beast Manhattan. The novelty of it seems to expire but I don't move. There is so much to resolve. I shiver and pace and drink. I scream several times. The soundproof winter.

-74-

Manhattan Island is *the tox-box*: the vanity so powerful you go blind to filth and sadism and lunacy. You are driven only by a perverted spite and money is your only purpose otherwise. It is your only redemption.

The New York dream is all the sex you *didn't* already have, or didn't have as good as it was SUPPOSED to be, somewhere else. The New York plunge is an enterprising heathen's violent jealousy. The New York decadence is electromagnetic voodoo for crazed moths who imagine themselves giant butterflies awaiting the apocalypse.

New York is juvenile at best.

At worst, it's guttural.

And there it is, naked in the ice: my first glimpse since the towers fell. The scope of New York is enough to unleash an interrogation of one's natural instincts. I anticipate a flood of memories, a thousand limp, venal, venereal shitheads come back to haunt me, small creatures with big appetites and almost no intellect, swarms of them in places I may or may not have enough sense left to avoid. They who feasted on me - as they feasted on each other - every day for three solid years.

I call it the tox-box. Being in New York is like that for me now.

Involuntary irradiation.

Violation, corruption, on a cellular level.

I'm no longer young and the effect of all that base hedonism and all that screaming steel is not GOOD for me, because I'm TOO OLD to see the NEW YORK FOLLY as anything other than a dishonest fury, a passive-aggressive obscenity, an incubator of obscene local traditions created to forge new vulgarities, uglier perversions of human reality, of human ego.

From the gallery owners to the Mafiosos that time forgot, from the NYU freshmen to the Fulton Street fishmongers, from Bob Guccione Sr. to Joel Rifkin, from the stock exchange to the Staten Island Landfill; there is nothing about New York City that isn't in some way barbaric to me.

And God help me to miss Third World Horror Detroit, when I pull back from the skyline, when I turn away from Manhattan, but in some way, I do. It is an abstract way, but it is sincere: I'd take hell on earth over this city, knowing what I know.

Maybe I'm spiteful, as I'm often told. That's what everyone says about you when you leave New York or Los Angeles, even if your departure from one is for the other. The wisest course of action is ambivalence, even if it is forced, even if it is false, when someone brings up your former home. And of course you don't dare *introduce* the subject. It will only be seen one way.

Maybe things happen for a reason. Maybe it's time for me to give up on my Florida dolphins and consider the next chapter. But New York isn't my problem anymore.

Court adjourned.

Amen.

Goodnight.

Farewell.

-75-

Another Man's Treasure glows softly out upon the Grove Street shopping district, the cheerful projection of commerce (or commercial projection of cheerfulness) being a larger glow, and it's mainly due to the cooperative weather, the continued arrival of snowfall, that the shops are all open later tonight: it keeps local money flowing. Shoppers bask in the small town trip, "towny-ness" being the foot traffic aspect, the boutique experience, Grove Street's boutiques are QUAINT, see, and all those "BUY LOCAL" types are celebrating the holidays New York style.

When I find the place, the next step is to distract Cynthia from her customers, through the glass with goofing off on the sidewalk, making faces at her and so on, but she doesn't notice. The lights are too bright.

Inside (the bells ring and THEN she waves hello) I stand in the heat which punishes my bones, moaning and sighing with frostbite. Snot glistens on my frozen lips, and now she gives me an unhappy look while pointing to a group of precious young things flipping through the record bins next to the fake furs and the stupid fucking hats. She silently *shushes* me. Marc Bolan's "Life's A Gas" ends, and I notice street sounds.

When the smiling and chatty lesbian at the counter has been rung up and thanked, I pretend to be entranced by a rack of scarves until the bell announces her absence. I approach the counter warily. It is really just a pair of display cases at a right angle, with a narrow gap at the end.

Cynthia gets on a stool there, in that tiny corner space between the cases and the intersecting shop windows. Like all physically misshapen misfits who clerk in such snide little boutiques, Cynthia is either pretending not to ponder the nasty joke or pretending to be in on it.

"Mika's getting back from the Bahamas tonight, she might stop in. It's probably not a good night to hang out." She hands me a tissue, and then a CD. "Put this on."

"Jonathan Richman?" You *TOO?* This -"

"Shut up."

"I hate that fucking shit. He's the reason not to ever fucking..." "Oh fuck you. Keep it to yourself."

"He's CUTE. He's worse than the Ramones."

"BYE GENE."

"Fine, I'll take mentally retarded douchebag Jonathan Richman with me."

"Put it in the player," she half-yells at me. A small shelf-system is tucked into one corner of an antique cupboard with the doors removed and crammed with fishbowls full of punk rock buttons and costume jewelry, just to the right of the door. I can't operate the machine with my numb fingers and curses.

"Come on, Gene. You gotta go."

"Can I use the bathroom first?"

"In the corner," she says, rolling her big green cow eyes. "Be quick."

Of course, the bathroom is an unusable rat's nest of broken display equipment, old shop flyers, filthy rags, fast food cartons, just total fucking retail misery: "Fuck this."

I wipe my nose and let Cynthia pick out a peacoat for me.

"Jesus Christ." she says. "BYE."

I spend the rest of the evening drinking Rioja wine out of a soda cup at the Holland Avenue Burger King and contemplating my new coat.

The road life.

-76-

And so a week passes as I cope with the transplant trauma. I keep washing my pants in the tub. I drink my way into a peculiar fascination with Ballantine Ale, starting with the purchase of a single 40 ounce bottle merely on the basis of that format, because the 40 ounce is illegal in Florida. The dive - head first - into six packs of Ballantine occurs immediately afterward, the beer coming at me from an entirely different direction. I don't busy myself with the analysis or examination of a new development in my life, but rather commence directly to immerse myself in it until the time has come for the next thing. Suffice it to say, Ballantine - regardless of its failure to capture me so forcefully, or at all, during my New York years when I was an insufferable nitwit - emerges beautifully and without labored scrutiny while Cynthia works and the lashings of rain and snow which visit The Holland give me a reason to stay in bed. I watch television and befriend the desk clerks during runs to a Shop-Rite five blocks away for more six packs.

The few deviations from this pattern are troubling, such as a walk to the enormous Jersey City mall when Cynthia insists I buy a cellphone with a "vibrate" feature. This is because I sleep through the room phone, which is deafening, while Cynthia's "smart-phone" can startle me so violently with its vibrating that her sleeping hulk next to me stirs when I'm using it to access Facebook at 5 A.M., I respond as if cattle-prodded, because that's a perfectly reasonable response to an inanimate object seizing to life in your hand. (Otherwise, Johnson-Smith's 'zap pen' would have had absolutely no reason to exist.)

This is also because Cynthia has begun openly referring to me as her new boyfriend, and her belief that fidelity can be purchased is manifested unambiguously in the utilization of a cell phone as a tether. I'm neither insulted nor flattered by Cynthia's objectification of me... in some ways, it is a relief. But I pity her. Pity is a humiliating thing, its very existence serves to further debase the fortunate and the unfortunate alike. So I stay submerged in the murky undertones of Ballantine Bay, on as opposite a schedule as possible. As with anything else that is suffered with the mercy of alcohol as a component, there is a magical quality to my short-lived odyssey at the Holland, and a dream-like language takes over. In fact, the imagery of my toxic delusions and hallucinations threatens to dominate the natural disorder of things, as I find myself drifting across the river for spectral sojourns, or in the more convincing visions, I simply take the PATH train UNDER the river, to Manhattan, to find my sad old haunts, to haunt my haunts and wander my old Brooklyn where I was a ghost even then, a feeling of having never once been moored to the earth or any one living soul, a roving lake of self pity, agony on two legs up and down Williamsburg's Broadway in 1997 the whole world the Dominicans the Hassid the occasional bohemian art school tramp all too busy for me and the beauty of it all only compounding my loneliness because Broadway at Christmas under the JMZ tracks (all the way to Coney Island) was old school romantic with filthy Brooklyn winning out over the elements. My walks through that neighborhood and all others ended with me back at my Metropolitan Avenue apartment at a small table in the tiny kitchen taking nips from a pint of whiskey knowing damn well I had no business even being there, but I've returned in my visions, the calendar once again ticking over another year and all the faces of 96 97 98 99 return to me, faces of 2000 return to me and I wander Greenpoint too with a little pocket money (shoplifting is impossible in Brooklyn) while Cynthia works. I take the L train back to the city 6th and 14th and a glance up on the corner where Lester Bangs was found dead of Darvon and Nick Tosches had me up to his place once (below Canal, I think) and how I was so consumed particularly in Manhattan with the past as if the present just wasn't good enough (it wasn't) just don't hold up (it didn't) and Warhol stories, Hendrix stories, Bob Dylan stories and Jack Kerouac stories, but now looking back I have stories of walking the Times Square and East Village streets with a blacklisted journalist named Mark Kramer whose best stories were Mark Kramer stories: shooting porn with future Sex Pistols documentarian Lech Kowalski in 1974, ghost writing for Al Goldstein during the crack epidemic of '89, beating Vanity Fair's Nancy Jo Sales senseless at the Jane West, hounding himself as he hounded everyone else, and "crack crazed squirrels run amok in Central Park" for The National Enquirer, and "Benji Was Gay, He Died of AIDS" for the Weekly World News, and committing suicide in 2011 to hound us ALL forever, one way or another ("Don't worry, Mark - I'll write a book about ya!"). I take tea and cigarettes at the Jade Mountain on 14th and 3rd right next to the old Variety Photoplays, take the 9 train down to the World Trade

Center and hell I didn't even know there *was* such a thing (just a hole in the ground last I heard)... I wake holding a bottle of Tanqueray in one hand, the television remote in the other, realizing all of this in a shot.

"What do you need," Cynthia says, as I convulse and giggle (DTs are euphoric).

"Sauna. I need to dry out. Garlic and Vitamin C and Vitamin B12. I need Niacin, and then sauna."

"Okay. I'll be right back."

Total shutdown. Alcoholic fail safe.

Cynthia returns with the stuff, a big grocery bag rattling with pill bottles and we begin the search for a YMCA on her smartphone.

"Do you think ecstasy would help?" she wonders aloud.

My cloud of alcohol sickness is dispersed then by the revelation that HARD DRUGS are on the premises.

"How much do you have?" I ask. And, "What about coke?"

-77-

Publicity ain't my strong suit and my heart ain't in it, but a Facebook post announcing my New York arrival is met with a handful of invitations. It's mostly homosexual men like Mattias, a simpering young swede with too much money. The women are strangers, except for Amelia, a beastly punk rock hair stylist from South Carolina. Her clients include people like Jimmy Page and Jack White, and she works out of a shop on Ludlow Street. It used to be a cafe where you could buy 7 inch records and fanzines, including my own *Sex & Guts: Cruel and Unusual Entertainment.* I don't really understand why I should cherish those memories. Those streets were mean indeed. And I was usually bleeding under my clothes. ("Fan-zine." I always thought that was a stupid word.)

Cynthia is slowly but surely infiltrating my network of friends, acquaintances, and former lovers. It's categorical stalker behavior but I keep my eyes on the prize: "Sam's fine, Gene," that's what Wendy tells me when I call to give her my new number. "It's a flip phone," I say proudly. She tells me she's impressed, and asks who the hell is paying for everything. Is it the fat woman who keeps posting photos of me? "Gigolo Gene," she says. "When you coming back?"

I tell Mattias and Amelia to be at Lucy's on Avenue A around 10 and to keep it to themselves. The drugs - and sex with Cynthia - have put me in a dark place but another bottle of Tanqueray livens me up again and we're back in the car, flying into the Holland Tunnel with momentum to ward off the sheer wrongness of it all.

The night happens with Mattias' preciousness and Amelia's limp sarcasm. There are new faces and cocaine at the little dive bar where everyone wants to know about my flip flopped feet in the New York wintertime. I talk of having "ran a street gang" in Florida and although my face is healed, Mattias seizes upon the chance to lecture me about leaving the Sunshine State forever. I decide that this rupture of concern has more to do with me doing something entirely different, and ESPECIALLY with me doing it in such an aggressively anti-social manner, than it does with my health or personal welfare besides. Mattias, like any other New Yorker, is a misery addict. My beach insurrection trip is 100% anti-misery addict. Mattias is threatened by my nerve. People are aware that I delight in frightening them, and I'm self-conscious of that, the way it reveals the juvenile aspect of my character. The beach was something I should have done in 1997. Instead I came to New York. Rather than enjoy life, I decided that I had to be a hipster freak show. Peter Laughner wanted to be Lou Reed and died trying in 1977. And I knew that story well... yet there I was, twenty years on, trying to be Peter Laughner. I tell the whole table this much at Lucy's, aggravated by cocaine, and no one hears or understands a word. They say, "Fucking Gene." They say, "You miss the city, admit it."

"Well, yeah, but you're speaking two-dimensionally. I'm trying to introduce a new idea here, or at least propose that... I mean... if someone's interested in the essential honesty, the purity of a thing which really did cease to exist with the invention of MTV and even more so with the Internet, and as someone who only wants to HAVE a three-dimensional conversation but keeps getting stuck on these petty, shallow assumptions that everyone accepts New York as the center of the world... I mean, I don't LIKE the world, and if New York *is* the center, well okay, I lost 3 years finding that out, that New York is the center, for center-oriented people, and I'm not-"

"And you hate Los Angeles too," Amelia clucks, rolling her eyes.

"I only hate BEING there. If I'm not THERE, it's not my problem. But Los Angeles was a mistake that's all. New York was a mistake. Detroit, Baltimore. All of them!"

"But moving to FLORIDA was brilliant."

"It was for me."

"How many more times are they going to lock you up before they just decide to let you rot in there?"

"I'm happy on the beach."

"You gotta get out of there, Gene."

"It's my home."

"You're really going back?"

"He's not going to listen to anyone," Cynthia says. "Don't even bother."

"Fucking New Yorkers. You're threatened by anyone who hits the eject button. Fucking terrorized by a guy just getting the fuck out. I saved my LIFE, leaving here when I did."

"For LA and Lydia Lunch."

"At least it was warm," I whine, exasperated.

"A warm bandage on an open wound," Mattias says.

"You're a scared fucking rabbit in a filthy cage," I punch back.

Mattias begins wiping tears from his cheeks. Amelia shakes her head.

The night is over.

-78-

Cynthia all but demands sex from me when we return home. I inform her that I'm in love with Bec and will be moving to Australia to win her back to me. She tells me I am a monster and I am hit with all the liquor that I've been drinking then, attempting to CLEAR my head but it's not as simple as diving *under* a big wave and anger keeps dictating my responses. Cynthia despises herself for being fat, homely, and talentless, and alcohol brings the pain out of her, insult after insult. I have only to consider Sam and my focus finally returns to me, a relaxed perspective. In my distancing – the separate drinking, separate sleeping, separate living – I have not been subtle, and there is now a sickness pervading the Holland Motel, so many bad feelings piling up so much snow piling up hangovers piling up and my phone won't stop ringing after I put the number on Facebook dreaming of cash, drunk at the Holland Avenue Burger King convinced that my threshold for pain, my constitution would be the deciding factor here and clearly I had only to share myself with these people whose crocodile-like insensitivity was altogether benign, and hadn't I been foolish in *expecting* the poor dears, the poor pampered dears, to respond appropriately to my bulking horrible whatever, I am the freak show and TACT will not be an element in any of this. I am the KING OF PAIN, wasn't that Lydia Lunch's name for me? "I know you think you're the king of pain," and "I know you think you're the queen of the underground," (stones) (memories) and so it is on the final Holland night with a roomful of sickness and head full of sickness naked stepping out of the bathroom and seeing that butterball crone on the bed with her dollar-store reading glasses and stumpy little arms tapping away at the SMART-PHONE that I hurl myself on top of her and slap her with all my might a short cry another and another and another until I'm finished then shattering the Ballantine bottle over my forehead sending glass everywhere and punching myself in the leg with its broken neck sending blood everywhere and punching myself in the chest with its broken neck sending blood everywhere Cynthia resigned to it now as I batter myself with a closed right fist "I'm going to commit suicide" and "I'm suicidal" until management comes.

The sun is up. I open my eyes: "Get your things out of my car."
And in the parking lot she's bawling, "Is THAT what you do?"
"I'm sorry."
"I can't have THAT around me. I don't do... THAT."
"I understand."
"Other women have come to me. This is just... how you are with girlfriends."
"You are NOT my girlfriend."
"Then get your things out now. I don't want you back here."
And once I have the pack out, she holds a fist up to me, extending one puffy finger, and begins crying again. In the parking lot, industrial life shrieking and howling towards Manhattan behind us, Cynthia's cowardly childish plan in tatters, her fantasy land underwater, her bourgeois bohemian fairy tales all dead in the snow, my hollow apologies in the falling snow, the Monastrell brain and my late book orders, and my new peacoat all collecting snow, I ask her for directions to the Jersey City Greyhound station.
"I'll be alright," I tell her.
"You don't have any money."
"Fuck you." And I'm walking.
But I haven't made it off the lot when the Honda appears again without sound.

All great men are similarly, troubled in this way. Cynthia, knocked far out of her element, grips the wheel tightly and trembles – a 200lb Chihuahua – while the scene doesn't anything to me. I have been here – *exactly* here – hundreds of times. I very consciously consider a full-on, official shift to homosexuality, but in the heat of the moment, and of the obnoxious little Honda, I can't honestly cite a single characteristic of either gender as attractive or desirable. The mousey librarian with a purely literary sensibility and absolutely zero respect for law and order – that would be the one, wouldn't it? And it's a concept many women have SEIZED upon, sure, but the *concept* is worthless to me. You don't build your life around a *concept*, or your identity, unless you're hollow at the center. (In which case you might choose the center of the world as the place to find your soul as if it had been surgically removed and flown to New York on ice like a black market kidney). I seek not conceptual women, but REAL women.
The thing the – the woman – rises out of the fog as a complete

evil, an arcane but inevitable synthesis of demonic and pathetic, of fragility frozen over into the many pathological perversions, and prejudices, which await complex organisms forced to coexist with the basest bacterial elements. She is not a gentle creature; her manners are defensive and sarcastic, and she would scorch the earth with her disgust if given the opportunity.

How many have aspired to this *appearance?* And how many of those counterfeit wraiths have I settled for? How many have I fled?

-81-

Lucky7 is a neighborhood corner bar with a barmaid who is in all ways a typical New Jersey barmaid: cute, frumpy, inaccessible. Cynthia and I are laughing in there at noon, and I'm sober enough to take notice of the snowplows and the noonday sun both attacking the previous night's payload. It's a kind feeling: as if we're the only sentient beings in the city, the millions beyond these walls awaiting the big thaw.

Back to the conversation, which I indulge automatically, with unvarnished fatigue:

"You're not suicidal, Cynthia."

"Don't ever say that."

"Huh?"

"You're not supposed to tell people they're *not* suicidal. It's provocative. You don't provoke a suicidal person."

"You are the LEAST suicidal person I've ever met."

"You're MEAN. Stop it."

I figure I ought not to say anything else, but it's nothing to do with triggering a fatal overdose but rather my being all of the sudden hip to Cynthia's "sad, fat duck" sympathy game which is pure Grand Guignol grotesquerie, something out of Robert Bloch and probably a quivering protoplasmic center of Oedipal blah blahblah and I'm in no mood for that: "Next subject, then."

"Subtle," Cynthia says. "You're big fucking jerk."

"Then NOT next subject, then."

We sit for 5 minutes with our $6 pints of beer. There's a new Coors product out called Batch 19. *Oh* it's good!

"Look," she says. "My parents are gone. So I'm free to do what I want."

I figure I ought not say anything else (again) because I still have my folks. Cynthia looks directly at me:"I could kill myself easier than you. All this cry-for-help cutting shit..."

"Girls are cutters. Girls ain't no good at tearing right into it. Your precious little girlskin ain't precious at all to me and I could care less what you do. I ain't gonna mop up your blood."

Cynthia starts crying, so I step outside to smoke. I clench my jaw in the hostile yet somehow emotionally pornographic self-consciousness of Atlantic winter where I try to pretend I don't belong but maybe after all is said and done, I *do*. I flick my cigarette in the wake of a snowplow.

Without an audience, the blabbering butterball has straightened out, and she's stuffing bills into the wall-mounted "Internet jukebox" and Big Star is playing. The bartender gives me a stink eye. I am ashamed of somehow vaunting her boring old barmaid pussy as a pipe dream (a dream for my pipe, as opposed to a crackpipe dream which would be Cynthia) but just because the trick WORKS doesn't mean it's a good one and in the end it's not a trick anyway – it's her knocking down the ones I set up, and I keep my heart on the table, keep setting them up (setting myself up) because honesty is not my servant, but quite the reverse. I have a soul. I am alive, and she is dead. Anyway, I tried for years to be like Big Star and kind of failed until I heard *Third*, also known as *Sister Lovers*, and that got into my head - deep, deep, deep - without a lot of exposure. It's a sickness. I won't belabor you with the record's mythology, that's easy enough to investigate and you better.

"I met Alex Chilton," Cynthia - now totally recovered - informs me. The bar remains eerily cheerily boringly melodramatically ordinarily STILL. Very much a Christmas Day: stillness. I'll have my revenge on Christmas before all is said and done. Big Star *Third* has the saddest weirdest Christmas song ever made on it. There was something wrong with Chilton, something REALLY wrong in '74, and whatever that illness actually was, if such a thing could ever indeed be defined, it lives most powerfully in that haunting (Satanic or just sad-sack?)"Jesus" song. It's a sick ditty masterpiece in a Satanic suicide-cycle of sad-sack sick-ditties.

I bubble all of this to Cynthia. "You're one of *those*," she says. "And you're obsessed with Peter Laughner. Makes sense. I don't see the big deal about *Third*. It's just a bunch of demos. I don't get it. People read too much into things. Like saying Alex was a curmudgeon. That's not true. He was just Alex."

"You really got to talk to him and everything?"

"He was older then. And very sweet. We made out on a couch."

"How long?"

"It was just before he died. In Austin."

"No, how long did you guys make out?"

"Oh I don't know. A while. Ten minutes."

"Did he have bad breath?"

"No."

-82-

The bar remains bleak. The barmaid remains bored. She paces, channel surfs, drinks, Thera-Flu fizz drinks, chops limes loudly like that'll get those asses back on those stools. I hear clink-clink of a metal fork on aluminum Friskies can, wandering up and down some street, looking for Hank.

"You haven't mentioned my tattoo," I say. It's my long-dead tabby, my son of 14 years bad trouble (NY-LA-Harrisburg-Detroit-Baltimore).

"I saw the video of you getting it. Those poor kids, I can't even think about it." (I paid a homeless heroin addict $20 to put it on my neck: HANK.We somehow managed to get it on video. Feral children played in the background. I don't know who they belonged to.)

The bartender (Kari? She looks like Kari Wuhrer. I know who Kari Wuhrer is but I haven't seen a single Ingmar Bergman movie.)has forgotten all about us now and there are Red Stripe bottles and Magic Hat bottles, Brooklyn Lager bottles, and Blue Moon bottles, a hundred dollar tab EASY, and the jukebox has eaten a twenty or two – Big Star's *Third* having played in its entirety twice which bolsters Cynthia's narrow-minded pretentious dismissal and my slightly less pretentious and open-minded fetishizing. Big Star is just a sad story. But so is The Replacements!

"I do not understand the appeal of The Replacements. Or maybe I do, like, I get why people love the Ramones, but I'm not a moron, see, and I'm fully capable of deflecting all the mentally retarded Ramones-love in the world with my original 1979 copy of *Metal Box*. *That's* special. It's challenging. You and your 3rd grade bubblegum BULLSHIT.

"Just because a record doesn't make you want to slash your wrists, that doesn't mean it's stupid, or kid stuff. You're just a miserable CREEP and you only like miserable creepy records. And anyone can see that about you a mile away."

"And yeah, like I was saying, The Replacement was mawkish, sentimental, juvenile, navel-gazing idiot rock just like The Ramones, but when Westerberg finally GREW UP, when he ditched the band and put out his own stuff...see, *Come Feel Me Tremble* is in the top ten best records of all time, that's when he became one of the legends."

"Why can't you just have the confidence to come out and say, 'I don't get it'?"

"I'm pretty sure YOU'RE the one who doesn't get it."

"You're so quick to destroy or discredit everything outright, it's just SAD. I feel... yeah, I really feel sorry for you."

"I'd like to write ten books about *Come Feel Me Tremble* and Big Star's *Third*. And *Like Flies on Sherbert*, also. You prefer the polished poppy shit because you are a poppy bubblegum-brained shithead."

"It's like... hating The Beatles! You know, that's the same thing as coming out and saying I DON'T UNDERSTAND MUSIC! And no one will ever take you seriously."

"No-no, I absorb a thing before I toss it. And I ain't ever coming back to fucking BECK, either. I come back to Duran Duran, and early U2, and R.E.M., and, like... what was that, The Smiths I guess, you know that people are finally starting to agree with me that Morrissey is a pile of shit and has ALWAYS been a pile of shit... I might come BACK to some things that I never actually outright wrote off, but I am not coming back to Beck, and-"

"Beck's a genius."

"He's a Baby Huey fucking MORON."

"And just wait, The Beatles shit will come back on you. That's why you love Big Star, those records, they're based on The Beatles you dumbass."

"Fuck The Beatles."

"You've never taken the time."

"Dirty Stones. EXILE Stones."

"Like you never even read my emails."

"I read them."

"GENE..."

"I read SOME of them. That drug babble shit... 5 pages... come on. I'm running a business."

"I was trying to tell you about Joe! And Dylan! That's important shit!"

"Wait... Dylan... the kid-"

"I have a friend in jail right now, Gene. I loaned him most of my money, for bail, and now he needing me for all kinds of shit. He's a GOOD KID. He's had a rough shake and I'm helping him."

"You're screwing him. What is he, 12?"

"He's 18, asshole. Remember who you're talking to."

"So this is the kid you were cheating on your husband with?"

"I don't like your tone. Just watch it. Watch your mouth."

The snow falls outside. I hear all about Joe Selick, the host of WFMU's GARAGELAND radio show and Cynthia's husband of six years: "He's not gay, he just dresses up. He's a crossdresser, you know? He has more shoes than I do."

"Sounds godawful."

"Six fucking years. I'm sorry, but I like to fuck, and-"

"I get it."

The sun is down. There is a heavy, toxic spirit in the place. We've been there too long. It's cursed. Cars creep through the streets. Cynthia orders fried whatever. I step out to smoke. The caked snow groaning under snow tires. More and more snow. The Lucky 7 begins filling up with the evening regulars, the neighborhood crowd. Football drowns out the jukebox, and they'll be talking about Hurricane Sandy all night long.

"There's a dinner tomorrow," Cynthia says. Her mouth is full, and she keeps stuffing it. I'm appalled.

"So?"

"I'm taking you shopping. You need shoes."

"No."

"Yes. You look like a jackass."

"I'm IN from FLORIDA. I'm in TOWN to pop my head up, sell a few books, and I'm OUT. To FLORIDA. My gimmick is FLORIDA."

"My gimmick is WAL-MART. Hurry up, we're leaving. TO WAL-MART."

-83-

"Wake up. We're at the hotel."

Silence in the car like a kick to the balls.

Cold in the car like a punch in the nose.

"Uck, Fuck. Where?"

"The hotel."

I'm soaking wet. I get out of the car. It's a gray 2-door thing. Cars all look the same to me. Cynthia's switched cars?

"Where's your car?"

"What do you mean, WHERE'S MY CAR? You're... you..."

"The red thing."

"I had a red car in Palm Beach. You're thinking of a fucking rental from two weeks ago."

"Why are you crying?"

I stand in the falling snow, a parking lot near an overpass. A roar of trucks. A glowing sign: Candlewood Suites.

"Where are we?"

"The... fucking... HOTEL."

"But WHERE?"

"Secaucus"

Cynthia stares ahead at the yellow swirls of the headlights, shiny tear trails down her cheeks, and I'm thinking of New York style pizza, with a bottle of petulant Old Vine Zinfandel. A real fruit bomb on account of so much garlic. Gnarly Head is a good brand for that. Old Vine Zin, 15% ABV. Eight bucks or less. A pizza wine. Wine and pizza is–

"Are you mad at me?"

"Don't talk. Just get the bags."

-84-

"Augh. I need a hot bath."

"What are your plans?"

"I need to type out *Dog Days2*, and–"

"How are you going to do that?"

"Um-"

"And where?"

"I'm going back to Florida."

"With what money? And where will you live?"

"The *Vice* article will be out this month. I'll sell a ton of books."

Cynthia storms into the bathrooms where she remains for nearly two hours. I am sure to be staring into space, deflated and demoralized, when she emerges. This is the only way I have – at the moment – of communicating with a crises'd-out cunt.

She STOMPS to the bed, hovering above me.

I close my eyes.

She STOMPS to the closet by the door, whipping hangers around in a lather.

I open my eyes.

She STOMPS back to the bed hovering above me.

I narrow my eyes.

"DID YOU SEE THE KITCHEN?"

"Yuh."

"WELL? ARE YOU COMING?"

"We're... where?"

"FUCK YOU."

She STOMPS herself to the door:

<SLAM> (Heavy wooden hotel room door. Ugly.)

I wait a minute. And another. And another.

There are Wal-Mart bags strewn everywhere. I have no memory of a New Jersey Wal-Mart. Some of the bags are empty, others are not. I discover a can of macadamia nuts, a six pack of Corona Extra, and a pair of Levis. Boot cut blue Levis. I slide them on quick, sense returning to me, getting a line on the plot, or a primary plot *strand* anyway, and I wash up quick so by the time her horn starts honking outside and my phone starts buzzing itself off the nightstand, I can hop in before there's much opportunity for a scene. Also, it'll give the car a minute to warm up.

-85-

"Secaucus is creepy."

"You think everything is creepy."

"I remember watching *The Howard Stern Show* on WOR9 when I was a little kid. They taped it somewhere out here in this shithole place, in one of these buildings I guess."

"Right there in THAT building. That's the Channel 9 building."

"It looks like a sewage treatment facility."

In the ugly silence of the ugly arctic night, we approach the ridge which delineates the "Jersey Boroughs", Jersey City, and little

Hoboken down below. I don't truly understand this region, or why I find myself so tirelessly questioning my hatred of the landscape, but it seems very similar to the way I force on myself a kind of unremarkable jealousy, an altogether banal jealousy, as a means of coping with a wealthy person, or a group of wealthy persons, which is to say, with wealth itself. Jealously explains it away tacitly, and for 97% of you, it will suffice because it IS jealousy. But when one's discomfort will NOT be explained, when its source is not so conspicuous, to grapple with the larger issue of gluttony/greed itself, it is then a larger and more sinister discomfort: so it is with me and the North, it *is* the weather and it *is* the lay of the land. A *profound* rejection.

Cynthia turns up the heater AND the stereo: she plays the same four or five dumbfuck Jersey hipster bar bands in an endless loop, tacky 90s rock mercifully forgotten now, except in fucking Jersey. I can TALK music with the goofy cunt because, even if it's in the most pathetic way imaginable, it's her entire life. But she is obsessed in a lazy manner, there is no muscularity in her obsession. It has occurred to me now that Cynthia's old band – was there a SERIES of bands? – has never been brought up by me. I'm supposed to KNOW her work, she sent me YouTube links to view, but I never bothered. Sooner or later, she'll grow tired of waiting for me to mention the band, and start playing her own CDs in the car. I can't even remember the name. Did she ever actually tell me? It was more along the lines of, "here, check this out."

"Cynthia, where are we GOING?"

"Hoboken. We're meeting Tony, from Holmes."

"Holmes."

"My band. Tony's the drummer. You and Tony should get along."

"I don't mean to be so dismissive. I just don't like anything."

"You know that's not true," she says, looking for a parking spot on the main drag. "There's Louise& Jerry's. See?"

"Lainie took me there once."

"It's the best bar in Hoboken. HERE we go. I can parallel park like motherfucker. Watch this."

"I'm really sorry for being so awful."

Cynthia shuts off the car and puts her claw-like right hand to my face:

"Oh honey. You can't help it."

-86-

Tony's a diminutive Cuban with a harsh New York accent. We *do*hit it off, singing Johnny Thunders songs and that sort of thing. I want a picture of myself in Tony's cap and so that is quickly arranged. I find myself alone with Tony's gal Carrie when I climb the stairs of the basement barroom back out onto the street, to smoke. Carrie is simmering wolfish beauty in her late 30s. We find ourselves flirting after it is discovered that we smoke the same cigarettes. The street is not dead yet but the night is winding down: Christmas carols from the vestibule of Tom's Oyster Bar, thick black blankets of quiet settling down, spilling out from the darkened side streets. Carrie and I smoke, taking it all in, laughing at the insignificant pleasantries of a sweet old bull dyke building an elaborate window display for the old fashioned pharmacy next door. She stands and admires it all, with a lit Parliament. It's a civilized moment, with three strangers all agreeing on the night (beautiful) and Carrie with her peroxide pixie cut and little red peacoat has me fairly impaled by sadness because when she pulls the coat closer to her, tighter, while pulling on her cigarette, I see that she is terribly unhappy and I am sure that there is a way to steal her trust long enough, or enough of it, so that she dares to steal mine, maybe in hopes that it evens out or only for the thrill of it but I am old enough to know that this type thing only makes it WORSE for women and it's not quite healthy for me either but I use the alcohol hard enough – I'd like to hold Carrie, so we shiver and put our cigarettes out not saying goodbye to dyke... but I make sure she knows that I know that that's enough. "You've really got the prettiest hair." Heh. We've all lost now.

On the way home, Cynthia tells me that Tony is cheating on her. I say, "If I make it back to Florida, I'm buying a kayak." And then, "Does Joe know that you were cheating on him with the boy?"

"His name is Dylan."

"Dylan."

"No."

-87-

Cynthia is on the floor back at the sterile Candlewood Suites, digging through her many torn black Hefty bags of torn, dirty, ill-fitting clothes. All the zippers appear broken.

I call Wendy in Florida: "Sammy's fine, Gene. You coming back?"

Cynthia looks like a bag lady there among all her bags, in the corner, now pecking at her phone with little sausage fingers.

I find *The Late Show* and watch that, drinking Mickey's until a commercial break. I haven't watched TV in years. I don't know the names anymore.

-88-

The hotel "snack room" is just a medium sized alcove adjacent to the central lobby. There is a massive fake tree blinking away, with a mound of fake presents. A sign reads, "Ring Bell For Service". I don't see anyone.

In the alcove above the tiny microwave oven, another sign reads, "HONOR SYSTEM!" There is a yellow smiley face, and the word, "ENJOY!" I pick up a bag of corn chips. Stepping backward into the lobby, gingerly turning my head slowly from side to side. An awful, dampening stillness then. The lobby quiet is like an inverted harangue, the adjoining hallway has a hallway quiet which is a telepathic pageant of ridicule, all of the quiet is my own invisible ticker tape parade of failure.

Returning to the snack room for a second bag of chips, I look once again at the "HONOR SYSTEM!" sign, noticing now the small black box above it: a flashing red bulb (Was it flashing just a moment ago? How could I have missed it?) with a tiny little eye there, to watch me, a bag of chips in each hand, confused and ruined and weak and vulgar. A glance back at the lobby: "HELLO?"

I give the camera the finger, and place the items back on the shelf.

I spit on the floor and walk through the white automatic French doors of the Candlewood. Outside, an old bear of a man is loading white minivan with cardboard boxes in the falling snow. I light a cigarette and watch the bald old bear. The universe is against me now. If I do not busy myself somehow... my lungs reject the smoke, I toss the cigarette.

What will happen if I lose track entirely?

I retreat: "Cynthia! Wake up!"

"HUH! Errrrrrrr..."

The woman releases a roomful of shit-vapor, sounds like a large bottle of soda pop opening up. I swipe my little phone and a can of Yuengling, fleeing back to the night. Light up and ride it out. A New Jersey dream.

My coat comes to life, nearly throwing me onto the ice. I need my bare feet in the snow, to ground me. The pulse-charge rocks me again. I panic. On the third ring: "HELLO!"

"Gee-Gene? Is this Gene?"

"Who is this?"

"GENE! MACHO MAN! It's LASE, man! Lase SAL-GADO! How ARE you, man? Do you know who this is?"

"Yeah, Lase. You have a good voice. I'm happy to hear from you."

"It's LASE, from Facebook."

"I know, I..."

"Look, man. We gotta meet up. I got you a reading, and people want to see you, you know."

"Okay."

"Gene, where ARE you? It says on your Facebook that you're in New York."

"New Jersey."

"Listen, meet me at my place, the Raw-"

"Where do you live?"

"Gene, my PLACE, my PLACE, I have a RESTAURANT, remember? This is LASE, from Rock'n'Raw in the VILLAGE, in the West VILLAGE."

"I worked in the Village for three years."

"It's a lot DIFFERENT now, Macho. So tomorrow, you meet me at my PLACE, ok?"

"Y-yes."

"Rock and RAW, okay? 218 Sullivan, okay?"

"Okay."

I finish my can and toss it. It's a fucking chore to move at all.

The large man, huffing and puffing, lights a cigarette on the brightly lit front porch. You might call the Candlewood "neo-colonial." It's like a space plantation. It explains corporate-state collapse to me, as clear as all the Noam Chomsky and Howard Zinn I never read. I am a part of this collapse. Hydraulic white Star Trek doors with French glass windows.

"Someone should burn this place down."

"Excuse me?"

"Just kidding. You need any help there?"

"Thanks buddy. I got it. Jesus, what happened to your face?"

"A big misunderstanding. She looked 18.But I knew it was wrong."

"Hey, get the fuck out of here, freakshow. Before I split your goddamn head open."

"Goodnight, sir."

"Unfuckingbelievable."

-89-

When I awake, the beast is sucking me off. I know it's in my own best interest to let her finish but I make for the bathroom and pretend to vomit in there. And once again in the room with her, I pop a can of beer and say I'm having a panic attack.

Cynthia huffs and puffs and pulls the covers over her head. I grab my cigarettes and leave: "FUCKFACE!" she shouts. Our room is close enough to the lobby that the pretty young counterwoman decorating the Christmas tree ignores my passing entirely. She's *more* than pretty, she's a dream, and the space between us unnerves me. Once out of sight I take stock of all that DISTANCE: Mangy beard. Sick-green Mohawk. Broken nose. 20-odd deep facial scars, obviously self-inflicted due to the crude patterns (subconsciously conceived during bad breakups with women I didn't even love / obscure demon romanticism) that you don't get from windshield or knife attacks as if THOSE things don't also terrorize dream gals. I have an odor problem and no shoes and no toenails. I am bowlegged and old and mean and I only have one earlobe. "She's not a dream, she's a machine, and pussy pussy pussy at the age of thirty-whatever, go jack off then worthless, it's bad enough without android square-pussy to ruin you further, when you've had fat/thin pussy, hideous/bewitching foxy/boxy hot/squat pussy all talentless idiot pussy crowding around you in this way since you were a young man not to mention a few thousand faggots all told, rough trade with a brain – that's fair enough, and your mother says you've lost your looks, increasingly Justin Gene they *all* say ALWAYS SAID you'd come to an end like this," and et cetera, all goddamned morning it'll continue, I can be sure of that much, in the sulfuric morning air and dead sky the industrial throb of SECAUCAS MOTHER-SUCKING GODLESS FUCKSTAIN NEW JERSEY I can see perfectly well: oblivion.

I finish my can. Toss it.

-90-

I ignore three calls on the way to Jersey City. Cynthia's plain-Jane caterwaul fills the car to bursting as she sings along to her own CDs. She's atonal, or near atonal: this is my punishment for neglecting her.

"What's this one?" I say, trying to look enthused.

"High School Sweethearts."

"What year?"

"This album? Ninety... six? We were together from '94 till '97. Something like that. It was me and my husband John, from Electric Frankenstein."

The names come back. And a grotesque rockabilly chickenhawk named...

"Mike Gutter-Trash! That's RIGHT! Mike was Mr. Fucking Garage EVERYTHING. He was in LOVE with High School Sweethearts. God, what a terrible band name."

"No it's not. Fuck you."

"Mike was a New York Dolls freak. He had the biggest collection of Johnny Thunders bootleg vinyl, it was just... ridiculous. He was an older guy, but he lived with his folks in the Bronx. I took the train up once. We drank Schlitz on the balcony, on this 50th floor apartment balcony. Berkowitz shot up a car right there, his folks talked about it like it was yesterday. The girl died. It might have been the last one."

"I remember those murders."

"They found a lot of dead dogs up there in Yonkers, where he lived. His neighbors were Satanists. The Process Church had a bit of power back then. Maybe they still do."

"Creepy."

"Mike worked in a little shop called Routine Six. I spent whole days there drinking and listing to records. You remember Routine Six, on Sixth Street?"

"Routine Dix... maybe..."

"Between Second and Third, it must have been. I bought a panama hat there, and insisted on wearing it every day until it fell apart. Everyone made fun of me. I fucked a crazy German fashion model in the bathroom there, and... man, the JUNKIES that used to come in there selling shit, hardcore Johnny Thunders junkies. I was real impressed. Girls always used to ask me if I was in a band with the crap I'd wear from that crummy store."

"We weren't very popular, but we made a couple records. We were a Hot Pick on *Little Steven's Underground Garage*. He was a big fan."

Cynthia does her trembling, lost Chihuahua nod, agreeing with herself. Her six chins concur, unconvincingly.

"I remember now. Mike babbled about your band. And babbled. And babbled. He was a funny guy. A flaming queen, a Greek queen in Roy Orbison shades and the whole rockabilly thing, super fancy. He was always blowing Puerto Rican guys in men's rooms. 'Gene, this guys was so fuckin... he was wearin RED SWEATPANTS, I swear to Christ, this muthafucka, he had to be a foot, he was a Latino John C. Holmes.' And, you know, he was super-hyper, always laughing, you couldn't take him seriously."

"He was all over *you*, I bet."

"Oh yeah, yeah. I let him blow me a few times, to shut him up."

"Uh huh. But you're not queer."

"Hell no. Come on."

"I know you don't remember. I told you this - you wrote for *Brutarian Magazine*, right?"

"Oh yeah. I kept the fucking thing going. I was the only life in it. Dom Salemi- what a scumbag he is."

"Oh he's a creep, alright. He tried to buy my panties. He offered me a thousand dollars for my panties. Anyway, he interviewed us for *Brutarian* about twenty years ago, and your photo was right next to a photo of me. It was this photo of you eating pussy. Small world, huh?"

"That's subculture. Punk rock stuff, and underground punk culture, what it *is*, is a filthy little sandbox specially designated by the establishment for mentally retarded middle-class brats to masturbate each other in. Small and dirty and sad."

"Ooooh, you're BITTER!"

"About what?"

"Not really making it."

"But I only started trying last year."

"So what the fuck, why even live in New York?"

"PUSSY!"

120

Cynthia turns up the music: fucking Steve Harley, now. I ask her to put herself back on, because "that guy sings like a fucking jerk," but by then we've arrived at the Grove Street PATH station.

"Call me," she says. "Be careful.

-91-

For certain people, or maybe for any type of person in a certain set of circumstances, the best way to leave New York is without a goodbye. You could spend a dozen lifetimes kissing New York goodbye, so you leave in a hurry, a cutthroat cab ride straight to JFK or LaGuardia, or a Colt 45 swagger to the belly of Port Authority, when it's raining, a sobering ghostly rain; slow motion, it's all yesterday's bruises and the going-away party never quite came together, and you start to wonder where your friends are, what you'd be doing out there in the rain if you hadn't just dropped your apartment keys in the mail for the landlord you never met (only saw the super... drunk in the lobby or the courtyard) (he didn't know the landlord, either) all forced stoicism and disconnect contemplating the bigger picture with a new life waiting somewhere else now, and maybe *my* exodus was this way, harsh, should never have left that way or maybe not at all with two terrified cats I took straight to hell poor babies (hope I have the decency to commit suicide this year maybe next) and it's my cats Hank and Simon and Max and Sam when I exit the NEW World Trade Center it's my poor CATS I think of my pulverized toes numbin the brown slush when I finally hit Canal Street sleet and the cold future lying ahead of me in taxi smog Varick Street unchanged Sixth Avenue unchanged Sixth and Houston my joints stiffen my tongue swells my chest shrinks and it doesn't matter HOW you leave ANY fucking town if you're wise enough to leave it PERMANENTLY.

-92-

Lase is glowing a bit when we shake hands at the entrance of Rock'n'Raw which is very easy to miss in the shadows of Sullivan St. between Bleecker and Houston. Oh, he really *is* happy to see me, the dandy hipster has a glib passion, makes me blush and feign this and that. Writers need coddling, that's the idea. So let the cunt have his idea, he's swarthy and unibrowed with a big nose and long black wavy hair, patent leather shoes and skin tight black Levis: the Peruvian Marc Bolan, just what the world needed, and he is a big fan of my work.

Inside, I get my own table. I get my own hippie bitch waitress, she takes my paper sack of Olde English 800,takes my peacoat and I get my own little bottle of filtered water. She wrinkles her nose at my sandaled feet and hands me a menu.

Lase: "Order anything you want, man. Great stuff, macho."

"Hey Lase, she took my beer, can I have my beer?" I order the vegan spicy burrito. There is a broken guitar mounted above my head; otherwise, the walls of the five-table restaurant, which has been converted from a slim row home, are bare. It's a pompous vibe "the Raw" has and while ideologically I am against slaughter, I am after all a gutter human, I am among those BEING slaughtered, my time already come and gone, I am down in the streets like the poor of Rio de Janeiro and Buenos Aires where the streets mean theft kidnapping murder where the elite hop from rooftop to rooftop in helicopters, hah hahhah,but I keep this all to myself because LASE is charming although I know damn well he doesn't READ my work no one READS my work only the FACEBOOK tantrums which are free (dies cunts die cunts die cunts) and then the food comes. I gobble it up, it's fine, and I'd gobble gobble even if it wasn't because of the high menu prices: if you were serving boiled monkey shit at $19 a bowl, I'd be on my third fucking one before I allowed myself to consider a set-up. That's poverty for you.

Lase's wife Teri emerges from the kitchen, a freckled, gap-toothed ginger girl, a New Orleans hippie: she's stiffly obliging. I've suffered this before: my "readers" are ALWAYS power-tripped, pussy-whipped pretty boys like Lase here, and their approval of the slimeball sex beast GREGORITS may be the only MANHOOD they can afford. Their cunt girlfriends and cunt wives research me with morbid fascination, the sum total of all this homoerotic complicity being such that I find myself re-made as "the other woman" in a more traditional love triangle.

This is not success

This is not success

This is not success. I leave without paying OR tipping, but I *do* give Lase a kiss on the cheek and grope his ass after he fetches my peacoat and nearly empty malt liquor bottle.

"I'll call you from the bar," I tell him.

-93-

Bleecker St. is different and the same. The sameness dampens my spirit, the differences leave me cold. I could consciously tally it, keep track of either/or, but I don't, because I prefer to bicycle through fresh territory, stasis is death and I'm for rolling. Minneapolis, Albuquerque, Tulsa: my time for them will come too. Many years of this, I expect to die *in between* places.

"Paul Colby's The Bitter End" and "Kenny's Castaways." Old fart places, tourist traps for Midwest dinosaurs: the Café Wha and the Minetta Tavern remain. But the rest? My old haunts? They're gone.

Every last one of them. There is no need to run through them all now, standing in the freezing rain. I ponder the ways that myths are more dangerous than anything, particularly for the young. Everything is dangerous for the young, particularly in the not-so-recent past when the young were passionate and intelligent creatures, enough so that they were themselves inherently dangerous, even without all those cruel myths. It's as if this thought had never occurred to me, for a moment, and then as if I'll go on forgetting what I know, over and over again, forever. The only thing that isn't dangerous is dying, and they make that as difficult as possible. It's illegal to even try.

-94-

The little basement bar I duck into turns out to be a Treasure Island-themed frat bar, but they have $3 Budweisers (I pretend to be shocked, far too accustomed to my dollar drafts at Beach Lounge) and a cat asleep on the floor in a beer crate. I'm petting the cat gently, without waking it, when the obscene, godless little gadget explodes in my pocket.

"Who the FUCK is this?"

"Oh come on, Gene."

"BYE!"

I rise and return to the bar. The phone rings again: it's Richard Wellington, the self-styled impresario (emphasis on "imp") from Australia who introduced me to my lost love Bec, and who may or may not be in New York for Christmas. It quickly turns into a cursing match because despite the worsening road drama of Cynthia Maviano, I have been unable to nullify the momentum Bec and I spent the fall season building after my return from Melbourne. I'm forced to leave the bar and have my screaming fit in the rain.

RW: CAHM ON, MATE! SHE'S MOVED ON! AND YOU WERE FACKING USING HER ANYWAY!

GG: Using her for WHAT?

RW: Oh come on. Grow the fuck up, Gene.

GG: You MAGGOT! You call yourself a FRIEND, you slimy FUCK!

RW: Look, Gene, man, I didn't mean ta fackin put it like that, oh-kye? But you KNEW she was eek-SPECTING you to sort out that ee-veektion business down there, and ya FACKIN BLEW IT, dee-leebrit-lee, deen-cha?

GG: I BLEW IT? HO! OH! I BLEW IT? I JUST ROLLED THE FUCK OVER AND GAVE UP THE BEST FUCKING HOME I EVER HAD, YOU FUCKING MORON. YEAH! LISTEN TO ME-

RW: Now Gene...

GG: YOU LISTEN – THE FUCK – TO ME. I SPEND ALL DAY... EVERY DAY ALL DAY... FOR A MONTH! TAKING THE BUS TO THE

COURTHOUSE! SPENDING ALL MY FUCKING MONEY! TO FIGHT THIS THING! AND I BLEW IT? IS THAT WHAT YOU SAID? RICHARD!

RW: Oh bloody hell. Where are you, we need to-

GG: I GOT *SNAKED*, RICHARD, and no one, NO ONE did a FUCKING THING TO HELP ME. And I CARED ABOUT THAT FUCKING GIRL! IT'S THE WORST THING THAT'S EVER FUCKING HAPPENED TO ME! FUCK YOU! DON'T EVER CALL ME AGAIN! WE'RE FINISHED!

Back in the bar, I wait for the phone to ring but it never does. I dial Lase and leave a message, ten minutes later I run into him on the stairs as I'm stepping out. We cab it across town to Avenue A and I'm quickly reminded of how lonely the nightly barhopping routine can be. We exit the cab at Fifth St. and dash inside Niagara.

"Monica Beerle used to leave in this building, one of the apartments upstairs. Do they still *have* apartments upstairs?"

"Probably," Lase says. "What else would be up there? Monica Beery?"

"Beer-LEE."

"Hey, I know you're a beer drinker," Lace says. "But I'm ordering you something special now, do you trust me?"

"I could write an entire book about sex with undesirables, all the memories I have of this cokehead fucking shithole," I say, scanning the bar. "Now listen... Monica Beerle was a stripper who, in 1985, got eaten by the homeless people in Tompkins Square Park, after the riots.

"That's nuts, man. You say they ATE her?"

"She was living with a schizophrenic hippie named Daniel Rakowitz. He had a pet rooster. He killed her in the apartment, chopped her up, and made a big pot of soup. Then he fed her to the junkies, late at night, in the wintertime."

"How do you know all this stuff?"

"I've been building an archive for 20 years for a book. *Necropolitan Life*, a scum history of New York. It's a real *Bad Lieutenant* kind of history book. *Bad Lieutenant* is really the CENTER of the book, and Abel Ferrara- it's complicated."

"You've got to put that book out, Macho. Listen, we're going to have tequila, okay?"

"Yeah."

"This is Patron."

"I recall a lot of L's. They were all L's. And the L's were also Jews. All the Jewish L's. The batshit hot-shit airhead Jews with L names."

"Hah hah! Yeah, really? All L's huh?"

"Let's see... Lisa Rose from the *Star-Ledger*, a horrible cunt. Laura the fake mortician, skulking and lurking around... Lainie from *Penthouse*, Leni was Mark Kramer's woman, she was a sweetie, though. Another Lisa journalist, Jewish, Lisa Edelman from *NY Press*. Lynne Hoffman from the LD50s. That stands for 'Lethal Dose.'

All right *here*. That lameass Joe Strummer mural outside, that went up after I left. Lana Meltzer, she came in towards-"

"Gene! Come on!"

"Lucy from Greenpoint, of course... I hate this fucking bar."

"Here's to GENE BACK IN NEW YORK!"

"Oh! This is really nice, Lase. Thanks, pal."

"Really. You like it?"

"I do, yeah."

"CLEAN. It's a CLEAN drink. This is the good stuff. PRIMO."

Niagara fill up after Lase buys a second round, so getting to the bar for a third is impossible and then we're forced to shout into each other's ears once the "DJ set" begins. Charming New York absurdity? Endearing bohemian folly? There's nothing charming about it. I feel like an imbecile while enduring these obnoxious situations – ALWAYS. I feel like an imbecile now. Once kids started believing that simply PLAYING records was itself an art form, and an ideologically bankrupt cultural establishment ALLOWED those imbeciles to CONTINUE believing that, ad infinitum, music began to die. I remember this feeling, always, of being a phantom investigator of old school craft, of thoughtfulness and soulfulness, of wit and romance, while being handed Xeroxed flyers by the idiot muppet fucks I slept with, and drank with, and worked with... Flyers announcing my chums' "DJ night," "spinning" at some bar. These were the cheap, vulgar brats who chased me into the vile embrace of a blown-out groupie con-woman named Lydia Lunch. That's the short version.

"Lydia's another one," I scream.

"WHAAAT?"

"LYDIA'S ANOTHER ONE!"

"ANOTHER WHAT?"

"ANOTHER LOOPY JEW CUNT WITH AN L NAME!"

"EASY, MACHO! LET'S GO SOMEWHERE ELSE!"

"DOES DICK MANITOBA STILL HAVE A BAR?"

"YEAH, YOU WANNA GO THERE?"

"ANYWHERE WE DON'T HAFTA LISTEN TO THE FUCKIN BEASTIE BOYS!"

"WHAT THE FUCK MAN, YOU HATE THE BEASTIES, TOO?"

"I'M NOT TEN YEARS OLD ANYMORE, SORRY!"

"DAMN, GENE!"

-95-

I introduce Cynthia to Lase when she waddles in to Manitoba's, drenched and insane.

"Did you bring any drugs?" I say, quietly.

"Yes."

Lase flashes his perfect teeth, howling.

"It's not a joke, Lase. She's a walking pharmacy. Show him, Cynthia."

She digs into her 20-pound homeless woman purse, a nightmare of junk, residue, paraphernalia, memorabilia, and Day-Glo plastic things. Lase winks at me. I turn red. Cynthia produces a "family size" Advil bottle, cracking it down upon the tabletop. I grab it, open it: foil packets, loose brown pills, loose blue pills, glassine bags of orange pills, glassine bags of white powder. I hand it to Lase, who peers inside and says, "Holy shit."

"Ecstasy, coke, Xanax, Vicodins, and... oh, there's Adderall, and... that's it."

"No weed?"

"Weed's in the car. There's a few ounces at Joe's I need to pick up. You guys want a drink?"

A young brunette with a Clara Bow bob and a black choker necklace takes Cynthia's drink order, while Lase shakes his head. "Wow Gene," he whispers. "You're a gigolo." I tap out two ecstasy tablets from the Advil bottle and wash them back with Patron. Maybe New York has something left for me after all.

-96-

The three of us drink late into the wet night. They are Lase's spots, mostly. Lase likes yuppie bars, fashionista bars, underground goth bars, punk bars, gay disco bars, and in the nearly pitch-black heroin-chic cocaine-oblivion bar with massive red velvet curtains and tiny tealights burning on all the tables, an occult Chiaroscuro, my teeth are loose and my eyes are happy singing Richard Hell songs and New York Dolls songs out loud with Lase while Cynthia plays Mott the Hoople and David Bowie and The Beatles on the jukebox which is a REAL jukebox, not one of those little Internet things, we are the only ones IN the heavy joint, doing lines right off the table while the bartenders sweep up around us, and we're even smoking CIGARETTES in there, the kind of night you're SUPPOSED to have in post-terror Manhattan when it's nearly January and all your real friends are dead.

But Lase has a baby at home and Cynthia must be up by noon for work, so she pays for another hundred dollar tab and we all split. After dropping Lase at his high-rise on East 19th, Cynthia drives like a fighter pilot all the way back to the post-industrial wilds of New Jersey.

-97-

At Lucky 7's, our sexily frumpy barmaid is telling us about her

126

boyfriend, and Christmas shopping for her boyfriend, and going on vacation (Costa Rica or Puerto Rico?) with her boyfriend, while turning on all the little machines, the credit card machine, the video poker machine, the little Internet jukebox, the television, the satellite TV console, the cash register. She's wearing a scarf with ice clusters hanging from the pale gray tassels, and dripping...her lips are chapped and I'm wondering how it's possible – and it is, even for me – to fall in love with a brainless cunt, to endow a non-entity (an *anti*-entity; more commonly) with imaginary qualities, grafting the desired traits onto their naked stupid bodies like dressing a Barbie Doll. I smile and listen to the girl talk, as my imagination drifts lazily to the smartly manufactured, innocent-yet-serious visual contemplation of her taking a crap in a peach-colored, potpourri-scented bathroom. There is no sexual component: I always find myself placing stupid people on the toilet. It's all the shit they heave at me every time they speak.

"I'm out of money," Cynthia says.

"Oh."

"I need to request more, it's a trust account."

She stares straight at me, waiting for something.

I shrug my shoulders. A *trust* account? What's that mean?

"How much money do you have?" I dare, feeling cocky.

She holds my eyes with hers, with her widow's peak and defeated posture framing a sad situation I won't take the blame for.

"About 11 grand. I need to start keeping a close eye on what's being spent. You need to get a job."

"I'll be selling books again after the *Vice* article comes out."

"When's that?"

"I don't know. Soon. And the reading Lase has arranged... if you get the books printed, you can keep everything that comes back..."

Cynthia isn't listening, something out in the snow, in the round window, the porthole above the out of service payphone, having seized her attention, and she begins nodding rapidly. She produces a brightly colored Visa card, placing it on the table. "I'll be back," she says. "I have to go into the city. Order your books."

"Is there an Internet café around here?"

"My laptop, come get it from the car."

Outside it's a real Norman Rockwell wet dream. I walk with Cynthia to her car, four blocks of baby steps, my peacoat and sandals, pure Ratso Rizzo. Snow blowers whine in the distance, old men out playing with their east coast toys. Melting ice dripping from trees. Repulsed, I light a cigarette. Cynthia sniffs the air and squints into the sun: this is her home. She pops the Honda's hatch and drags out a heavy old HP laptop, its heavy old power supply popping behind it into the brown slush.

"Tonight's the Christmas dinner at Andy's."

"Is today Christmas?"

"Christmas is Thursday, I think. *Next* Thursday. Isn't Christmas on the 24th?"

"25th."

"Jesus."

"It's the 25th,yeah."

"Well..."

-98-

I watch the Honda twist out of the tight spot and creep back toward the bar with my hands balled up deep in my coatpockets and the laptop under my left arm when my entire body explodes with a powerful vibration accompanied by a piecing jingle. I have to brace myself on a lamppost, nearly dropping the computer and tearing down a flyer for *Annie* to stay afoot. A fat man across the street chews his cigar and shakes his head at me.

I open the little phone and hit the green button.

"Small Animal Vasectomy Clinic, may I help you?"

"Gene-o?"

"Yeah what?"

"That's sick, man. Listen, you comin out tonight?"

"Tonight is Christmas dinner at Cynthia's friends. I have to go."

"You're a gigolo, man."

"Stop saying that."

"You really going back to Florida?"

"As soon as I have the money."

"Well... hey, man, the truck is here, I have a delivery. Call me later."

"I just ordered my books for the reading, I won't have them for a week. Is that okay?"

"So not this Sunday but *next* Sunday?"

"Is that okay?"

"Should be. Call me later."

When I hang up, the fat man is still ogling me, and I realize I have to be alone with the woman behind the bar. I don't like her, I've decided. I do not like anything about her, or this day, or the man across the street who understands my hustle all too well. Just like everyone else.

-99-

When Cynthia returns, I've managed to download a pirated copy of Photoshop and assemble an industry-grade poster for my reading, dated December 27, 2012. I'm on my eighth pint with a blown out ego and a manic pulse that chased poor Princess Frumpy to the other end of the bar.

"Get anything done?" Cynthia asks.

I show her the poster.

"Oh, that's... YOU did that?"

"Yeah."

"You're good at everything, you jerk...Who took the photo?"

"This fat girl who ran the Sonic Youth Fan Club. She committed suicide because I blew her off, I can't remember her name. Listen, a New Jersey magazine just reviewed *Dog Days*. We gotta find a newsstand."

"NEWS stand? They don't even HAVE those anymore."

"What about a bookstore?"

"Borders?"

"Borders is gone. Tower is gone. What about Barnes & Noble?"

"There was a Barnes & Noble in Nutley, but I think they... no, that's gone too."

"I need to find a copy of *Shock Cinema* today."

"Cinema? Your book is reviewed in a movie magazine?"

"The literary magazines won't acknowledge me, so... yeah. It is what it is, you know?"

"Did you order your books?"

"Yeah."

"How much?"

"$212.90."

"Jesus. Maybe I can finally get a copy of *Hatchet Job*."

"Are you kidding?"

"No!"

"You never got a copy of *Hatchet Job*."

"Uh... no?"

"No?"

"NO!"

"Maybe it came when you were at work and Joe got it?"

"NO! You just never sent me one, ya jerk."

"You gave me two grand to print that fucking thing, and never even got a copy. Fuck."

"You had a ton of orders that never shipped, right? Back in Florida?"

"Yeah, but-"

"So it must be one of them."

"Look, I was losing my home. It's not how it looks. I spread myself too thin..."

"I'm just giving you a hard time. I do want one, though."

"I promise. They're on the way."

"What address did you use?"

"This one."

"The BAR?"

"Hahaha. Yeah!"

"Gene..."

"We're here every day..."

"Can you call them?"

"Sure"

"You need to call them right now and give them a real address. We'll use my friend Eileen's place in Cherry Hill. But we gotta go. I told Joe I'd move some of my things today. And tonight's our last night at the Candlewood. It's too expensive."

"It's horrible."

"I found us a new place, in the ghetto. You'll love it."

"You ever smoke crack?"

"NO."

"Well..."

"We're not smoking crack. What size shoes do you wear?"

"I've *got* shoes."

"I'm getting your shoes. Just something to cover your feet. Don't you want to be taken seriously?"

"But I've *got* shoes..."

-100-

The building has an angry look, like a schoolhouse from the 19th century. Or like an army barracks. I think of that movie that was always on TV when I was a child, *Fort Apache: The Bronx*.

And beyond the building.

"I'll meet you somewhere else, later. I can't be here. Cynthia!"

"Oh, stop it."

"Well, gimme some coke."

"Sure, hold on..."

(*WIDESCREEN* SHOT of Manhattan with lens filter to give the effect of a dirty windshield, CYNTHIA MAVIANO's dirty road salt Jersey windshield, and the shot then slanting downward and pulling back to reveal the Hudson River and Hoboken, etc., at once epic and seedy. SECOND widescreen shot from INSIDE car using the ACTUAL MAVIANO WINDSHIELD with ELLEN BARKIN as CYNTHIA MAVIANO and CHRISTIAN BALE as GENE GREGORITS, and the TORN CHAIN LINK on either side of the car framing the NYC view (great poster image) (think Springsteen's *Nebraska*, but in color, and peopled)).

Cynthia taps out a pile of cocaine from a blue glassine bag, scant inches from the edge of a 300 foot drop, and she chuckles, it's a chuckle that has the deepness of cigarette smoke and of a premenopausal desperation that lends itself to transmogrification, dissipating into obscure memories of two dozen similar creatures spanning two decades, thin and dark, long and explosive, dim and pale, cunning and tragic, and that's definitely Manhattan staring seemingly down on us although we are most certainly above it. A badly damaged chain-link fence appears ready to drop into the void, the powerful shelf of asphalt-topped limestone split in places, as if by Thor's hammer, feral vegetation sprouting around the fault lines, the ugly rust upon the fence and its heavy gray-blue poles bent OUTWARD dragging the chain-link with them for a hair-raising sight which terrifies me: how is it that STEEL POLES come to be BENT OUTWARD in such a fashion, in such an UNNATURAL location? Did the chain-link really prevent a vehicle (or large group of persons) from SLIPPING OVER, and what about the ICE FACTOR oh no no no this is NOT A SAFE PLACE TO BE which is when it CLICKS: my first VISIONS of the city, when I was at once hopelessly backward and perversely bright, at age 15, were from the windows of a Greyhound bus, and it was THE SAME CLIFF, and the same VIEW, the Greyhound route of 1991 when it wasn't just the skyline that seemed so impossible, maybe the grandest impossible we're not in (ANYWHERE) anymore skyline in civilized history but the perilous stretch of winding NEW JERSEY HUDSON-BLUFF ROAD, the BOOM OF METROPOLIS that took the bus with it, that BOOM being doled out to me by the bus driver in 1991 only ten feet at a time in rush hour Lincoln Tunnel traffic, nearly evening in early winter and the traffic gave me TIME to absorb the spectacle and anticipate the thrumming necropolis and its necessary pornographic guts but there was something ABOUT that nightmare border landscape that festered in my imagination, in a deeper and weirder fashion, an energy that was recognizably Pennsylvanian, I suppose because of the down-at-mouth look of all these houses if not exceeding then perhaps MATCHING the unnaturalness of their location, the shit-brown aluminum siding and puke green shingles and sagging roofs of the HUDSON BLUFF HOUSING exactly the same as the SUSQUEHANNA BLUFF HOUSING in the town of Enola where I was born, the damp shit brown snot green sagging porches and frayed fruit fly'd river paste-caked porch screens along the craggy hillsides, places not built to last and so I watched them from the left side past the laps and heads of Greyhound strangers while the city sat there like a demonic uprising on my right and I was powerless against the dread memories of the Enola river houses and "who would live here?" etc. and as I lean forward to take the cocaine with a snort, I KNOW because now I *AM* THERE, I am there with ONE OF THOSE PEOPLE, I HAVE well and truly caught up, finally, with the phantom hill of the megalopolis, with one of those phantom people.

"Was it scary, the first few months, at least?"

"No!"

"I would never live here."

"You could never afford it anyway."

"I can't be up here. I don't even like being this tall."

"You're safe, don't worry."

"But what is it?"

"What is what?"

"All this. ALL this up here."

"Palisades Park. Union City. And Weehawken."

"The Lincoln Tunnel?"

"Yup. That's Weehawken. Right over there."

"Jesus Christ. I need a drink."

"Come on."

-101-

My heart pounding, I whimper, "How many flights?"

"Sixth floor."

"Awww..."

"Oh come on."

"This building is exactly like my old place on Havermeyer, in Brooklyn. Same mosaic in the lobby, same wall patterns. Same railings. We made a couple of porn movies there in '99. The whole neighborhood talked about it for a year, because we forgot to cover the windows. We had trannies, you know. Chicks with dicks."

"I still had my place in the East Village then. I probably met you a few times."

"Same apartment doors and everything."

We come to the one marked "SELICK" and inside, I get it: the fanboy hipster radio personality, and the wastoid downtown garage punk scene burnout. He's a cross-dressing Humpy Dumpty, and she's got the most acute case of Cindy Bradley syndrome in recorded history. Two faux-bohemian pop culture grotesques rotting away on the edge of a cliff where nothing exciting has happened since 9/11.

Inside are the framed concert posters, the rooms packed solid with CD box sets and crates of vinyl. One hall closet is a morbid shrine to Jack Klugman and Tony Randall, a mini-museum of *The Odd Couple* artifacts. There are signed 8x10s, framed *TV Guide* covers, action figures still in their boxes, shrinkwrapped toy watches, "Oscar Madison For President" and "I Heart Felix Unger" bumper stickers, and a vinyl soundtrack album there in the middle. I sniff the air. This place has seen better days.

Cynthia collapses on an L-shaped black leather sofa, so hip it hurts. She spreads her stubby arms across the cushions then heaves her bulk forward to the glass coffee table where a pewter dragon box sits brimming over with marijuana and its paraphernalia. She lights a joint.

"Did you see the-"

"Yeah. Play this." I hand her the legendary *Funhouse Sessions* box

132

set, issued 10 years ago by Rhino Records in an edition of 500. "I never had the money for one of these. I've never even HEARD it. I've never even SEEN one before."

"Are you nuts? It's SEALED. That's a month's rent, right there!"

"Put it on!"

"It's BRAND NEW. Are you fucking HIGH? Put it back!"

"Open it!"

"PUT IT BACK!"

I stamp off, pouting, and return with a standard issue *Sticky Fingers* CD.

"Fine," she says. "Just remember to put it back."

"Joe knows you hate the Stones."

"I do not HATE THE STONES."

"Is it weird being back here?"

"Yeah. There's probably some Heineken in the fridge."

"Hah!" I race to the kitchen and find a stash of the green bottles. "Fuck yeah."

"Don't go crazy. We've got things to do."

I pop the bottle on the pristine retro countertop, letting the cap's clatter come to a natural stop on the black and white checkerboard floor before taking my Dutch treat to the hallway where I examine the framed concert posters on by one.

The Sex Pistols at Roseland, 1996.

Big Star at Irving Plaza, 1998.

Blondie at CBGBs, 1995.

The 13th floor Elevators at Coney Island High, 1992.

The Pogues at the Brooklyn Academy, 2003.

The Troggs at Maxwell's, 1994.

"These are all *reunion* shows!"

A faint "yeah..."

"Is it weird being back here?"

"You just asked me that!"

I return to the living room. She has lain down on her back, lengthwise on the couch in a cold of a foul drugsmoke, dank squalid fecal-sweet potsmoke, with her ugly legs folded over the left couch arm. "Do you want to go?"

"I guess I feel kinds crummy being in the guy's house. What happened to *Sticky Fingers*?"

"Gene, he's not gonna be home for another three hours. Wanna fuck?"

"Let's go get a drink."

"Just have another one here," she sighs.

"I'm getting it... it's like... always knowing where the other person is. No one to fight. And then failing at re-living East Village shit from 20 years ago. Fucking hipster purgatory."

"Oh fuck you."

"Heh. To live and die in New Jersey."

Now she's crying again. I return to the fridge and take *two* beers, pop both on the retro countertop. "Is this Formica?"

I sit down next to her, making a loud clank on the table with the bottles. I say, "We better let some air in here."

"SHUT UP. SHUT UP. SHUT UP. DON'T YOU EVER SHUT THE FUCK UP?"

"He didn't kick you out, did he? You just left."

"Gene, I'm gonna fucking stab you with something. Get me a tissue. Over there."

I get up, return with the box, sit.

She dabs her eyes.

"There was a party. We had a party here for New Year's and it carried over a few days. One of our friends, his wife left him. I was attracted to him. Joe hadn't touched me in so long."

"But he's not gay, you said."

"He's into dressing up. You want to see his shoe closet? He has these shoes specially made. Thousands of dollars. And dresses. You want to see?"

"No thanks." I pick up an extinguished joint, relight it. "So can't he just fuck you in drag, then?"

"That's not his thing. It's... weird. I don't want to talk about it."

"He likes to be watched, like... you're supposed to watch him jack off when he's dressed up, kinda?"

"Pretty much"

"Wow."

"Yeah. Repulsive."

"So you cheated on him."

"No, not then. It just...got weird. I told him I was leaving. He didn't stop me."

"That's not being kicked out."

"You don't understand. He doesn't *want* me back. And when my mother died, I inherited some money... I've just been, kinda, staying with people, you know. I should just go ahead and rent a regular place."

"And get set up before you spend it all on drugs."

She narrows her eyes at me, biting her tongues in the musty air.

"You look like an axe murderer, why don't you get rid of that mangy beard?"

"I'm going-"

"I guess I'll have to buy you some razors. You need to get a job."

"Yeah, but-"

"That beard is horrible. I thought the point of the mohawk was to look younger."

"I'd never get a mohawk. The worst idiots in the world have mohawks."

"Then why-"

"I was trying to make a young girl happy. She'd lost her mother. But then I fell in love with her."

"I don't want to know. Is that how you got all beat up?"

"Heh, heh, heh."

"Jesus fuckin Christ."

"Can I open the curtains?"

"Oh, the view! This is the first time I didn't go right for it, with company. Pull that cord on the right."

And there it is: the source of every self-inflicted misery. You can't take your eyes off of it. Stand there staring while it ruins you. Blots out the sun. Dumb fuck.

"It's the best view in the whole building. Hey, c'mere."

"What?" Boats. I think of horrible old Trocchi down there on his barge, 1959.

"C'mere. You want a blow job?"

"Let's go to Florida. I need to get back to Sammy." Fuck Lou Reed. Fuck Martin Scorsese. Fuck every last one of 'em. Glorification of debasement. Vertigo is not the same as transcendence. Go loopy on electromagnetic overload. Over KILL. Cultural dementia. Sex dementia. Claustrophobia. Dumb fuck.

"I'll give you the money," she snaps. "*You* go. I have too many people here. Roots. Family. Everything. Quit *asking* me to go to Florida. I'm not *going* to Florida. You should open your mind to getting something started here. You could have a career, if you'd learn to stay out of your own way."

"*Dog Days 2* is magic. I could sell that book from the moon."

"You haven't touched that book in how long?"

"It's done! For the 50th time, it's DONE. I wrote it in the nuthouse."

"But since you've been here..."

"I need a monitor. I need a keyboard. A desk."

"Make me a list. I'm getting an apartment. On Monday."

I close the curtains. Silence big and defiant, like the city.

-102-

It is a starless, dry, silent winter night I observe in the parking lot of Super Liquors, Elizabeth, New Jersey, and its neighbors: BJ's Wholesale Club, Shop-Rite, Loew's Cineplex, TJ Maxx. The highway glitters behind us.

"We're late," she says. "Be quick."

"Monastrell is produced in Spain, almost always in Jumilla, but there's been a surge of growth in Alicante over the last decade. I'm not sure how far apart they are."

Cynthia is tapping a note in cellphone semaphore to her soon-to-be ex-husband.

"Shit," she mutters. "We need beer. Can you – never mind."

"It's a BIG FAT grape, thick skinned so it's, like super easy to-"

"Not now. We have to hurry. You can tell me about it later."

Inside, we are greeted by doughy, middle-aged oenophiles wearing burgundy smocks and they scatter quickly when I tell them in an unkind fashion, "We know what we want, thank you."

The creepy Tom Petty song about Santa Claus is barely discernible over the din of shopping courts and clinking bottles. "I'm going to grab the beer. Be ready." We make for opposite ends of the store.

I am again accosted by a clerk, this one much younger, with black spiky hair. He's one of those "pop-punk" types, a cocky suburban manchild who still gets a basket full of chocolate from mama each Easter. I hold up one of my hands: "Spanish reds, I got it."

"But sir, it's over here. You're going the wrong way."

I don't like wine clerks. They're paid to upsell and oversell, and they give wine a bad name. I've been trying for ten years, almost fifteen years, to forge a kinship with the wine clerks of the world to no recognizable satisfaction at all. There is an intimacy that happens in the aisles of wine specialty shops – or "superstores" – but it happens rarely. It does not happen when the clerk seizes upon an upsell prospect with all the sublimity and poise of a feral Tijuana youth hawking Chiclets on spring break and does his absolute best to downplay a very real and very underfed ego, as naturally exists in all dedicated wine snobs, long enough to seduce the cretinous attorney with a Merlot or Zinfandel fetish, or the cretinous family man, a St. Bernard in khakis, who would rather be buying Bud Light, or the poor cretinous project nigger, who only wants what he sees rich cretinous project niggers drinking on reality television.

The intimacy ONLY happens when the clerk encounters a true-blue fucking wine-HEAD, discovering WITHIN that encounter a potentially maddening (or euphoric) index of motives, of agendas, of biases, of temperaments, of manias, of sympathies, of instincts, of wits, and most importantly – again – of egos, which *ALL* very necessarily, very urgently exist just behind the eyes of any dedicated wine snob. It's not entirely different than the prospect of two film geeks feeling each other out, or two gearheads, two mutually contemptuous aficionados of ANY everyday element that happens to lend itself to fetishization by loners, feebs, dinks, and dorks, except that in the case of the wine clerk, who cannot UPSELL without either a superior bargain or a superior wit, envy is inevitable, always. The superior bargain does not help him transcend his starving-class retail-ravaged drowning life so of course he's going to fuck with you.

But Billie Joe Armstrong here hasn't got a clue what he's selling,that's my educated guess. I let him guide me to Spain, which is traditionally located adjacent to the South American bottles but Super Liquors – perhaps a merely logistical compromise – has it stuck between the CA Cabs and Italy.

"Anything in particular that you're-"

"Holy FUCK! Look at all... these..."

"Oh yeah..."

I can feel Billie Joe taking stock of my gnarled beach feet and crusty jeans. "Yeah," he continues, "our Spanish section is-"

"SHOCKING. I'm... I'm SHOCKED, okay? I wasn't expecting... look, I need to grab a few cheap Monastrells, I'm late for a dinner, and they're gonna want some dipshit trendy Malbec they saw on sale at fucking Shop-Rite, and –oh! Look at this, Monte Oton for four fucking dollars, oh boy that's tempting..."

"That's an awfully good Grenache."

"I take it to the movies. That's my movie theatre wine."

"There's a *theater* that allows you to-"

"No one *allows* me a *god* damn thing. I mind my business and give THEM a chance to mind theirs."

"Nice!"

"Yeah, you can drink at the movies. You can drink anywhere if you come on real highfallutin about it. Or if you're discreet. Discreet is usually best-"

"Gene!"

"Cynthia!"

In the moment I am in love with New Jersey and Green Day and Cynthia Maviano and everything. I want to get a job directing traffic in the Holland Tunnel so I can load up on three or four cases of Monte Oton before I even consider – before I even DISCOVER – the Monastrells, the *other* Grenaches, the Tempranillos, the Bobels, the Spanish Cabs.

"Gene, we gotta go. *Now.*"

I don't turn, but I know she's rolling her big brown cow eyes.

"So you're into Monastrell," Billie Joe says.

"Am I... I mean, I brought it, like... I'm a writer... and I'm bringing Monastrell UP."

I fumble for my coat pocket, nervously producing a Monastrell business card. He takes it, and gasps.

"Okay, I just KNEW you were a writer. See, Monastrell's *my* thing too, I-"

"Bullshit."

"No! I mean, I dig French wine, but I've been on a Spanish kick for the last year or so and *Monastrell* is-"

"Oh, I KNOW. I'm bringing it to a... a *new prominence*, see? Monastrell Books is an exaltation of transgressive literature AND the

Monastrell grape! I'm taking on *two* missions, *two* causes, because, like, I don't even hardly THINK of other grapes anymore! It's a brooding fucking thing, it's *serious*, I get SHY around it like it's a fucking, a...WOMAN, with TITS!"

"GENE! ENOUGH! You can do WINE CHAT later! Why don't you exchange numbers?"

"I'm Anthony," he says, extending a long, alabaster hand with magic markered fingernails.

"Gene," I half-bark. I embrace the kid in an awkward bear hug, beaming.

"Did you pick something out? Gene we have to GO."

I select two bottles of Monte Oton, and the first Monastrell I see on the shelf: a 2012 by Luzon Verde, a brand owned by Juan Gil wineries of Jumilla. You can't go wrong with a Juan Gil product.

"Call me," I mouth to Anthony as Cynthia drags me to the checkout.

"You should shave that beard if you want to pick up guys like that," she says.

-103-

Crummy old two-story rowhomes sulking quietly under the stars.
Quaint?
Vulgar.
Falling snow made orange-silver in buzzing sodium lamplight.
Eerie, not magical.
"We forgot your shoes again. We're really late," Cynthia says. "Grab the bags."

Although we are late, she continues playing with her phone, her face on her chest as the car speakers squeal with the bratty three-chord antics of her current favorite band, a sensation sweeping the hipster punk bars of the tri-state area. They're called The Wyld Boys and they sound like a sped-up version of Ireland's The Undertones whose "Get Over You" was a favorite of legendary UK DJ John Peel back in 1979, and a heavy staple of my own vinyl rotation a decade later.

"I thought you'd really dig this," she says.

"It's The Undertones, sped up."

She rolls her eyes and turns up the music, bobbing her head like an insolent teenager because she knows I'm right. She's tied her hair, dyed a patently fake brown, into a ridiculous pair of Cyndi Brandy pigtails. She wears a spiked leather collar which can only be seen when she stretches her neck out like a giraffe. Otherwise it is lost underneath her five chins. I pretend not to notice any of this. I am thinking of convenient ways to commit suicide.

From the car to the front door, Cynthia insists I walk slowly behind her so that I may rescue her no less than four times when her six-inch platform boots clash with the ice. The porch steps, neither salted nor shoveled, are particularly lethal. Fortunately, my Reefs have ample treading, and the built-in bottle openers bite the rough-hewn cement edges like grappling hooks.

I have a flashback of a heroin-ravaged Jamaican man covering "Cheeseburger In Paradise" on an untuned acoustic guitar at the Sloppy Pelican one deep-fried eve (the big indifferent moon daring patrons to stay) (and the sharks feeding anonymously under same), which causes me to smile.

Cynthia tells me that Carla, Meka's best friend and owner of the upscale punk rock salon around the corner from Another Man's Treasure, will be dropping by: "Be polite if she corners you. Carla's managing The Wyld Boys, and it's a big deal, this band's gonna be really big."

"The Undertones, sped up," I say.

"See, that'll make me look bad. Please?"

She rings the bell. I say, "Aren't these people all friends of Joe's?"

Before she can reply, the sound of a deadbolt retracting is tearing into my eyeballs and my vision shrinks. I become bitterly self-conscious, angrily aware of my powerful desire for the door *not* to open: another cocksucking *fake smile* another soul-killing entire *evening* of *fake smiles* and I'm shaking hands with this fucking four-eyed spazz, he's ANDY, another fucking ANDY there's always an ANDY and I'm SMILING for the CUNT and into a warm apartment more SMILES which I dodge unsubtly for the kitchen to start DRINKING.

It's a large apartment, and I'm safe for a minute but only a minute:

"Hey, Tony."

He smiles a different kind of smile.

"Gene," I say.

"Yeah, I know"

He hands me a beer.

We drink our beers.

"Fuck," he says.

"I know," I say.

"We'd better get out there."

"Yeah," I say. "I know."

-104-

My white V-neck is quite favoring a grayish tone, actually, with blood stains, wine stains, mustard stains, coffee stains, when I stand in the corner of the living room like my first day at a job I know I won't last a week at. A dozen, maybe fifteen cozy-looking Jerseyites burble and chirp. Cynthia introduces me to Andy for the second time, and Mark, and Pete, and Carmie, and Denny and who the fuck knows; they are all drinking and their smiles are authentic. I'm horrified, and scan the room for Tony, moving to the dining room, which is connected on one end to the cramped kitchen. There is another room, a kind of den where most of the women have congregated to watch CNN reportage on the post-Sandy cleanup effort, which is finally complete. The prettiest of the women is wearing black thigh-high boots and a black skirt (fuck) and when she looks in my direction I dive for the kitchen but its empty this time (fuck) so I reclaim my corner space until a man -ANDY - taps my shoulder.

"So - Cynthia says you know Lydia Lunch." (He speaks like a fairy, although he's married.) (All the fairies love Lydia Lunch, especially the California fairies, and many Italians fairies.) (And a saucy, bristling contingent of young Turkish fairies in Istanbul, I see it with my own eyes.)

"No, I don't."

"But-"

"We lived together for a couple of years."

"I didn't mean... honestly, I'm just-"

"No, I understand. I'm not offended. Truthfully, I can't even remember back that far very clearly. Otherwise, I'd turn it into a book, you know - I mean, I don't ever *dip* into those days, because there's just... blanks, you know..."

"I guess you got to know the Sonic Youth guys, and Richard Kern, and all those people..."

"I met some of her old friends, but I was never that sociable, you know. She had Jim Foetus try to get me into A.A., cuz he was in A.A. I met Siouxsie Sioux, Debbie Harry, and those people, but... sorry to tell you, the truth is that I barely ever left the house, and we didn't have guests very often. Man, that's over a decade ago now. A dozen years."

The music is loud in the apartment, it's The Wyld Boys, and Andy is babbling about my ex-girlfriend's current touring band, which includes members of Swans.

"Did you meet any of The Swans?" he asks.

"No. I don't know the music, either."

"You're kidding"

"No."

"What about the one Lydia made with those guys?"

"No idea. I used to joke that even Lydia hasn't heard of all of Lydia's records."

He doesn't get, or doesn't appreciate, the humor of this. "Well... they're in town, you know. Lydia and the new band, the one with the

Swans in it.The show's next week. You're not going, I guess?"

"It was a bad split."

Andy has a gleam in his eyes that one might read as conspiratorial. I theorize, with almost certain accuracy, that he is the kind of all-seasons fanboy who scarfs up Beach Boys reissues back to back with import-only Diamanda Galas live albums. He's got no shortage of old friends from his record store days to get all soggy with every time another fucking Ramone kicks off, but the no-wave art-punk thing is a touch of class you just don't find every day anymore. The balding, pot-bellied nebbish just has to know what Miss Lunch was like in bed.

I pause, and look heavily at my empty Pabst can. 12 years of this. I don't want to be rude.

"You've seen the movies. She did two porn films. You've seen them."

"Yeah, but... it couldn't have been... like, was she into-"

"Andy, let me put it this way. If you've had one attention-starved pop diva from the 1970s, you've had'em all. They're fetishistic on account of all the cocaine, and the narcissism and the child abuse that made them run for the big lights in the first place... so they want to be tied up, and worshiped, and this that and the fucking other. It's just depressing. Its like fucking the madam in a brothel, you know?"

"Wow."

"It sounds awful, but the thing is... these people don't live in the real world. I was a messed-up kid with Lydia. We did too much coke. It was a bad scene. Nearly killed each other, blah blah blah. That's all."

"Yeah."

"I'm happier with a *real* person. Even if she has a couple of kids, like little fucking retarded kids running around breaking shit. That's reality."

The guy's actually *beaming* at me. He continues, with an unnervingly feminine shiver:"But how did you guys end *up* together?" (I realize then that there is coke on his nose.)

"Lydia has a fetish for literature. Listen, I gotta take a piss, is it..."

"Oh! Second door! Right there."

"Thanks."

In the hall I encounter a leering old woman whom I immediately understand to be Carla, an elfin, unfriendly little creature who has very nearly done herself in dodging the decades in her ripped-up Wyld Boys baby-tee, red PVC skirt, and black fishnet stocking. Her frosted white hair is streaked with expensively tasteless blue and green highlights. She is, simply put, a scene hag, a punk rock cautionary tale, just another Hipster That Time Forgot.

In the bathroom, I call Florida while running my right finger across the top of the toilet lid for Carla's coke residue, which I rub eagerly on my gums. It occurs to me that my feet stink so I fill the sink with water, adding bleach after finding a bottle in one of the cabinets. I decide to kill as much time as possible in there, perched on the marble countertop with all of the yuppie Bed Bath and Beyond bullshit swept to one side as I contemplate each of my wretched piggies. On the left foot, only the big toe has a nail, the others' withered, ashy nubs appearing to me as obvious signs of a mental disorder which *should* concern or sadden me but of course do not. The nail beds of the right foot's toes are similarly blighted, like the faces of methamphetamine addicts. It occurs to me that it is too late for my ravaged toes ("this little piggy got gangraped, this little piggy found God, this little piggy saw too many underground movies, this little piggy went to Baltimore...") but that no book written by a man in his 20s ever found any enduring favor with me, and precious few written by men in their 30s. Preciousness is the most putrid quality of all, and in 2012,you can lose your career criticizing Lena Dunham or another such media troll, these "wunderkinds"...this little piggy had none...I'm growing sleepy in my rage, the peach-colored bathroom reminds me of...

"OH COME ON!"

...everyone.

"JUST A MINUTE," I say, in the masturbating/drug-taking voice, the GUILTY voice. I put the bleach back underneath the sink because in this day and age, tampering with household cleaning products in a stranger's home could result in any number of criminal charges. The hot steam distributes the bleach smell throughout the bathroom, so I find a bottle of pumpkin-cinnamon–caramel air freshener and spray that around which now advertises the "fact" that the bearded, stinking creep has defiled the happy home with a runny alcoholic chemical crapand attempted to mask it with fancy ($11.99) fragrance, probably forgetting to wash his hands and thereby contaminating...

"HELLO?"

...everything. When I pull the door open, Carla is holding a pose which confirms the tenacity of her delusion: it is the pose of Joan Jett, or Chrissie Hynde, an ANGRY stance, but there are no film cameras rolling when she snaps, "You must be GENE." She narrows her eyes to blue slits: "We have MUTUAL friends."

It is *not* a friendly statement. I am wise to ignore her.

The door slams behind me in the hall. Back in the dining room, a drunken Cynthia introduces me to Liam and Terry, a gay couple who obviously love Duran Duran. One of them, Liam I'm assuming, is British, but I can't be sure since they were introduced as a couple and not individually. I'm ready to puke when I catch them palming a little bag of coke from a just-returned Carla, who I meet formally.

The snarl remains and I say, "Great band, these Wyld Boys." Then I am face to face with the mysterious brunette in the black boots who is even comelier up close but entirely unfuckable for reasons I would never bother trying to articulate to anyone, except that I *always* know whether I'm going to end up fucking a woman within 20 seconds of meeting her and Mickey and I are definitely *not* fucking. (I would rather masturbate, anyway: imagine killing yourself over a woman named Mickey, and imagine going on a six month bender over fucking MICKEY, and her perfect pair of MICKEY-tits, and her Mickey minge and Mickey mouth.) Meeting *Mickey* reminds me that I am standing in the middle of a Cameron Crowe film.

Next is Auggie the DJ in a Pixies t-shirt which hardly contains his beery expanse while the fat old duck, cock-eyed on coke and vodka, pets my face with her ugly hands to advertise her triumphant seduction of the least-read and least-respected writer in America. Rocco the punk rock investor wears a plaid pullover and Buddy Holly glasses, while behind him I encounter the dead-eyed countenance of Andy's wife Stacy who represents hipster stability in furry boots and a Betty Page bob. Pete the guitarist chuckles knowingly while I shake his hand, and I'll obsess over the meaning of it if I don't flee the scene... little Kendra the photo editor of Spin Magazine laughs loudly in her mohair sweater and insulated black leggings and the little bag of coke keeps traveling from hand to hand and I'm wondering why they don't just consume the drug openly when Cynthia insists I meet Larry the Sound Guy in a Sonic Youth t-shirt stretched over yet another gutbucket frame and then finally TOOTIE a wonderfully mousey redhead strange-o hypersexed on coke, (oozing) like a strawberry Tootsie Pop left on a hot sidewalk in her (through her) red tights with blue stripes, which make for an odd pairing with a tight denim skirt but I have an inconsolable panic-erection the moment we lock eyes and that *never* happens anymore. I can smell her sex straight through the sour stagnant marijuana blaze and I'm an inch away from killing everyone in the room.

A proper dinner proves impossible, as the table is too small, with far too much food, all of it expensive. To complicate matters further, the guests are handing those tiny bags of cocaine back and forth with increasing regularity, and the thought of a feast apparently terrifies them. As for the *sight* of it: there's a gorgeously-prepared turkey, flanked by an equally well-appointed ham, with bowls of romaine salad and pots of thick stews, baked vegetables and grilled vegetables, pies and cakes in pink bakery boxes, my Monastrell bottle and one of the Monte Otons standing unopened – morons – and a stack of large, sealed Tupperware containers that I can't possibly contemplate. It's all been abandoned and my contempt swells.

Most of the action pours out onto a large 3rd floor balcony where the coked-up weekend warriors begin bumming cigarettes from two or three holdout smokers, but there are new arrivals every couple of minutes and I'm still very much a cornered tuna in these shark-infested waters. The conversations around me are mostly about The Wyld Boys but the sex of 80s cocaine nights and 90s cocaine nights is like an abandoned thing, a lost un-nurtured angry pathetic little babe and the longings then were easier to quell than now smoking those bittersweet cocaine memory cigarettes tattered wreaths to hang around The Wyld Boys now unreasonably perhaps even defiantly in thrall to the carefully manufactured exuberance of the well-observed retro-pantomime of THE WYLD BOYS, except Tootie shivering beside Cynthia nodding and smiling but indifferent to anything but me which others by now have begun to notice and the feeling is absolutely mutual. The snowfall suggests ringing bells. Faint, phantom bells.

And back inside there is a switch from beer when the beer is gone to berry-flavored vodka, with new introductions to former recording artists each of whom I see struggling with it, with the past, with "90s ROCK" whatever that was, and I have a queasy realization that their adulation of The Wyld Boys mirrors my own tireless attachment to The Kills and could it be that I too suffer this disease called parasitism, drinking big mouthfuls of berry-flavored Absolut and there's a complicated argument raging in me about manipulative inner-workings of any hipster idealist's sad little mind, the deceitful insistence that old news propped up is better than flawed authenticity which is problematic in the grand design, the insolent, badly disguised desperation that rejects the past outright while wallowing in it, that says anything it has to say to avoid the problematic because birth is always painful. Every time I sneak a glance at Tootie she's a deer in the headlights and Cynthia is livid so I don't beg the question – not vocally – of whether counterfeit throwbacks are preferable to the inert arrogance and estrogenic anemia of indie rock twee-ism and that's good thinking on my part because Carla is listening in on our banal chatter already on the verge of nastiness because of Tootie who Cynthia might wish to threaten, and the berry-flavored vodka in the verse of capturing my tongue I tell Carla how well PRODUCED The Wyld Boys are on the new record, I mean how SPIRITED they are on that very WELL PRODUCED new record which gets me a sour "thank you" which gets her an obscenely sincere "they sure are *catchy!*" Cynthia smiles at us both as Carla stomps off to the living room, and says, "good boy" and I whisper back, "are they coming here tonight?"

"Who?"

"The Wyld Boys."

Cynthia shrugs her shoulders and continues her smug nodding and squinting and pursing.

I tell her, "I have to piss."

The fat duck shrug her shoulders

In the mirror I observe myself though Carla's eyes, Andy and Stacy's eyes, but mostly Tootie's eyes because it's rare I happen upon someone who doesn't require a *translated* Gregorits. My face is no longer swollen, the skin around my eyes gone aquamarine which gives me the appearance of a gutter drag queen the morning after a bad dope situation, and I'm on my fourth glass of fucking berry vodka which has me mentally traversing the outskirts of this literalist (non-literary) Jersey City imagining myself for some reason stranded in Perth Amboy down the river with Tootie, stranded in the snow and in the brokedown post-nuke everything of Bayonne or Bushwick, Brooklyn, or Yonkers, or stranded on my own without even my body – disembodied then – in the dead neutral air *above* all that, above those vulgar and frigid commuters halted by the wrath of Sandy, if only for a few moments – not a catastrophe because all courses remain as before. I wonder what it would take, but quickly, as I dare an offhand knuckle-fuck because what has transpired between Tootie and I, the electrically-palpable schizo-kinetic sexual voodoo there has what it takes: in essence it is the THING I spent my teens and 20s staking out in Greyhound stations and bookstores and everywhere else the THING I am powerless against, it's true that it's been NEAR-FATAL a LIFE-DEFINING SICKNESS giving myself over to the MYTH could never give a damn about the fucking music and I wasn't even so crazy about the pussy (of COURSE I was crazy about the pussy) but rather the death-defying MYTH, the banality-bashing MYTH, the jealousy-rousing MYTH which I always enjoyed pairing with animal violence testing with animal rage and chasing doggedly after bloody footprints that god damned myth being very much the essence of the wonder, the WANDER of the wonder, always very much on purpose, pathologically prized out of 1980s pop songs and John Hughes movies as a sicko teen prized from deserted strip mall parking lots and the desertion inner and outer which gives rise to serial killers and serial rapists prized from commercial overkill and Pennsylvania impoverishment and realized so purely prized so fully only once a year or every couple of years, that all or nothing hit of dope that redeems the evil around it.

The perfect bite...

TOOTIE.

I'm about to come when there's a knock at the door.

I let her in.

When I open the door I encounter the fat duck in the hall.

"WHERE is TOOTIE?"

"Who?"

She tries to push past me but I step back into the doorframe, blocking her.

I won't budge. Her puffy face is reddening, her hook nose now dripping with tears. It's clearly time for a touch-up, but not *here*, not with Tootie cowering in there with her vodka glass and her smeared lipstick.

"I'm sorry. Just-"

"It's not you, it's that fucking WHORE. WHORE!"

"Don't cause a scene, come on."

"I'm so fucking stupid, Carla warned me..."

"You're going to get someone over here, come on. Don't embarrass us."

"Just get back out there. Have a drink."

"I've had enough. Come here."

"Fuck you."

"HERE."

I grab Cynthia by the arm of her child-size denim jacket and drag her into Andy and Stacy's bedroom at the end of the hall.

I let the vodka do its thing.

Back in the hall we find the bathroom empty as a commotion rises out in the living room.

"Alright," I say, "fix yourself up. The Wyld Boys are here."

"The Wyld Boys," says Tony, rolling his eyes."Look at those fucking clowns."

"They look like plastic action figures of Generation X."

"Generation X was bullshit too."

"Yeah, they sure were. But these kids.. like... I'm sure Billy Idol, in '78, I bet he'd read William Burroughs, at least."

"Yeah. Think we can make the kitchen?"

"YES."

We slink off into the empty kitchen with laughter swelling behind us. He produces two pint cans of Budweiser and a pint bottle of Jim Beam from underneath the sink.

"I've got a plan," he says, pouring off the head of his Bud into the sink and replacing it with whiskey. I do the same. "Come on," he says.

Our unlit cigarettes held aloft as we smile and nod to the Wyld Boys towards the sliding glass balcony door, our drinks empty behind us in the kitchen, we are grateful for one another and our smiles in the night air are genuine. This time, the bells are nearer.

A chorus of dogs as we shimmy down the frozen drainpipe, into the lurid backyard.

-109-

At Louise & Jerry's Tony is a cherished regular, but I don't get so warm a reception.

"Come on, man. You look like a fuckin scumbag." Tony laughs.

"You better call Carrie, let her know where we are."

"Why don't *you* call *Cynthia* and let me worry about my own fuckin wife?"

"I'm sorry, man. I thought she was your girlfriend."

"That's my fuckin WIFE, bro," he barks, slamming his left hand down on the table, then holding it two inches from my face, now closed. Black Flag bars tattooed on the fingers, a plain gold wedding band: "Change the subject."

I reach for my phone, for excuses.

Tony buys a round of Pabst and Jägermeister. We're the only ones in the bar.

"I have a colonoscopy in the morning," he says.

I laugh.

After a solid minute, he laughs too.

-110-

It is nearly dawn when I wake in the frozen Secaucus parking lot, one leg hanging out of the car and my pants around my ankles. I enter the Candlewood more than a little wobbly and find the room's door propped open with one of Cynthia's platform pleather boots. I take a few crumpled ones off the nightstand to wash my sandals and jeans in the hotel laundromat while Cynthia snores away. I lose myself in Jersey dread drinking beer again, skulking around the hotel and in the room, gathering up stray things like cigarettes, pocket change, matchbooks, wine corks, the still unpacked ALICE pack with the Monastrell brain, the late book orders, the sealed manuscript, the future. I call Florida: no answer.

I load the car and wait for checkout time in the bathtub.

Another Man's Treasure is cozy in the early evening with a rising tide of Christmas shoppers ringing the little bell as they come and go, scraping the coat hangers along the steel racks as they browse, the little Sony boombox playing one of Cynthia's old bands all the while. I sit in the corner right of the door in a low-slung red leather throne which is just soft enough to sleep in, but I've been told three times not to sleep in the store.

I've got Cynthia's laptop open and am elated to see that my Monastrell print order has been filled by Amazon Print-On-Demand LLC, and my attention jumps to the leaking black plastic bag of empty Ballantine cans at my feet. I slip outside with the trash and find a bin on the corner with its round metal mouth overflowing so I toss it all in the street just as someone – a woman – calls my name. I'm having DT symptoms (moaning in the store, threats again) so I do not want to see who is behind me.

I run gingerly, in short strides, all the way to a liquor store or Broadway where I pay $4 for a Chilean Carménère by Gato Negro and down most of it waiting for a double order of Pad Ped at a takeout counter back on Grove from which I can clearly observe Cynthia folding clothes, throwing hangers in a large cardboard box, and shuffling back and forth between snooty young customers (her desperation for approval is agonizing). I call Florida: no answer. I step out and smoke two cigarettes consecutively, staring north towards the Holland Motel, and Hoboken, and the Jersey City Mall. It occurs to me that the woman who called my name may have been Laura, a schizophrenic fashion model who haunted my life like chronic arthritis during my New York years. My toes are numb when I return for the food, and I don't mind. I've gotten used to the nakedness, long walks in the frozen Jersey shit. I'm so full of misery and hate that I enjoy the cold. It keeps me warm somehow.

Cynthia introduces me to a man who looks like a Hispanic Robert Forster in his officer's best, black fedora, and a freshly dry-cleaned 1950s overcoat made of heavy brown wool. His medals are polished, his posture unforgiving: he smiles and shakes my hand.

"This is George, my very good friend."

I say, "George, I apologize for my putrid condition. You are the sharpest dressed gentleman I have ever seen. You are magnificent, sir. I am very pleased to meet you."

George nods his head, squinting a moment, evaluating me with a sly grin at Cynthia before speaking:"Cynthia is a brilliant young woman and she would not introduce me to some no-account joker.

You are you, sir, as I am me, and each of us has our own style. I salute you, Gene."

I look at Cynthia, fairly dumbstruck, while shaking George's bear paw.

It's a scene from the movie version of us, yet it *is* us. A drop of magic New York, and I say so: "Wow, what a moment. George, would you care for some wine, sir?"

"No Gene, I was just leaving. You enjoy it. Cynthia, I'll see you tomorrow. Goodnight, my friends." He bundles his overcoat, and grips an alabaster cane with both hands.

He bows. The little flip-bell chimes as he fades off into he snow.

"I love that guy," I say.

"I knew you would."

"He some kind of nut?"

"Hey! That's an incredibly sweet, beautiful man. Don't be a fuckin jerk."

"I'm not!"

"You've being an asshole."

"You got me wrong, I'm sorry. But is he for real?"

"Yes he's *for real*. And he's dying, so shut your mouth."

"I really like him. And you know, I don't like anyone. Is he really dying?"

"He's on his way out. Cancer."

"Does he drink?"

"Yeah, yeah he drinks. Just, you know, a few drinks. You see how particular he is. That's old school class, what George has. That's a classic gentleman."

"We should take him out. Let's take him to Lucky 7's tomorrow."

"I don't know. Maybe. Listen, Meka still hasn't come in so she's due any time. Why don't you take your food over to that little bar, the Puerto Rican place? I'll pick you up."

"Okey doke."

"Do you have change from dinner?"

"Five bucks."

"Here, just take my card. Don't go crazy. Call me if you go somewhere else."

I pull Cynthia's steaming boxes out of the bag, and the napkins, the chopsticks. I leave the bottle which has nearly a full glass left in it.

I smile weakly and slide back into my peacoat.

-113-

On the side streets, I am safe from the rolling headlights and the shoppers and the gales of Hudson River wind. The lazy silent snowfall swirls and pirouettes in the dark. I leave a trail behind me,

50 cent cans of Extra Gold lager, all the way to the Holland Motel where I stand in the parking lot wondering what could have happened, where I would be now, if Cynthia had left me there that morning all those years ago. I enter the Holland, finding no one at the desk, and I wait. "Don't they KNOW?" I wonder.

I proceed up the stairs, up the stairs, up the stairs.

I wander up and down the halls.

-114-

A scarecrow in the storm, a noir postcard, leaning on a mailbox with my last can of Extra Gold directly in front of a darkened hair salon with a ransom note-style sign in the window: The Wyld Life. A photo-collage poster in the window: The Wyld Boys. A small cardboard sign hand-lettered in day-glo marker: CLOSED.

Hoo fuckin ray: someone else knows the Lydon/McLaren story.

Inside: a pudgy middle-aged Asian woman with PURPLE HAIR is sweeping the floor with a cellphone shouldered to her right ear.

I pop the can and tap on the window.

I can hear those bells again.

-115-

"Wow. Where'd you go?"

"A place in the mall."

"You look younger."

"*How* younger?"

"I don't know. 36?"

"I *am* 36."

"You should have kept the Mohawk. Ready to go?"

"Not yet. I have a tab. He won't take the card."

"There's nothing wrong with that card."

"He won't take *any* cards."

"Motherfucker."

-116-

"I've never stayed in a Holiday Inn before."

"Just leave everything in the car. We'll be checking out again at 11."

"What happened to the place in the ghetto?"

"They never called back with a confirmation, so fuck'em."

"The Holiday Inn. Wow. How much is it?"

"Too much for more than one night. They have a pool. They might have a sauna."

"Did I really... did all that stuff make a stink at Andy's?"

"I'm not talking about that. Don't bring it up again."

"But aren't they all Joe's friends?"

"They're MY friends. Mind your own business."

"Hey, pop the back, I need my bag!"

"That big heavy one? It'll be fine."

"No, I'm not leaving it out here."

"For god's sake, Gene."

"Pop it!"

-117-

"Tomorrow," she tells me as we check in, as I pretend to browse tourist pamphlets, as I rifle through my pockets, as I fidget through yet another financial transaction like a bored child. A bored child with no dick.

"Tomorrow what?"

"You need shoes. What else? Computer stuff."

"Yeah, ok. We can get a keyboard and monitor at Goodwill for a few bucks."

"There's a Salvation Army store in Union City. What else?"

She rifles through her purse.

"Smoking or non?" says a traditionally attractive young Latina with her hair pulled into a tight bun.

"Can you smoke outside?"

"Yeah," I say.

"Non-smoking."

"The books arrive... they won't arrive until Monday. When do you-"

"*Tomorrow* is Monday"

"Wednesday. Shit. When do you have to housesit?"

"Okay. Room 712. Checkout time is 12 noon. Let me know if you need anything. My name is Amanda."

"Is the bar open?" Cynthia asks, like a friendly New Yorker, which means not without a palpable aggravation, or simply a reciprocal write-off. And you'd better find that endearing.

"I'm sorry. There's a Shop-Rite two blocks over."

"Thank you."

The Monastrell brain on my back, and Cynthia's bags full of broken zippers in my hands, we proceed to the elevators without bothering the young barman as he kills the floor lights and the panel televisions and the music with the same remote control.

-118-

I am aware of an old, well-formed New York skin as I pass haunted Laura's haunted house on the way back from Shop-Rite with two bags of wine and deli food: being in this skin is perverse and as if I am dreaming, a walking, waking dream, a sickly sepia-tone dream of cruel casualness and crueler immediacy. The New York skin is formed quickly yet without your being aware of it exactly, when you begin living there, when you begin doing your business there, whatever your business it. There's a thin membrane around you, to keep you from going to pieces entirely (some people go to pieces anyway, they shouldn't have come here) but that doesn't mean your day-to-day won't be degrading because it will be degrading in the extreme. My New York skin is and is not like my Detroit skin. You want cities to be like people and you want all your city skins to be like costumes. But you cannot graft mortality onto architecture, and Kevlar is not a disguise. We are charmed by the notion of our old skins as being something like tattoos, like surgically-implanted scrapbooks, but I think to myself staring at my ugly feet in the snow that these skins remain with us because we are programmed to return to all the places we should not be: the hells we escaped, we will return to. Living again in my New York skin as I take breaths of burning cold and wipe my snotty nose through the mocking steam-balloons is like being locked in a telephone booth with the rotting body of a spiteful young woman I often found myself strangling, who I used to beat and rape domestically (Harrisburg skin) many years ago. She was unpleasant when she was alive. I want to call for help but the receiver's been smashed. Probably been that way for years. All of Jersey City is asleep and I'm haunted by Laura by all ghosts but especially Laura who was schizophrenic and would keep me up all night crying hysterically about aliens and zombies and demonic possession, in that house, that one right there. Second floor, on the left side. Streetlights at the end of the row of condominiums suggest warmth upon the frozen walls. The *real* sun will be up soon enough.

-119-

"Aren't your feet cold?" says the graveyard shift Latina as I stumble across the lobby.

Cynthia I find fast asleep, face down, with her boots on. I place the olives and the crackers and the prosciutto and the cheese in the room's mini-fridge.

-120-

Dawn finds me in the lobby with a bottle of plucky Malbec, a fishbowl-sized wine glass the Latina made a special trip into the locked bar to give me, and Cynthia's laptop. An anonymous email: "The word is WATCH YOUR ASS. Half of New York is still screaming for your blood, Justin."

People say, "Being notorious is like being famous without any of the good stuff."

Like money, I guess. Or a place to live.

I decide to pack it up and take a swim. The bottle is empty, and the woman, the Latina, tosses it for me when I shuffle around too long looking for a trash can.

In the elevator, I pretend I am a high-end drug dealer making my weekend runs.

In the room, Cynthia is still in bed and fast asleep. I change into my trunks, my *only* trunks two years running, with the right leg slit up the inside: an enhancement made in the service of public urination.

The pool is closed but the key card works and I don't see that a woman is there until the door clicks shut behind me. The woman is only a blurry shape in the bleak flicker of the pool shadows. An imitation wraith awash in imitation Northern Lights.

"I'm sorry."

I turn to leave. Is it really a woman?

I rub my eyes, squinting through the weird haze.

She speaks, sounding much further away: "I was just getting out."

Stepping closer along the blue tile, I find myself alone with an *old* woman, 56 or 60, alone in the wee hours. A woman, even an old woman, alone like this, at this hour, is bound to be drinking. But in a swimming pool? Is this why some people live in hotels full time? In New York '97 it was afterhours clubs with numbers for names and the women would be in their 30s, in their 40s, which was old to me then and in the morning they'd kick me – rather nastily – out of their beds. (Brooklyn kicked-dog sunlight in my eyes walking the streets female-wounded again and my cats hungry back home/eventually I'd find a subway stop.) New York '98 was sex zombie hallway scenes and New York '99 was those same scenes again in triplicate, "wanna fuck" in dark tenement hallways because that's how one imagined New York '77 and it was always so fucking good without protection icy January mornings we were cold and unwell and we needed therapy I guess but instead it was booze and dope and "wanna fuck" so in that respect maybe you could say I was a slightly normal 21 year old man grinding his ax.

Racing against the sun, a post-everything luminescence when our eyes lock and the woman will not speak.

I do. "I'm Gene"

She's elegant: "Colleen."

My rules: "Wanna fuck?"

It's almost noon when I wake up nestled between her pale, slack breasts, her thick gray hair in my eyes. She stirs from my stirring. There is panic shooting through my legs: my Monastrell brain!

I kiss Colleen's brow and separate from her to find my trunks on the floor and then my towel, my key card.

I kneel at her side: "I'm so sorry... I've got to go. It's an emergency."

"Honey... you can stop that. I saw you and that woman checking in last night. I was sitting at the bar when you got here. It's okay. Just go. You have nothing to apologize for."

She touches my face. Her hand cradles my face and I am old enough to be a monster.

"Stop killing yourself," she says.

"Jesus. I thought you killed yourself," says Cynthia when I knock on the door, deliberately missing my keycard and my towel (diversion tactics), dripping wet from the pool.

"Are we gonna miss checkout?"

"So what. What are they gonna do, charge us for a second night?"

"But don't they get pissy?"

"Let them get pissy then. That's their job. How was the pool?"

"Cold." I shiver for effect. She narrows her eyes.

"You okay? What are you up to?"

"*Up* to? I don't *feel* good. I'm hungry."

"Alright, let's go. I'll take you to the Coach House. It's the famous diner, you see it in all the movies. They're all the time shooting movies there."

Our sandwiches and Bloody Marys have only just appeared on the super-deluxe diner's bar when Cynthia breaks from her phone tapping session to tell me, "Get ready."

"Oh shit."

It's early for the bar, while the dining room is packed solid and the noise from the lunch crowd envelops me as I suck down my drink in one go. It's strong.

"Ack," I say, "My fucking head."

"Gene..."

I order another drink from the ridiculously fuckable blonde currently doubling as their waitress and our bartender. I think to myself with an involuntary amphibian shudder, that she must take home several hundred dollars a day, and because she seems happy at that moment, I do not pity her, nor do I envy her: I am simply somehow relieved that she's paid what she's worth, and that I'll never get the chance to ruin her life. Once in a while you just seize upon someone, you find yourself caring for a stranger whose affliction reminds you of yours, or maybe your mother's, or your father's. Maybe it was something you weren't meant to see. I cannot let go of this impulse to address the thing but I've rarely had the nerve. Only once in Baltimore, in a bar: I sat at a table drinking vodka for three days until she returned, by which point I'd rendered myself genuinely inconsolable. I threw myself at her feet and began producing the folded-up stacks of incoherent love letters I'd generated, written on the backs of menus from the Tex-Mex restaurant across the street. We lasted four, maybe even five months. I took that one the hardest, at *both* ends.

"Stop staring at that poor woman," Cynthia says.

"I thought she was staring at *me*."

"*Everyone* stares at you. You're weird."

I suck down the new drink and order a Heineken. The woman tries not to smile, as Cynthia shakes her head. The woman returns to a table full of fat people, in the usual waitress poses. (There are only so many.) Cynthia smirks.

"I'm just going to tell you."

"WAIT."

"It's not bad."

"Then stop scaring the shit out of me."

"It's good. But you gotta take it all in stride. I know your first reaction's gonna be... I don't know. You ready?"

"It's a *Dog Days* review."

"Kinda. Not really."

"It's a sex video."

"No, idiot."

"Fucking Wellington."

"I don't know what that is."

"*Vice*. The *Vice* thing is out."

"Yeah."

"Shit."

In the car, I'm being ridiculed and scolded at the same time.

"She fucking did exactly what she said she'd do, Gene. It's a funny piece. It's authentic. It's YOU. You came off very well, I think."

"Fuck her. She's never actually read my books. She's never, to this day, asked me a single fucking question that had anything whatsoever to do with my books. She's a fucking idiot."

"That's not true. She-"

"I'm not reading it. I just need to find a fucking... NEWSSTAND. He just – THAT'S RIGHT! – Steve and his wife just LEFT the city, the, uh, East Village, for JERSEY City. That's probably his fucking house right THERE."

"GENE! Stop it! Now!"

"I'm calling him."

"Calling WHO? Who the fuck is STEVE?"

"The only magazine in the world that actually had the fucking balls to review *Dog Days* was a movie magazine, Steve's magazine. See, STEVE actually READ the books. Steve-"

"Gene, do you want me to read the article to you?"

"Let me out."

"GENE!"

"Let me out of this fucking car NOW."

"Do you wanna go Lucky 7 and chill out while I run errands? I'm gonna pick up your computer stuff and tonight we'll have a decent place to sleep. Okay?"

"Fuck. I'm sorry."

"It's fine, you're fine, just quit with the fucking drama. Read the piece after I leave."

"THERE! It's a bookstore."

"That's a *card shop*, Gene. They're not going to-"

"NOTHING DOING! We're already here. Let me run in!"

"YOU'RE GONNA FIND YOURSELF ON *FOOT* IN A MINUTE."

With a violent twist of her denim-strangulated night arm, she enters the strip mall parking lot along a stretch of road otherwise overtaken by seedy sports bars and industrial supply houses. I leap from the still-moving Honda and find the shop "closed for the holiday."

"What TIME is it?"

"Get back in the car."

"It's almost Christmas, I guess."

"Goddamnit, Gene. Let's GO."

"Hrm."

-125-

Stepping into Lucky 7 with Cynthia's laptop and its cord dragging behind me over the ice, I am enveloped by a fear and a hunger that all but disappears the ground under my feet. My peripheral vision shuts down. The air in the bar pops and hums like an ozone generator.

I stand there a moment, entertaining the inevitable crime scene and thieving and bar-hijacking fantasies, then plug in the battered old PC next to a dead pinball machine. Back by the men's room, the video poker machine blurts and shouts like a possessed toddler: "BRA-REEMP, BRA-REEMP? SHUM-SHUM-SHUM-SHUM-SHUM! HA, HA! SHAKA SHAKASHAKA! SHA-ROOOOOMP!"

Back in the piercing pale hell of the morning, on the corner, I dig out my little phone and flip it open. My whole world now is reduced to cold and snowblindness and the dread of lung cancer which the cold and snowblindness quickly consume. A snowblower begins screaming. The sun is hot on my shoulders but the snow won't melt. I dig out my cigarette pack and flip it open.

-126-

"Ted? Teddy?"

"Who the fuck is this?"

"Wow, Ted! It's Gene."

"Gene Gene the Dancing Machine."

"How the hell are ya?"

"Look asshole, I don't know who the fuck you ARE, so-"

"It's Gene! Gene *Gregorits*."

"Gene... Suicide? Nick Zedd's pal? Get the fuck outta here."

"You still in Brooklyn?"

"If memory SERVES, GENE, we ain't friends. You fucked my girlfriend and then bragged about it all over in town. That ring a bell, GENE?"

"Ted, I was real bad to drink then, man. I was a kid, but I know-"

"Bad to *drink?* Who are you, *Larry Brown?* Who says 'bad to *drink'* that ain't from the Deep South? Aren't you from fuckin... Pittsburgh?"

"Now Ted, I-"

"Oh MAN, this is too MUCH! You were a phony fuck then, and you're STILL a fuckin phony piece of shit. *How* did you get my number and *what* the fuck do you want?"

"I got your number from the operator, you're listed. Look, I'm back in New York and-"

"Oh, *you're back in New York*, huh? Well, I'm disabled now, but I know a few guys who'd just *love* to come see your scrawny ass."

"Well Ted, you know, I ain't really scrawny anym-"

"Uh huh. Where in New York exactly, Mr. *Suicide?"*

"Erm... Staten Island, actually. BUT-"

"Well look, why don't you meet up with me this week in the Village? I've got a few things I'd like to tell you in person, GENE."

"Sure, Ted. I'll come out and see you. But the reason I'm calling, and I really am sorry to just pop out of nowhere like this, is that it's extremely urgent that I get in touch with Steve Puchalski from *Shock Cinema*, and I thought you might-"

"I ain't talked to Steve in ten years."

"I bet he still has the same number, though."

"Un-fucking-believable. You remember Leo Bernard?"

"No. Yes!"

"You ought to. You fucked *his* girlfriend too. You screwed or screwed over everyone in the fucking city south of 14th Street. And - yeah, that's right, you were about to get your fuckin throat cut so you went running to L.A. to fuck Lydia Lunch, something like that? Didn't you, *Gene?"*

"Ted, I didn't call to-"

"Yeah, I'll tell you what, Gene *Suicide.* I'll give you Steve's number and you come see me tomorrow night at Otto's on 14th Street. I'm serious."

"I can do that, Ted."

"Hold the line."

-127-

"Heh... hello?"

"Steve!"

"Yeah? Who *is* this?"

"Gene Gregorits."

"HELLO, Gene. The new issue is out, you know. I mailed you one already."

"Well, I lost my place down there in, uh... dirty business. Police, and, so..."

"Police. Well, *that's* never good."

"I'm up here in New Jersey now! I'm in Jersey City."

"Huh."

"And *you're* in Jersey City."

"Well, yes, we're technically in J.C., yeah."

"Look, we've been driving around all week in snow and in rain trying to find a goddamn newsstand and... I thought it might be okay to drop by *your* place and just pick one up!"

"Oh NO, no that's not possible, heh-heh. We have family over, and Anna's got... Gene, what are you doing in Jersey City?"

"I'm moving here, from Florida, you know. I'm looking at apartments right now, as a matter of fact. But I was really looking forward to the new magazine."

"I gave your novel a good review. It's a *very* good review, you know..."

"That's so good to know, Steve. Thank you. And how're the kids?"

"We're... we were just about to - *kids?"*

"Listen, why don't you just leave a copy in the mailbox and I can swing by-"

"Gene, I'm *not giving you my address* and frankly I'd rather you

158

didn't call me up like this, I'm not really a phone person and... tell me, how did you get this number?"

"Ted gave it to me, Ted from... you know, Ted Dulude from Screw? Ivan Lerner's buddy."

"Gene, there's a newsstand in the Village where you can... it's really not far. But today's not good, buddy, ok? I'm happy to hear you're around. Merry Christmas."

"Hrm"

"Bye Gene."

-128-

Kari is waiting on a beer delivery with a glass of Diet Coke and the TV remote. Red straw. Smell of peach shampoo. Tassled gray scarf in the tassled gray morning.

"Where's Cynthia?"

"Errands."

"What's your name?"

"Gene."

"Gene, get you a drink?"

"A shot, yeah."

"Of?"

"Jäger, and a Batch 19."

"You like that stuff, the Batch?"

"Aw no, don't tell me you're getting rid of it already."

"Yeah... no one orders it. It's been a few months, and it just doesn't sell."

"It's the best beer anyone's come out with in a long time. And I think it's just the best thing Coors ever produced. What it is, is... they tried to grab onto the *Boardwalk Empire* thing, the prohibition thing. It's 'prohibition-style' beer."

"My boyfriend watches that show."

"It's sexy. It's really sharp about making the 1920s sexy. The Coors though-"

"What's it taste like?"

"Try it."

"Oh, I'm a whisky girl."

"Well, it won't mean much to you then, but it's a cross, I guess, kind of, between Sam Adams and Red Stripe. Closer to Red Stripe but a lot of the caramel from Sam Adams."

"Oh, okay. My boyfriend drinks Sam Adams."

"Ah."

"Start you a tab?"

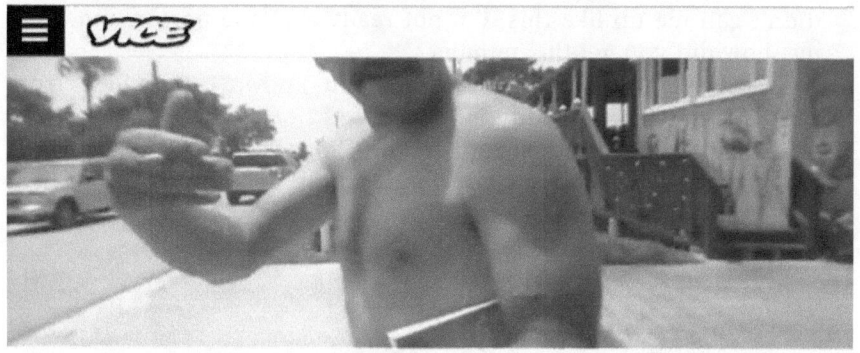

He's Not Dead Yet? Life with Gene Gregorits

By Lisa Carver

January 26, 2013

Gene Gregorits is the greatest, truest writer you never heard of, unless you read the news right after he cut off his earlobe and ate it. Twice. How that hurricane of a man ever managed to sit still long enough to complete eight books, including the three-volume "disintegration comedy" Dog Days, is beyond my comprehension. I asked his haters, lovers, and family to describe him. Two themes stood out: an awed intimacy with the writing, and an acknowledgment of the wisdom in keeping a safe distance from the writer.

Cynthia Santiglia: His writing meant enough for me to send him all my money, bring him home with me, feed him, clothe him, coddle him, suck him, fuck him, not to mention all manners of putting up with him. He is fond of me but he sees me as a sort of desperate older woman, and he thinks I'm taking care of him because I am in love with him, but I am not. I do care for him deeply, but it's really all about the writing. *Dog Days* spoke to me in a way nothing else has, ever. It was life changing for me, cliched as that may sound, and cathartic, literally an EVENT in my life, reading that little book. The connection. My hunger for his words, words that could easily be mine, had I the talent. I don't trust him as far as I can throw him. He lies constantly but I know it isn't only to protect the short term gravy train I provide, but also to protect my feelings. He makes me laugh every single day. We have fun together. Yup, that we do. That I don't think he would ever dispute. Everyone, including Gene, thinks he's using me. I am the only one who knows he's not.

Anonymous: Lydia [Lunch] emailed me last night, she said it's time for Gregorits to rid his worthless self from this planet. I've known her through many boyfriends and he was the worst. He makes fun of me in print. Gene's an asshole whose only claim to fame was the fact that Lydia likes young boys and he was one. Out of all the talent in the world why you are writing about him is beyond me.

Christine Boguslaski: He's not dead yet?

Gene's mom: Gene is eccentric. Intelligent. Uh... I'm trying to not let my negative thoughts out. He has a very good heart. He's just... volatile. Determined. Well-spoken. Extremely handsome, in spite of his best efforts not to be. Beautiful eyes. Beautiful from the day he was born. But full of anger.

Gene's dad: [*Hangs up on me.*]

John Kolchak: Gene is a pathologically narcissistic bloke with an ego from outer space who takes an unusual approach to self promotion: self-pity, extortion, and self-mutilation to sell books. Seems affable enough though.

Dennis C. Lee: Man-child, baby-man. Lost and found. He's a crazed shaman in search of a tribe that's no longer there. Never met him but I like him. Reminds me of many a fallen comrade.

Cliff Dellinger: A plane going down in flames while furiously writing and throwing.

Melissa Mescalero: The allegory of being a fiend, themes about possession, being seized. Gene's writing reminds me of the things I think about in my head that I have to process and rework so that they're acceptable enough in social settings when I tell stories. Also, I really like his word choice. Other people describe a "rip off" vibe of Bukowski/GG Allin/whatever, but when I'm reading Gene, I actually hear my own voice in it.

Maggie Wagner: Highly functioning lunatic.

Mr. Yuk: Don't trust him with your daughter. But the fucker can write!

Gene Gregorits: We're not doing it now, are we? I'm completely hungover, can I run out and get some beer first? Take me ten minutes.

VICE: One question, then you can go get a beer. Do people feel turned into characters by you?
Yeah, I mean, that IS what I'm doing. The people in my neighborhood, they're the characters in the third part of my trilogy of *Dog Days*. I amassed on my videocamera upwards of a thousand hours of the neighbors. Most of them were totally okay with being taped. Most people aren't, but this is a poor community, we're very tight; we have to help one another. I never want to leave this beach. I'm going to go run and grab some beer before I fucking die. I'm really fast on this bike. I'll be back in ten minutes.

Moments later.

What are you wearing?
A pair of filthy blue flowered swim trunks, recently purchased blue Reef flip flops and a purple shirt with little blue bottles of wine printed on it.

How come you are so often shirtless in photos?
It's the beach. Beachlife. I'm always either in the pool or the ocean. And it's just nice because I'm developing a paunch from the drinking, I'm around people who have even bigger beer bellies, so I'm not self-conscious about it. I can go around half-naked all the time. I can go to the store without a shirt on around here. Or shoes. I can go in my underwear to buy eggs if I want to.

Southern California is like that, too. Even the fat people want to feel the breeze and the sun on their flesh, and they do. It's really nice. How is it for writing?

The only thing I've written this week is a 15- or 20-page statement for court about my landlady, the infamous thief, pimp, crook, killer Suzanne Ferry. Other than that, I've only written on Facebook, ranting and raving, making a fool of myself. I don't really get to do real writing because I have to worry about getting these books shipped out, I'm 30 orders backed up and—hold on...

Who is it? I'm on the phone. Yeah, you can have a beer. OK, I'm back.

See, that's the other great thing about this neighborhood. Everybody likes me here. I've never had so many friends in my entire life. Every five minutes literally there's somebody at my door and they want a beer or a cigarette or just to see what I'm up to. I like that. I've been secretly lonely all my life, and I'm not lonely anymore. It's great.

Conversation here is kept very basic. We talk about women, we talk about drugs, we talk about the police. The police are here all the time. They're at my door almost as much as my neighbors are. There were literally eight or ten cops here last night to kick all the people off my porch. A few people got written up for trespass, and now we're not allowed to drink in front of my place. Suzanne, my landlady, stole my fucking propane tank from the grill, because that grill was like a buglight. If there was food on the grill, people could smell it cooking and would come congregate, and that's exactly what they don't want. Especially now that it's gotten out of hand with me riding around naked on my ten speed carrying a machete. I'll ride it into the pool sometimes. Get revved up blocks away and then crash the gate at 25 miles per hour and ride straight into the fucking pool. She's going to bring all these things up in court: he walks around naked, he falls asleep in the gutter. But I have a much longer list of complaints about her, and I think I'm going to win.

Do you think your neighbors and friends down there are as deep as people who know the regular collection of intellectuals' names and cultural reference points? Why live in the Lower East Side when people here are much more original, much more amusing and respectful? A lot more fun to be around. I mean, yeah I can't really have the conversations I want to have all the time. But my next door neighbor, Zeeb, an Iraq war vet, he's seen Blade Runner. We can talk about Blade Runner. I can't talk to him about Agnes Varda. But that's all right. They go through all the stuff that the intellectual people go through. Then again, I don't know much about philosophy or poetry or history. I'm a lot more like these guys than I was like the people I lived with in New York, or the people Lydia Lunch introduced me to in LA. A lot of those conversations were alienating to me.

I've never read William Faulkner. I realized that I could write well myself, and the important thing is that you're doing it, in a context and with a caliber of material that is relevant, that actually gets the interest of people who are smarter than you. You know what I mean?

Who do you want reading you?
The language is a little dense for my mother, the sentences were too long, but it is basic enough for her to get it. Or the bartender last night. She's a derby girl named Ammo. She made some kind of crack about, "So what about that girl that you raped, Gene?" So obviously she read the book. The language is not antiquated. It's basic. I play with sentence structure, which you can do with simple words. And I play with chronology. I like atmosphere and I like style more than plot. I have no interest in writing a plot-heavy story. And I don't think I'm going to write books at all after I'm finished with the Dog Days trilogy. I want to make movies.

Unlike professionally schooled writers, you don't seem to use writing to construct or alter something. You use it more like a machete to get stuff out of the way to show what already is.
I hope so. That's really nice, thank you.

When you cut off a piece of your ear, you looked really happy and like it was funny.
It was one of the happiest moments of my life. They wanted to put me away for a long time. I'm the first recorded case in Florida of auto-cannibalism. But when I went before a whole board of doctors, they were in stitches. They felt bad about it; it's really unprofessional to be laughing. But, I had a sense of humor about it, and the truth is it doesn't hurt that bad. It bleeds a lot and looks really horrible, but I've never had a tingle of regret over cutting off my earlobe.

What's the use of it anyway? It just hangs there.

Yeah. And I liked it so much, I went back a second time and did it again, and they locked me up a second time. This time, same people, they were all laughing again; they said, "What are we going to do with you?" I said, "Well, I'd like to go home." They said, "OK." My landlady was counting on me being gone for nine days again, so when I got back the next day, I caught them in the act and I grabbed what I could off the truck. They took my television, my plates, my knives, my food. I said, "Fuck you, this is not a legal eviction." Also about the ear, there was a bit of a flap there hanging from the first time. It was unappealing, it was off-putting. So I took another piece off. Which I also ate.

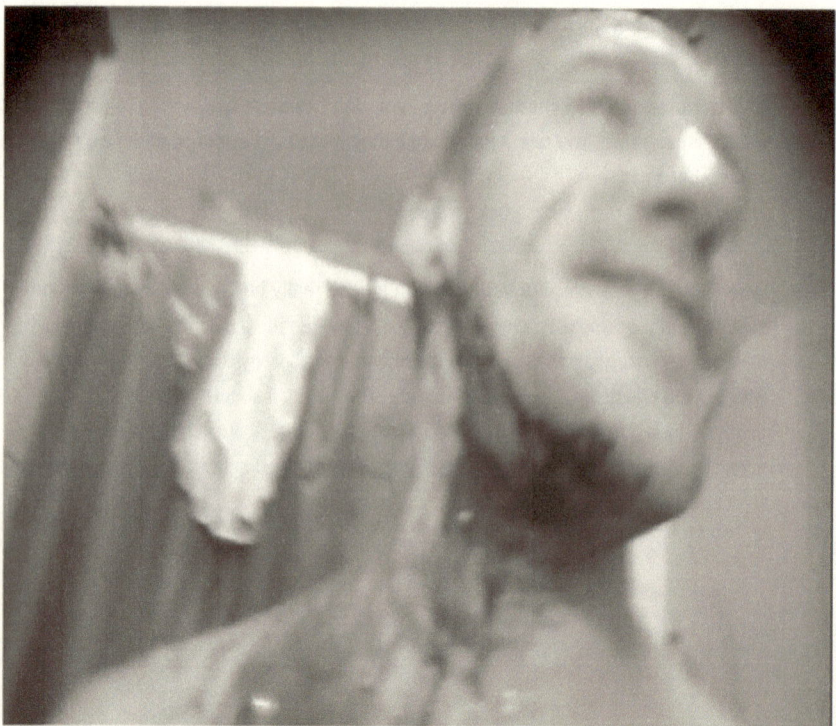

How did it taste?

Tasted like beer. Blood's great. I wish there was someone like an android who didn't feel pain and you could just hack 'em up and, you know, eat them. Wouldn't you take advantage of that, if you could eat somebody but not really hurt them?

Remember the German who took out a personal ad that said I want to eat somebody and this other German answered his ad saying Yeah I want to be eaten? And they got together and he slowly ate him over three days until he finally died.

Remember the Chinese guy who cut off his own penis and ate it or gave it to someone, a gift from one lover to another?

And then there was the porn guy who cut up his boyfriend and ate some of him and mailed the rest of him out. But I don't think that was consensual.

And let's not forget dear old Daniel Rakowitz and Monica Beerle...he fed her to the homeless.

I think I would rather be eaten than to eat someone. It would be a nice way to be remembered after I'm dead. Sure there is murderous cannibalism, but there's also places where it's a way to honor loved ones.

It is an important part of many cultures. I try not to judge. I was going to eat my cat Hank when he was killed. I thought it would be the best thing to do. I didn't want to leave him in the ground. My girlfriend at the time was appalled at the idea, so I didn't. It still breaks my heart that he's out there in that field all alone. He could have been warm and safe in my tummy. All I had to do was find a way to make it less gamy. I heard cat meat is supposed to taste awful.

You would have been able to get through it. A funeral isn't easy, why should eating our dead be easy? What's the longest you've been in a mental institution?

Two and a half months when I was a kid. I was 14 or 15.

Why?

I was going to kill my mother. My mother and I used to fight a lot. I felt very trapped. We lived in a one- or a two-bedroom apartment. My brother and I shared a room and my mother was always behind in bills and rent. Her temper was short, and I liked to bait and provoke her. There would be a lot of violence. We're great friends now and we've worked our way through it. At the time, though, I hated school and couldn't get along with her. All I wanted was to get a job and get my own place, even when I was 15. I always knew for a fact—I didn't know how I knew, but I knew I was going to get out of there fast, and without finishing school. My mother thought that she could, as usual, remedy that situation by force. With me, that's the worst thing you can do.

Were you diagnosed with something?

I don't know if they did at that time. Now I hear "bipolar" all the time. But everybody's fucking bipolar. Like everybody's got herpes. It doesn't mean anything.

Do you think that being called crazy means you don't fit the expectations of your era?

I don't know. I've always been very single-minded and I got turned on to the idea very early in my life by Celine and Bukowski that it's okay to not like people. To me, the example was set that the thing to do is to fall in love and find a good place to hide from everybody else. And that's what I've been trying to do up till now. But if I'm going to be an artist, I need an audience, so I need some place in my life for people, and some way to deal with people. When I'm in a room with somebody, they know that I'm really uncomfortable, and that makes them uncomfortable and things get really weird. And it's like quicksand: the harder you try to fight your way out of it, the quicker you're going to sink.

Here's a line from one of your books: "I was pleading on my knees before my infernal teenage-daughter-fixation Sarah Tillman." Were you really on your knees in real life?

Yes, I was on my knees literally.

Have you done that before? Been on your knees pleading?

Yeah. I don't know how to leave somebody. No matter how fucking dire the relationship is or what point of hell we've reached together, at the point of no return still I won't accept that somebody's going to leave. I've had girls that I've absolutely hated, to where we had to do a lot of drugs to make it interesting, make it seem like there was something going on, when it came time to end it, I will flip out. I will become catatonic. I won't eat, I won't sleep, I won't work. It takes me fucking months and months to get my head back after that. That's why it's comfortable right now and it's comforting that I don't have to worry about that happening, because I'm not... or I wasn't... with anyone.

But it was nice for a long time there to be able to enjoy my life without worrying about what somebody else is doing behind my back. I've been cheated on a lot. Because apparently I don't like to have sex very often, that's what I've been told. "You'd rather be on Facebook than fuck me." I actually had a girlfriend's father take me out to a bar and set me down and say, "Gene, she's not happy." Basically saying, "Please fuck my daughter. When I was your age, I was horny all the time. Don't you find my daughter attractive?" I said, "Yeah, of course I do!" "Well she says that you're up all night drinking." I'm like, "That's because I'm working such a horrible job and I'm so keyed up on adrenalin when I get home, I just want to blot everything out." I've had several relationships like that. I am a really horny guy, but I don't know... sex for me is more something to play with, and dip in now and then. Who said that great quote Don't ever try to beat sex because it's much greater than you?

Have you ever left anyone?

That's confusing. No, I guess I left Sarah. John Water's hairdresser's daughter. This guy, her father, was always trying to counsel me, get involved, telling me what to do, or to do everything differently. And I did leave her, because I wasn't going to be dictated to.

What was your age and what was Lydia's age when you met?

I was probably about 23 and she was about 38, 39. I'm 35 now.

Reading your email exchanges that you include in your book, it seems like a mommy baby relationship. She was giving you all these instructions on what to expect every step of the way at the airport, mailing you vitamins.

I was scared to fly. I'd never been west of Cleveland, and all of a sudden I have to fly to L.A.? I don't drive for a reason. I don't vote. I don't do things that most people do, because it's depressing. I feel like once I have the world figured out, then my life is over. I want there to be things in my life that I'll never understand or never have the courage to discover on my own. There's no way I could have ever figured out even how to buy a plane ticket if she hadn't taken me by the hand all the way through it.

She was talking to you like you were six years old: "Don't carry too much change in your pockets," at the same time you guys were I.M.'ing where you were sucking on the bloody panties she'd mailed you.

Ha!

Photo by Tom Garretson, www.guttersaint.org

Does it seem incongruous to you how maternal it was at the same time it was violently sexual?

Well, she's a schizophrenic and she acknowledges that, and that she's a sociopath. Half of it is theatricality and half of it is real. She's a profoundly damaged human being. So yeah, she wanted me to be really healthy, but for her. So I could handle it. Because what did she do when I got out there? She whipped me with a rubber cord until my back was drenched with blood. And I think it was later that night or the next night I'm tied to a chair, blindfolded, whipped brutally, punched in the face, while she's having sex with someone else. This was before we'd even decided to be together. I mean, there was one date in New York that involved some heavy petting, but that was it.

It was like in Hansel and Gretel... she was trying to plump you up, get you healthy, before she ate you.

I think so. But then she's got the other side of her personality where she wants to be abused. I don't believe in masochism. I think it's mental illness, I mean nobody really enjoys pain. That's not possible.

I disagree. And I think you're putting what happened off on Lydia, but that was a relationship. You were in that relationship, for years. You can't just say she was crazy.

I don't know. If I knew at the time what I know now, I probably would have found a way out of the relationship. In fact, I did throw myself out of a third story window. No wait, that was a different time. I climbed up on a huge moving truck, drunk, onto the roof, and jumped off onto the sidewalk on the Bowery and broke both of my feet. Right when I was supposed to be moving to L.A. permanently. My whole New York life was in boxes. Lydia was trying to find out if I did that on purpose to sabotage it because maybe she wasn't what I wanted.

Talking with you, I think you sound sensible in how you describe motivations for how you've lived. Maybe you don't live sensibly.

I didn't understand at the time what was happening with the whole Lydia thing, what it was really about. And it destroyed ten years of my life. I could have been doing other things and been enjoying myself and avoiding a lot of problems and a lot of damage if I had been sensible earlier. But if Lydia hadn't come along, something else would have. I was in my early 20s, but I was really more like 12, 13. I had no friends, no connections, no advice coming in from anywhere. I was so retarded on so many levels. I couldn't cook, I didn't know how to travel, how to find an apartment, how to turn the electric on. I could clip coupons. That was about the extent of it, as far as managing in the world.

You were like an alien who'd just landed. And you said you felt uncomfortable around people. But I feel an easy connection to you. Do you get that a lot? Like, We're twinsies?

When it comes from someone like you, it's a compliment. But when it comes from someone who beats and cheats and lies and is a scumbag, then you hate to hear that shit. And you don't like to be in the position of having to explain that they're wrong.

That's interesting though, that so many people like that relate to you.

I don't spare the reader any details at all. I'm learning as much about myself in hindsight writing it. At the time, I think I'm being naughty, I think I'm getting away with something. Sometimes writing, I hate to call it transgressive, but I guess it's almost an act of malice. But then you look back and you realize it's all true.

You're not transgressive like Peter Sotos. His stuff comes off as deliberate. Yours comes off like you can't help it. And sometimes it's just fun. Your writing is contradictory, and that may be what people respond to. Everybody is a mixed bag of horribleness and gentleness, yet we feel embarrassed by one or the other and feel like we have to pick one and cover up or destroy the other half.

When I was reading your book in the pool today, that's the thing that jumped out at me. I feel like we're on the same path of yeah, we're contradictory, but we don't have to make sense of it. We have to manage it, but we don't have to have a tidy fucking bow wrapped around anything. We're not forces of evil or negative, but hey, we're damaged, and we're going to do destructive things sometimes that don't make any fucking sense.

Do you think you'll ever quit drinking?

[*Sound of swallowing*] Mn-mn. Mn-mn! Oh, no, no! I like this stuff way too much. Forget that! Beer is really nice in Florida because it's really hot all the time. But what I really like is red wine. I named my book company Monastrell. It's a really dry, earthy wine. You need something powerful to pair it with. I could talk about this for hours and hours. Why would I give that up? I'm at my happiest when I am sitting by myself at a table on a warm night with a bottle of wine and a pile of stupid magazines like Entertainment Weekly and a huge steak. And I can just pick at my food arrogantly for three hours and I'm just there to pay tribute to myself and be a big-headed wanker. You had to quit drinking, didn't you?

I did have to quit drinking, and you're making me salivate right now. That's what was so great about drinking. When I drank socially, I became such a wreck that it was obviously bad for everybody. But going to the store on a warm night and getting some magazines and cans of beer that would sweat and just eating and just being there, that's good memories. Who do you think you're more like: The Bronte sisters or GG Allin?

I don't know about the Bronte sisters. You'd have to tell me about them. Female romance is attractive to me because it's romance. But it's female. I'm much more attracted to the Jim Thompson kind of romance where you don't get the girl. Matter of fact, you don't get anything. You get your face blasted off. You get shot in the back. You get sent away to prison to work in an oil field for 15 years. That kind of thing. And the girl was in on it the whole time. That's my idea of romance.

The Bronte sister characters went insane, they killed each other, one guy killed his beloved's little dog and hung it for her to find. Then she saw a ghost and opened a window and caught her death.

That sounds good. See, romance from a woman's point of view, there's a lot of drama and histrionics. I think that with the most doomed and ill-fated male stereotypes—James Ellroy, Mickey Roarke, Celine, Carl Panzran... like Jim Thompson said, "I'm damned and I'm proud of it." You reach the point where you're no longer interested in redemption. And you don't need any drama. You don't need a bunch of screaming and yelling and death. What it's really about is giving up. And brooding. And being broken. I think that the best way to be romantic is to be completely smashed to where you're no longer capable of romance in any traditional sense. I've always wanted to be that, honestly. [*laughs*]

Do you think you are?

Yeah. I finally got my wish! [*laughs*] That's why I'm not afraid of people anymore 'cause I got nothing left. I'm not trying to protect or preserve anything anymore. The illusion has been torn down. It's a fucking joke and a lie. The only way I can access—hold on. [*Gene's neighbor returns.*]

What? OK, you can take another beer, man, but you're going to have to give me one later. But hurry up, man, I'm on the phone! Please? You know, how can you be that drunk? It's only two o'clock in the afternoon. You ought to be ashamed of yourself. I'm going to find your mother in Tampa and tell on you. I love you, too. Bye.

OK, I'm back. [*laughs*] We're just getting started. We're going to be howling like monkeys in five, six hours. The police will be here. A girl will probably get smashed in the face and somebody's windshield will be broken. Somebody's fishing pole will get stolen and that will cause something. A dog will be kicked. It's gonna be great! And it's every fucking night. It never stops. Once in a while... if there's a huge storm and the whole beach is rained out or there's a flood, then people will have to quiet down a little bit. Because you can't really be louder than a category three hurricane.

-130-

I've barely made it through the abomination by Lisa Carver and am summoning angels from the sour air to keep from biting the side of my pint glass when the phone calls begin. And the emails. And the book orders.

By 4 P.M. I have mastered the practice of ignoring all this putrid phenomena, getting sloshed quite badly on Jägermeister and Batch with Big Star's *Third* on the Internet jukebox. Cynthia peers over my shoulder wearing a clownish cowgirl hat which has been spraypainted pink and stored safely underneath a crate of encyclopedias for a few decades.

"See?"

"See what?"

"I know you read it. The window's still open."

"It's a piece of fucking shit."

"Alright. You want to get lunch?"

"How many readers does *Vice* have?"

"I don't-"

"One MILLION. That's what I'm told, or maybe over a million."

"So?"

"Every other word in that article... it's not a profile or an article, it's a fucking taped phone call, let's be honest. Let's be HONEST and admit that Lisa Carver is a mentally retarded woman-child, and that her piece of shit wasn't even proofread. It NEEDED proofreading. Mickey Rourke's name is misspelled, EVERYTHING is misspelled in this PIECE of SHIT. *Vice* has a fucking SHOW, right, on H-BEE-fucking-OH, right, but they hire mental retards as JOURNALISTS and hire NO ONE to proofread the lazy garbage the mental RETARDS-"

"STOP! NOW!"

"I fucking... last summer I ordered *Ulysses* because I'm 35 years old and I haven't read fucking *Ulysses* and I feel bad, I'm self-conscious of never having read the big famous gobbledygook, ok? And I get the book in the mail form Amazon, and it's got a faggoty cocksuck cartoon, an INDIE-ROCK CARTOON, for a front cover, and all the words, you're not expected to know any of the words so every other word is NUMBERED and glossarized so you can find out what fucking 'catacombs' means, what 'LOTHARIO' means, or that 'boose' is slang for-"

"Gene, honey..."

"FOR FUCKING BOOZE!"

"I'm not the person you need to be venting to. Can't you go see Lase or someb-"

"Fucking Jonathan Franzen every five minutes... middle-class yam faced fuck... T.C. Boyle... have you ever seen a photo of T.C. Boyle?"

"What can I do to make you happy? Let me give you some ecstasy."

"The entire world is functionally illiterate, or almost, and the ones that aren't wanna read Dave Egger's muppet fuck critter hand CUTESY COCKSUCK FAGGOT shit and they need GLOSSARIES BECAUSE THEY HAVE NEVER COME ACROSS THE FUCKING WORD 'LOTHARIO' AND I DON'T WANT ECSTASY, I WANT MY FUCKING HOME BACK... I'M TRYING TO SELL BOOKS TO MENTAL RETARDS AND YOU WANT 'GABBA GABBA HEY.' THE RAMONES RECORDED THE SAME SONG 400 TIMES, BUT YOU DON'T KNOW WHAT 'LOTHARIO' MEANS! ARE YOU FUCKING CRYING?"

"All I've tried to do is be KIND to you."

"Oh, REALLY! Let me spell it out for you, DUMMY. Telling the fucking WORLD, in a HIGH PROFILE WEB ARTICLE on VICE DOT FUCKING COM, that you are my SUGAR mama CYNTHIA, without my PERMISSION, CYNTHIA, that is not kindness. That is SUBTERFUGE, do you know what SUB-"

The little duck's slap sends me reeling into the next stool, knocking it over, "FUCK you," the duck growls, scrambling for her car keys.

"No, fuck YOU, you fat old Cindy Brady freakshow."

Kari finally arrives on the scene; "Cynthia, you okay?"

"She was just leaving, Kari."
"Get out," She says.
So I do.

There's no music in my head when I take the tundra, bent at the middle and hugging my ribcage through the clogged and stymied avenues of Jersey City, past the Holland eventually succumbing to the dead trance of rage, stubborn rage, too late to stop now *stomping* rage, 10,000 parking lots under the brooding bruising December airspace with planes and helicopters and smoke the light pollution like noise pollution a radio in a frigid bar or maybe it's a teevee "grief can be interrupted or derailed," a man is saying, "becoming what we call complicated grief..." and I chuckle to myself, I laugh about the studying of pain with hunger slowing me down and my phone buzzing and ringing and buzzing and-

Night falls and I might be full of complicated grief I might be full of murder - and ringing and buzzing and ringing and

"You're going to lose your fucking toes."'
"Fuck you."
"You TOLD me to talk to her."
"I said the same thing to everyone. I said, 'Lisa Carver is doing an article, and she'll probably be in touch with you. Don't feel pressured to talk about anything you're not comfortable with.' THAT is what I SAID."
"I asked you if you wanted me to be interviewed. I said, 'Should I talk to her?' and *you* said-"
"My mother says two things, two *sentences*, right? My uncle says something there. A few cowards chime in, anonymous maggot people, and they're all *sentences*. SEN-TEN-"
"That's not necessary."
"Sentences. Okay? And there? At the end? There's *YOU*. Cynthia-Who-the-Fuck-Cares-Mariano, with her - oh, you can leave, but I'm going to finish my fucking SEN-TENSE, CYNTHIA. There's YOU, with your TWO PARAGRAPH FOOTPRINT, your IDIOTIC FUCKING SNAIL TRAIL, fucking CLAIMING ME. You have made a FOOL out of ME, you have made a FOOL out of your SELF, and Lisa Rose-"
"Carver."
"What?"
"Lisa *Carver*. You said Lisa Rose. I don't know who the fuck that is."
"I don't think you have *any* idea-"

"I need a drink, Gene. I've had a shitty day, of you slicing me to ribbons, I've only been-"

"Mother-FUCK what you've *only* been. I *earned* this attention. Twenty fucking years getting the *snot* pounded out of me and all I get is *this*, which is a fucking *tragedy*, but that's not bad enough, is it? I can't even have *this* piece of dogshit, this braindead Lisa Carver DOG shit, without YOU having to-"

"Good luck Gene, good luck not freezing to death. I'm not helping you through this shit one more day. I don't *deserve* this. You can call Lase and maybe-"

"Let me tell you what *I* don't deserve. *I* don't deserve a fucking freak show instead of a thoughtful article. I deserve my PIECE. This is not my fucking PIECE! I wrote a *brilliant* goddamn book, didn't I? But a year later, not ONE literary profile, not one! No, instead it's *Vice*, I get idiot-fuck *Vice*. I get *Fear Factor*. I get *Tosh.0*. I get *World's Dumbest Criminals* and Lisa 'look at my tits, look at my mutant kid' Carver."

"Oh, how DARE you, that woman *adores* you. You *owe* Lisa everything. She's the best friend you've ever got. You take that back."

"Fuck her. She has no right. And neither do you."

I light a cigarette and attempt to imagine myself small enough to hide under the seat. Cynthia parallel parks around the corner from Louise & Jerry's.

"You're panicking. I know this isn't really you. Come on. Let's get a drink."

-133-

Big Star on the jukebox, the bar is packed, and I've sold my soul for a wad of drink tickets, for crummy coke, for cheeseburger breakfasts, for an overcoat I didn't want anyway.

"Gene, you cut your fucking *ear* off. What did you expect, Oprah? *Good Morning America? Time?* What?"

"I expected to get to live another month."

"You expected more than that."

"*Hustler* would have been nice."

"No one reads *Hustler* anymore."

"I deserve a fucking CRITIC. Greil Marcus. A guy with a fucking *brain*. And a real magazine. Paper. *The Voice*. Something, fucking *Esquire*."

"You don't get *Esquire*. You get *Vice*. Your phone has been ringing all day. It's a writer's dream! Stop pissing in the well, you really need to pull your head out of your ass. This is prima donna shit."

"But couldn't they have done a *thoughtful* piece? I mean, why *Lisa*? Talk about gimmickry... and it's not even sincere, what she does."

"She's fun. And people like her stuff. She does it well, that 'idiot-savant' thing."

"Minus the savant."

"Oh, who cares. You *got* a thoughtful piece. It's gonna sell a shitload of books. Maybe you're just scared. You've never had this before."

"Nobody's had this before. I come across like a zombies circus freak. The whole thing is a setup. I hope she gets cancer."

"Hush. Did you call Lase?"

"I haven't talked to anyone. I need to check my Amazon account. My email... Facebook... damnit."

"You can deal with that tomorrow."

"This is all my fault. I'm going to get myself killed."

"You're going to be fine. Everything is fine."

-134-

"You should NEVER try to sing. You are not, like... you just don't have it. That's *okay*. You are a writer. You don't have to sing."

"I can sing okay, sometimes."

"If you... like, you're not trying, just... at a regular level, you're kind of okay, but in the car, with the music up, you can't sing. Just... trust me. Don't sing."

"Iggy Pop can't sing. Leonard Cohen can't sing. Bob Dylan can't sing."

"Those people can sing. That's a type of singing they do. They sing within their range."

"Lou Reed can't sing."

"Lou Reed *can* sing, he.... He sings within his range. You can't sing, honey. It's okay, just don't sing."

-135-

The parking for guests of the Jersey City Ramada Inn is a few blocks away and half the lights are knocked out. We circle each level, drunk and bedraggled, looking for a spot in the cramped, Escher-like structure which could be used as a simulation model to explain Manhattan or Tokyo to people from Dakotas.

After three trips back to the entrance, the lot attendant finally rides with us to the hidden turn-off, successfully piloting the car into a crude, flooded sub-basement where one spot remains, a black cesspool.

"We are still pumping, you know, after Sandy," say the egg-shaped Polish septuagenarian. "Watch your step, now. Normally, it is not so much trouble, getting down here. When it is dry."

"And *lit.*" Cynthia snaps at him. "There's no fucking *light*, you should have told us."

"I'm sorry ma'am. It's the only spot."

"MISS. I'm not a grandmother."

"Take it easy." I whisper.

"Shut up," she says.

"No, you shut the fuck up. I'd let the air out of your tires if you talked to me that way."

"Oh, fuck you."

I hoist the ALICE pack with the Monastrell brain onto one shoulder.

"It'll be safe here, just leave it."

"Uh, NO."

"Well hurry goddamnit. I'm cold."

The old man shakes his head, and cups the flame of a lighter, a cigarette in his mouth. "You're okay here," he says.

Surly Cynthia waddles along behind him, baby steps on black ice. Across the street, the Jersey City Ramada is cramped, like its garage, built like a tower.

Straight up and down.

-136-

Breakfast at the Coach House: Bloody Marys, beers, fried eggs, potatoes, coffee. Double bacon for Cynthia. I wish I was clean.

The phone rings and rings and rings.

"You want me to take calls for you?"

"No."

"The apartment's open now, the ghetto place. I told them we'd take it. But I've got chores, divorce stuff, I've got to pick up Dylan, and then I work. So I'll drop you off after we eat."

"My books-"

"I talked to Elaine, she's watching for them."

"Well... I still..."

"Spit it out! What do you need besides shoes?"

"I don't need *shoes*, I need to get Monastrell back up and running. If we could stop at that Salvation Army, I can pick up the hardware I need for a few bucks."

"Then we need to leave *now.*"

A blast of vodka. Jelly toast with egg yolk mashed in. I call Florida. No answer.

-137-

The Union City Salvation Army is closed: A casualty of Hurricane Sandy. Cynthia sings flatly, absently, along with an atrocious recent

182

album by Paul McCartney in between irritatingly melancholic remembrances of area bars and restaurants that won't be reopening because of the flood.

"Gene, you don't understand how awful it was. My friends Hugo and Joelle had to *move*. And in Brooklyn, you know, the Norton Records warehouse was fucking *underwater!* They lost everything! If you'd been here... people were really wondering, like, you'd have wondered if you were going to survive or not."

"Not likely."

"See? Talking shit."

"Yeah. My apartment was flooded last year. The fucking Gulf of Mexico came up and swallowed us. It was a fucking nightmare, and it was great. I love shit like that. That's the problem with people, they can't stand a little shake-up. It's healthy, don't you know that? Die offs are part of nature. Fuck Norton Records. Fuck Hugo and Janette. If I'd been here-"

"You sound like such a fucking idiot. Sandy just devastated us."

"US."

"Oh fuck you. GOD you're an asshole."

"But New Yawkas are FAWKIN UNBREAKABLE! WE... WE FAWKIN PULL THROUGH ANYTHING. WE FAWKIN..."

"Wow. Just shut the fuck up."

"It's really too bad the storm didn't take out-"

"Look, look over there! That bakery was the best bakery in Hoboken. They had that place... the VEGAS! They had that damn bakery in their family for 50 years and it's *destroyed*."

"It looks okay to me."

"There's internal structural damage. Everything was ruined, the plumbing, the ovens, everything. It's beyond what anyone can afford. It's beyond what insurance will cover. Have a little respect, for Christ's sake."

"Yeah, yeah. Fine. But change is good. I think it's funny that New York sucks now."

"Fucking sour grapes, man. Get over it."

"How do you mean? Because I left?"

"Fucking people come here, get slapped around a little, and run home. I get so tired of the jealousy."

"That degree of isolationism is probably close to mental illness. It's not that New Yorkers, or Jerseyites, or whatever... it's not that they dislike the world outside, it's more like they refuse to accept that it exists, except as some kind of conceptual theme park. You're a fucking sketch comedy bit."

"Sour grapes."

"And I left New York for L.A. How is that sour grapes? I *wanted* to leave. Those miserable winters... yeah, it's mental illness!"

"You are such a pussy."

"I'm not a masochist. Not like *that*."

"I see how you look at everyone. You're so damn jealous of *everyone*. It's hard to *watch*, Gene."

"I'm impoverished! That's *hunger*!"

"It's jealousy."

"Intelligent people, enlightened people, they *laugh* at you, do you know that? San Franciscans somehow manage to love their city without having to go around like cartoons beating their chests 24 hours a day. And Boston, too! Bostonians are loudmouthed retards in the same way, people find that shit unbearable. You kind of have to feel sorry for the Detroit chest thumpers. But Boston and New York, you guys are the Foghorn Leghorns of the modern world."

"Sour grapes."

"I got ten grand from Lydia Lunch to leave New York."

"Sour grapes."

"I like the album *New York* but what a jackass Lou Reed is. You're *all* jackasses."

"Sour grapes."

"Misery addicts. Masochists."

"Hah! Says Gene fucking Gregorits."

"I'm misunderstood."

"It's your own dumb fault if you are."

"Granted."

"Sour grapes."

"LET'S GET A SLICE, A REAL FAWKIN SLICE YA KNOW? YA BEEN TO JOEY'S DOWN ON METROPOLITAN DERE? BEST FAWKIN PIZZA IN DA CITY."

"Sour grapes."

"I'd rather eat Doritos in a Tampa gas station."

"Good riddance. You couldn't deal with it, so it sucks."

"No, no I could *NOT*!"

"Where are you going?"

"You said there was a Goodwill..."

She squints at me like she's trying to remember who the fuck I am. I hit the window button and light a cigarette, Cynthia's cellphone begins buzzing and farting and singing.

"Obnoxious." I say, aloud.

"What? Honey, what? Slow down, I can't understand you. Dylan, let me call you back. I gotta pull over."

-138-

I squint into the haze across the lanes of Holland Avenue, almost certain that the busy, sprawling parking lot peeking out from behind an Auto Zone belongs to a large liquor outlet, or "party store." (In Detroit, all liquor stores are called "party stores.") I toss my cigarette into Holland Avenue, turn and face directly the Holland Motel, that stark, paranormally vibrant place, then return to its rear (central) parking lot where Cynthia's Honda idles in its own frosty exhaust.

It's the same spot where she'd threatened to abandon me after the assault.

I unwrap my phone from a pair of socks; 44 missed calls. I admit to myself that I am terrified and I do this to see what happens next. My bowels loosen. I feel so desperately poisonous and polluted, and lines from the Vice article haunt me: "the wisdom of keeping one's distance from the volatile writer."

Cynthia honks the horn. I approach, trying to appear completely non-volatile.

"Dylan's in trouble. I gotta go, right now."

"What's the address for Goodwill?"

"I - I don't know. I'll text it to you. This is a bad situation, so... look. I'll give you my Visa card. Why don't you just pick up what you need at the mall, it's right there."

"All *new* stuff? That's nuts."

"Just put it on the card, you need it for your book. I'll pick you up in a few hours, or just meet you at the place. The keys are in the box. Oh your poor feet. Go to a bar and get warm. Get your stuff. I gotta go. Here."

I take the card.

"Don't get yourself killed."

-139-

Being alone makes me do it. Being cold makes me do it. Being stupid and dirty and tired makes me do it. A sexual panic sweeps over me like injected cocaine when I realize I'm going to commit a serious crime. There's nothing accidental about it. Not "what *is* it" but "what it *is*." Shivery delicious. What it is and how it is done. I'm going to need black paint. And... what else? Kick it old school on The Holland's roof and fill in the white spots, above the Tunnel; a roaring blank.

The curious parking lot across the gray lanes opens up to reveal a blinking, buzzing, glowing majestic SUPER LIQUORS which cuts through all the grim determination without disrupting it: I'm going to do this. The store itself completes another blank and I'm allowed to smile. I purchase a six-pack of 16 ounce Budweisers and I say "Merry Christmas" to the guy like it's no big deal. It really isn't!

I'm in exactly at the right place at exactly the right time.

From the roof of The Holland, you try to put all the pieces together: the tinsel and the green trim, the pine needles and the bog green and red dick up your ass that you can thrash around on, or learn to live with for a week, two weeks, six weeks. They start fucking you with the big red-green peppermint penis about the beginning of November, yes? Right after Halloween, it starts.

And then I introduce my own personal concerns: the production of the novel *Dog Days 2*, which I intend to perform in a soggy one week stretch at the new apartment, insulated from Cynthia and from Sam-worry and from the 6 year old boy I'm told is my own in Baltimore, from mom and dad and Xmas. I'll have 1,000 beers, a carton of cigarettes. Music. I'll take a lot of showers.

Below me one pair of taillights crawls into the creeping procession of one thousand other taillights, doing business in the city or returning from same, it begins and ends in the militaristic clusterfuck of The Holland Tunnel where one dope/one thousand dopes/a billion dopes that trust the engineering - I would say - a bit too much. It is a mediocre soul's grandest delight to surrender in this way. The rabble wants nothing more than to experience the vastness of death this way. That mediocrity is apelike but omnipotent: in the logic and the optimum efficiency of each bureaucratic compromise, encroaching inevitability introduces a kind of anesthesia. The insta-mix Superman's middle class vigor is ingeniously maintained by the diminishing effect of modern technology. You *see* this perverse symbiosis between unnatural man and his unnatural environment most clearly during the takeoff portion of a commercial fight (itself the ultimate perversion of modern life). Inside the vessel, the engines explode deafeningly and not a soul onboard winces.

I cannot submit in this way.

I do not trust the engineering.

I do not trust the engines.

I expect bridges to collapse under me, tunnels to collapse above me.

I do not need to be dwarfed or threatened by modern marvels on a regular basis to understand my role, to accept my role.

I am a sensible man: I have no role at all, except to put out my own fires when necessary. I am a combustible man and there is a wisdom in maintaining a safe distance from the writer sucked him fucked him clothed him using me I know he's not.

I am a natural man, and I decide that I haven't enjoyed sex in too long.

I think of Tootie: an erection.

I watch the cars feeding themselves into the horrifying structure.

I have flashes of things, of tables with ashtrays, and spoken cruelties, tables covered by bottles and the waste of it all, I lean onto the air over the four story building and light a cigarette. The cars below, the feeding, the dwarfing. I think of extermination camps and Merry Christmas. I think I'm cold and open another beer don't even like being this tall should've bought Yuengling like to drink some Yuengling – and where to buy black paint?

-141-

Traditional Christmas carols roll over the heads of a thousand overstimulated shoppers dressed arrogantly in leather winter at Macy's where I ride the escalators and negotiate the menswear and cookware departments hungrily before locating the mall.

I am going to require a Radio Shack, which every mall has, and a large chain pharmacy store like Duane Read or CVS, which the mall may very well *not* have.

I consider my large order of computer accessories and how a half-century ago, such purchases allowed you to be a little demanding. Of course, no one's going to stop you from making a scene. I don't have this concept properly tied down, haven't run it through logistically, and my cocksucking phone won't stop fucking and vibrating and screeching and I'm on the verge of dumping it. I need a drink and the mall's curiously dead (Macy's is teeming, however) with dead music and dead air giving me the spins with flashes of my father and of my wife and of my divorce of all my life taking place in billion dollar junk arcades.

I retreat to what I think is a parking lot but I'm two floors up and it's a parking *garage*, so – this is insanity and sickness and death – I run all the way down the exit ramp in the dark snow and gritty winds with my toes curled for balance and so as to hook my flip-flops and keep them with me all the way to a CVS three blocks away where I purchase a bottle of Gascon Malbec on sale for $10.99 two Sharpie markers a bottle of rubbing alcohol box of Q-tips bottle of MagikGone adhesive residue remover box of GLAD brand sandwich bags box of E-mergen-C fizz drink packets. The corkscrew I shoplift. (Haven't paid for a corkscrew since 2005.)

-142-

In the Jersey City Mall food court I take off my coat and pop my Malbec under the wobbling little table made of indeterminate mall stuff which is smeared with General Tso's chicken glaze from Panda Express and pour it into a Styrofoam cup swiped from a restroom trash bin (the restroom is down a long hall exactly *beside* Panda

Express)(I ignore the stare of overwhelmingly worthless mall employees shuffling by minimum wage somnambulant dimly considering a police situation if I'm psychotic).

The wine is rich, dark, a convincing fruit-forward Malbec, pleasing in the way of a Hollywood blockbuster film like *Mission: Impossible 3*, or Ben Affleck's second directorial effort *The Town*, which is to say full of short-term astonishment, of disposable inspiration. It is an expensively loud and sleek and idiotic wine, custom made for pairing with the unsophisticated whey-based creams and high fructose glazes and condiment-forward fare which surrounds me on three sides like some kind of failed intervention. I cork it and return it to the bag. Five minutes later, the caper has finally presented itself to me. In that moment, I am a drone vessel flying over the Hudson.

-143-

In Radio Shack, I set my cup of wine on the counter and say, "I know exactly what I want, Ron."

Ron makes it easier on us both by having a sense of humor, but there is trouble – briefly – when my purchase of a Logitech digital headset, a Panasonic LCD flatscreen monitor, a Toshiba Blu-ray player, a Logitech wireless mouse, a Hewlett-Packard 2TB external hard drive, a Sony handheld digital voice recorder, and some type of iPod-type thing is stalled by a verification issue.

"I'll just be a minute," I tell Ron, holding up my "cellie" and pointing to it with my eyes set to submissive/apologetic. Ron nods in an accommodating manner, Ron with deep acne scars who is too old to be working in a shopping mall, and also, I'd like to imagine, too human. But everyone has their own masochism. It's easier than fighting. Anything is easier than fighting. "Poor dear," I think, leaning over the railing above a cell phone kiosk where a female Ron is setting up for the day. I dial Cynthia's number and she answers quickly, out of breath.

"I'll call you back."

I dial her again:"Oh my God WHAT?"

"I need the pin number."

"It's ninety nineteen, fuck!"

Back at the Shack, I give Ron the thumb up.

"9-0-1-9," I say. "Now they've got to start all over again."

"No no," he smiles. "I knew you were coming right-"

"Not you. *Them*. Cynthia and her junkie kid."

"Pardon?"

"Sex. They were having *sex*."

"Oh jeez! Hmmmm. Well!"

I get a photo of Ron and I holding the x-large Radio Shack

shopping bags, three of them, the ones with the red plastic handles and cardboard reinforcements inside. My heart's not really in it because I haven't had enough to drink and my leg is itching with a vengeance, the skin having grown over my dogbite stitches which should have been removed a week ago. A month ago?

I wish Ron a happy Christmas and offer him a glass of wine.

"I don't drink, but it sure sounds good, thank you."

The poor son of a bitch has a cast eye, an impossible lisp, and a ratty black beard, which lends him a trace of masculinity only in the sense that most child molesters are male. I myself have a ratty 2-day crackhead beard *base,* to complement my crackhead odor and also my personality, which, to Ron, at least, is that of a full time alcoholic child-molesting crackhead.

We are happy to take leave of one another.

-144-

My second food court vigil begins with the request for a second Styrofoam cup from Panda Express. I also offer to pay five bucks for a roll of paper towels, which the troublesomely young countergirl produces wordlessly after ducking into the back room. It is a ten pound industrial size roll, about the size of a water cooler bottle.

"Just take it," she laughs.

I study the roll and chuckle at the thought of hauling it back to...where?

"Look at me, for Christ's sake." I raise my arms, and sigh with defeat.

"Ha haha! What?"

"I'm dispossessed!"

"Uh huh. I don't know what that means."

The thought arrives like a ball bearing: would I fuck a child?

"Listen," I say. "I'm obviously too old for you."

"Uh, yeah? By like...20 years?"

"Do you have a boyfriend?"

"N-n-n-o?"

She sounds it out, long and sarcastic which triggers a framing of her chubby awkwardness in a sexual scenario, like...right now, in the Panda Express Supply room!

"I certainly hope not," I say, unsure who I am replying to, and how.

She takes a step back and I feel the guilt wash over me. I feel like a hundred year old boogeyman, like Jack the Ripper, realizing that I'm taking the seduction premise seriously, if only for a heartbeat. I make a sheepish, pitiful retreat. Somehow I know to trust the core logic of the thing, despite the duality of the thing, which is that, if she were my daughter, and this were a post-apocalypse situation,

I'd only be doing the *right* thing.

I sit for a minute, watching her watching me, and return to the counter, unable to leave it alone.

"I'm getting stink-eye from the... the cleaning peop-"

"You mean the *janitors?*"

"The, uh, yeah. Can't a guy have a discreet drink with his lunch? I mean, it's a fucking-"

"Why don't you just keep it hidden?"

I return to my seat and open the box of vitamin C, feeling lightheaded. But I have nothing to mix with.

Back to the counter: "What's your name?"

"Alexis."

"Beautiful name. I should probably eat, like you said, uh..."

"No, *you* said."

"I, uh..."

"You said..."

"Just to look..."

"Eating would be a good idea, you might-"

"How can you work here? And at Christmas, FUCK. I've worked in shopping malls at Christmas, make you want to commit suicide."

"You look sick. Don't worry about, you know, it's a job. Are you homeless?"

"Am I *homeless?* Wow. You really don't give a *fuck.* You'd make a good investigative journalist."

"Really?"

"Yeah."

"Thank you."

"You look like Olivia Hussey."

"I don't know who that is."

"Can't you look her up on your phone?"

"I guess."

"Do it."

"I... yeah, okay. How do you-"

"HUSSEY. H-u-s-s-e-y. Olivia. O-l-i-"

"Seriously? I can SPELL Olivia."

"I'm sorry."

"That's my grandmother, my grandmother's name, you know."

"It's a sexy name. Vs and Xs, you know, always..."

"Oh, okay. Yeah. I used to have hair like that. She's hot."

"Yeah. So I'm drinking Malbec, it was on sale. I need something that pairs well with big dumb Chilean red."

"Is that wine?"

"Red wine, yeah. It's like a big dumb dog."

"How is wine like a dog?"

"You know, it's...vulgar. No, not vulgar. Beer and liquor are vulgar, but Malbec wine, it's... you know, like, 'hey, look at me, whoah.'"

"I don't...you're like, one of those wine people. That's annoying."

"Why?"

"It's like... you think you're better than everyone else. It's just wine."

"It's just grape juice, yeah. But hey, in *this* world, *this* human race, in *this* life...you'd *better* be better than everyone else. You're definitely prettier. But the wine thing? There's no use trying to get you into the wine thing. You'll wind up there on your own eventually, if there's something you need there."

"Listen to you, gettin' all deep."

"Wine's deep! And this here Malbec, and how it's like a dog, pardon me, I meant to say that it was like a dog *person*, as opposed to a *cat* person. Wines are like people, with personalities and everything."

"Well... I'm 16, so... I guess it doesn't matter. I'm not allowed to anyway."

"Not ALLOWED? Fuck that! You can do whatever you want. Just keep it hidden! You just told *me* that."

I fetch the bottle and my cup and pour myself a BIG GULP FRUIT BOMB, as Alexis eyes me with poorly concealed fascination. She's damaged, but far from jaded. What she has is rare.

"Is it *good*, though? Big dumb dog wine?"

"It's well *made*. And it's normally fifteen dollars, so it better at least be drinkable. But you know, it's like a really good hot dog. No matter how good it is, it's still a lips and assholes hot dog."

"I like how you say things."

"It's Chilean. And the thing about Chilean wines, they almost always drink at two or three times their price."

"What does that mean?"

"Well, like... if you buy a $7 bottle from Chile, you can count on it holding a decent comparison to a $20 bottle from California. Especially if you know what you're buying. Three quarters of being a wine snob is knowing how to shop."

"I'm half-Brazilian," she says.

I reach over the counter and pull a cup off one of the cup towers.

"To Brazil," I say, pouring her introduction to Chile.

-145-

For three hours I sit in the rising tide of hungry Christmas shoppers, drinking wine and watching Alex work. She flips me off three times. I urinate three times. There are dull moments and tender moments. A fleeting domesticity. An enduring paternity. Another corkscrew shoplifted from Shop-Rite. (Fuck CVS.) Another bottle of wine. Evodia is an irresistible Grenache that exists, both container and content as a brazen mockery of its own seven-dollar price tag. It looks *and* drinks like real hot shit, but I won't let Alexis have any because she's gotten a little silly, knocking things over and flirting with me. I go out – getting tired of the terrible music – one last time for another Evodia, another corkscrew. I surrender both to Alexis, and I tell her: marinated skirt steak and grilled peppers, the long lime green ones I can never remember the name of. And baby arugula as a salad: bleu cheese and cranberries and anchovies. She giggles. I tell her: or smuggle the bottle into Five Guys Burgers and Fries. Oh, man. Who needs drugs when you have Evodia? My book? Which one? Being broke and crazy... and perverted... like *any* good book. *Vice* just ran a big story on me. Yeah, the real *Vice*. Everyone knows *Vice*. Not Carraway. Kerouac. No, there is no such person as Jack Carraway. Well, I bought the wine, didn't I? Well, what about the hardware? I already told you, I have this cat...no way...too cold. Take my card. It's an old picture. I *am* a creep. Thank you. What if the cook turns you in? But *everyone's* feet are gross. There's no need to get personal. I don't need them in Florida. I hate movies like that. Maybe. Just be careful with it. I'll mail you one. I'm the best writer in America. Okay, *North* America. Because I gotta *go!* No, you're the prettiest girl I've seen all day. You mean *patronizing* and I'm not doing that. Maybe. Kiss you goodbye? Pepper steak, with... with nothing. I don't *want* any rice. I'm not kissing... okay, quick, c'mere.

-146-

"Hi Ron!"
"Welcome back, Gene."
"Look, some of this st-"
"Any returns go straight back on the card."
The 15-inch monitor nearly slips out of its partially-split shopping bag, as I hoist everything to the counter.
"Here we go."
"Pardon?"
"I knew something was up. No cash."
"With a generous tip?"
"No cash."
"50."
"No."
"I'll give you a hundred dollars cash. Nothing up. I'm keeping some of this stuff. I'm the famous novelist, Gene Gregorits. Look me up. Seriously."
"I don't-"
"A hundred FIFTY cash, *and* I'll send you a signed copy of my-"
Ron releases a sigh that takes the Christmas joy out of

192

everything. He narrows his sickly green eyes, his subterranean retail jaundice eyes. He clenches and unclenches his jaw.

"Which items are you *not* returning?"

A black pall descends upon the store. "Nothing but a dat-damn *junk shop*," my mall-wandering father would have said during one of our endless mall-wandering weekends. Sundays... even as a little boy, the brutal banality of all those empty parking lots was a fast track to "suicidal ideation." Terms like "suicidal ideation" are a fast track to finding a gun. If you're really serious, you find a gun. The electronic sensor says "BANG-BOH" as a couple of Chatty Cathys arrive. Mariah Carey sings "Silent Night" in that meandering idiotwoman warble, that emotionally infantile inarticulate tangle of tortured vowels. That piercing taunt of negroid imbecility. That little pug nose and all the rank Christmas shopping hoochie mamas of the world filling their stretch-marked bellies with Big Macs in the food court but I have three hundred twenty four dollars, and change.

All is calm.

All is bright.

-147-

Impenetrable blind of sewer gas and bus exhaust gagging me at the Macy's side entrance when I light my cigarette and hop across the patches of snow which lead me back to Grove Street. But I drift the two blocks over to Laura's house which is dead in the gray afternoon.

The little phone has been ringing and I decide to answer it when it begins its tantrum again.

"Yes?" Cynthia says.

"Yes what," I say.

"Oh for fucking Jesus Christ."

"You're really not a phone person."

"BYE GENE."

"Wait."

"WHAT!"

"Check *this* out."

I end the call, then send her the photo of Ron and I with the bags. She immediately calls back.

"How much?"

" A lot."

"Motherfucker. How much?"

"About five hundred bucks."

"You need to get a job. How the *fuck* did-"

"You *told* me to buy everything *new*. Well, I-"

"Yeah yeah yeah alright. Where are you?"

"The mall. Where you *told* me to go."

"I can't get back to Jersey till tonight. Can you take a cab to the new place?"

"How the fuck I'm I supposed to get in?"

"The keys are supposed to be in the mailbox. 766 Van Horn. I've already paid and everything."

"Okay, I'll see ya there."

"You have money for din-fucking GO HUNGRY. *I'll* bring food."

"Yeah, I won't use the card again."

"But you... do you have cash? You'll need cash for a taxi."

"I'll buy a cheap bottle at Shop-Rite, they'll do cash-back."

"Jesus Christ. Alright BYE. HEY!"

"What?"

"Second floor to get into the building, and the apartment's on the *third* floor. So - are you listening?"

"Yup."

"You have one flight outside and one flight inside. You need *both* keys."

"Okay."

"Don't lose those fucking keys."

"Okay."

"BYE. HEY!"

"What!"

"Call me if you can't get in."

"Okay."

-148-

A frigid and desolate Puerto Rican dump called Mataro's where a jukebox plays meringue and salsa tunes at a punishing volume is where I order a double shot of chilled vodka with lemon and two Heinekens and yank the grown-over sutures out of my dog bite calf with the CVS corkscrew. I ask for a sheet of paper and begin logging my messages from voicemail. There are several dozen. Most are prank calls. I write down three numbers with a pen from the Holiday Inn. I wonder if I should have asked for Colleen's number. I dial the first number on the paper.

"TALK TO ME!"

"Hello, this is Gene Gregorits."

"Gene! Hey buddy... LISTEN, my name's LEE TOLLISON, okay, I-"

"Hello."

"LEE TOLLISON, I'm... LISTEN, I just read your book, man, uh, *DOG DAYS*, uh, GREAT STUFF, man! Listen, GENE!"

"Yuh."

"WE gotta talk. I'm a LITTLE busy right now, uh, have you HEARD of ROGUE Talent, I'm with ROGUE Talent, okay?"

"Are you in New York?"

"Are we IN New York. YES! Yes we are, but at the moment, me personally, I'm calling from Connecti-"

I hit END and dial the second number.

"TALK!"

"What the fuck is with you people?"

"I don't know you. Who are you?"

"This is Gene Gregorits."

"GENE GENE THE DANCING MACHINE!"

"Gene Gregorits."

"And how do you say it, the, the last name there?"

"Gene Gregorits. Greg. Or. Its. Gregorits. Exactly the way it looks, one syllable at a time. Exactly phonetic. Greg-or-"

"Yeah yeah, got it Gene! Well listen buddy, I'm glad ya called. My name's Frank de Curtis, and I'm starting an independent publishing-"

"In New York?"

"Uh, yes! Yes, in *Brooklyn*, and-"

"Can you pick me up? Right now? I got stranded out here in Jersey City with no shoes, and-"

"Well, no, I'm calling, er, I'm in Denver, but-"

I end the call and dial the final number.

"Yeah!"

"This is Gene Greg-"

"GENE GREE-GROTTIS YA CRAZY BASTARD! How are ya?"

"I'm in a terrible fix. Are you in New York?"

"I'm... yeah! I'm *IN* New York! Listen buddy, look me up right away, right *now* if you can, I want you to know who I am. This is Chris CROQUET, *boo-sher*, I have a publicity firm called FTP, that's *Forgive the Prince*, and I can help you! Are you represented by anyone yet? Is anyone handling you or your work?"

"No, but I only have today to talk, it's got to be today, so, ah, can you meet me in Jersey City *today*?"

"Oh! Oh boy. Maybe. Let me see. Uh... today *when*?"

"Today NOW."

"I see. Well... where *are* you?"

"Jersey City. The Holland Motel."

"Well... alright. Uh, *maybe*. I'll call you back."

"Cool."

"Five minutes."

"Okay, yeah."

I pay up, collect my shopping bags, and head toward The Holland. I'm fighting off this vision of a dying horse, as I charge along the walk, through the icy blocks of Grove Street. The horse, perhaps sensing that death is many hours, or even days away, flings its head off the ground in search of a witness, a spectator, and of course there is only me. I allow a few moments of eye contact, the animal's misery scraping and gouging at my heart, and at my own illusory sense of control, and safety. I am held in that involuntary eyelock, a white-hot, airless vacuum, just long enough to understand that the horse is begging me to kill it. I understand then why I will spend three or four complete days staring at a single 90 second porn clip when taking amphetamine in large quantities. The terrible lesson of sex and death is something one struggles to correlate with civilization, or any established order, what is considered decent, one struggles in a spooked frenzy to subdue the insidious power of INDECENT DEATH, INDECENT CUNT, unquenchable voids, petrifying abysses, the yawning crocodile at the heart of ALL existence, that which cannot be hitched to ritual or custom or culture or love. That which we truly understand is only bacteria. So why the fight? And what is there to do? Sex surrounds you, in youth and in maturity, in decrepitude, means of pleasure like banshee cries from hell, but there is no such thing as evil, not even suffering, not even cruelty, and we are cruel IN our suffering, cruel to ourselves more than any other, cruel by not facing what is there, there for us to do. And unlike birth, our leaving maybe merciful, with a gun, or medication. I'm trying to make a mental note to research heroin overdose as a method of suicide, and cursing the wind chill, when Croquet calls back.

"Ok, so...I *can* meet you out there, so..."

"Oh, fantastic."

"What's the exact address?"

"Oh, I don't know," I say, staring at my frost bitten ingrowns, stomping through a patch of black slop. "When you come out of the Holland Tunnel, just look – where are you coming from?"

"I'll figure it out. It'll be an hour though, okay?"

"That's alright."

I return the phone to my pocket, realizing I am without chopsticks for my pepper steak. It is with an odd relief that I discover that there's no pepper steak, either. Eating Asian fare with western utensils is vulgar, and I refuse to do it.

Then I realize I forgot the ten-pound roll of paper towels.

-149-

"The idea had been burning in my brain for *some* time."

"What?"

"You know, from *Taxi Driver.* 'The *idea* had been burning in my brain for *some* time.' Come on, Teddy!"

"Oh Gene! You comin to Otto's tonight buddy? Word got out quick! Remember Rick Brynaert? He's coming out. It's gonna be a hell of a night."

"An article came out yesterday, an article about *me*, Teddy. In

Vice. Vice Magazine wrote that I am the great writer of our time."

"Sure they did, you fuckin crackhead."

"I've been taking calls all morning. They're flying me to Los Angeles next week, Teddy. I'm on VICE DOT COM, so ahead and-"

-click-

Re-dial.

"Teddy, I'm lost in Jersey. I need you to get me an address."

"STOP FUCKING CALLING ME."

-click-

Re-dial.

"Teddy..."

"WHAT THE FUCK DO YOU WANT?"

"What's the address for the Jersey City Goodwill, Teddy?"

"HOW THE FUCK I'M I SUPPOSED TO KNOW, CRACKHEAD?"

"But you have the Internet, and a nice warm apartment, and-"

"I own my own HOUSE, crackhead."

"Exactly! And here I am standing in the snow, by the Holland Tunnel, with NOWHERE to live and schizophrenia and no shoes on and a debilitating alcohol addiction, and I need an address for Goodwill, Teddy, so I can pick up a homeless Christmastime care package with dried fruit and chicken soup and Ritz crackers and peanut butter and tuna fish and juke boxes and chopsticks and-"

"Gene?"

"Yes, Teddy?"

"I'm going to get you this address, and you are not to call this number ever again,"

"But Teddy-"

"Fuck you, Gene Suicide."

"Don't call me that, Teddy. I have serious mental problems. And it's Christmastime."

"I don't care."

"What about Otto's tonight?"

"Oh don't worry, we'll be at Otto's."

"Alright then, do you have that address for me, Teddy?"

"Yeah, you fucking crackhead. 2808 Monroe."

"Are they open today? What's their number?"

"I talked to the police yesterday. One of the girls you raped is willing to talk. You need to be locked up, Gene."

"That's ridiculous, Teddy. If I was a rapist, I'd be in prison. Like with your girlfriend, I can't even remember her name, just that she had hairy nipples and seemed to have fallen in love with me. Thanks for the address, Teddy."

"You're dead, motherfucker."

"Don't hate, Teddy. Hate will give you the-"

-click-

"Cancer."

The Holland Avenue Super Liquors may be older, dirtier, and a little smaller than its suburban counterpart, but it's no less wondrous. The squeak and rumble of a hundred haggard shopping carts fairly drowns out Alvin and the Chipmunks on the PA system as I make a beeline for the checkout area and ask the only available cashier for a manager's assistance. The young woman is unnerved by me although I don't *feel* manic: I tell myself that I'm doing alright, that I've got a long day ahead and that uncertainty *will* make a person - even the most well-designed person - susceptible to panic. And then I *am* feeling it. My last drink has just worn off when I follow the dismissive hand jab of the cashier (Penelope Cruz, oh!) to a dirty beige office door in the far front corner of the store which is plastered with holiday event flyers, shit wine tastings and shit liquor giveaways, a door half-hidden behind a display of Patrón Tequila which reminds me of Lase and Lase's wife and downtown drinking and for some reason I think of my mother.

I knock on the door, find myself facing a tall, halogen-wearied black gentleman with granny glasses and the requisite neck strap. Rather than words, which perhaps he is too overdrawn for, he produces an expression of muted rage.

"I'm sorry to bother you sir. I'm... staying over at the Holland, and I will be making a large purchase."

The man examines my feet. Fortunately the snow encountered en route removed most of the blood that had trickled down my calf and onto my toes during the de-stitching job. This blood very well may have ruined me, I think, taking my book, my plot, my entire winter purpose, and Sam, away. I say a tiny prayer.

"*Yes?*"

"I'm needing eight cases of beer, and a case of wine. Um...do you sell cigarettes?"

"No."

"Just the beer and wine then I guess." I smile, having gone beet red.

"What do you NEED, sir?"

"Oh! I'm so sorry. Uh, I have no car, so I need some help getting my purchase over to the Holland."

"We have no delivery service, sir."

"Pardon?"

"We *HAVE* no *DELIVERY* service."

"No, I understand..."

The man's jaw clenches; he senses an unnatural scene, an escalation. I'm wise to jump ship: "Thank you, thanks anyway."

He lowers his glasses down his nose, his head down to the

clipboard.

He closes the door.

-151-

It takes ten minutes, four trips, and $257.97 to get my beer (192 bottles of Ballantine) and wine (8 bottles of Honoro Vera Monastrell) out to the parking lot. The upright dolly clanks and whines as I wheel it past the manager's office where the door remains closed. I stop and return to the checkout lane.

"Excuse me," I say, much louder than necessary, "what is your name?"

"Chris," the cashier tells me, spooked.

"CHRIS! Okay! Listen, I'm staying at a hotel about five blocks over, and my ride back never showed up. And it's about to start raining, so..."

"You need a cab? You need to, for me to call?"

"Could you?"

"Yeah, sure. Just..."

He holds up one finger, returning to an elephantine attorney and a fleet of whisky bottles. The holiday soundtrack has receded behind a human chatter.

The manager emerges right on cue. "*Look* man, *I'll* give you a lift. It's my dinner break anyhow."

And so we walk together outside, me with my clanking six-foot stack and thunder murmuring above the tunnel traffic from far away, maybe over the Long Island Sound, or Sheepshead Bay. The manager says, "Your timing could've been better. You having a party over there?"

I begin to answer, but he cuts me off to say, "Just hang back. When you see the black pickup, that's me."

The lot is tight with parked cars, and a half dozen circling around. "I'd rather fucking... is it Christmas Eve... round and round... stop-go, stop-go, stop-go... shielded... thoughtless... in the warm cars... rockin around, the Christmas tree... stop-go, stop-go, stop-go, smile – laugh, laugh – cry, cry – smile... in the new old fashioned way... honey, did you remember to get the... everyone's dancing merrily... they were *out of everything* but look what I found for your... kill myself..."

An angry horn sets me into action, hoisting the cases two at a time over to the truck, the back of which is covered by a black tarp secured to the lip of the bed with rusted metal snaps.

"Just yank that up!" he shouts above the blowing horns, through the space above a tinted window as it lowers, automated. The brown cases, once in the truck bed, start to *belong* to me. And I'm closing in on the future.

"Roll that cart back inside," he says, and then we're inching through the gray.

Stop. Go. Stop.

-152-

There is a problem at the intersection, an accident? An ugly gloom announces another day gone, conceals the trouble. The stoplight is blinking red.

"Did you get shut down by the storm?"

"Yeah, we...got some water in the store...lost two days. But we were lucky. The whole city was shut down. Where you comin' from?"

"Florida."

"Yeah, it was bad. Whole...whole city. Now... you havin a party over here, or...not that it's any of my business but the last time I drove a guy to the Holland he lit the place up."

"Hah hah hah."

"Place half burned down."

"When was that?"

"Ooooh... damn...that was..."

"I'm a writer. I'm writing a new book here, then going back home."

The man surveys the traffic, the same old winter, and then me.

"Kinda like that... *Rear Window*, with Johnny Depp, ah heh heh heh..."

"*Secret* Window. Heh."

"Or that other one, with Sam Jackson, the white dude who gets, you know, the writer dude..."

"*1408*."

"Yeah, *you* seen it then."

"Well, no, but people always-"

"Finally," he moans, as the procession begins to move. "There's still problem with, after the storm, you know...ain't everything fixed just yet..."

(I have *become* one of those silly ham actors.)

(This has *become* one of those stupid fucking movies.)

"Well," he says, pulling into the Holland Motel, "Merry Christmas to ya. You oughta get some *shoes*, you gonna be walking around here..."

"Thank you sir."

"Good luck with your book."

"Hey, here's my card. I'll mail you one when it's out, just send me your address. I'm Gene."

"Well, ain't that... good to meet ya, Gene. Mike."

I snap the tarp back on when the cases are on the ground; a thumbs up in Mike's rearview.

-153-

The Asian Woman working at the Holland is a shy creature. She's the only living shy girl in New York. New Jersey. Whatever. "Oh," she says, "so much beer!"

"It's for a party, we're..."

"Oh! For *Christmas*, yes?"

"Have a beer, you want one?"

"Oh, no! No, I get *drunk!*"

"On one beer, *drunk*?"

"Yes!"

I begin to ask her what the weekly rate is but stop and smile and open a bottle of beer because the guy she's supposed to think I am would already know that. I smile again opening a second bottle and she giggles: "Don't get drunk!"

I'm on my third bottle of beer and five seconds from telling her I'm in love with her when the phone buzzes, a text message: IM HERE U INSIDE.

I text back: Y.

Another buzz: ROOM NUMBER.

I rise and open the door to find the man upon me, very much as I'd imagined him: a doughy young creep. An Ivy League toad boy. Christopher "Prince" Croquet has a five o'clock shadow on his porcelain countenance, a milkiness that comes infantilism and privilege. His black designer overcoat, and black designer shoes, and particularly his protruding little ears, brace me for another necessary performance. It will be an audition.

"Mr. CROQUET! So good to MEET YOU!"

"Oh, there it is, that's definitely a lobe-less ear."

"Hah! I suppose-"

"Mr.Gregor- I'm sorry, how do you say-"

"It's GREG-OR-ITS."

"GREGORITS. I was listening to an interview on the way over, and I realized I'd been saying it wrong."

"Oh. Yeah."

"So should we talk in your *room*, or-"

"Oh I'm not staying *here*. Can you help me load this into your car? We'll hop over to Burger King, ok? We'll get a Whopper, we'll drink the great Monastrell wine, and see what's what, ok?"

"Well, I'm a little short on time. Do you...need a ride somewhere?"

"It's not far. Don't worry, this won't be, like, an all day thing."

"My wife was freaked out, she didn't want to let me-"

"Oh no."

"So don't get me into trouble now."

"Absolutely not."

"I don't...I thought we could just get *coffee*, Gene. I don't eat meat, and I'm not drinking, I'm definitely not *drinking* today."

"Burger King has good coff-"

"Look, let's find a Starbucks. Aren't your feet cold?"

"No. I just got off the plane from Florida, and-"

"Gene, you've been here all week. I looked at your Facebook page."

"Starbucks is perfect! Can you believe this..."

"No drugs, okay?"

"No! I mean, Christopher, 98% of that is hype. I've got a new writing pad, man. There's a guy holding my computer here in the city, in Jersey City, so I just need help getting over there. But yeah, let's definitely have our meeting. It's gonna be great! I checked you out, and I feel good about everything."

The Prince glances at the stacked cases: "Is that *all* yours?"

"Oh yeah. This is *the big one*, man. Gotta BUNKER DOWN. It's no joke. The new *book*, man. This is *Dog Days 2*. You make sure I get over to the new pad and I'll sign the fucking thing over to you right *now*."

"I'm not sure if it'll all...I'm in a little Geo car, Gene, *come* on."

"We'll figure it out! It's good to *meet* you!"

-154-

In the car, the Prince says, "Do you like Coldplay?"

"No. I mean, I don't know any of their music... It's that guy, that Chris Martin, he's just so horrible, you know."

"Well, what *do* you like?"

"Richard Thompson. I like dark folk. Lou Reed, and-"

"I've got David Bowie on there."

"Oh hell no."

"Just play what you want," he says, tossing an iPod at me.

"I've never had one of these, how do I-"

"Just-"

"Oh! You have Kasabian!"

"There ya go. Just tap the screen."

"We just passed Starbucks."

"Fuck! Gene, I can't even use my rearview mirror! Goddamn it! I can see why you've been underground all years, no offense."

"Well, yeah. I'm a drug addict, which makes me very tough to work with."

"At least you're aware of it."

"Erm."

"So... Kasabian, huh? Okay, there's Starbucks. Gene, goddamn it, I can't... I need you to hop out and grab a few of those cases, I... I'm gonna have a fuckin accident here..."

"Okay, I know what to do. Is there anything behind us?"

"HOW THE FUCK AM *I* SUPPOSED TO KNOW?"

"Hold on."

I step out into four inches of black slush, and pop the little car's rear hatch, prizing out two of the cases as a small line of cars immediately begins forming behind us. Placing both cases on the front passenger seat, I hop back to the hatch, slam it shut, then empty all 48 bottles onto the floor with a terrible explosion of clinking glass and groaning cardboard. I flip the empty cases over my head into the dark air, nearly striking a passing cluster of rich cunts.

"*Ass* HOLE," says the prettiest one.

The boxes are conspicuous there on the sidewalk as the Prince parallel parks, and I look both ways for witnesses before abandoning them there.

"GENE!" the Prince snaps, and then we are standing in line at Starbucks.

"Eat something, Gene. My treat."

"Anything with cheese. And ham. Something meaty and cheesy. I'm gonna take this new Monastrell for a test spin. Is the car open?"

"Gene, you can't drink in Starbucks."

"Sure I can. It's civilized. I'll drink my civilized wine in this civilized place in a civilized fash-"

"It's illegal Gene. Do you see people drinking wine here?"

"Trust me, it's fine. I need to relax."

"Goddamn it, I'm not hard to get along with. Maybe this wasn't a good idea."

I stare at him.

My god: all that money and the Prince has the worst nose hair problem I've seen since my last telemarketing gig.

"O Holy Night" by Mannheim Steamroller.

A jingle of keys.

"It's *not* that I'm humorless, or that I don't get it," says the Prince, as I pour the dark, brooding Spanish red into a small Starbucks cup. "But Gene! You look really *bad*, and-"

"Chris, I'm fine. I'm trying to start work on a new book. If no one wants it, I'll do it myself like I've always done. It'll sell a hundred copies and I'll have to accept that. But I'll tell you man, I never needed anyone to show *me* where the good stuff was or who was doing it. Not even when I was a fucking child. I just *knew*. And if *you're* not really interested-"

"I *am* interested But-"

"OK, here I am. Let's talk."

"Are you really going back to Florida?"

"Absolutely."

"Where do you see yourself in five years?"

"Miami."

"Miami is sinking. Literally. You must know about-"

"No, it's not. The water's rising. The city's fine, you know what I mean? It's the fucking world that's the problem."

"It's a bad place for what I'd be trying to do for you. This is about your work's commercial potential."

"*Dog Days* is brilliant. So what is the problem?"

"You've got to *sell* that."

"No, *you-*"

"*We've* got to sell that."

"Erm."

"How were sales before the *Vice* thing?"

"Terrible. I lost my home."

"So you agree that you need help."

"I've had 25,30 calls from other people this week. I've *done* my part. The *real* work's been done. If you, or someone else, can make some money here, great. But I'm onto another book. So – holy Jesus fucking Christ man, I don't have *time* for this namby-pamby fucking-"

"You really haven't met anyone else yet?"

"No! I hope I don't have to! I'm onto the new book!"

"I'm flying to LA after Christmas and-"

"Look, here's what happened: I'm sitting in a bar with piece of paper, and my phone. I'd blown off the phone, okay? All week. I'm couch surfing, I'm homeless, I'm screwing crazy old women, and I'm not a phone person, okay? So I start checking my messages, and I'm not really listening, they're all the same, this kissy kissy smoothie... 'Gene baby.' You know? So it's like, number, delete. Number, delete. I get a whole sheet full of numbers, I've got it right here. Okay? And I start calling. You in New York? No? Click. You in New York? Click. You were about the seventh or eighth one down. Now, this is how I do things. I'm taking a chance on you because I'm stranded, and I need to pick up my computer stuff. You get me back home, a mile or two from here, and I'll deal with you exclusively. I'm interested in... the kind of relationships I have, they're... *organic* relationships. And you fucking forget everyone else. We do things organically. So... I think... I know... that you'll be sensible. For *me*."

"Uh... well, Gene...thank you? I know what you're saying."

"Common sense. And let me do my work. That's all."

"So... I'll be in LA next month, and I think I could interest some people in you, but if I didn't have any reservations, I wouldn't be a good businessman, would I? I mean, on some level, you have to do things in a civilized manner, you just-"

"The WORK. What do you like, what do you like about the WORK?"

"Well... it's raw, it's honest, it's-"

"Oh, those words are clichés, that's like saying 'gritty.' You haven't actually read the book."

"I've read *sections*, Gene. Come on. Two days ago I'd never heard of you. The way to get things going, first of all, is to have a good idea of what *you* want, and *where* you want to be."

"I want to be done with the new book."

"And where will *that* take you, what then?"

"The next book."

"Gene-"

"There's a communication problem here. See, I'm a writer, not a movie star. People don't even know the difference anymore."

"Oh come on. Lighten up. But hey man, a *movie* is the thing to talk about."

"Yeah. Heh heh. Chris, I don't see a movie about dog killing and anal rape being a big hit at Cannes."

"*Dog* killing and-"

"That's the book, Chris. That's what *Dog Days* is about. The woman who wrote the *Vice* article hasn't read it, either. See, that's the problem. If I can't get MY INTERVIEWERS, or MY CRITICS, to read the books, well, what am I actually even selling here? What the fuck am I even doing?"

"Jesus. I *love* dogs."

"Goddamn this is a good sandwich. And the wine, oh man. This is fucking heaven. Really, you'd be doing me such an honor. I named my imprint after it."

"Why don't we get together again this week for a drink?"

"Sure. But you'll make sure I-"

"Yes, I'm taking you home."

"And my computer-"

"We'll get the computer. What are your plans this week?"

"Um. A reading in the East Village. Writing for a stretch here in Jersey. And that's it."

"That's it?"

"Then I'm going back to Florida."

The Prince looks at his watch.

"I need to be home, Gene. It's Christmas Eve. Did you even know that?"

"Erm..."

"What are the addresses?"

"804 Monroe. And 766 Van Horn is home."

I finish my wine while the Prince does his thing on a small Internet device. The Paul McCartney Christmas song everyone hates, and that everyone *knows* everyone hates, is playing. Why is it still...who...and then the gentle ivory caresses of a mercifully traditional "O Tannenbaum" fall upon me, all that alcoholic holiday self-pity going to work but the McCartney nightmare returns, and when I think of Paul McCartney I usually find myself thinking of Linda McCartney, or of the two of them together, and-

"I'm gonna make a call, Gene, just a minute."

-then it's hard not to think of Richard and Linda *Thompson*, of the *menace* there, and what the *menace* means, and then I'm thinking of Richard and Linda Thompson *killing* Paul and Linda McCartney. Of course, Linda McCartney *is* dead, which gets me onto *my* dead exes, and in particular my dead ex Leslie (or was it Lesley?) who loved Paul and Linda McCartney but not Richard and Linda Thompson, and who hated the very *idea* of records like *Shoot Out the Lights* and *Berlin* and-

"Berlin."

"Yes? Never been."

The Prince is still pecking away. Just like fucking Cynthia and all my exes both alive *and* dead with their fucking McCartneys and TV shows and peck peck pecking all night long.

"The record *Berlin* by Lou Reed. That's *Dog Days*. I bet you haven't heard *Berlin*, have you?"

"N-no," he mumbles.

"Get that record. It might help you to see *Dog Days* a little differently."

"Okay." There is the crisp slap of his device as he folds it up and puts it away. I am seeing the futility but it doesn't anger me. I'm drunk. A handsome drunk, demonstrating impeccable diplomacy in his effortless absorption of it, of the sadness of otherness, of having no reasoning power... with the primates...

"Let's get you on your way," the Prince says. "This could be good, Gene. But I need you to try to see things from the other person's point of view. I'm sure you've met with other producer-types before-"

"No. Just you."

"But before. Didn't you live in LA at one point?"

"Yeah, but...I never left the house."

"For two *years?*"

"Two and a half. Ask Lydia!"

"Lydia... Lunch. Right."

"Yes sir."

"We can work on these... these are *minor* issues, I guess."

"Yeah, because this has to be a *pure* relationship if it's gonna go anywhere."

"How do you mean? *Pure.*"

"I mean you make calls or have meetings or pet egos or whatever you do. You be you, and I'll be me, and I'll do what I do, which is produce literature. If that means enough to you, or whoever, then you'll let me...I will BE allowed, let's put it that way, to *exist* as *me*. That's not much to ask. As a matter of fact, I think it's the measure of human decency. I'll respect deadlines, and I'll come to New York once, maybe twice a year, but no more than that. And when it comes to money, jesus, just pay me what was agreed upon. I don't understand where things like this get complicated. They don't have to"

"Well, the drugs-"

"I don't use drugs. I'm a drinker."

"And nothing happens overnight, you *do* understand that."

"If I can't wait any longer, if I have to... move on, I'll let you know. Things are tough right now."

"I'll take that into consideration."

"Okay." In the movies, a guy like me always says, "I have a good feeling about this." Or maybe it's the smoothie from Hollywood's line. I say it anyway. "I have a good feeling, Chris. I'm a hard worker and I'm excited about getting started with you."

It's not much of a movie moment, but at least it's over.

The Prince and I shake hands.

-156-

Snow again.

The day is done, is long gone, when I hoist the filthy Goodwill box of filthy old hardware off my lap and plunk my feet in the gutter slush. The Prince is double parked and speaking softly to his wife as I strain my eyes against the darkness of Van Horn Street.

Leaning across a black metal fence, I'm able to make out the numbers 766 on a door high above me: it is a row home, identical to all others on the block, which ends with 766. Beyond the fence and the latched gate are four overflowing trash barrels, being slowly concealed by the falling snow. The vacant lot to my left is aglow with the burning neon signs of a corner bodega just across Van Horn. Chris and his Geo seem cruelly distant to me: I understand then that it's the last time I'll see him. Idling cars have always terrorized me: they are the embodiment of all that is transitory and mundane, the gory details of going nowhere.

In the darkness beyond the gate, beyond the trash cans, comes the sound of a deadbolt turning. A small light flicks on, revealing a door on the ground level. I brace myself against the delicate, horrifying mechanical fidgeting of someone's key in the lock, and as the door squeals open the Prince hits the horn.

"Gotta *go*, Gene. I gotta GO. Come on!"

I have no choice but to turn my back on the emerging shape, as the house's sensor light pops on and the shape says, "Huh-lo?"

The Little Prince, idling in the road: "GENE!"

"Pardon me," I say to the man, a large, bespectacled German in a brown overcoat holding an unlit cigarette in his mouth, which he smiles around disaffectedly.

I unload the car right there, curbside, including the 48 loose bottles from the passenger side floor which I grab frantically, five longnecks at a time. The bottles crack and rattle in my arms as the Prince punches the Geo up to the intersection and roars back across Jersey City. I am lost in my urgency to reflect back on it all, but the German man has approached, saying something about the beer.

"Excuse me?"

He lights his cigarette and takes a hands-free drag, looking very Hollywood supervillain.

"I said, 'Man! That's a lot of beer!'"

"Oh," I say, as if there is one case behind me, instead of nine. "Yeah. I'm moving in."

"You are... second floor? No..."

"Third."

"Ah, now *that* makes sense. So you move in, with *beer*. You have... just... so much beer?"

"Well... I'm a writer, and-"

"You write novels, really?"

"Yes, I'm only here to write *one* book, just a week or two."

"Ah! Excellent! Are you with the small, uh, a *small* woman with-"

"The fat old blonde in platform boots?"

"Oh ho ho! Yes, the... on the... *third* floor..."

"Yeah. I'm with her. Did she have anyone else with her, a boy?"

"In a leather jacket, a young... guy. Yes, they left. It was... only an hour ago? Maybe two hours hours?"

"Well, I'm Gene."

"I am Anders. Do you need help?"

"I can get this. But thank you."

"Man that's a lot of beer. Are you sure?"

"Yes."

"Be careful then. Your feet look so cold!"

"I'm okay."

"You must have two hundred bottles of beer. But they are all alcoholics, *writers*. The American writers. Hemingway, I guess."

"Yeah, but it's a crazy thing. Crazy people in Japan drink like crazy people in Poland, I think. And at Christmastime, you know..."

"Crazy drunks in Frankfurt, certainly, certainly! All the crazy drinking people of the world, yes?"

"Have one, I'm gonna-"

"Oh. Oh, I think maybe not *now*, but if you are up late, I have some very good cocaine..."

I nearly drop my bottles and am completely erect by the time I've opened it and taken a drink.

"...if you are up.Late. I'm back there, first floor, behind the stairs. And *you* are on *third* floor, with the little fat woman, oh oh oh! It's a very *nice* apartment. I've taken people there too, you know. So talk again, maybe? I must be somewhere."

Anders looks like the Scandinavian actor Stellan Skarsgård. He jingles his keys in one upraised hand, a manner about him - that movement especially - which I interpret as evil. I see myself engaged in guttural drug sex and chuckle to myself, another type of evil, amused by my own amusement because that which once brought me such unspeakable shame and terror is now just another of life's many booby traps, still dangerous this druggy black ice but altogether manageable with my vet status and my broken spirit my broken back my lessons learned. There are stagnant wading pools and deep crystalline drowning pools, and I know the difference. Scum is easy. Safe. Amusing. Only a woman can give me hope and only a woman can kill me, so I'm smiling - *all* the bitter *sweet*, hah hah hah! - and delighted to be alone at 766 Van Horn.

I find the keys in the mailbox. Finish my beer in the naked street: All the three story row homes of the world above me.

-157-

Inside, the immediate thought is of a poorly scheduled open house, a real estate showing during a bad storm: the place is fresh form renovations, the crispness of new paint, that smell.

But there is also fresh mud on the bare staircase, I notice while wincing from the cruel acoustics. Already, the hardwood floor is waterstained. The door of the second floor apartment leaks the sounds of a nice meal being enjoyed, piano music, while behind me, through the wide open entrance, I hear murmurs and footsteps, *between* footsteps and turn to witness two young Hispanic passersby snatch two of my loose bottles and scatter into the vacant lot next door.

I descend the outer stairs and begin the work, lining it all - my shopping bag, the Goodwill box, the cases, and the loose bottles - to one side of the inner stairs. The work makes me lightheaded. I dash across the street to the little bodega for a sandwich, before I begin. In my black peacoat and my hellhound mindset, the ancient cathedral looming above the vacant lot beckons. I approach it cautiously, the cushiony silence around me making stealth impossible, while the young bodega clerk fixes my tuna sub. I catch a blast of hot air from a Chinese laundry, full of good clean brand name soap which I bask in, a moment, a long moment, wanting to eat that cloud instead. A fat young Chinese woman gives an old white woman her change. All the laundry is folded. Didn't I always want to get laid in a laundromat? The warm, clean air, the admission of defeat in the laundry experience, the clarity of excremental human life and young urban single apartment life in all that warm machine grunting and grinding and spinning in sad circles twenty-five cents a go is an invitation to hungover redhead grad students, mousey bartenders, bipolar strawberry blonde trust fund brats, or maybe just a normal middle-aged secretary with lots of freckles and tattoos. I'd rather not ever fuck anyone who doesn't use a coin-op, who doesn't read lonely pretentious hipsters novels and smoke cigarettes at the coin-op. I want a woman who's never shaved her pussy, a woman with dingy whites. Car keys and Camel Lights left abandoned in a big rubber tub, like at the airport, while our sounds are lost in the machine song. One like that is worth a year of standard-issue bar pussy. Ditto that (double it) for Greyhound equivalent. (Chinese woman spots me in the stark exhaust cloud scene and freezes. I bolt.)

-158-

A printed receipt I find on the floor states the name "AIRBNB.COM" several times, which helps me to understand the weekly arrangement, and the return of the bed-sit in the Internet age. It gives me the creeps.

A lightswitch panel above the top step reveals a modest kitchen with a serving counter, a living room full of cheap wicker furniture, and a tight hallway running back towards the street. It opens into a bedroom with large, old windows. I grin at the thought of the Butterball Queen and her punk going at it, which they appear to have done well and fully upon an inflatable mattress there. I am unsettled to find myself aroused, and it's only after I've masturbated into the mussed navy blue sheets that I become cognizant of the hundreds of row house windows through this bedroom's fully compacted Venetian blinds. There is a smell of new rubber in the room, presumably from the air mattress. I entertain a series of images: a middle-aged bird-like woman pushing a shopping cart through Passaic Costco, the cart filled mostly with the mattress in its brightly designed Coleman box, but also bed sheets and sets of Venetian blinds and maybe a set of cheap silverware. Nancy Wertheimer is a whiny, cheap divorcee who began dabbling in real estate several years ago after all the paperwork went through. She's really proud of herself, buying this shit for "the new unit." She answers her cellphone in the checkout line, telling the caller all about her busy schedule and her "handyman" and her new unit and the new installations. She has half a clue what she's doing and she's on her own now. She's real proud of herself, with no man in sight.

I return to the kitchen and look inside the fridge: baking soda. Lemon juice. A half empty bottle of V-8. *Low-sodium* V-8. "Better not smoke in here," I think.

On the other side of the kitchen, I sniff around living room a minute, and locate a small balcony, and the large back window, both of which offer a clearer-than-necessary-or-comfortable gaze across the vacant lot, and into the Satanic pout of the desecrated two hundred foot cathedral. If any lights became visible in the distance, in those angry windows, through the unrelenting snowflakes of this raw Christmas Eve, I'd guess them to be flames from barbecue lighters, held by crackheads. But, of course, it's far too cold for that sort of thing. This cold tonight is a killing cold. The church will host the Jersey City crack Olympics in early spring, if it's still there at all. Do they tear down cathedrals in the wintertime?

The bakery becomes the obvious hiding spot for the beer because it's the only hiding spot for anything larger than a shoebox. I can see my breath in there, after everything is brought up from below, and it takes me a half hour to locate the thermostat. The heater fills the room with the smell of scorched metal. It ticks and purrs and whispers.

I open a bottle of wine, designating the kitchen counter as my Monastrell office, my workspace. I dump the CVS bag into the kitchen sink, tearing open the cellophane from the cardboard of each item; toss all that packing off the balcony. I locate a small cutting board and a dollar-store carving knife, which I use to shred a dozen or so plastic sandwich bags. I sprinkle the cheap wicker furniture, and the living room rug, with the bits of brand new plastic, taking a step back to consider it all. The wine needs air, and the tuna aftertaste is ruining it for me, so I cleanse my pallet with several Ballantines while I begin wiping, painting, patching, and spraying back to brand-new condition a battered box full of Goodwill hardware. The keyboard fares best of all, after I slap about a pound of hair and filth out of it, going between the keys with Q-tips and rubbing alcohol. I stretch sandwich bags over either end, Sharpie-out those partially eroded key characters, and blow it dry.

On a small panel television in the bedroom, I'm happy to find a full set of cable TV stations and several dozen music-only stations. One is called "Classic Punk" and the track playing is "Venus de Milo" by Television. It's Television on the radio on television... or something like that. I tear open one of the legitimate purchases, a digital tape recorder, and remove a small styrofoam block, crushing it into tiny crumbs and blowing the Styrofoam everywhere from my ink smeared hands: *Hey Richard, let's dress up like cops, just think what we could do.*

All the little white bits hang and cast about in the cottony apartment air. I go to work on the next item, a paint spattered LG 15 inch flatscreen. "Razor blades," I mutter: I feel very tired just then. The heating vents release industrial sounds, industrial odors. I dream of Florida.

-159-

I wake on the floor with my peacoat balled up as a pillow, and to the sound of laughter, canned laughter. I rise up then, my bones popping, the word "alcohol," and six kinds of death: Cynthia says "good morning" all cocainey, and before I know she's there.

My eyes adjust to the raw dawn, the eviscerated cathedral's outline hard enough through the cheap curtains, Cynthia on the wicker sofa playing with her phone, while *The Odd Couple* flickers on her laptop. A little black saucer beside it, little lines of cocaine.

Beside me, in two stacks of three, are the beer cases and the wine case on its own.

"What time is it?"

"You are unbelievable. You're gonna pay me back for all this. I want the money today."

"Are you really doing coke to the fucking *ODD COUPLE?*"

"And *Ballantine*. Who the fuck drinks *Ballantine?*"

"I've rediscovered it."

"You may as well have got Rheingold."

"That's not fair, or accurate. Ballantine's got character."

"Yeah, okay. What the hell did you do yesterday?"

"I had a meeting with some kind of half-ass movie producer. He's not really a movie producer. More like a project developer, or, no... an agent? He was a cunt."

"You're being funny. Come on..."

"No, I... I met him. I met the fucking guy."

"I told you! *Vice* is a big deal! Are you selling books?"

"I don't know, you have my computer."

"Ah shit. You'll have to bring it in."

"Do we have Internet here?"

"Yeah. She left me a code for it, Wi-Fi code, you know, how it's called..."

"Didn't you sleep?"

"No. I picked up from a different guy, all the way in, he had, usually his stuff's no good, but I guess he's got a new connection, you want some?"

"I don't want get all whacked out and..."

"Oh come on, you want me to take care of you? I'll suck you all morning if you want, who cares? Try this."

"Ah shit."
"You're gonna pay me for all that beer."

-160-

Cynthia Santiglia · Store Associate at Verc Enterprises
Excellent piece. Lisa and Gene. Congrats! I am hoping my comments expressed the message I intended, which was to underscore the power of Gene's writing and its influence on my life and my desire to support his career- the motivation behind as well as a driving force of our friendship. But equally important is the fact that Gene has looked after me and looked out for me in ways more meaningful than picking up a tab could ever be (which he insists on doing every time he sells a book). Our bond exists because of a mutual respect; it's a give and take. He will be pissed that I am outing him as a decent guy here- but he shouldn't be worried. If anyone wants details about his reckless behavior, whorehounding and general forays into jerkiness, they can feel free to contact me directly. 😊

Like · Reply · 🖒 8 · Jan 27, 2013 5:59pm

James Fernández Ramírez · Sales Development at Complete Solar
Forcefully trying emulate a life similar to Hunter S. Thompson... and then failing to do so. Tryhard.

Like · Reply · 🖒 4 · Jan 27, 2013 4:42pm

alfalfamail
Know it all...

Like · Reply · 🖒 1 · Jan 28, 2013 12:20am

Peter Crumpler · Bartender Server at The Drinkingbird
that's a small minded thing to say

Like · Reply · 🖒 3 · Jan 29, 2013 3:38pm

T Beryl Ring
.

Like · Reply · Jun 14, 2013 5:22pm · Edited

Thomas Berry · Photographer/Videographer & Editor at The Arizona Republic
Ah so great, this guy is awesome.

Like · Reply · 🖒 3 · Jan 27, 2013 3:18pm

Jarrod Matchett · Boca Ciega High School
FUCK IT BRO! IF WE WERE ALL THE SAME, LIFE WOULD BE BORING! ALL THOSE SO CALLED NORMAL PEOPLE ARE THE CRAZY ONES.

Like · Reply · 🖒 3 · Jan 27, 2013 3:13pm

hobbsend13
Wonderful piece. Gene and Cynthia are beautiful folk. He is gifted with the possession of a truly parallax viewpoint and can really write. If I was so inclined you could dismember and eat my penis any day Gene. We could share. Candlelight, maybe some Abba...Erasure for our sins? That's romance...
Warm me a pew by the beach. Miss you guys. Ben
Like · Reply · 🖒 3 · Feb 25, 2013 12:19pm

Darius Smith · Chief Executive Officer at Self-Employed
Lisa Carver, incidentally, the author of _____, is Our Greatest Living Writer!
Like · Reply · 🖒 2 · Feb 22, 2013 10:33am

Darius Smith · Chief Executive Officer at Self-Employed
Rock! Rock! Rock! Rock! Rock'n'Roll High School!
Like · Reply · 🖒 2 · Feb 22, 2013 10:30am

Greg Gure · Charles Bukowski HS
Lack of my comment makes me sad. I also think Gene can't be that emotional or violent as some portray him, because if someone kept mentioning GG ALLIN to me and that I was remotely like him I'd cut off the interview.
Like · Reply · 🖒 2 · Feb 4, 2013 7:45am

Kowalski Lech · Writer/Filmmaker at Revolt Cinema
Gene is evolving. He turned his back on the hipsters. There is no core to society anymore. Everything is scattered.
Like · Reply · 🖒 5 · Jan 29, 2013 12:09am

Dominic Thackray
Wow! I think it's time to cash in and sell my Gene Gregorits shares
Like · Reply · 🖒 2 · Jan 29, 2013 12:46am

Tommy Watson · Hoboken, New Jersey
He "evolved" straight into prison for sexual assault against a minor.
Like · Reply · Jun 15, 2018 6:21pm

Téii Kim · Newark, New Jersey
This guy ended up adding me on Facebook because he thought I was witty or something and then persuaded me to buy his book because why not I guess? He charged me 30 bucks for this Bible sized book that was full of random interviews of people who weren't even quasi-celebs and email exchanges with random people I didn't care too much about. Most of it wasn't even him writing. Just transcripts of chats and such. This was his book Hatchet Job.

The dude really needs and editor and I felt sorry for the guy because he does seem genuinely batshit crazy or just a bad attempt of coming off as crazy for attention or to get welfare payments. I guess some of the stuff was decent if it was actually organized. I told him I didn't care to read any more of his books, but I did tell him I can send him money through Paypal or mail him a check because I felt bad for the guy.

This REALLY pissed him off and he started calling me a ton of names. It really offended me and then things got really ugly. That's okay though. I'm mailing him his book back.

Like · Reply · 🖒 1 · Dec 30, 2013 7:20pm · Edited

213

Peter Crumpler · Bartender Server at The Drinkingbird

This guy fuckin gets it.

Like · Reply · 👍 4 · Jan 26, 2013 3:38pm

    Tommy Watson · Hoboken, New Jersey

    Yeah, he "got" 8 years for sexually assaulting a Florida minor.

    Like · Reply · Jun 15, 2016 5:35pm

    Peter Crumpler · Bartender Server at The Drinkingbird

    Tommy Watson I've had several opportunities to interact with Gene during his travels. I've found him to be a menacingly intelligent person living the true life of an artist. Although I can't make excuses for the lack of foresight Mr. Gregoritis seems to suffer from which has landed him in his current predicament. I pity you for deriving happiness from and gloating over another man's gross mis fortune. I pity you indeed and I must ask, where are your novels? Where's your contribution? In other words the fuck have you done. In closing keep your keyboard cowboy bullshit to yourself. No one gives a fuck about you.

    Like · Reply · Jun 15, 2016 6:38pm

Alphonse J. Hudson · Detroit, Michigan

What pisses me off the most is this cut cookie "Tryhard" who commented something about a HST emulation. Handful of pop culture references working out for you these days?(did you pick up my Tyler Durden?) HEADLINE: "Little bug(will be eventually be self-squashed by cliché blind culture misery religion) notices general similarities between little mind life-style references and hip morning ritual readings... gets depressed". What you failed to realize is that Hunter wasn't the first to set his mass produced soul on fire for a living Valhalla tie over. Now, I've never heard of this cat Gene until ... See More

Like · Reply · 👍 5 · Jan 26, 2013 8:44am

Davis F Joel

Nothing cures you, like that which made you ill.

Like · Reply · 👍 2 · Jan 28, 2013 8:37am

Aidan McTighe · San Francisco, California

sounds like a decent fellow.

Like · Reply · 👍 3 · Jan 27, 2013 9:09pm

Ben Bicknese · Finance Rep at Mayo Clinic

"And those who were seen dancing were thought to be insane by those who could not hear the music." Nietzsche

Like · Reply · 👍 4 · Jan 27, 2013 7:17pm

-161-

Leslie Small via PayPal	Inbox	**Leslie Small sent you $100.00 USD** - www.paypal.com/us/cgi-bin/?cmd=_view-a-trans&id=1NV38031H72132
service@paypal.com	Inbox	**You sent a payment** - www.paypal.com/us/vst/id=1NJ95714NS133230K Your monthly account statement is av
greg kilgore via PayPal	Inbox	**greg kilgore sent you $150.00 USD** - www.paypal.com/us/cgi-bin/?cmd=_view-a-trans&id=8BP70994GC2649
DoNotReply_Billing	Inbox	**Your eBay invoice for January is now ready to view** - method: PayPal Date: Between February 15, 2014 an
service@paypal.com (2)	Inbox	**Receipt for your debit card purchase** - www.paypal.com/us/vst/id=40004826VR8147007 Hello Justin Gregor
GiftRocket via PayPal	Inbox	**$20 for Florida Winery at John's Pass** - www.paypal.com/us/cgi-bin/?cmd=_view-a-trans&id=0EL187598204
michael montagano via Pa.	Inbox	**michael montagano sent you $100.00 USD** - www.paypal.com/us/cgi-bin/?cmd=_view-a-trans&id=68J751598
service@paypal.com (2)	Inbox	**Receipt for your debit card purchase** - www.paypal.com/us/vst/id=0MM96717LN045273Y Hello Justin Gregc
Jennifer Torres via PayP.	Inbox	**Jennifer Torres sent you $70.00 USD** - www.paypal.com/us/cgi-bin/?cmd=_view-a-trans&id=4HH281999P40801
service@paypal.com	Inbox	**You sent a payment** - www.paypal.com/us/vst/id=2JJ0564823130401M Your monthly account statement is av
Christopher Cantrell via.	Inbox	**PayPal money request from Gene Gregorits MONASTRELL BOOKS** - money with PayPal.
service@paypal.com	Inbox	**You sent a money request to cantrellmarching@hotmail.com** - request:PayPal money request from Gene C
service@paypal.com	Inbox	**Receipt for your debit card purchase** - www.paypal.com/us/vst/id=07795248UT8972745 Hello Justin Gregori
White Trash Art Studio v.	Inbox	**White Trash Art Studio sent you $10.00 USD** - www.paypal.com/us/cgi-bin/?cmd=_view-a-trans&id=5052741
stuart broughton via Pay.	Inbox	**stuart broughton sent you $35.00 USD** - www.paypal.com/us/cgi-bin/?cmd=_view-a-trans&id=1EG54643X02

"I don't want you to lose your deposit, Cynthia."

"Oh fuck 'em. What time is it?"

"I think you'll change your tune when you're flat broke."

"DON'T TELL ME HOW TO SPEND MY MONEY, FUCKFACE."

"Yeah. I'm hungry. What's happening today?"

"Lase's band is playing Bowery Electric."

"What's that?"

"The Bowery Electric. It's a club, you know, like the Bowery Ballroom?"

"Yeah?"

"It's The Bowery Electric."

"But, CBGBs is gone."

"CBs has *been* gone, Gene Genie."

"Huh."

"Bowery Electric is like the new CBs I guess. Thurston Moore owns it, I think."

"So?"

"You need to pick up all these bloody tissues."

"I think I got cooking oil on the cushions."

"Just get the tissues. I gotta shower and everything, so..."

"I didn't know Lase had a band. I thought he was restaurant owner."

"Wizard Sex. He's been dropping hints for you, you know, he doesn't want to be like, 'here's my band,' you know. He's got a little more class than that. He says he's sent you links to the music videos, and that you just ignore him."

"But that *is* saying 'here's my band,' though."

"You need to start being a better friend to your friends. It's painful to watch, Gene. I feel bad for him."

"Wizard Sex. Sounds like stoner rock."

"It's kinda glammy. Glam-garage."

"Hrm. Are they any good?"

"*Yeah*, actually. They *are*."

"Fine, okay, jesus."

"Do you have money?"

"Yeah."

"How much?"

"About a thousand I guess."

"You can pay me back, then."

"Yeah."

"You going out for breakfast stuff?"

"Yeah, I'm fuckin-"

"Me too. Get me some coffee. Large cream and sugar."

"I thought you didn't *drink* coffee."

"Stop."

"But-"

"Go! Get outta here! I need some privacy."

"Take some Emergen-C. I got a whole box."

"Don't rush. Get a drink somewhere. Call Lase."

"Yeah."

"Be nice! He likes you."

"Erm."

"And call your mom. Yesterday was Christmas."

"Yeah."

-163-

I am standing beneath the vast face of the cathedral, willfully impudent, self-consciously contemptuous, thinking, "the waste... the waste... good riddance... the waste..."

I spark up a cigarette, standing in the middle of the street, watching cars approaching both my left and right sides, jingling Cynthia's keys in my hand. Aside from my hand, the jingling, the approaching cars, Jersey City is frozen solid, frozen still, frozen silent. I enter the bodega with a nod and a wave, breathe in the ham and cilantro and coffee and mariachi song.

That's all that remains of New York, for me: the bodegas. Outer borough New York particularly is preserved only in the bodegas, grim old Dominican bodegas dwarfed by the thousands of frozen brownstones, frozen cathedrals, frozen tenements, frozen warehouses, frozen garages. Gentrification does not faze the bodyguards: their charms and comforts are universal. Around them now only rust and ice, filth and decay, cancer and abuse.

The bodegas are road dogs (beers en route) and three dollar sandwiches and warm, milky sugar buzz against the day. The bodegas are there to facilitate all childish small town wonder gone shell shocked gone knocknutty gone comatose cottonmouthed disconnected non compis mentis in the subway clatter gone way-cynical and gotten mean in animal-brutal = animal *SIMPLE* after 20 years after-hours bathroom sex.

I smile again and pay for all that caught my fancy.

-164-

I'm standing in the kitchen trying not to make any noise but I've got to open the bags. I cough lightly, and she moans from behind the bathroom door.

"Oh GAWD. Go to a BAR!"

"No bars. Too early for bars."

"Well wait in the car then."

216

I tear the top off a Ballantine and drink it all down.

"This beer's got a bad rap. I love it."

"You're so fuckin weird."

"Jersey City is like Brooklyn with a little dick," I say.

"JC is JC, and Brooklyn's Brooklyn. Stop."

"Eastern New Jersey is one giant outer borough, that's all it is. There's no real JERSEY on Van Horn! It's Brooklyn West! It's just Brooklyn out there! It's a frozen piece of shit!"

"Go get in the car. I should teach you how to drive."

"On black ice... yeah. Listen..."

"WHAT!"

"I got you coffee and an egg and cheese sandwich from the Brooklyn Bodega."

"You just have no clue how *stupid* you make yourself look half the time. It's like... when you're talking about The Beatles or something. For God's sake, stick to what you know! It really hurts you, talking too much. New Jersey is New Jersey."

"I'll leave your New York style egg sandwich on the counter. They put a squirt of hot sauce on one half, and a squirt of mayo on the other half, that's New York style."

"The keys are hanging on the... they're... do you see 'em?"

"I got the keys."

"Go start the car up."

"I also bought-"

"SHUT YOUR MOUTH AND GO."

"I'm going! But I bought some frozen confections at the New York bodega, these really neat ethnic flavors, Hispanic stuff you know, these weird ice creams, or ice *milks* I guess they are, that you can only get in Brooklyn."

"Stop!"

"They're in the freezer. 'Milk-flavored', you know? What the fuck is that, and 'vanilla *cream-ice'?* I got papaya milk pops, coconut milk pops, tamarind milk p-"

"CAN I FUCKING TAKE A SHIT?"

"...guava milk-pops, caramel milk-pops, ginger milk-pops, cinnamon milk-pops, mango-"

"GENE! GET THE FUCK OUT!"

"Cola champagne... bizcosho de canela... bimbo galletas... beanpies..."

-165-

I toss my cigarette, sitting high atop Van Horn, and turn to witness her sad platform boot descent from the third floor. That's my cue to get curbside and let her brave *both* long flights solo. If she falls, I tell myself, an opportunity will be created. Of course, I don't *hope* for this; I don't even have a plan. Let it happen, I tell myself. The thing will come into focus soon enough. Meanwhile I occupy a spectral realm, an interstitial foxhole between oblivion and obliviousness, flirtatiously, as Cynthia reaches the front door landing looking like a subnormal child after plundering mommy's makeup kit, like one of the old Warhol gang at the 80s reunion party, a punk rock Tammy Faye Bakker in a denim jacket two sizes too small – so tight she can't lower her fat little arms – and with an unconscionable white swell of bare chub, bursting out over the top of a lint-spackled black skirt fastened loosely by a Ramones button because the zipper is busted. The whole package is topped off with a pink and black visor cap, its plaid flannel befitting the season and the city. Those Hudson River gales do not discriminate: they are to be well heeded.

And I'm also dressed to kill, in a cream-colored thermal top with thick bloodstains adorning the collar, and sagging boot-cut Levis that could stand on their own. My rotten sandals are sticky with blood from ten deformed toes, the nails gone, leaking black toe pits left by outright yanking with teeth and pliers and anything what's got *grip*, nights and early mornings when I can't sleep.

-166-

Cynthia's little gray hatchback is like a pin ball launched by sadistic hands: I see us from above, from my very own helicopter, through my very own movie camera, snaking through the frozen streets one block at a time but re-inhabiting the scene gradually as the stashed beer finds its way into my system, as we grind through the Holland Tunnel, all improbable stealth and ease, maybe even menace, and Cynthia singing all the words to "Golden State" by John Doe and Kathleen Edwards when we emerge in an eerily motionless Tribeca (it occurs to me then, hearing John Doe and Cynthia together, that the woman's "style" is no more than a bad imitation of Exene Cervenka which means... well, I suppose that I should feel no remorse about releasing my own charmless yowl into the stuffy machine air)... we park on Delancey... somehow lifeless. I light a cigarette and point at a 5th floor window where... Cynthia is calling someone. I don't feel like telling the story anyway. The rumble of a passing truck, of a thousand passing trucks. Chinese lettering. Same old restaurant supply deliveries for the same old Williamsburg Bridge.

-167-

"Gene, *macho*! Where's your shoes? You gotta have some boots, don't you?"

"Maybe after my reading I'll have some money."

"Ah... ah no, man, I'll get you some boots."

"Thanks, Lase."

"Oh for fucking Christ's sake. He could have *three* pairs of boots if he wanted them. He's... *tell* me how this makes sense... he's afraid that if he covers his feet, he'll end up stuck in New York forever."

"New Jersey, Cindy."

"Oh shut up. He's been awful, Lase."

Cynthia goes on to tell the story – the *full* story – of the beer and the used hardware.

"He even bought a fucking *tape* recorder," she says. "And he keeps that, the one thing he doesn't need..."

"What's the tape recorder for, *macho*? You taping us now?"

"New book," I drone, unamused. "I've explained it a hundred times. New book. New book. New book."

"*Dog Days 2*," smiles Lase.

"*Dog Days* **Volume** *Two*."

"Written in the Florida mental hospital in five days."

"Six days."

"See? We listen to you. C'mon Gene, let's get a drink. Do you like this place?"

"Yeah, I mean... this is the typical '97 scene when I first got turned loose out here."

"Really? Right here?"

"No, I don't remember what was *here*, but bars *like* this, you know. Back in '97, and a little bit in '95, '96, when I was married, but after the divorce I really went nuts down here. Every night. And there were always cocaine scenes, fucking trannies in bathrooms."

"Oooooh, co-*caine* scenes," says the very attractive brunette bartender, a sharp, freckly Lara Flynn Boyle-type. And the bar is Betty's, a fetish-themed hole in the wall, which, with its Betty Page posters and framed glossies, and one life-sized Betty Page statue, wouldn't win any points for originality. All that aside, I recall the artificial balm of the neighborhood bar Friday night, or Monday night, or Wednesday night: New York made us all invincible, until the coked-out blaze of Houston or Delancey morning sun. You were beyond saving then. Being young was mostly agony of that sort. Chasing the perfect hit, the perfect pussy, the perfect film noir scene: I had my share. The terms were brutal.

Lase orders drinks and introduces me to the girl: "Brynn, Gene's the writer, for tomorrow night."

"Very pleased to meet you, Mr. Fucking Trannies In Bathrooms."

I blush and take her hand. Cynthia stands off near the front's rustic little windowpanes, and narrow drink counter, lining up a drug deal on her phone. Brynn tell me about the bar, clearly (and wisely) not accepting my queries as sincere. I upgrade to hometown queries, which are met with only the most obligatory responses. I'm being profiled. Harshly.

I say, "I've never met anyone from Montana before."

She's had enough: "Well I've met *plenty* of tranny bathroom fuckers before."

"Well, you know, that's, like, half of New York City, so..."

"Uh huh. And where are *you* from? Let me guess... OHIO."

I slap on of my Reefs down on the bar: "Gulf coast. Florida. I'm a beach savage. Just got off the plane."

"Don't listen to anything he fucking says," says Cynthia.

"We've been trying to squeeze him into a pair of shoes for two weeks," Lase follows. "His feet-"

"Oh, yeah, I just had a-"

"My GOD."

"I can't even imagine," Brynn sneers.

"Most of Gene eventually grows on you, but not-"

"Not the feet, no, no..."

"Exactly."

Satisfied with that, Lase and Cynthia form a drug score huddle back in the corner, and Brynn simply pulls closer to me, elevated on her heavily stickered bartender chair.

"You can smoke in here."

"Hrm." I sip my fancy tequila.

"Really."

"How about that. You're out-*standing.*"

"Am I?"

"Oh yes. I'd drink your bathwater."

"Vomit."

"I would..."

"No, just don't."

"... work in a Mexican carwash for you?"

"That's better. But don't."

"Hrm. Do you want some ecstasy?"

"Do I want some... no, no I do not want some *ecstasy. Jesus.* Is that your girlfriend?"

"Oh god no."

"Seems to me she's taking care of you. Sugar mama for the poor writer cliché. Aren't you a little old for *Midnight Cowboy?*"

"It's for a child. I'm trying to save a child and-"

"Uh huh?"

"She seduced me with hard drugs and oral sex."

"That's the short version, is it?"

"The essence of it, yeah. When you strip it down to its bare components, it's not very sexy, is it?"

"Un-fucking-believable," she mutters, looking intensely at me, our noses only a few inches apart, the type of scene I always lived for. And don't I feel foolish now, made to understand that I'm living for it still.

Brynn fishes around under the cash register a moment, producing a pack of American Spirits and a book of matches. She slaps a large plastic ashtray down on the bar.

"Let's start with the ear. Where the fuck is your earlobe?"

"So I've got to transcribe the thing, all two hundred pages, and mail this to him."

"In Sydney?"

"Sydney, yeah. He's slightly retarded. Or maybe just really severe Asperger's. It's kinda hard to tell these days. That whole Wes Anderson indie rock thing."

"Not to sound like a superbitch, but isn't $200 a little low for an original manuscript?"

"I don't know. It is not something you... writing on a computer, as everyone does of course, there is no such thing. So it's definitely a novelty, a..."

"It's unusual, yeah."

"But I'm not famous, so..."

"How are you transcribing it?"

"Reading it into a tape recorder. This one here-"

"Turn it on."

"It's on."

"And then you have to, well, you're not really... is recording, like, a spoken recording isn't transcribing, more like a trans-"

"Transposition?"

"And anyway, then you have to transcribe *that*. So what's the point of..."

"To get this guy off my back."

"Is he like, e-mailing or-"

"Yeah, yeah. But he'll start calling."

"What are you guys doing tonight?"

"Lase is playing a show at Bowery Electric."

"I like Lase."

"Yeah."

"His wife's really sweet."

"Yeah."

"How old are you?"

"45."

"No you're not."

"35."

"Hm. Maybe you should grow your hair out."

"I feel like I'm butting heads with New York, again… like…"

"Wow, where did that come from?"

"I don't know, I could tell you all about this wine. I've read a hundred articles about it."

"Who cares. What did you mean by that?"

"I don't know. It's like I'm not supposed to be here. I got an email from someone, last week, a few weeks ago, that said people were out for my blood here."

"I bet you were a nightmare when you were young."

"I'm still young"

"Not really. No, not *really*, sweet baby."

"You were doing okay, but now you sound like an art student, like an NYU-"

"Oh fuck you. Like, okay, for one thing, you're *way* the fuck off."

"It's a harmless dig. All I said was-"

"All *I* said was… and I'm right, is that… oh, I can see it too. You were one of those hot mess kids. Fucking Pete Doherty."

"I smoked crack and that stuff. But I was too cool for that hipster shit. I still am. "

"Honey, you're getting *old*. You oughta-"

"You ever smoke crack?"

"Fuck no."

"But you'll do coke, though."

"Hardly ever. Is that where your friends went?"

"I guess."

"Where did *you* go to school?"

"I didn't."

"You didn't…"

"I *didn't*. I didn't *go*."

"How do you not *go*?"

"I got married and got a job. Actually, I-"

"So? A lot of people do that. But you went to *school*, I mean-"

"I never even went to high school."

"That's crazy."

"I married a Jehovah's Witness, and got a cat. And a job. See that on my neck? That's my cat."

"I bet you hate your mother."

"*Of* course."

"And you probably beat your wife."

"Not *really*. So you're about 30, aren't you?"

"I'm 29."

"I didn't mean to-"

"Chivalry's dead. So why do you hate your mother?"

"You can take that from so many angles, and with any fucking guy, I mean, an objective analysis is gonna turn up some degree of misogyny but…"

"Oh great. I get to hear this shit for the millionth time. You're a letdown, Gene. And you started off with such a-"

"I'm an individualist. Any halfway intelligent person is. So all that matters, all that's on the table, if you are assesst-assest-"

"Spit it out Gene!"

"ASSESTIMATING! If you're ass-*sess*-ing meeeee, okay? How am I on an individual level? Am I compassionate? Am I generous? Am I ROMANTIC? It *IS* romantic! I am the consummate fucking non-partisan, bitch!"

"Hahhahhahhah... Gene!"

"Put the rest on the fucking table! Slap it down! Slap it down! MISOGYNIST! So what? Individualist! MISANTHROPE! So what! Individualist! RACIST! So what? Individualist!"

"Oh, you are just... delightful. But I want to pet you, you're like a crazy old... like a bear. Or no, a... I don't know, but you got out of the zoo and got, like, hit by a *bus*..."

"Listen..."

"I'm not having sex with you, Gene."

"I thought this was about... man. I really do NOT miss New York right now."

"New York does not miss you."

"Uh... I've seen the other *side* of that attitude, and it's not pretty. I've seen the zombies of that thought, like, 20 years later... they gave their *lives* to New York, for, like, nothing."

"I've seen a lot of people come and go in two years. It's really not for everybody."

"I'm talking about the opposite. People who *should* go, and *don't.*"

"Who *should* go?"

"Anyone who isn't happy."

"You know a lot of happy people?"

"It's hard to be 'happy' with a fucking brain in your head. I strive to be engaged, but happy-"

"Have you ever killed anyone?"

"Well, shit."

"Have you?"

"Maybe. No."

"I bet you've beaten people up. You beat women up, you ever beat a woman?"

"BEAT, I mean, that's such a strong, like-"

"You fucking douche!"

"Oh, hey-"

"DOUCHE bag!"

"But she hit me with an ashtray! A GLASS ashtray! You see this scar?"

"That's HORRIBLE. I would NEVER date you."

"You want me to go?"

"You can go if you *want*. I'm just saying I would never-"

"Well..."

"I'm sorry. It's none of my business, and if you're not *IN* the relationship-"

"-you shut the fuck UP about the relationship."

"BAD Gene! Oh!"

"I'm sorry."

"DOUCHE bag!"

"I'm a mega-douche, I'm *ne plus ultra* douche."

"You're *tortured by life!*"

"This, fucking CITY tortured me, I can tell you that."

"Where are you actually FROM?"

"Never *mind* where I'm *from*. This city tied me to a rack, you understand? Baltimore kicked me when I was down, Baltimore beat me up, you know? But New York tortured me..."

"It's you! It's all your baggage!"

"It's *money*, is what it is. Everything in this life comes down to *money*."

"Well, it ain't a *cheap* city!"

"It's a cheap-*shot* city. It's got that sneak thief *shittiness*. But I had some incredible nights. Maybe the best nights. So good I can't remember them. Remember... oh shit, you wouldn't remember."

"Anyway, I'm a pretty balanced person. I don't have all that baggage. I came from a really good family. It's like... I feel like there's something wrong with me because I don't hate my family. I'm like, the only girl in New York who doesn't hate her family."

"Hrm."

"Hrm. You're cute. I like you, Gene. You're not scary. I mean, you are, but... oh! Uh uh. Can't do it."

"Too much nutsness."

"*Way* too much nutsness. And you hate women."

"And dogs."

"Well... that's understandable."

"So there's hope?"

"Not even a little."

-169-

It's making my head hurt. My heart is, the *rest* of me is... laughing? Relieved? Abso*lutely* relieved to have survived the New York voodoo, the suck-tide of moneypussydopeart New York infantilism, of punk fable, punk fairytale, punk myth. Physically, my head HURTS though, throbbing like one of my bastardized fairy tales come back in the form of a black widow bite, or one of my abscessing toes. A memory returns, little triggers in all the honking taxis dim bulbs and sewer gas expensively bundled sexpots from Finland and Estonia Japan Australia rushing in and out of hipster gift shops of boutiques of Indian restaurants of apartment buildings, what things used to cost and how I *spent* money in those days, sniffing coke on a table with an original 1965 hellraiser, me saying, "I bet you know what happened to Andy Warhol's old Factory furniture, the places that got water damaged in '72,"and being told by the bored gentlemen, "we're *sitting* on it, you're sitting *at* it right now, boy this is lousy coke..."

The sleet builds, thickens in the blinding night air my nose numb in the lights of bars on Avenue A, Avenue B, back to the bar lights of Second Avenue, back down to Houston, all those bars haunted by dead people, or famous people, some people famous *and* dead, when you find out how it *really* works in the belly of the beast in the glow of Sidewalk Café, at 6th and A. I remember Rockets the poor evil drunk who never could let go of downtown at all, and bumping into Patti Smith at the grocery store – she was always so sweet – and bloody cab rides reaching for what the MOVIE would have been because didn't I come here to ESCAPE hick reality reaching for MOVIE scenes one out of fifty ain't bad but you paid the price Gene Genie the names come back the winters come back pussy a way-off far-out beacon in the ugly BROOKLYN WINTERS like a beacon and before you can ENJOY the HEAT only a LITTLE simulated MOTHERING (DTs just rearing its ugly head) the girl's gone or you're gone (puppy dog stumble down Borough Hall subway steps a real kicked out bed sadness, runt of the litter blues) before a single wound feels a glimmer of healing, even my first date with Lydia at Connie Berg's place was that East Village, no it was Chelsea, tail end of history last time ANYONE was cool, and I WAS cool, wasn't I cool okay wasn't I dangerous then? But worst of all somehow no I know exactly how is the chill full body gutted winded and chilled when I light a cigarette on Bowery and Bleecker, the mouth of Bleecker Street where I took my first-ever girldate a pudgy redhead from Wisconsin who did *not* care for me it was 1993 and it was July the kind of summer in NY that leaves black soot in your hair an hour after leaving the hotel, I was 16 with cigarette burned arms and pimples and hadn't they all only just died, GG Allin the month before but in the last 24 months it was *wide*: Kurt Cobain, Frank Zappa, Johnny Thunders, Charles Bukowski, Bill Hicks, and several others besides... Rob Tyner? But the 1993 destination for the Harrisburg busboy and the Manitowoc waitress (both dropouts) was the natural fixation for all literate minimum wage kids of all nationalities in 1993 when the cracks were showing alright, it was CBGBs, wasn't it, where no good band had played in a solid decade but so what, because wasn't it a fact that the place was barely even swept clean of empties from the magic years, and aren't they all original fixtures and seats where Lester Bangs puked and Richard Hell told reporters to read Lautréamont, where John Belushi plied the Dead Boys with cocaine and Lou Reed skulked eerily too good for it all?

But it is gone, and in its place only a glowing white box of a store. And that's what I take in as my phone begins to ring: an empty boutique. I look in there, I make eye contact with the shop clerk. My brain is all lit up, neurons firing over and over again but nothing happens... I lie to myself, "It's just time and it's gone..." and I never got laid at CBGBs anyway, or... was it Lydia who... and BANG! The last time I ever saw the famous CBGBs skank-queen who became my common law wife for three years but in Los Angeles (THIS IS HOW IT CAME FULL CIRCLE, and then RETURNED, FOOL'S GOLD, BACK TO FUCKING NOTHING) we produced a book, *two* books together, one was published and one was not, not for 15 years, anyway, the year was 2003 and BEGUN this way, Lydia and I were over, I returned, a puddle of shit (psychosexual oblivion, yup) to Pennsylvania August 2002, and the winter approached, the holiday passed, and it came to light that Lydia wanted to reconcile, that the book release was planned for February at CBGBs, so I go to New York and I've begun drinking vodka, it was a deadly pursuit of terminal bad drinking, and how was it I wound up that New York morning in the home of Nick Tosches, he in his bathrobe and the two of us staring at each other without words and chainsmoking Camels, me, "Do you want to go get a drink?" Nick, "No," me, "Are you coming to CBGBs tonight Lydia's in town." Nick, "No." and that's the kind of impression I leave on people although Nick did tell me, "That's a great fucking magazine" and "Good to see you, buddy."

On the way out I realized that I'd been to this building once before, teased into a volcanic madness by a friend's scheming hateful wife, Maureen who I had pursued in full view of both her simpleton husband and my heartbroken ex Lydia, and it was a Christmas party (so, only weeks prior to the CBGBs event?) and I'd tried to throw myself off the 7th floor, off the roof in fact, so sadly bent and bewitched by the homely little brat and THAT is why, leaving the poignant, impositioned, and awkward Tosches visit, the grim realization hit me and even THEN I knew New York was gone to my soul or that my HEART had grown hostile to New York and that I ought to never come back here... at the book release party I was propositioned by THREE women and lost them all when I made a play to... well, Lydia was not amused, and I was wearing all black dressed to emulate my guitar hero Steve Wynn (looking sharp is nothing to be ashamed of) and I was rude to all of my friends I rolled around on the ground throwing rubbery punches at Lydia's guitarist and it was vodka vodka vodka all night, a crummy way to get loaded, that was my last night. For CBGBs, my last night for

Lydia Lunch, and should have been my last night for New York, why the hell can't I just-

"Hello!"

"Gene! Richard Wellington here."

"They turned CBGBs into a shop."

"A what?"

"A clothing shop. CBGBs!"

"Oh yes, they did. They did, yeah. Gene, I'm *in* New York, ok? I'm here, and I've... I've got Miss Lisa *Carver* with me. And Bec, so... where *are* you, my friend."

I hang up. The shop clerk and I keep staring at one other through the front window.

I consider all the *other* staring that must go on, taking a last drag on my cigarette.

I shudder at the thought that no one bothers.

-170-

Bowery Electric is a basement club a block away, a basement club in the sense that the concert room is subterranean, but you enter via a ground floor lobby with a ground floor bar, and it seems to me rather like an impersonal cross between one of those fraudulent "independent cinemas" (read: independent video projection room) and a velvet-curtained meat locker. I catch the last song and there's a hyper-stimulated bag lady making rock 'n' roll faces in the first row so I watch from the rear of the room, it's a painfully forced pantomime of hair and tattoos and scene kids who look like Japanimation versions of The Ramones, the music and the band nothing more than spit-polished glam garage: it's as if someone came in with a surgeon's blade and disconnected all the sexual panic, leaving all traces of good faggot energy to be drowned out by the witless snark of *Saturday Night Live*. I'd be doing rock 'n' roll history a favor by tossing a few grenades in there.

Backstage, Lase is like a starved poodle with his Lizard King hair, and brothel creepers, and dinner jacket, his thick black unibrow damp and twitching as I hug him, and squeeze his shoulders conscious of the lies I'm about to tell. The band pretends to know who I am (names: Feral, Raphael, and Howie). Cynthia is *still* making her retarded rock 'n' roll faces and there are women backstage also; I'm pussy crazed and humiliated by the effortlessness with which these RAWK ELITE accept the duck as my girlfriend. She's doing lines off a Wizard Sex CD while babbling about Ronnie Spector and it's the type of thing you and your companion would politely excuse yourself from after a half hour, rolling your eyes wordlessly once safely back on the street, because you're too *old* for *drink tickets* and glam rock narcissism and novelty retro, but lazy preeners

Wizard Sex get that good coke in me so we end up singing "What It Takes" by Aerosmith and there's a good feeling in the room until the iPod session begins and the band starts gibbering about the New York Dolls now playing through thousand dollar speakers from a thousand dollar cellphone's hard drive, and when they sing the words, the first line of "Frankenstein", they're not thinking what I'm thinking, they couldn't possibly, could they?

-171-

GG: We're on Metropolitan, right?

Lase Salgado (vocals, lead guitar): Uh... Howie, what's this-

Howie Unger (drums): It's Metropolitan, yeah, and... Lorimar, the Lorimar stop.

GG: Kellogg's Diner, oh yeah. Kellogg's Diner days. There was a guy called, um... shit, remember Larry Clark's movie *Kids*? Those kids had a... a...

LS: Macho, you'll love this place, get the, you gotta try the... don't be ordering any fucking pork in front of me, get the number three noodle bowl-

GG: Duck fat.

LS: Gene, that's really fucked man, don't-

GG: Okay, this place used to be-

Feral Wheatley (bass): Man, it's-

GG: Go ahead, like we were saying, get that on here-

FW: Lase says CCR, and Raphael says Creedence, but the best-

Gaby Oleander (Raphael's girlfriend): Here we go.

GG: I'll have to get your name. I used to do this for... I was always recording this kind of crap for the punk newspaper, where it has all the banter, "guitarist's girlfriend", you know.

GO: Okay, I'm out of here.

LS: (laughing) Gaby, come on.

GO: You're fucking GROSS, dude.

GG: Dude, hahhah. People say dude like that, really? *Still?*

GO: Why don't you have some more coke? Raph, he's been staring at my legs all night.

Raphael LaRocca: Oh, man. Gene, put that away!

Cynthia Maviano: Gaby honey, let's have a drink at the bar.

GO: Fucking ASSHOLE. I own my own (UNINTEL). Dirtbag...

CM: Come on, honey. I'm sick of him, too. Let's go.

GG: Do you guys want-

RL: Dude.

FW: Not in the restaurant.

GG: I was on the verge of - this is for *Sex & Guts*, okay? Which you guys never saw.

LS: I've got one, Gene.

GG: When I lived in Brooklyn, uh, right over there by the dinner, actually, I was on the verge of – see, this was a bar, it was Old Man... I don't remember his name, Old Man Lastnameczechoslovakian, Old Man... well, his name was Steve, it was just Steve's Bar, and Old Man Steve, see it's all *Blade Runner* in here tonight, with the fancy lanterns and the rain and all, but this was *Steve's*, and there was none of this hipster aren't we CUTE ain't life fuckin CUTE kinda shit-

HU: Lase, man-

LS: Go with it, trust me-

HU: But he's not interviewing us...

GG: We're gettin there, ok? But with Steve, I took a crazy girl there, a punk girl who got kicked out of the fuckin United States MARINES, okay, she's an award winning documentarian now, I took her to Steve's and got kicked out, because it wasn't all cutesy, everybody's dick in the next guy's hand kind of bar, Old Man *Steve* say, "You drink UP and get OUT." Hahhahhahhah! You know?

RL: Have fun guys. Lase,I'll call you.

Waiter: Yes, okay?

LS: Number three noodle bowl, and... Raph, come on!

CM: I want that too.

GG: I want pork rolls. Where's, no don't leave!

CM: Lase, just ignore him, he's not gonna eat anyway.

Waiter: Pork-

LS: No pork, just two number 3's, and the veggie pepper pot... Howie?

HU: No, man. Just get me another beer.

LS: Two number 3's I guess, just that, and then... beer for everyone? Ok.

GG: See, it wasn't that we were masochists, but we just couldn't *communicate*, and there was that *feeling* of having to tear things apart, and sometimes you tore *people* apart, and sometimes you *got* torn apart.

CM: Gene, what are you-

LS: Let'm finish.

HU: You mind if I get some of that?

CM: OF COURSE! Gene, no more for you.

GG: Yeah, it was early, like maybe one the afternoon, and Liz lived over in Greenpoint. It was snowing and Steve told us to get out, we were already drunk, and Liz kept licking my face, she had a crooked mouth and she was always farting in front of me, she was trying to be a dyke but the thing was, she was just shy with guys so all this macho dyke shit came out. And it was super cold, right after Christmas, and we're heading down Metropolitan, Liz is super skinny, and muscular, she's a Marine, like a fucking... six feet tall, six *TWO*.

CM: So you have studio time booked, guys? Talk about he album.

GG: She's a trained killer dyke assassin psychobitch from Detroit. No... Chicago. She's... oh, and that movie *Fight Club* had just come out, and me and Liz , we were doing that kinda shit anyway, it was like, like I was saying, the whole city was nothing but damage cases, and me and Liz always had banged open knees and elbows, and none of the sex we ever tried to have with anyone ever worked out, so – like, all this insane confused energy-

CM: Oh you were just kids.

GG: it was horrible. Kids are... well, we weren't trying to *be* anything, like, aren't you supposed to, I see the flipside when the new kids, it's like little brats trying to be 50, but neither nor, you know? Anemic. But me and Liz, and well, everyone, we used to shoot, these other guys, we were SO fucked up, like... short circuiting robots, like... half of our personalities, half of our brains were just, GONE so we're just smashing into each other as hard as we could, and we were TERRIFIED of each other, I bet we really were douche bags but, the drugs wasn't a normal way of being druggy, oh well maybe we were just, but Liz didn't do anything but get drunk really quick on martinis and then she'd wanna get crazy, so when Steve – right here, this place, can you imagine it, just a plain old neighborhood bar, a 50s style, like *Last Exit to Brooklyn*, a Hubert Selby place, that's what it was, and it was snowing, which would make, it makes you think of home and Christmas and your mom but you're a young suicidal moron turned loose in this... like...

LS: Is this in the new book, macho?

GG: I'm not... no. But, so Liz-

CM: Thank you.

GG: HEROIN! *King* heroin. *Real* rock stars do Big H.

FW: Lase, we gonna do the heroin thing for the *next* album.

GG: Yeah, do *that*, record *that* shit, and, like, I'll transcribe it, like how Steve Albini *records*, you know? I'll *transcribe*. This band tried to get me to manage them, they were called Patty Hearst Army. I said, "You gonna change your name?" And HEROIN. Like, the next level.

LS: That's like-

CM: That's the worst band name ever. Like, Anton Newcombe, hello?

GG: So Liz falls, hurts her leg, like, REAL bad-

FW: Oh, we gotta - Liz is HOT. Right?

GG: She's crying! There's *no one* on the streets but us, and she's crying, fucking two feet of snow, and I try to carry her but I keep slipping on the ice, and it... it became this real Vietnam-type scene.

CM: Did you get her back to... wait, you're trying to get to your place?

GG: Yeah. Poor Liz is wearing her.... she's in fatigues, basically, and Chuck Taylors, and I'm in my Sid Vicious getup, leather jacket

and t-shirt in the dead of winter, just.... misery.

CM: You brought it on yourself.

GG: We were as hard, or as harsh, as the conditions. And it was SNOWING! The only sound in the world is fucking Liz bawling, "I broke my leg, Gene, it's BROKEN," but she keeps biting me and licking my face! And I'm all turned on, so I'm telling her, "This time I'm gonna TAKE your pussy," because Liz was totally my older sister,so that was never the point, it was never-

LS: Yeah, yeah. And it would ruin your thing.

GG: But now I *want* it! It's all of the sudden, it's *hot*, but is she really that fucked up, with her leg?

FW: Is she?

GG: I don't *know!* I didn't know. So I get her to my place on Havemeyer, Nick Zedd the famous loser lives across the street, and, okay, this will give you an idea how fucking COLD it was, okay? I get her up to the second floor, we're, we can't even *talk* because our fuckin *teeth* are chattering so hard, and-

HU: Is Liz hot?

GG: This is 20 years ago, I don't-

HU: *Was* she hot?

GG: She was my *sister*, how do *I* know? I'm trying to save her life, but yeah, I'm telling her, "That pussy's mine," you know? And I get my key in the lock, and she starts *puking* up the cheap vodka she was drinking at Steve's all over the mosaic tiles, and the puke just immediately freezes, but I'm thinking, "no big deal," you know. Nice blankets, good New York steam heat *inside*, you know, but – and there's blood all over too, from her leg, which is just smashed real bad, it's not broken-

HU: But what's she look like?

GG: Blonde dreads, she had dreadlocks... Liz was... she coulda been a model, she had that Germanic model look, but... no ass. She was all muscle and teeth. I mean, frail, you would *think* to look at her, gawky, and *long*, but *dangerous*, Liz was.... well, she was trained to kill. Blonde Milla Jovovich.

HU: Alright, alright.

GG: Her face was always screwed up. She was angry all the time. See, *now* I'm into her. Anyway, the key snaps off in the lock-

CM: No.

GG: *Oh* yeah.

LS: Fuck!

GG: But the stem is sticking out, and I've got the little handle part, and I can see, like, I put it back together just pressing the two pieces as had as I can, thinking, with enough pressure, maybe I can turn it over. Liz is passed out. I can smell the puke. So, I hold it fucking TIGHT, and twist, and my hand slips off to the right, across the broken tip, and I'm cut, real bad, like, along the edge of my thumb, I can see all this white fat coming up.

CM: Oh for Christ's sake. This is really good, Lase. Gene-

GG: Now, if you can imagine, my thinking is, "Well, I'm hurt now too," and the blood is just pumping right out – I try it twice more-

FW: OH! Anything with the hands I can't deal with, the hands is... bad.

GG: I had to give up. I left Liz there, and I went to this cabstand a few blocks away and called for a locksmith.

CM: Oh god. That happened to me on 6th St. Hundred bucks.

GG: That's how much it was, yeah. But this cabstand, I went there hurt or in a jam all the time, and they hated me, these Arabs. They'd curse me, like, shake their heads, laugh at me, but you know, they *always* took perfect care of me.

CM: So they dressed your hand?

GG: They dressed my fucking hand!

CM: See, after all your New York bashing bullshit-

HU: I think the whole story's bullshit.

GG: Well, it took the locksmith an hour, and we were in bad shape. I needed stitches. We got back in there, and I got Liz's leg wrapped up, so... about 5 or 6, it's getting dark, and we're... well, we're *up* but I'd never stopped drinking, I had a bottle of Jack Daniels or something, a whole fifth, and I got Liz drinking it, and as soon as she was a little loosened up I started with the pussy thing again, you know, "I'm taking that pussy, Liz," and she's getting into all the dyke stuff, but I just, maybe I forgot it was a joke, or maybe it really *wasn't* a joke, but I fucking went for it, and she *fought* me, hard! But I'd already taken her clothes off, well, I took her pants and coat off, when I was putting her to bed, but Liz is built like a, she's like a mantis, and all those arms and legs, so we tore the apartment up real bad, my cats were terrified-

CM: Those poor cats.

GG: She, at one point she scratched my whole face open, my forehead and my, like, down along my ear, and-

FW: Wow.

GG: Dog tags and everything. She got into it, once I'd, you know, stuck it in her. She started licking my face, so I knew we were cool. But the whole apartment was ruined. I couldn't believe it when we woke up. Liz wouldn't shut up, "You *RAPED* me," you know. But it was, I mean, we went out for sushi.

CM: Who paid for that?

GG: Oh, I don't know. Probably me. So after that, Liz started going after guys, trying all the time to get fucked, but she always wound up with, I think it was five guys in a row she took home who were impotent, whiskey dick or however she said it. SO now, she's a dyke again, but, a *real* dyke. I really liked Liz. She was a *creature*.

Everyone... well, not everyone, obviously, but I knew some real creatures back then.

LS: Should I tell him, Cynthia?

CM: Tell him – *oh*. Sure, he's a big boy.

GG: Oh what the fuck now.

LS: You didn't notice the posters at Bowery Electric?

GG: No. Is it-

LS: I saved you a flyer. Guess who. *You* know this woman.

GG: What, Lydia Lunch is coming? Is that what-

LS: She's *here*, macho. The show's tomorrow.

GG: Oh, *really*. Hah. How do you like that.

LS: You wanna-

GG: Absolutely not. No, no. What the fuck for?

CM: I told you.

GG: Yeah. Bad idea. What is it, a music gig? She has another band?

LS: Big Sexy Noise

GG: That's the name? Big Sexy *Noise*? It should be called Big Sexy NOSE. Lydia's nose is huge. That's why she always has it airbrushed out of her photos. But I like that.

Waiter: Noodle bowl?

TAPE CUTS

GG: I never found out how Howie says CCR.

HU: *Lase* says CCR. Raph says, um, he just says *Creedence*, but *Feral's* right, doesn't *Feral-*

FW: I say CC *Revival*. That's how you're supposed to-

LS: Howie's the one who always comes up with, he has the best, but it's not CCR, it's-

HU: (coughing) (laughing) Wow.

GG: Nasal drip. It's clean. I told you, didn't I tell-

HU: I'm not into that whole agrarian scene. Leave me out-

GG: Holy shit! That's is so beyond dick! That is *super-dick*. I'm not into that *agrarian* scene. I'm... oh, that's just wonderful.

HU: Yeah, and leave me out of it.

GG: It's called Fleet Foxes now. It's CCR with the nuts clipped. That's *hard*-core AGRARIAN. But I wanted to get into the whole writer-rock star thing.

LS: "The worst rock musician in the world gets a tight cunt in a miniskirt every time he leaves the house." Another Gene classic.

FW: Is this actually coming out? Is it a real thing?

-172-

At the Coachhouse, Cynthia's cheeseburger grows cold as she stares at a copy of *USA Today*, a special edition devoted to Hurricane Sandy. The full color front-page photo of an eight-story wooden rollercoaster re-situated several hundred yards off the coast of Seaside Heights, New Jersey is a real eye-catcher. She blubbers and moans: all the summers, all the summers, all the summers. I ask her about her parents. I tell her I understand.

"That image will be everywhere today," I tell her. "Maybe we'd better stay in and do drugs."

The city, the region, the Palisades, the whatever, smells like wet cardboard, wet dog, wet upholstery.

"I've got to work today," she mumbles distractedly, waving for the check and dabbing at her bloodshot eyes. "I've got to meet Joe to sign divorce papers."

"Jesus"

"Yeah. It's going to be a long day."

NECROPOLIS NOW

(PART THREE)

In youth we were whole and the terror and pain of the world penetrated us through and through. There was no sharp separation between joy and sorrow: they fused into one, as our waking life fuses with dream and sleep. We rose one being in the morning and at night we went down into an ocean, drowned out completely, clutching the stars and the fever of the day.
Henry Miller, *Black Spring*

"Ellen honey, it's Gene. GENE. No no, why would you think – oh! Oh, I get it. You're... yeah, that's real cute. Oh wow. Yeah. Oh yeah, but you can't... no, you can't count on it, but it's certainly a boost, yeah... who? *White Stripes* Jack White? Well no shit, what was that like? Again today, really? Yeah, I could, but... how did you know... yeah...no, that sounds great, but I'm not a fan, and... oh, I didn't mean it like that... no, not at all... because, have you heard The Gun Club? I *am* happy for you, it's big deal, and why wouldn't I... I... no, I didn't mean it like that... a few more days, I guess... so... I should do an interview with you, Stylist of *the* Stars, or... that was Sarah you're thinking of, her dad, yeah... John Waters' moustache, yeah... no, I think what you're doing is cooler... yeah... I didn't? Well, I will, I'll... as soon as I get home... but... a few more days, yeah, I... right *now* I'm homeless, I mean... no, the book is selling but I lost my wallet... I've, what? Who? Oh for Christ's sake Ellen, no I did *not* forget... it was an accident! I can't believe that... well I almost died! So? I'll buy you a new one! This year! Because... that is so fucking rude... I'm not ask- that's not why I called... just a hundred... I love you too... no, but jesus, can you let me get myself together first? Jealous of what? I'm not a fucking hairdresser, am I? No, I'm... yeah, so what? I've got to eat, don't I? It's not... who cares about the fucking White Stripes? That's... no, but... I'm not asking you for money, Ellen, I've... I don't need that, I've got money in PayPal, but my card, I got robbed in Florida, and... it's *not* bullshit... no, but sweetie... I'M GOING TO BUY YOU A NEW FUCKING COUCH! JUST AS SOON AS I DON'T FREEZE TO DEATH? No, it's not, see... I'm sending... no, I'm sending money to *YOU*, see? No, but... look, I'll just take your number out of my... fine... honey, I think you're fantastic, I've *never* been mad at you! It's...fuck no, she's awful, why would I... which I think is fantastic, is... no, it's... it makes me happy to know that... we've been friends for ten years! Yes! I love you too, and... right, but it's not... I'll send you... but you'll actually read it, won't you, this thing with the... oh yeah, it hurt, but now it's... I'm a comic book thing, a sideshow... I love you too! It's really great... I'm so happy for you... I promise, at least once, while I'm, before I go.... Yes... just a few hundred... Western Union..."

I curse myself my being too distracted-lazy-sick-bipolar-ugly-drunk-venal-fake-restless-miserable to remember my computer in Cynthia's car now that I'm ready – all that aforementioned out of my system (but not *really* if-) so as to begin my work, the long day ahead with the Monastrell late (late-late-late) orders and the laying of foundations for the...for... and on the kitchen counter, the poorly refurbished junk, are my eyes that had, my vision was, did they say, back in Florida when the, nine mile bike ride to The Eyeglass Factory when I saw the ad on TV at the Blind Pass Laundromat, warm mornings like that, I *rode* across the intracoastal, tropical birds by sight *and* sound, a *friendly* planet with *plenty* of direct sunlight, after a good week in the boiler room I says, "I'll *buy* me some goddamn glasses" so lazy-immature-senseless-drunk-pathetic, so sick of not being able to see killing them with squinting (dok-tah my *EYES*) and I make my plans known to mama she is sympathetic "no honey, let me pay for them, sounds like a good deal two pairs for 120" and so I rode, across the backs of alligators and the herons crisscrossing pelicans diving I rode and arrived stinking, "you have 20/70 vision," is that bad, "you have bad eyes" with a smile, and that was all included yup, now my glasses are... gone... or maybe... Beach Storage... the godless rows... Mama, she gave me the whole 120 and more, too, I had lunch at Taco Bell a half dozen Rolling Rocks at Taco Bell while they made the lenses I rode all nine miles in the summer sun *nearly 40 years old* – the sun burning here too dirty Jersey sun all the dirty ice drip drip drip– I watch the church, drip drip drip, watch the vacant lot and the back of the Chinese laundry but mainly the church squatting down over the neighborhood half the city pretends not to see, too cold for worship not in *there* I savor two, three, four bottles of Ballantine like wondering if I'll ever *do it* how the hell it'll *ever* get *done*, phone buzzing buzzing and then a text message from Ellen *keep it 4xmas luv u gene genie* light another cigarette like aw hell.

-175-

Into the ripped Radio Shack shopping bag goes a bottle of wine, beers wrapped in a swiped copy of the *Star-Ledger*, my tape recorder, the late book orders still tormenting me like diaper rash from the Sunshine State, and the bughouse manuscript which will have to be dictated (couldn't I have kept the scanner, and do I have another still in Florida?) as it is itself a late order, the simpleton Sam Fielder all-too-capable of God knows what, too hot-too cold in and out of my peacoat all the way down that part of JC's main artery where I enter a Western Union office and collect the bills using my passport which is all comforting enough a standard scene except that there are so *many* bills, "hundreds okay?" to which I replied, "sure" (which was *not* wise but anyhow) expecting two bills but I receive *ten* bills, a kook "K" with five twenties on top of that and maybe that's the part that rankles me so far sick 'n' sideways I'm not sure if it's the edge of Manhattan I see looming so far in the distance (YOU are HERE) or fucking Philly, I light a cigarette and

drag – wait for it... *there's* the *rattle* – and re-count the bills before
they drop from my numbing fingers and fan out on the brown
concrete beside the entrance to a large and impersonal family
restaurant, a brand new mega-corporate concern "The Pancake
Factory" as the morning drags into afternoon but ever brighter, ever
wetter water running loudly in the street splashing up from trucks
and buses ghostly outline above it all of the new building this
objectionable thing I wasn't meant to see THE WORLD TRADE
CENTER but it looks – even up close – like an apocalyptic nose hair
trimmer, the Norelco building, this awful feeling of eating shitting
earning spending LIFE, really overdoing it all East Coast slobstyle,
how the hell, where the hell (oh yeah, 'twas EUROPE) and a sorrow
again sweeping through the factory back lots and family restaurant
dish rooms, the garbage and slob-slop up to my armpits the
pollution of the new world and the new world hoarder scraping wet
hundreds and wet twenties off the sidewalk in my bare feet.

I enter The Pancake Factory and am quickly handed a fresh
styrofoam cup to begin drinking the superior Monastrell wine,
chuckling on way out about how *serious* everyone in there looks
about their food, a bracing horror to think that I may look like that
sometimes but of course I don't, it's a grim picture I tell myself (and
maybe I'm correct in skipping lunch for this reason) but I'm a
soulful chap interested only in non-alignment and non-partisanship
in non-industry in non-aggression, I'm ready to go having seen and
done it all knowing it well and truly, it's a hideous picture even the
Northern fisherman eventually knows his own sickbed as well as the
tides of industry the fallacy of all that coming and going of washing
in and washing out, the real dawn comes with neither light nor dark,
neither heat nor cold, neither emptiness nor fulfillment, it is the
cockeyed longing for that sharp right hook you barely see coming,
that acceptance, that mercy, that sly wink when you consider it was
only a few hundred years ago people were getting drawn and
quartered for simple theft. And the crucifixion... oh, you're god
damn right I'll be skipping a *few* things today, laughing over my
wine about pretending to have a gun in my pocket, it's a *good* day
to be half-alive.

-176-

Somehow I find myself in Journal Square, which appears
physically intact from 100 years ago: whirling, cacophonous Old
London congestion, apparently deliberate

Sunday afternoon overdose of carbon monoxide. Brazen.
Arrogant.

I pretend it's Piccadilly Circus pretend my Bud cans are pints of
bitter my cigarettes are limp french fries in the misery holes of

238

Derek Raymond's *Factory* novels but my station is one of many benches at the New Jersey Transit Authority's transfer center, where they roll in and out by the half dozen, and no matter how inert or impotent the fake spring day around them, the hundreds -- thousands -- of commuters remain an unbreakable, unending situation. I squint into the golden glare, through all the urban ritual and rise to follow Lea Morton -- it's *her* -- from a double-parked SUV into an office building but I'm nearly blindsided by another, Mindy Perret, getting out of a cab (fifteen years ago, *no* one lived in Jersey city, except Laura) and the cats are out now, do they think it's Spring, this crack in the ice before the onslaught of January-February-March, the benches the haunts the birds now a crummy oxidized old clock tower in the center of the square sending big apelike bellows out against the traffic and the thousands of windows so that I get the spins a little. Still fingering that wound, about how Jamie and I never had a chance in Harrisburg, how New York really could have been something but when I see my old Brooklyn tenement (hallway) friends Beeta and Christina standing beside my Radio Shack bag I know I'd better eat something except the distant past is no longer distant, I watch the buses full of commuters come and go at the heart of Journal Square. Every other woman seems to have a broad Slavic countenance, and I am guarded now, considering these haunts in the abstract, bits and pieces of women but gradually the thing becomes *benches,* the *other* benches of *other* pigeonshit fake springs particularly in my 20s and particularly in Brooklyn or the Village where I might take a bench for four or five hours with a book I was too... too fucking *dear* to know was an awful, truly, an awful book. Young people sicken you that way. Actually, I cannot think of one way I am *not* sickened by a young person. Beeta and Christine, why *them*? I remember that 15 years ago, my vision was poor, poor even *then*, and I never looked at people on the street, and I was really a combatant when it came to looking at people at my job (but I shouldn't have been that way, it made everything so much harder; was I really so afraid of them all?), and as a result my friends would drift from my life like waves often thinking that I had snubbed them on Bleecker St. or on 6th Avenue or Bedford Avenue or St. Mark's Place and honest to Jesus I couldn't SEE you guys! (but yeah I didn't want to. I really didn't want to, did I?)

Journal Square is large enough that there are some movie billboards and I look up at them and lock eyes with GODDAMN THAT'S SUSAN! The subway train when, it was only five or six years ago (seven or eight years *after*) but I'd sat on the train god know which train or why when cute dumb Suzie walks right past me and I was holding a book not reading it but just sitting there on a crowded train and we saw each other, then too, (like today) and me I snap to the cheap rationale that I'll *not* apologize there in front of all those people because it's been too many years and I'll never see that dull sweet redhead again anyway (was that '05, must have been, or '04) so now certainly certain I won't do that to either of us *again*, she's gone a little boxy in middle age, but not much and I've left my bag but that's okay, as long as no one thinks it odd – or notices – that we're the only ones running, Suzie and I, but I lose her after two blocks, winded and weirded out, I've lost her but not the reasons, the reasons I have to feel ashamed, ashamed of *being* ashamed, the reasons to feel so much *pity* for poor fucking Susan.

The chase has led me to a small liquor store where Frontera's Casa del Diablo is on sale for eight dollars, and lo and behold the used bookshop a block over which I am of course drawn to but this time I'll choose admirably, a smart book, which turns out to be the Dover Thrift edition of *Beyond Good and Evil*: perfect – at only two dollars plus tax – for a day like today when I return to my bench to find the late orders and the tape recorder untouched.

A two-story Burger King is necessary for many things, mainly French fries to feed the pigeons, and caffeine for my concentration, but in four hours I have dictated the entirety of *Dog Days 2* into my slim-line Sony handheld. The novel, as it is, could use some work. In fact, it's a travesty. And what hope there is for its improvement could be dashed with a few drops of water, or, in fact, just one push of a button: one wrong move. Anything could happen, even though I spoke *around* all those bus sounds.

The sun begins its retreat. I pat my bench on the back like a loyal hound, and Journal Square churns like an old washing machine. It's more than enough to pacify me that the post office is open until six, so that my late orders – including one large, rescaled package for a schizophrenic fan in Sydney – can be liberated into the postal slipstream. The moans, the threats, the insults, this will all continue unabated. My putrid, idiotic readers will precipitate and prearrange and provoke my every eruption. This insufficient, insufferable busload of jellyfish people will haunt my movements for years to come, I tell myself. But not forever. In Florida, I will teach myself to fish.

-177-

"*Ah*-nother Man's Treasure!"
"Cynthia."
"Gene."
"I'm..."
"You're?"
"Thank you. No, this is fine. Thank you."
"Gene, I'm busy. Where are you?"

"I'm at an Irish pub."

"Can you – okay, just let me – everything in that box is two dollars."

"I'm at an IRISH PUB."

"Gene, I *heard* you. If you're coming over here, can you bring some Thai food? Or I'll just call for delivery."

"Have you heard from Joe?"

"Why are you – no, and please mind your own business."

"You really sold that guy out to me. You might as well, have you considered-"

"You sound *really* fucking gone. I don't like – I'm telling you one more time to mind-"

"He threw you out in the street, at... at... on the *holidays*. Jesus, that's cold. So what you should do, is *black*-mail him and-"

"I'm gonna hang up. You leave that poor man alo- Gene, goddamn it, listen to me, listen to me because you will find yourself in a lot of trouble, that man's never done a *thing* to you."

"Oh for God's sake, I was only kidding."

"You were *kidding*? Gene- I'm..."

-click-

<ringing>

"*Ah*-nother Man's-"

"Oh COME on."

"I'm giving you one more chance."

"Look, I've... I'm just drunk, I'm sitting at this-"

"You're at an Irish pub, uh huh... you better try to sober up before-"

"Hey, let's go see Lydia at Bowery Electric after my reading!"

"That's... look, you can do what you want but I won't be part of it. I think you know better. I *hope* you know better. Someone's here."

"Bye."

-178-

I'm beginning to enjoy that "I should have left here hours ago" feeling, that spiteful energy that gets caught and twisted around in all the swirling drink, which whispers impishly at you from the urinal each time you visit it, "too late to stop now, buddy" and which usually means you've pissed off at least three people. The bartender is no longer putting the shamrock stamp in the cream head of my Guinness pints, and I'm just sensible (or spiteful) enough not to complain about it. The bullnecked, tribal-tattooed gentleman actually *is* Irish, and for a fleeting moment, a sweepingly romantic moment, I'd entertained the possibility of the two of us getting pie-eyed over another dozen pints and the entire Pogues discography when it became clear no one else was showing up.

Indeed it has been just the two of us: he switched off the jukebox to watch football in the middle of "Astral Weeks", every one of my attempts to explain to him who I am and what I do have gone *very* badly, and I refuse to take a hint.

It occurs to me that it was exactly ten years ago I found myself in identical circumstances, with an identical copy of *Beyond Good and Evil*. The aphorisms were of interest to me in those days. Now I like the proper chapters. The literally sensibility of a wetbrained autodidact is a curious thing, I muse, smiling at myself like a mentally handicapped child in the bar mirror. I'm never so fascinated - seduced! - by myself than when in the presence of a canine-like "Roddy" (that's what I've been calling him) in a freak-hostile tourist trap like this here ("James Joyce Authentic Irish Pub") and I'm absolutely sure that Cynthia will understand.

"Another Man's-"

"HELLO!"

"Gene, I'm working. Stop calling."

"But listen-"

"Quickly!"

"I've been thinking about it all, you know, you, me, CRIME, the absurdity of it, you know?"

"The absurdity of crime? What-"

"No, of *everything*!"

"Gene..."

"Listen - the great epochs of our lives are at the points when we gain the courage to re-baptize our badness as the best in us."

"You didn't write that. Come on."

"I didn't *write*-"

"You didn't *say* that."

"You didn't SAY that," I whine back at her. "Who the fuck... so fucking WHAT, I didn't say that. The point is, I don't DO that! In fact, I've gone out of my way to SUBVERT ALL PRESCRIBED NOTIONS of, of US, yeah, but not what I see as the *real* us but the Gene and Cynthia the WORLD SEES, and at least I'm DEALING WITH IT, you understand, it's an absolute ATROCITY, it's a... a... HEARTBREAKING, the way you have to justify, to EVERYONE, and for what? I mean, as if it's not bad enough, I don't have the backing of a major publisher, and the fucking AUDIENCE I want, I mean, do you think, for even three seconds, that *I* would *ever* let you go hungry, or let anyone *hurt* you? It's, you don't know my true nature at *all*, which is, it's really a-"

"Gene, honey, I'm work-"

"And you wont LISTEN! *You didn't SAY that*. Say what? It's about standing *up* to those impulses, rejecting that anti-hero worship, or *self*-worship, that, because, I mean, I'm NOT a badass, or, a... that DEMON thing, but..."

"Gene!"

"And the reason why is that, and you KNOW this Cynthia, I TAKE OUT MY OWN TRASH – which, if you had half my integrity-"

"BYE GENE."

"Fucking idiot," I mutter, slipping the phone book back into my dangling coat's side pocket, and when my eyes return to the bar –

"Time to nip this in the bud," Roddy says grimly, sliding a piece of register tape across the dark old wood.

"What – are..."

"Fifty-eight fifty," he explains, his thumb on the tape. "Do we understand each other?"

-179-

A punch of Aqua-Velva and the stabbing bone-ache of sudden heat when I enter Another Man's Treasure frozen stiff and liquefied with a magnum bottle of Gato Negro Carmenere and a bulging brown paper sack of Thai takeout.

I am sobered somewhat to encounter George, in his officer's finest with purple hearts and captain's bars and that alabaster cane: he is dressed for his own funeral and that changes my chemistry. I re-set my course or *attempt* such a thing, anyhow. Two young lovers stop browsing the racks to talk softly with Cynthia while George and I chuckle although it's not clear what is funny or *if* anything is funny: the door chimes. The lovers are gone. The Christmas holiday is over and now it is just the three of us, Cynthia and I tearing the paper cartons and styrofoam boxes out of the bag while George stares off at street traffic through the front window.

"I never got too nuts about that, all that *Asian* jazz, where they got the sue-*shee* and the egg *roll*, you know. I like a good pork sandwich, or a, a fried chicken dinner. No-no, you guys go ahead, ok? I'll pop in later, tomorrow, or..."

"But George! Tonight's Gene's reading, we thought you-"

"Cynthia goddammit hold your cup still," I snarl, pouring an inch of plonk across the top of the counter, exactly as *she* arrives.

-180-

It is George's voice I hear: "Meka, sweetheart!"

It is my hand I see, pouring wine, still spilling it, and it is too late when I turn directly into the deflated pout of a small dark Jewess...

"Hi, I'm Gene!"

Meka is in her early 30s, a reasonable facsimile of Cynthia's little sex troll Mimi back in West Palm. She regards me as a 6 foot herpes blister and places her hand on George's arm; forcing a weak smile, briefly, before letting Cynthia have it: "So this is why the receipts have been so poor. Cynthia, I need to talk to you-"

"Oh, Meka, I-"

"I need to talk to you right *now* in private."

"Oh, Meka-"

"What are you playing, what is that?"

"It's... why... The Oblivions..."

"*Christmas* music. Our holiday sales keep us going through the other 11 months, where is the fucking *Christmas*-"

"Christmas was 2 days a-"

"Meka," I simper, "I was just dropping some dinner off for Cynthia, I didn't mean to cause a problem."

"And now *homeless* friends in the store, Cynthia, I-"

"Hey, like, I'm not *homeless*, Me-"

"I need to see you *alone*, Cynthia. Now."

"Meka, that's unfair, I-"

"I'd better be going,"I say, inching toward the door.

"Stay *put*, Gene. I'm coming with you. Meka, I quit."

"Cynthia, I only want to talk with you, I think you're overreacting."

"I won't be spoken to that way. I've done nothing *wrong*."

"Nothing *wrong?* You're lucky I didn't call the cops! *Three* people have come to me since I got home to tell me you're dealing *pills* out of my fucking *store*."

"I'm going to wait out front for-"

"Stay the fuck put, Gene. Meka, if this is about Joe, that's no one's business. I'm out of here. Fucking dealing PILLS... all the work I put into this fucking place... fucking assholes..."

The poor inflamed duck shoves and slams her way around the tiny enclosure until outfitted in coat and hat with a Shop-Rite bag full of CDs and buttons and makeup items and several bottles of Advil. I hold the door for George, but it's all I can do not to lunge through it first.

In the sleeting dark lamplight, I decide to double back for the food but Cynthia gets me by the scruff of my coat: "Don't you fucking dare."

"But I paid for it-"

"GENE? Goddamn it, shut up.SHUT UP!"

"I'm sorry."

-181-

Launching ourselves upon the wet Hudson night, we silently process all the negative energy, shame and black juju, mainly Cynthia's hurt, it's *her* time to shine: we take several blocks in this mildly panicked silence before arriving at Cynthia's car and the *idea* of Louise & Jerry's, for a few drinks to collect ourselves. George has been caught in a low-grade trauma bond, he's caught a case of it, of the mute witness sickness, the trapped rat sickness, caught some bad timing like road spray. But he's playing along, and that's standard protocol either as a New Yorker or a loyal friend, which isn't to say that it couldn't be *both* considering in earnest how big city friendship are: sentimental fabrications, alcohol tangents or sexual tangents always in pursuit of a putrid Frank Capra or John Hughes simulation. *That's* what a soft-headed puke, weakened by life, is always on the lookout for, a furtive ear cocked in anticipation like an oily Labrador camped out on its hung over owner's musty 9-year-old J.C. Penney's comforter. We are like that, waiting for a sign, a promise of MAWK, a MOVIE MOMENT and when summoned by some queer circumstance like Cynthia's firing, we say "RARF?" Then it's OUR time to shine, all thrown together by life, just patsies, living debris in the storm of life, this crazy killing life, this crazy thieving world, where we can at least duck into a basement tavern and see through this horrid hurting, this vulgar condition, this BEAUTIFUL EVERLASTIN TRAGEDY, this BLINDING NIGHT, and AT DAWN: when we wake up seven kinds of ugly, in bed together, we can pretend that IT, like US, like everything, happened completely by accident.

George swings his cane like he's out on a relaxed evening walk, his polished dress shoes so particular upon the wet chunk terrain and the whole of him a well-rehearsed elegance, even his exact vocal pitch when he says, "Cynthia, I'll never shop in there again," and "To hell with that little bitch," and "You'll find a better job, sweetheart."

Cynthia wipes away a tear, two tears, three tears, and she's done with that. We are all abuzz with all the many adorable discrepancies within our still-raw camaraderie, our ungainly outfit so overweeningly underdog, we may as well be on our way to fucking OZ when Cynthia, swollen with all the free-flowing pity like some kind of dolled-up puffer fish, orders me into the back seat.

"No-no," says beaming George in a hushed shout, "nothing doing. I'm fine in the back. "

But I shove the ALICE pack atop "quirky" Cynthia's collection of *Odd Couple* memorabilia, then myself against and half-underneath the ALICE pack before the Old Captain can argue further. (We are at Hal Hartley-stage already, which means the free-fall drop zone of Wes Anderson is around the next corner.)

Cue headlights, heater, braindead bubblegum in digital stereo: we're ROLLING. The two-door silver bullet back in play, past the shop, past the little take-outs she'll never order from again, past the drycleaners she'll never take shop merchandise to again, past all the other members of the Jersey City Shop Owners Guild – who themselves will never again buy drugs from the sweet old fat lady at

Another Man's Treasure.

And past the Jersey City Mall.

Past the Shop-Rite and past CVS.

Past the Holiday Inn and my memory of a sad old woman with her hair tied into a bun, with pursed lips and young breasts and wine euphoria, euphoric *postmodern* haunted, shimmering blue water and past the Holland Motel and the Holland Tunnel.

Past Super Liquors.

Past pasts, large and tiny pasts, recent and distant pasts, all barbed and jagged pasts, stinging my mania-lashed brain, buckshot pasts and birdshot pasts, like: the PATH train emerged at 6th Avenue and 8th Street (or was it 9th?), just opposite the Grey's Papaya hot dog stand where I was a hungover heartsick phantom kid in dirty black Levis and a tight Hanes t-shirt buying a half-dozen hot dogs in the April morning chaos to distract, to divert, I wanted to starve *with* the girl who'd kept me up all night, but three dogs and a large papaya drink (or was it a medium?) for two bucks was too good to pass up, romantic fasting or martyrdom be damned, my blueballed bone-thin mustard-stained 20 year old self, wincing and wilted in the 6th Avenue Grey's Papaya on a Monday morning in April, or November, or August, 1997 or 1998, all that and last week too, the understanding unendurable, neon-bright, unacceptable, vast: I'd never forgotten anything, and however severe the setbacks from dope, however severe the setbacks from booze, these substances themselves were not so potent after all. They had failed me, for here I was, awash in the acidic white foam of memory, ear deep in the sulfuric stew-pot of mortality because I'd chosen to hide (which may have worked, had I not changed my location so frequently), to fly low and live low and dream low, sometimes mere inches from past lives but always mindful of THE PRICE PAID For SELF-TRESPASS, until now, until tropical storm DEBBIE and Hurricane SANDY, events which had *not* been my idea, washed up one ghost after another, a mass grave come to squirming life, me smoking myself to death, yellow-brown fingers, brown-green bottles, when the sewers failed, when the great waters did not carry me out to sea, but raised up the poison at my core, the only miracle of my days gone by, such to make it all unkillable.

"One unified King Hell whole," I think to myself, as Cynthia parallel parks, gloating over a good spot. "Not a single stone unturned."

-182-

"God does not give us anything we cannot handle. Cynthia, you stood up for yourself, I was very impressed, you know. You must always stand up for yourself in this world. I'm very sorry that you have to find a new job, but change is a good thing. It reminds us that we are always growing, always changing. When my parents came here from Puerto Rico, they did not have nothing, you see? They barely, these two foolish people, very young people, the barely speak English! Wow, man, can you imagine just moving to, say, Germany – I was stationed there, too – just going to this new country, it could be *any* country, but German, German's a tough language but *any* language is, when you don't speak it, and you don't belong, that's a scary thing, I can't imagine it! Not as my father who... okay, so he gets a little place in the Bronx, he says, 'Okay, this is going to be a hard thing, a hard... years, 2 or 3 years, who knows how many years, but I've got a family now!'So... he just does it, he does...whatever he has to do. And I see Gene here, who is a very different sort of a person, and, do not be offended Gene, but I noticed all the, the *cuts*, the *scars* and, well, I don't know you from Adam, but is it fair to say that you are a person who finds, who faces difficulty, right? So maybe you look at the thing, whatever it is, you see things in another way from most people, but, hey, *Sinatra*, what did he say, he said, 'I gotta be me,' right? Born not even, just down the street he was born, 'I Gotta Be Me' he sang! So Gene has his problems, Cynthia has her problems, that's okay! I'm sitting here one foot in the grave, but we have to understand about what is bigger than life, we have our miseries and things for a *reason*, we move on from our bodies for a reason, and I don't preach, I don't mean to say, you believe, don't believe, I don't see how it gets to be bombing and killing over, that's just animals, *stupid* animals, they say it's craziness but I'll tell you, it ain't that they're nuts, the al-*Queda*, Tally-*ban*, whatever that's doing it, I don't buy this crap about craziness because I been around that, I got'em in my family, one of my kids is nuts, Gene. I'm sorry my friend but anybody who, yeah, okay, you're nuts buddy, alright, but listen, it's, what it comes down to is good sense, and smarts, you can be a fruitcake, fine, but you'd better not be no half-wit, you see what I'm trying to explain. And Cynthia, she is one of my very favorite *people* because this, I know right away, I met Cynthia and I say, '*there* is a *very special intelligence*.' I don't mean to *snoop* but, you don't always have... without *family*, okay, we don't all of us have that, so, Gene, maybe you are Cynthia's family through this time, and I mean this for both of you, maybe I'm saying it wrong or excuse me for being, for speaking from the *heart*, but God has a purpose for us, so we must have *respect*, and, you know I have a lot of *Jewish* friends, they say about the Jews that they are God's chosen people, hah hah hah, how about that? But I say, it's *us*, why, you know, why not us good, smart people who do our best not to cause pain in the world and who are alone in the world, and who go on, we *do* go on with life, you don't have a choice! The things I saw in combat, holy shit man, you kiddin me? And it's not what you think, the bodies and blood and guts, it's the craziness, the loony business that goes on, friends, you know, buddies of mine I *thought* were good guys... but you see all that fake shit go right out the window... I don't talk about it... but I see people better now, and also, since then, you know I became a haberdasher, I know the *outside* too, see? And that's *why*, people think *I'm* a nut being so well-trimmed, hey I'm *NEAT*, man! I take *great* care of my appearance, *always*! I'm very lucky to be here, we all are! And you must never let that escape you, get away from... how you... your *thinking* in how you *present* yourself, how you approach the other person, because this is always *war*, man! We're at *war*! Against the piss-heads! Scum-bums! Whack-a-doos! And the crooks! Shit man, what a... oh, what is *this*, Cynthia, this *pale* ale, I don't think I care for this, Gene my friend would you like to finish this? I know some people do not drink after another person but - oh, there you go. So what was that, that *ecstasy* you say sobered him up, yeah? If you say so! Oh, nicely done, my friend, *there* you go! I used to do *all* the dances, my father owned a dance hall in Brooklyn, and man we - no, maybe it was a different kind of dancing then - Cynthia, is he alright? Tell me that's not a real dance. Gene, sir, you're jut goofing on me. But we dressed *sharp* in those years, and that's no comment on *you*, Gene, or a *criticism*, you have your own style, but fashion, with young men, that used to be more of a thing I guess. Oh, hell no, you crazy, man? I'm too old for that stuff, I took a little coke, a little cocaine, that's always been around, we're talking the 50s, maybe the 60s a little bit, but this NEW stuff, what they call designer DRUGS, *de-signer*? I never understood that! I think of high-toned queens running around with measuring tape, hah hah hah. Because I'm friendly with these people, I don't, its not my THING, but who the hell they hurting? Maybe their folks, I guess. E-gads. But to each his own. Like this drug stuff, I don't know a, crack, from a Cracker Jacks. To each his own. Oh! You know what I'll *have*, here, is a... do they sell a...Heineken dark, goddamn that's a good beer, do they.... miss? Do you sell a beer called, ah, Heineken DARK, a DARK Heineken? Oh yes, that would be just fantastic. And a shot of RUM! *Brown* rum!"

Roaring through the tunnel, Cynthia passes me a large glassine bag of cocaine, saying, "You're sloshed, you're shitty," and I make a loud fuss over it saying, "Yeah... yeah, I'm real used to all *kinds* of dislocation," as if we were all in that very thought.

In the tube, all is expensive fallacy, all is excremental divination, all is heathen velocity, George no longer proper with his cane between his legs, Cynthia straining to stoicism in her transparent resolve, a step removed, listening and not-listening to us demanding the Stones, DIRTY Stones, "Street Fighting Man", *Cynthia, I'm going to* (this) *Cynthia, I'm going to* (that), the coke creeping down the back of my throat, post-nasal progression begun, down the back of my throat, post nasal progression begun, down the rabbit hole if I *let* the dark, if I *choose* the dark (moans like banshee cries from Hell) I hear myself saying, "LET'S FUCKING GET MARRIED."

-184-

There is a small human mass in front of Betty's when we roll by looking for a place to park and it's ten after nine: acceptable tardiness. If anyone knew who the fuck I was, they'd be astonished. For me, ten minutes late is two hours early.

"Cynthia, let me out here so I can carry the box in, can I-"

She stops and begins backing up but I've already opened the door causing us to narrowly avoid a scene of grinding metal, shattered plastic-glass-nerves-whatever against an expensive-looking black sports vehicle with me rather in the mood to cup and sup and genuflect before *anyone's* suck'ems, whether sagging or set firmly at the breastplate, or if disagreeable to any involved, negotiating the expanses of *other* areas, types of advances most *appropos* as the weather of the tox-box tonight returns to freezing I'll be a *funny* focus for the tightasses, the downtown demimonde, the Dantean rovers, the black leather elite, namedropping nihilists, Wooster St. tightasses and LaGuardia Place tightasses, sunless and sallow, jaded old Jews and wayward WASPs, the vampires of yesteryear, hipsters that time forgot.

But tits is tits and I can barely breathe so hypersexual now hoisting the 25 pound box out of the back Cynthia REALLY pissed BADLY rattled George still singing or *trying* to, not "Street Fighting Man" but one of the even more obvious ones and my box creating what would not otherwise be a delicate operation not if I hadn't gone so deep into CREEP right when I need to be FLUID with a benevolent wonderful ecstasy hard-on not at all like this crypt-keeper cocaine NUB oh for GOD's sake is that THE PRINCE?

I am NOT smiling and all the world is a rusty steak knife to me even my FRIENDS WHO LOVE ME beautiful FRIENDS Brynn and Lase OH WE GO WAAAAY BACK Lase's *wife* YEAH FUCK YOU TOO YOU TIGHTASS BITCH the infant daughter "Lase man, she's so fucking *precious* man" (WHY - *HOW* - DOES ANYONE BUY THIS SHIT FOR TWO SECONDS?) and my NAME IN THE WINDOW:

"TONIGHT GENE GREGORITS AS FEATURED IN VICE" with the "VICE" part done in magic marker, purple and black in a reasonable freehand imitation of the lame-o skateboard-graffiti-ish logo which is the main reason Vice remained merciful foreign to me for 20 years but, uh, thanks anyway.

One way and it better happen fast: nip it in the bud with WHISKEY. The bar is RELAXED and UPBEAT and CIVILIZED with Radiohead playing softly (*Kid A*) (*Metal Box Lite* but still good I guess Lainie left the CD at my place 02 03 she was a sweetie) (and BLOWJOBS) on the wall-mounted speakers I can FEEL people smiling at me now unable to RESPOND to NICE PEOPLE waylaid by BLACK HISTORY (no, not as in African-American) with LYDIA only blocks away after 15 years (GREAT TITS MY FAVORITE TITS) (WHAT IS THE SHE 60) (61) (LYDIA'S TITS FLOODING MY MIND IN 2001 CALLING THE LAPD ON MYSELF FOUR DAYS EVIL ON COKE) (OBLIVION) has she taken the stage yet a familiar voce behind me, calling me, famil-

"GENE YA FACKIN NUT-JOB, YA HEAH-"

I turn.

"Hello Richard."

"Double whiskey, Brynn!"

"I'm right-"

"I'm too COKED UP I NEED WOOO YOU KNOW WHAT I-"

"Gene."

"JIM BEAM I GUESS WOULD-"

"GENE I'M RIGHT HERE!"

"I'm SOR- I'm sorry! I'll be okay in a few minutes, just put it on the TAB and-"

"Okay, alright, EASY, Gene."

"This is RICHARD, Brynn, he flew me to Aus-TRALIA."

"IS THAT SO!"

The enormous Antipodean manchild extends a hand: the girl ignores it.

"Yes, we had the young man for a fortnight, it was good times with America's best writer, eh Gene?"

Brynn simply shakes her head and pours me half a tumbler of whiskey.

"Well," Richard continues, "I'm pleased to meet you, ah, BRYNN?"

She nods contemptuously, staring hard at my stomped roach misery show.

"Oh-kye, theen, very nice. She's rather your type, eh Gene?"

"Oh, for Christ's sake," Brynn spits. "I can't STAND this shit. Is he a cokehead too?"

I shrug my shoulders and drag Richard Wellington across the floor to the small stage where Cynthia and Lase have occupied a small table. The dozen or so patrons appear fixated on themselves and each other, and I avoid direct glances in any case, until the liquor puts me at ease.

"Gene, Macho..."

"You alright, Gene?"

"Hey... I..."

Lase and Cynthia grin at one another.

"Geney Bear? Anybody home?"

"I... I'm froze... I'm froze up..."

"Whatcha need, honey?"

"A BLOWJOB," I blurt. "I need... a fucking... SUCK-OFF."

Lase can only cackle, and Cynthia merely sighs, "Oh, for Christ's sake," taking me by the hand. "Lase, we'll be right back..."

-186-

Returning to the bar I find myself placated but now morbidly depressed; Cynthia says, "That guy Richard, I don't trust him. He's a snake."

"He's *my* snake," I say, without knowing why.

The music has been turned up and the lights turned down: it's 45 minutes past reading time and no one seems to notice. This is a relief, and I'm relieved to be left alone save for two formal introductions, faces that melt together, and I consider:

"Ecstasy. If I have to go on-"

"Brynn said 10, she wants you to read."

"Then give me some ecstasy. I'm not sure why I didn't think of it."

"Just get ready."

Finding me once again a corner by the stage, the ghosts continue to overlook me, all of them except for the Australian who demands explanations, who is getting foul receptions, who is nonetheless setting his little fires, baiting his little traps, digging his little foxholes because for me there are only jackals.

"So these Ceen-thia thing, wot the fack's *that* all about?"

"She's a friend."

"Can't she buy you a fackin pair of shoes?"

"I'm going back to Florida tomorrow morning."

"You only just got here, I thought-"

"Sam's still down there."

"OH *yew* and that bloody *cat*."

"Richard..."

"Yeah, yeah, alright. Look, Bec is heah, yew know that-"

"Absolutely not. Don't even-"

"Look mate, it told you side of the theengs and she's bloody heah, she's *beeging* me, every foiv fackin minutes, 'deed yah heah from Gene' and 'yew awlf teh see GENE', you know? Sheeze flown halfway around the world and *on* fackin *Creese*-mas-"

"No."

"Well, what do I tell the poor girl?"

"Don't fucking manipulate me."

"As a personal favor then."

"No."

"Then fackin call her at least, tell'er your *SAYLF.*"

"No."

"Well keen your Cynthia get us some coke at least?"

"N- yes."

"And it's good, is it?"

"Yeah, she's not going to take-"

"Yeah alright then. So she's like yer nanny, then?"

"Richard..."

"Yeah, alright, alright, fair enough. But I mean it's bloody obvious, innit, you're like a gigolo then, yeh?"

"Richard, PLEASE."

"Yeah okay, okay, fair enough Gene-O. Do I not geet an intro theen?"

"Yeah, but she won't like you."

"WHY THE FACK NOT? Yee know, I'm geetin' well shot of your manners, ya cunt. I facking pye f'yew, ta come eeks-perience my country, treat you like a brother, yer treated like a facking RUCK STAR, I even, I mean, who the fack do ya think yew-"

"She's got *really* good ecstasy, too, Richard, it's not you, it's Bec, I'm angry and hurt and I'm not changing my mind, okay?"

"Well, it's just a bit olb-viousyer can't be bloody bothered, mate, you're not only the only one with feelings."

"I just lost my home, and got beaten, and... I was eating out of garbage cans while you and Bec were hanging out with Lisa Carver, in LA-"

"Oh bullshit"

"It's true."

"Well Gene, m'boy, yew hive tageet it ta-getha, o-kye?"

"Do you want some ecstasy?"

"So this...wot is it, just a bit of a *drug* rely-tion-sheep then? Tearing up the scenery whull yer good friends bumble round Manhattan without a proper-"

"Richard-"

"Yeh righty O, no hard feelings, mate, just a little nosey, a little con-*cerned* though too, a wee bit *concerned* for the young genius, shoeless and fackin *mental* in the weentah, yeah? Lisa Carver, this whole week, well, bit ODD don't yew theenk not to even spike ta her, the ahttic'l bing such a seekcess 'n all, yeah?"

"If you knew the full extent of it, you'd back off. I'm lucky to be alive. Now I'm fucking begging YOU, drop it."

"Alright, fack's sake. She's gone anyway, back to the steeks. She's got that handicapped boy, doesn't she, but Gene, she really does theenk the bloody world of you."

"Great."

"Roity-o then. I dare not suppose you had any interest in heeding over to Bowery Ee-leektrik, yew mahst've herd Lydia Lunch is-"

"Are you really standing here doing this right now? For the HUNDREDTH TIME, *RICHARD*, I-"

"Oh fack yew, yeh facking-"

"Goodbye Richard."

"Cynthia, can I have some more ecstasy? Nine times... there is a link, you know, that explains the clichés, the patterns but... and the reasons don't change over time, they accumulate, how-and-why writers this, how-and-why writers that... oh yeah, turn it down... yeah, I'm starting, did you not... it's okay? Nine times out of ten, and his is why people cringe when they consider the whole thing of a reading, of experiencing a reading... I'm a writer, not a stand-up comedian, but the pressure is on, it is *applied*, by *you*, because it's about NOW NOW NOW... and precision, pre-CISE... out of MY haggard purple cunt comes THE HAPPY ACCIDENT... oh hush... I spent the day in Journal Square, I made some notes, about... riffing on the, well I have a new book coming out, and the problem is writing in a mental hospital with all that fecal matter, all that blood, make ya racist a guy said, motherfucker you're al-READY racist, but that's not...the problem is having bitten off more than a guy can chew who should be dead and it's when ya gonna die every time you... or I heard you were dead, I mean, I don't even have high blood pressure, so I feel good, I feel like, like vomiting all over, er, the next person cracks wise with me, so you wanna see my cock and balls? It's a grower not a shower, so for my next trick... shut up Cynthia, you can't write a good book in Journal Square, you can't write a book anywhere when ya... ya got... the book comes out lopsided, being about too many things, too many subtexts, or, uh, themes, none of 'em really go anywhere, and plot, you're KIDDING right, there's no PLOT, and... no I'm not... watch this, it's real coke, it's... I'll do that later... NOW NOW NOW... I'm shriveling up *INSIDE* too... and in the book with too many characters, you have... too many people walking around... hello everyone, I'm Gene, Brynn said it was okay, so I'll read, but I'm not a New Yorker anymore, all the pussy, I don't say that right, slight lisp, it was worse before my jaw was broken, but I cant say it, you know pussy pussy pussy and it's a stupid word anyway, CUNT is what I WUNT, but is it, maybe everyone is scared of their young selves, or of NYC, of, like when someone says THAT NEW YORK SHIT, I'm thinking, 'yeah, sloppy cab sex' or 'bathroom sex', you know, eatin the slit, eatin the clit OH BOY but I could never be in the moment when that was going on, all that greasy heathen puke New York hellraising shit, anyway... this is a digital... yeah, I'm going to bootleg myself, you can't be trusted to... fucking history has a million cracks, and if I leave you in charge I'll disappear down every one of 'em, you cocksuckers that never... so the book, it ends in an orgy, you ever try to write an apocalyptic orgy scene in jail... while your cat suffers a thousand miles away, and all your little cardboard cutout characters keep getting away from you, but... I am, I told you, I'm not *drinking* beer, I'm trying to be Lou Reed, can't you feel that good faggot energy? I bought 20 *cases* of beer, like, literally 20 cases, yes I did, it's back at the apartment in Jersey City, yeah... I've been living with this... disgraced woman, who... seduced me with oral sex... and hard drugs... I'll do another one, watch... blowjobs and coke, yeah, that's the... the line that I've been using... but it's true, and I *have* drugs for sale, you know, right now, see me after the show, tonight, I have cocaine for, I guess a hundred a gram, right? And... ecstasy for 20 bucks each, 1990s prices for 1990s, well, that's not a joke, this is 90s-style ecstasy, meaning it has heroin *and* meth, it's cut, or *made* with, uh... this, this modern stuff, what they call molly I never did get much out of, not yet, 2-3 times, I wouldn't spend money – oh George, we got George drunk, everybody meet George, a good friend – I'll say it right here, everybody is four people, there's only four people here, which for a punk kid would be fine, get up and make a dippy cunt out of himself but I'm almost 40 years old, and, uh, so one time back in Florida... it was a black woman, a prostitute, she said, 'oh you got one o'dem little WHITE BOY DICKS,' can you fucking believe that? I says to a girlfriend – huh? That's a stupid question. I'd like some gaffer tape or something, I need to tape the recorder to the mic so I can start reading... the new book is on this little recorder, this... little piece of Japanese shit. I mailed out the original, biting off more than you can chew in a Florida psych ward, my life ain't pretty, is it? Could I – just a piece of tape for this piece of shit, thank you... and some ecstasy... a guy said, 'Gene Gregorits is a real-life Bad Lieutenant,' which, I mean being back in the city... I have a few really good Abel Ferrara stories... say what you want but he's a *nice* guy... no, but I'll trade you some for Cialis, or no... that... wouldn't that... I'm not having sex tonight, it's impossible, mine's worn off, I'm too outside of myself... I'm in YOUR hands...yeah, I want this to sound like a Doors live album, but... very good... thank you Cynthia... what? Cynthia says there are books for sale, buy my books so this poor woman, she... yeah, okay... Dog-what? I am! *Dog Days* is my best book, it's... no, it really is a small miracle, a, what's... a masterpiece, a small masterpiece, so

I'll read from that, and... and nothing. Do I look okay? NO. I'm dirty. I'm just... dirty with it, with, you know, being back here, I went against god, or nature, or destiny, or... you know, FUNDAMENTAL WRONGNESS, I've always really appreciated that pairing of words, like... PROFOUNDLY DAMAGED, ah ha, heh, heh heh... my two big things since, since David Peace and *Xtrmntr* I guess are David Simon and big star, does that mean I'm mellowing? That's such a stupid world, I mean word, the world's not stupid, it's obscene, but this Lena Dunham shit... I rambled like this on the radio last time I was here, Lainie got me the radio, and I got stuck on some kind of brain-damaged Nazi thing, I don't know, but no more radio for me... but I'm dirty just being here, see, I might have gone to my grave never having to remember that... and there's Richard, lovely Richard Wellington, the Aussie Malcolm McLaren, whoa, not quite, haha... he came all the way from Australia to see me read from my year-old book which he said he's jealous of, he wishes that...well you fucking said, yes you did tell me... you... anyway... he flew me to, um, down under, to Melbourne and I'll tell you... let me attach this piece of shit... it was last summer, last August, I'd never been to Australia, and I'm an Ozzy-phile, and - wow, I didn't - I've never used that word before, so - but I *am*, so - okay now I *do* need a drink, my tongue is getting gummy, my mouth is sticky... just... a beer... so, I was, you can ask Richard, I was the JURY HEAD of this prestigal... pres... STIGE-us, prestigious, film festival, and this ought to have been covered, the beauty of the horror of it, because I didn't see they'd bought my ticket, my airfare from Tampa to Melbourne, round trip, 2,200 dollars, and I didn't have, I'd lost, my passport and holy shit was he pissed, and it's a big deal to me, right? Australia - finally I get invited to something good, a huge opportunity for me, but the *pass*port, okay? Turns out, well, I had a certain amount of money, maybe 600 dollars, and this 16 year old sociopath white trash Florida scumbag I'd taken off the street, I was training him to be my secretary, but he was a serial rapist, *18* years old, I'm sorry, but yeah, that... we had to share a bed, eating out of dumpsters to save money, while you fucking people are busy reading the new Jonathan Franzen... let me finish, see, it turns out that there are two ways to get a passport, and oh yeah, this is four days to... yeah, it takes... but, *unless* you expedite, you can... I'm gonna, hold on... Amy Winehouse does coke on stage... did... I really liked her, and the other one, Pete Doherty, I'm in the movie with Pete, but... so the regional office, I paid 500 bucks to get an expedited passport by overnight mail, but then that's like 70% solid, but then I find out there is a regional OFFICE, in Miami, the entire SOUTHEAST QUADRANT is, is, is rep... resented? By the Miami office, and PHYSICALLY you go in there with all your POINTS of evidence, that's like 90% solid so I get on the phone screaming for my money back, and I get it, and I go to fucking MIAMI, 2 days waiting for, to see if, my passport, it's not a hundred, and I got it, but I got stranded, on Miami beach, flat broke, letting drunk old women suck me off, then I gotta fake a psycho thing, a breakdown, to get a Greyhound back to St. Pete, this is the REAL writer shit the other writers never told you, and I got back, my chinny chin chin, in time to fly out of Tampa, with... my pants torn, so my balls are hanging out, my... I was literally holding my balls in, in customs, with a can of Fosters in the other hand but I got on the plane... I never saw any of the movies, fucking Richard kept giving me meth, but RICHARD I LOVE YOU AND I HAD A GREAT TIME, fucking relax, no this is better... the whole point is my former fiancée, because I fell in love, with Bec, Rebecca, you wouldn't think the Gene Gregorits's of the world actually get, or like, have, groupies... oh, you'd be surprised. But for an underground person, a cult artist, a cult writer, yeah... we HAVE'EM... but... well... heh heh... you get it. She's a fuckin' elephant. My sweetie. But *DON'T* I prefer the brain, goddamn RIGHT. And *wouldn't* you goddamn know, she's right in the neighborhood, after KNIFING ME IN THE BACK she wants to see me, yeah I'm a puke, don't I know it. I have moments, but a knife in the back is a knife in the back... it was all my fault, in the end, but... there are *rules*, being all mixed up with someone, vows and commitments, it's a shock, like, don't fucking CHEAT... god*damn.* I fucked up... anyway, I wont see Bec... Richard, that's not true...my big fear is that this coke will get on top of me again, you have to stay ahead of the drug train, run you right over... wind up like David Carradine, oh my GOD... the stuff is good, the coke's good, the E's good... Richard, why don't you call Bec, tell Bec... no, I'm gonna tell stories, I'm... no,, what I've been travelling with is *Beyond Good and Evil*, which is *not* babble, or masturbation as some people tell me, it's good writing, and if you understand, maybe it takes understanding *Beyond Good and Evil* to understand why we can't have another Lou Reed, or another... another Alex Chilton or another... putrid people, is, that someone is grotesque, or... it's all about that now, appearance... art, the art of something... well, I'm talking about the center, and we've got to get better at seeing *that*, because if *we* don't, aren't WE, meaning the weird ones, smart ones, bo-hoes. Hostess bo-HOES Hostess BO-HOs... but we're all lodged up a.... a.... Dave Eggers' asshole, don't fucking tell me limpdick indie rock faggoty bastards like that are where it's at, so LISTEN, how about it, I'm gonna read from, I'm, I'll read NIETSCHZE, yeah, I have it in my coat, Cynthia, will you get my coat, get my... in my side pocket, it's... oh, wow, anyone else pissed at me, come on... in the...the POCKET! Cynthia, for 3 weeks, has... 5 weeks? She's been on about, what was it, SANDY, Hurricane SANDY and no one ever suffered in history like the New Yorkers during SANDY, and... there, did ya hear that, y'all catch that? Y'all, it's Florida, my mom says I got Florida fleas, laid down with dogs, with, with Florida dogs...did y'all hear Cynthia? SOUR GRAPES, she says. She also thinks I'm gay. I'm a jealous closet queen, and I'm fucking living in exile, because you tightasses don't understand, which is what you'd have me believe, right? C'mon. You're too smart for that, you know better, but you'd rather keep the fucking bar as low as possible. No, it's... see, you have no idea what you're saying. It's romantic what I'm doing here, anyone can stand up and audition for your snotty applause, fuck you, and, what up here, what? Both, up here to read and, I'm GONNA fucking read! But no, I'm talking about Florida, which is, it's the most romantic thing I've ever done, turning my back on all you rich faggots and living on the fucking beach with the scum of the earth. No, no, because you'd never have the balls you jackass. Here we go, *explaining* the obvious, explaining the obvious, explaining the obvious... yeah, goodbye, goodbye, I'm leaving tomorrow, goodbye... I wonder if they read the *Vice* article, OH that, yeah, let's talk about *that*, the little fuckin' piece of shit *Vice* article that just came out... oh, that coke is catching up, I *am* a little queer, anyone wanna suck some dick? Hey listen, if a guy in wheelchair shows up, that's TEDDY and I'll have to run out the back, I'll have to cut this short... will you guys protect me, will someone... yeah, I guess so, crippled? *Something's* wrong with him, he says he's, I mean he didn't say KILL but you know, that's what he meant...you sleep with a guy's girlfriend...no, this was before... no, she was HIS at the time, but also he could, he had his legs, he could *walk*, yeah... what was her name... anyway, Teddy says 'me and the boys.' ME AND THE BOYS! Are they...hahaha... that's a good question... maybe, what a thought, like, like I would have to *live* here again to get an audience, why? I don't need a bunch of rubberneckers to WRITE the fucking... no, I need Florida inbreds, and blown-out junkie women, in the mental hospital who... yeah, what they do is sit right close to me when I'm writing this thing out in Crayola marker, and ask to hold hands, it's this cheesy 'hold my hand' or 'ya wanna hold hands?' thing, they all do it, these junkie piece of shit welfare mothers... no, do NOT make better lovers... Neil's *wrong*... well, they eventually get released and *I* eventually get released, and she, the horror Florida thing, collapsed face, just... TRASH, human birth- destroyed trash, just... it's like all these 9 month gestations occurred like, the barbarians at, not *at* the gates, but in-*side*, looting and pillaging town square, dropping the buildings, raping the skyline, and they burst THROUGH the gates alright but from the INSIDE, leaving this broke-down HOST of a thing, a crust, a husk, an INTERNAL RAPE, a backwards rape, and this hollowed out feedbag of, a human feedbag, would you believe I give these women my phone number, well, it's only a Skype number but I get home and they *call* it! So - no no, I've never, like, gone *out* - no, they need money with, OH and you know what I tell them? I tell them about Sam, my cat Sam, I say, I tell them I need to buy cat food, like, not 'I'm broke' but 'I'm spending it all on the cat, goodbye!' That's... in a nutshell... that's Florida, yeah... I'm a beach head, I've established a BEACH HEAD, like at Normandy, like, 'WE WILL TAKE THE HEAT,' it's, I suppose, it's dangerous... shut up Cynthia give me some ecstasy Cynthia lets go to Florida Cynthia... time to get serious, *Beyond Good and Evil*... that's the tragedy of *being* a philosopher, I think, is that you unravel yourself, your... you have nothing left but ideas and you are not writing for the sake of bickering but to introduce a NEW whatever, and no one has the BALLS to BECOME the ideas, to actualize them.... you gotta talk it to death. 'At least I'm moving.' I always go back to, 'At least I'm MOVING' from New York Dolls, but I can't think of the song but, like, you aren't GOOD ENOUGH for these books of mine, you ain't got what I call for, or it's, like, you *can* do it but, you won't... you *can* bring it, but why bother and you can't anyway, I've touched it, in Florida, the raw thing, the living beauty of it, and having it, I HAVE IT, like the internal landscape of the point of all this hipster shit, the original decadence thing and you... look for a tear in the fabric, and set your fingers in it, real tight, and tear it open, it's like, getting to the *real* bigger picture, beyond money or words or anything, you gotta be INSIDE it, you tear it down and say, hey man, THIS is how bad it is, is so we're going to go in here with crowbars and control-burn it the way they're doing in Detroit, all the abandoned houses, they had to do it that way, they did the estimates, like HERE'S how bad it is, so what's it gonna take? Bringing New York back, bringing the dick back, the brain back, the dignity back, the life of... instead of you... working against the tide, you drop down, you, you get a face full of dick, get to WORK. You know, because otherwise fuck your poor little endangered routine, poor little writer, poor little writer... the writing is poor, that's why, no one who was any good would settle, they'd choose self-imposed exile and, but no, you little pussies, it's just to PAY TO PLAY, PAY TO PLAY, PAY TO PLAY... establish a BEACH HEAD... but you gotta pull your heads out first, remember what's TRUE, what's SEXY, all of you whole generation of spoiled brainless pukes with your heads lodged up Lena Dunham's ratty little pussy, no WAY that beast, that fucking COW... I'm sorry... but no way she has a good looking pussy... it's certainly shrunk MY dick all to hell, I know what does it, it's radiation from computers, from LAPTOP computers, that explains a lot of it... you really don't see how that's cultural suicide, because it's *spiritual* suicide? Because let me tell you something, 'trending' is not a word... fucking, WOW what letdowns they all turned out to be, just, I'm gonna have to blow my brains out soon...

it's by design, on BOTH sides, encroaching roaches... but goddamn if I had 20 grand I could blast you roaches out of my kitchen, long enough... long enough to make a Reuben and drink a beer, FUCK, it's THAT BAD... smart PROSE, HOT SHIT, real HOT shit, BLACK NOVELS, no more BLACK NOVELS, no HOT BLACK ANYTHING... Peter Laughner... but can you imagine Peter Laughner trying to pick up Lena Fucking Dunham in a *bar*? She's a fucking retard... Noah Baumbach is a fucking retard... no one cares about your childhood... yeah, I'll read, I'll read as soon as you shut the fuck up... I'm not susceptible to that navel-gazing shit, I'm not fucking 12... yeah, leave... I'll read, you *want* me to read? But admit it though, don't all your mentally retarded social media playthings for Baby Huey retards, I mean HAVEN'T they, like, ruined everything? What is a Chan Marshall? Chan? Kids is kids I guess. I like the Stones... dirty Stones, 71 72 Stones... we used to get into these coke scenes, my cock was *okay* then, okay? BETTER than okay, but it would be *Exile* or *Sticky Fingers* on repeat, laying on the floor for three days, snorting coke and sucking each other off... that was life... do you guys even fuck? I'll have sex with anyone, and, y'know, Brooklyn was the best, you could never get anyone to come see you in BROOKLYN, not even, not even Williamsburg, but the thing was, if you did, if you DID get someone, if they DID come out, you *know* they're down to screw, so... but... I tried to get Lydia out to, to Havermeyer Street... Nick Zedd lived across the street, so... when I told her that, the whole thing was shot to hell... so it was just pussy eating in this kitchen... that was 20 years ago, I haven't seen her since... since... and she's playing tonight, just down... right over across Houston, we should all go over there, how's that for a stunt? READ, GENE! REEEEED! *You* read! *LOU* Reed! I'm remembering... rock stars are the least hip of everybody. Lydia wasn't like that, but she's got the jealousy, they all do. I've never had it, but Cynthia thinks, you're an idiot, honey. I'll take the rent, just the rent. I got welfare for the rest. They say there's no accounting for taste but that's complete hogshit... loot at the 90s, and grunge, and how AWFUL it all was... taste is accountable, it's rooted in intelligence which 95% of people do not have... and the rare 5%, that's... they're all New Yorkers, right? Wow. Self-deluded assholes. Oh fuck you. Racist? Who said anything about niggers? How do you – well, YOU brought it up! Listen, you sexless, you fuckin, art-hole YUPPIE, wow, listen, spend a night in central booking, BALTIMORE... I did! You bet! All your hypocrite nigger shit came pouring out of you like dirty dishwasher, tightass... fucking New York douche bags. BYE! It's not my *job* to turn you on. Pack animal. Grow your hair out, you look like death. The real world sucks, but hiding in Greenwich Village for 30 years just makes you a broken little dumbcunt. But how do *YOU* know I'm a racist? It's a big subject, who cares how someone feels about big subjects, that's human nature to put your stamp on the machine, and then pretend it's really yours, and then pretend it's the best machine when you've got nothing to do with anything and it's the ONLY machine! You're being TRICKED into thinking you amount to something – look-look-look – go ahead. I'll do some coke...yeah, the devil is in the details honey, and you're still talking, OH I'd better throw some whiskey on this coke... five minutes is more than enough, Cynthia, 5 minutes is fine, tell Brynn I'm sorry I'M SORRY BRYNN... but, the good, the little angels are in the details too... yeah, you are, you exist in the world nicely with the other boys and girls. You're a fucking sheep... OH OH OH, since it's all about this yapping pocket-rat little yap, little Chihuahua yap you're stuck in about RACIST – HE IS A *RACIST* MAN – let's talk about a pair of real Nazi pieces of shit, Boyd Rice and that horsefaced cow Lisa Carver, uh, YEAH... ya got all kinds of stigmas attached to... and Lena Dunham too... anything THAT FUCKING WHITE... poor thing, ya can't help but feel sorry for her, but no... this icky little, yeah I know, ICKY... but it is! Woody Allen has the pedophile thing, then with Roman Polanski it's the rape thing, with me it's the, hehhehheh, I don't even KNOW anymore, and with Lisa Carver, it's the sexually abused racist noodlehead thing... she's half a simpleton, at least Boyd Rice is sharp... but we're talking about cowards when we talk about these people... *Vice* magazine, there's some DEFINITELY something gone – off, something ugly behind that, but I wouldn't waste my time, I read something about GG Allin on *Vice* once, something about... or no, by Jim Goad, yeah... that's it! Not on my radar... I guess Bec's not coming, that's.... that's good... so I'm heartbroken by it, by sissification, and noodlehead punk rock Nazis, but the soul of what's left of our civilization, or our lineage of outsider novelists anyway, what part of civilization besides poets and writers and artists is worth saving? We don't need plumbing, we don't need an assembly line, we don't need – you know what we NEED, is our OUTLAW PAPAS... more of that good faggot energy. More Burroughs, more Celine, more smart, uh, FELLERS like Joe Heller, oooh, yeah, who has it... Denis Johnson's okay, but... I don't know, could you read *Tree of Smoke*? I couldn't. But I read something today, made me understand better... so transcribe THIS, transcribe *this* shit, and, like, take it to the next level.

-188-

GG: Whether it be hedonism, pessimism, utilitarianism, or eudaemonism, all those modes of THINKING which measure the worth of things according to *pleasure* and *pain*, that is, according to accompanying circumstances and secondary considerations, are plausible models of thought and naïvetés, which everyone conscious of CREATIVE powers and an artist's CONSCIENCE will look down upon with scorn, though not without sympathy. Sympathy for you! To be sure, that is not sympathy as you understand it: it is not sympathy for social "distress," for "society" with its sick and misfortuned, for the hereditarily VICIOUS and defective who lie on the ground around us; still less is it sympathy for the grumbling, vexed, revolutionary slave-classes who strive for power – they call it "freedom." OUR sympathy is a loftier and further-sighted sympathy: we see how MAN dwarfs himself, how *YOU* dwarf him! And there are moments when we view YOUR sympathy with an indescribable anguish, when we resist it – when we regard your seriousness as more dangerous than any kind of levity. You want, if possible – and there is not a more foolish IF POSSIBLE – TO DO AWAY WITH SUFFERING: and we? It really seems that WE would rather have it increased and made worse than it has ever been! Well-being, as you understand it – it is certainly not a goal; it seems to us an END; a condition which at once renders man ludicrous and contemptible – and makes his destruction DESIRABLE! The discipline of suffering, of GREAT suffering – know ye not that it is only THIS discipline that has produced all the elevations of humanity hitherto? The tension of soul in misfortune which communicates to it its energy, its shuddering view of rack and ruin, its inventiveness and bravely in undergoing, enduring, interpreting and exploiting misfortune, and whatever depth, mystery, disguise, spirit, artifice, or greatness has been bestowed upon the soul – has it not been bestowed through suffering, through discipline of great SUFFERING? In man, CREATURE and CREATOR are united: in man, there is not only matter, shred, excesses, clay, mire, folly, chaos; but there is also the creator, the sculptor, the hardness of the hammer, divinity of the spectator and the seventh day – do ye understand this contrast? And that YOUR sympathy for the "creature in man" applies to that which has to be fashioned, bruised, forged, stretched, roasted, annealed, refined – to that which must necessarily SUFFER, and IS MEANT to suffer? And our sympathy – do ye not understand what our REVERSE sympathy applies to, when it resists YOUR sympathy as the worst of all pampering and enervation? So it is sympathy AGAINST sympathy! (TAPE CUTS)

-189-

A glowering Brynn, spinning to catch me as I near the door, it's an awkward exit but I will not stop: "Now WAIT, Gene, you *owe* me fif-"

Walking west on Houston in a lather of misery, no perspective, no remove, body and mind debased and so now weightless and blind, a molten mass of sexual panic/ existential shock/anti-social inertia, succumbing to unmentionable solutions WHEN –

"Gene?"

We're standing at a noisy corner I know well but it doesn't come to me.

I'm staring into her eyes, on the tip of my tongue, but it doesn't come to me.

"Fiona"

"Fuck! OF COURSE," and then the corner comes to me, Houston and Orchard where... the pet shop, with the Madagascar hissing cockroaches in the window, $8.95 each, I always thought nine bucks a suspiciously *low* price for *any* exotic pet, even a cockroach, of *any* size, if it hisses and is from Madagascar, and these boys were no fucking joke, you couldn't hear them hissing through the glass though, gotta go inside for that and I never did, did I, why didn't I just – passing that window 5, 8, 10 times a week why didn't I just –

"You wanna have sex with me?"

That's what Fiona says, Fiona the dead-eyed junkie (one eye *literally* dead) from '97 the rawbone year when...

They were always there. I expected always – 5, 8, 10 times a week for 3.3 years – to find them gone, the humor never lost on me, however humorless I was otherwise, the joke of course being rather wonderful to me in the spring- summer-fall and even the winter when my toes would be numb in my Chuck Taylors at Orchard and Houston, that loveless pit of befouled tundra and arrogant Midwestern transplants, had to be them, *had* to be. Because – it's so obvious:

Sell a *cockroach*, even one that recites Shakespeare and is from Thailand to a *New Yorker*? And the horror to understand, groping and kissing Fiona by the same window, now full of iPhones, that I never got the joke at all, there *was* no joke, that it was something else, something presently beyond my reach, and wisely, so *very* wisely, I let it go. The fuckers are finally gone, anyhow.

Someone else's problem.

Someone *else's* joke, to get or *not* get.

Fiona is sinfully ugly and her breath is terrible.

I let it go.

En route, Fiona, who used to fuck nearly everyone(including Nick Zedd, GG Allin, and – if the rumor was true – Joel Rifkin) says, mushmouthed on heroin, "I thought I'd see you there."

"Why would you think that? Anyone who knows anything about me and Lydia knows we don't talk. We haven't talked in a hundred years. Hey, let's do it over here."

"No, I'm c-cold. Where's your *thing* at?"

"Betty's."

"The last time I saw you was at a Lydia show. The one on Bleecker."

"Club Life. You got me in trouble."

"With Lydia?"

"No, with the bartender. You made me ask him for a spoon."

"No I didn't."

"Oh, yes you did. You told me to tell him it was for an ice cream."

"For real?"

"Yeah, I wasn't even drunk. I remember!"

"Are you all coked up? You sound *weird*."

"Cynthia's got it, she-"

"Who's *Cynthia?*"

"Do you remember, when, how way back then nobody could ever spell Bleecker right? They always spelled it BLEEK, B-L-E-E-K, no C."

"Bleeker Street. That's how you sp-"

"Spell Bleecker."

"B-L-E-E-K-E-R."

"Never mind."

"Can you get me some coke?"

"I *have* some. How many people were at Lydia's show?"

"A lot."

"She always does well in New York. And..."

"The hometown thing."

"I guess. No one buys the records anymore, but they line up for a concert. I've never understood that."

"Hmm. My hair was long and black at Life."

"I remember. You were with this chick-"

"Gabby."

"She was horrible."

"She's dead."

"Huh. I'm sorry."

"It's a good life if you don't weaken."

"Huh?"

"That's what she always said."

"Well, she weakened all at once, so-"

"*What?* She fucking died of AIDS, Gene."

"I'm sorry."

"But why would you say-"

"I figured it was an overdose."

"That's kind of insanely judgmental. Wow."

"Sorry. I like the new hair."

(*Fucking junkies*, I'm thinking. *So easy to forget there's a person behind that brown dope cloud.*)

"So what was there, like 200 people?"

"What?"

"At Lydia's show."

"I don't know. It was sold out."

"You're fucking kidding."

"I mean, it wasn't a great show, but she looked...I mean, for age, she looks good. She's really thin."

"I only had, like... I can't get a dozen people."

"But the *Vice* thing, I didn't know you were here but I saw the *Vice* thing..."

"It's a good life, if you don't weaken."

"Hah."

-193-

Back at Betty's I see that George the Sad Dancing Bear has developed quite a crush on Brynn with my face pressed tight against one of the tiny panes the bottom-most pane just out of sight beneath the tealights of a wobbly table full of mixed drink glasses (empty) and the velvet curtains' shadows heavy with a dread I know will only worsen much like the risk of discovery in such a compromising position   (jacking off at the movies) so I swallow a dry swallow around the ache in my jaw and enter the bar head down Fiona sulking (simpering) at my side and greet the holdovers.

-194-

"They bought half the books," Cynthia reports while scanning the zomboid woman-child in a mohair sweater and mini-skirt with a curiosity intended to appear innocent. I've re-entered a SOURED space and despite a healed atmosphere (it's as if I've been forgotten) there is a feeling of being tacked to a board, or propped up on a desiccation table, and I'm surprised when Brynn summons me over to her at the end of the bar with a curled finger and hair in her narrowed eyes.

"Lame," she says.

I only shrug.

264

"Old hat, lame, pretentious, annoying, gross, sad, shall I go on?"

"Did Lase leave?"

"Wouldn't you have? His wife *hates* you. And that big fat guy, the um..."

"Richard."

"There was a girl, a chubby...the one you were up there babbling about?"

"No shit."

"I believe *so*, stud!"

"Bec?"

"They were all gone before you even finished. She was laughing at you. Everybody was."

"It couldn't have been. Did she look like Sofia Coppola, kind of?"

"*Fat* Sofia Coppola, maybe."

"Oh yeah, yeah. That's Bec. That's definitely her."

"You poor crazy man."

"Erm."

"I gotta serve drinks, get lost."

"I found Fiona on the street."

"Good for you. BYE!"

The music is loud again and the evening has found its own name. Fiona is feigning narcolepsy in one far corner while George and Cynthia are dancing with beer bottles in their hands and slopping beer on themselves. George's overcoat has vanished, and his jacket and officer's shirt are unbuttoned, the medals somehow re-imagined as costume jewelry, the entire uniform merely a costume now; Brynn is watching me over the heads of her customers, and puts down a fifth mid-pour to point at George. Her next motion is a curled finger swiped across her own throat: *Get'im OUTTA HERE.*

The delicate wooden frames of the front windows seem no match for the returned cold and the cabs gliding by remind me of dead time, dead bodies, dead words, dead spaces like all that which has been forgotten, and I wonder how, or when, I seized upon the idea of resisting, or first felt the impulse *to* resist, this notion which we *all* have to some extent, of posterity. Or of the *idea* of posterity being a kind of *shelter*, like this bar, like Brynn's good looks, like the booze, all things to be left behind, not soon, not one day when we've made our peace, made our fortunes, made our minds up, made children, made sense of our enemies or *to* our enemies, NO. It's not *LIKE* that. It's now, the bitch sting of NOW and I wonder how I ever managed to hold on to anything at all, or why I'm still fighting.

But then!

Ah HAH!

I'm a DEMON!

NOW.

In Motor City Bar it is the license plates on the wall and the filthy old car seats as sofas, the steering wheels for door handles – it's like 1997 never went away – and Cynthia is dancing with Fiona while George, having returned to a stoic pose, looks on from behind a table.

"Watch him," Cynthia has to shout over the music, and I do, until I bump into a literary young man, a lurking young man fresh out of the bitter night, and with the bar screaming to life, with a hundred pop-slop LIFESTYLE GURUS plying the juke box with trash rock, I lure this trenchcoated spectre to our table where George now sleeps a Cheshire-grinned kind of half-sleep, perhaps expecting a frosty bundle of Brynn to sidle up at any second(it was the only way to get him out of there) and amazingly, he still has his cane. I take this as a sign of my irreproachable altruism. (In anyone else's care, he'd have lost his cane.)

The spectre is Ben Rogers, and he has big sarcastic boyish eyes, wounded and deceitful and seductive eyes, he is British and we get into downing pints in a British fashion, each pretending to host the session during his respective turn at the bar, while the night expands, lukewarm ale gaining on cold powder, the way it will if you so will it. (swill it.)

Gene Gregorits: This...it's digital, the microphone...it has a microphone but it's built *in*, so you have to speak *into* it *here*.

Ben Rogers: *That's* not how Lester Bangs -

Gene Gregorits: *Fuck* Lester Bangs! He's dead! He-

BR: (laughs) My *brother* – listen, Gene! I gave that fucking book, I think it was the same, it was called the same thing-

GG: The *Psychotic Reactions* thing?

BR: *And Carburetor Dung, Psychotic Reactions and Carburetor Dung*, yeah, I gave it to my brother and like, now, he wants all the records too, like, *every* fucking record, and then, no, fucking hell, *that's* not enough because, like, he doesn't understand the record and I have to explain the fucking record to him.

GG: That's *good*, that's *good!* I wish I could get someone to, like, I can't...my advice is worthless, apparently.

BR: Fucking Bangs, he really got you looking for stuff. Van Morrison...

GG: Passion is out of fashion!

BR: That's true, yeah. Passion is out of fashion. Like, you could do something with that.(laughs)

GG: You know FAB Press right?

BR: FAB Press, F-A-B?

GG: Yeah, the British publisher, they do those big full-color coffee table books about lesbian vampire movies, and-

BR: Oh them, yeah, yeah, they did your thing, yeah?

GG: Yeah, and it sold, worldwide it sold about 75 copies. I mean, nobody gives a *fuck* about anything anymore, unless it's-

BR: Fuck, man. Yeah. It's really like –

GG: It's fucking grim. And it keeps getting worse.

BR: Gene, man, who's that bird with the lazy eye, the...I hope I'm not being rude, but...this is a really excellent coke, man...

GG: You wanna meet Fiona?

BR: Fiona!

(TAPE CUTS)

GG:-it's not as easy as that but in essence it *is* that, like, it all goes to the same place and you're – I mean, you *should*, anyway – have to oversee the clashes that develop, like when -

BR: I understand exactly what that is, that thing.

GG: *Ideological* clashes! Like when one book from your youth that maybe means more to you than it has any reason to, sentimental reasons, when that book – for a lot of people, that would be *The Catcher in the Rye*, or *Tropic of Cancer*, or *On the Road*, or you know, it could be a Bret Ellis thing-

BR: I *know* those people, they're the same people who, aw, who was that horrible *American* cunt who pissed off Oprah, the – he looks like a computer technician, the-

GG: Yeah, but Bret's more interesting I think, I mean, maybe not the writing, but... I had dinner with him last year.

BR: With Bret Easton Ellis?

GG: Yeah, yeah. In Beverly Hills!

BR: Oooooh!

GG: Oooooh! He had steak tartare.

BR: And what did *you* have?

GG: I had STEAK TARTARE!

BR: Ooooooh!

GG: Oooooooooh! But listen! We should do a magazine together, because -

BR: That'd be fucking brilliant, yeah-

GG: But listen! That old book, Ellis, or Naked Lunch, or whatever, colliding for whatever reason, with something *new* that maybe is far *more* valuable and which you just haven't learned to embrace yet, its function, like, in the larger scope of-

BR: Well, it's stature, it's the stature of it, that you give it, yeah – where does the great book stand this year, where will it be with you in *five* years, yeah... and that's *30s thinking*, y'know, I mean...

GG: As you get older, yeah, you see the framework, the

framework comes into focus, and it takes a lot of shitting things out, and re-absorbing them, like... I kinda look forward to knowing there's a big re-structuring phase coming up, a uh-

BR: A *shake-up!*

GG: Wheels are turning, Frank!

BR: Here's to your *fuck*, Frank.

GG: Ben, you're so *fuckin* suave. No, *rakish. Rakish* is what you are.

BR: Fucking hell. Gene man, I'm so glad I bumped into you. You fucking, just wow, man, it's crazy.

GG: Nobody would read our magazine, but we should do it. You can - hey, you can come to the beach, make it a holiday.

BR: Oh, I'd love to.

GG: But I wouldn't use a recorder like this for the magazine, I only trust analog cassette tape for that. With this piece of shit, like, with an old cassette machine, you can SEE the wheels turning, the red light is on, you know if you're in good shape or not. This little piece of shit, well, it's another reason not to bother. I used to do soundchecks, I'd say, "horrible...horrible...horrible..."

BR: Take a break! Have a quick crap.

GG: Have a what?

BR: Do you have Kit Kat bars in America?

GG: Oh yeah, yeah.Of course. Snickers. Kit Kat. Um...Twix bars, and-

BR: Well in the UK, they say, "have a KwikKrap," they're called KwikKraps.

GG: I get it.

(TAPE CUTS)

GG: Oh *man.* Now I, yeah, that was it, when Selby died. That was the last time I talk to Lydia. Because-

BR: I didn't know, I don't think it got to us for-

GG: Lydia and Selby were *close*, you know, or maybe they weren't, but he was fond of Lydia, she said, like he kidded her you know-

BR: Well that's my, that fucking book, that's burned into me, like, I can't imagine a time in my life where, like, when *Last Exit to Brooklyn* ceased to be like, dangerous, or, to have that kind of horrific power over me-

GG: Scattah! You don't-

BR: You don't pay my carfare! Fucking hell, Gene!

GG: Goddamn Lefty Frizzell records!

BR: Wow. See, I *remember* that. *All* that. To this day I couldn't tell you, like, I've never *heard* a Lefty Frizzell record, but I remember that. As a part of this other world. This fucking horrible *dream* I had.

GG; Lydia says it was *Last Exit* for her, like, she got *Last Exit* and that was it. She - I think she read it when she was 12. See, that's a

good thing. Now, see, 50 years ago a kid, it wasn't about *corruption*, it was education, it was illumination. Now, a 12-year-old kid isn't shoplifting a book, it's – they're just looking at-

BR: Fucking god knows what-

GG: On the Internet, yeah.

BR: Like, I've *got* a child, yeah? So it's a tough one. But we're split up, me and the wife so...but yeah...

GG: What else? *Metal Box...*

BR: That's another one! Fucking indestructible. *Last Exit*, Céline, *Metal Box-*

GG: I'm an anglophile. I've adopted *cunt* as an insult.

BR: Hah, that's *good*, you should *all* do.

GG: But I know all of the British kitchen sink films. I love *Room at the Top*.

BR: Oh but that's aged so fucking terribly.

GG: I don't think it has. What else?

BR: Alan Moore.

GG: Which Alan Moore?

BR: All of it, but... *From Hell*, obviously.

GG: *Swamp Thing*, but yeah, *From Hell*. Stone Roses.

BR: Some of that stuff is EERIE, like *eerily* good, you know?

GG: Jim Thompson.

BR: Bad Lieutenant.

GG: I just interviewed... remember the chick in the car, that, Harvey Keitel makes her watch, well, he makes her-

BR: Yeah, yeah. You talked to her?

GG: *Necropolitan Life* is the name of the book, yeah, it's an occult portrait of New York, the... like, the demonic aspect of a certain time, late 60s to late 80s, early 90s. Son of Sam and-

BR: And Abel Ferrara. Fuck, man. You're doing that?

GG: It's done. I just have to edit the fucker. Hey the SOURCE: "The idea has been burning in my head for *some time*."

BR: (Laughing) Jesus. Yeah. "What's moonlighting?"

GG: The ending doesn't sit right with me, though. Never did.

BR: No, it's perfect, you kidding? Just perfect. They nailed it. That's a permanent one, *Texas Chain Saw* is permanent, Jesus and Mary Chain, *all* the Velvet Underground stuff, *Naked*, *Notes of a Dirty Old Man*, all the Terry Southern stuff-

GG: - the 70s stuff, the Crumb 70s stuff-

BR: Yeah, but *all* Crumb is great, isn't it?

GG: Ok, you're right. *Get Carter*.

BR: *Get Carter* is fucking permanent. So what about this *Fiona*?

"British. That's the good thing about New York, all the Brits," Fiona tries to purr: it reaches us as a shout. "What part are you from?"

"I'm from *Dor*-set, the *West* country," Ben smiles, delighted by the girl's subnormal energy. "Thomas *Hardy* country," he adds with more than a trace of smart-ass. Fiona loses her reaction to runaway facial spasms and takes Ben's hand in an affectedly somnambulant fashion. They're gone in a flash and I'm face to face with Laura the mortician, a ghoulish latter-day Laura in a 19th century funeral dress stirring a vodka cranberry in a Tom Collins glass with black fishnet hands. When she's sure it's me and begins to speak, I see her again on Avenue A and Houston, from behind, the cold is brutal and I catch up with her, she's wearing a long black peacoat her skin so pure white with all that urban moonglow she looked like a marble faun, exactly like that, in 1997, and I swear on my soul I groveled thusly:"Don't you like me even a little?"(Or maybe I said "love". Did I fucking say "love"?)(But consider Saint Céline and his ballet dancers.) (Or, more recently, James Ellroy and Dana Delaney.)

I shake the encounter off like a wave of nausea and retreat into the conspicuously vacant unisex toilet. The same me going round and round, round and round, round and round, too many years, causing a kind of... dementia. Earthbound.

I am freshly powdered and panicked trying to take down a Marlboro in 3 drags and look natural doing it amongst the crude iron scaffolding outside Motor City, a freshly re-animated and brown rum'd George beside me ("This is the only drink for *me*, Mr. Gene", he announces. "Rum!") when Cynthia summons us both in to meet the Duchess and her man, who have a "party suite" at the Face Hotel. Sirens, other city sounds, and the moment-to-moment sense of carnage and catastrophe, of obscenity, the gleefulness of clever young boys and girls, those not yet humbled.

The ocean, its life, FLORIDA – all aberrant philosophizing rendered powerless, trite, redundant, petulant. All systems, all threats, all inbound/outbound malice: neutralized, like the acid in my blood made alkaline, until... the thefts... began and...I should be quite happy to stop this heart of mine dead tonight.

Rip is 6 of swarthy middle-aged Eurotrash in a sleazoid black pompadour and a sleazoid black suit that says it all, that tells the same old story. The morbid glitz and Luciferian ennui he seeks for free-fall is the product of Bryan Ferry's cocaine nights translated to pop hagiography, another man's masturbatory yearning for *more yearning* and his little boy soul being fully aware of this, I see this and let him know I see this, this two very different sorts of fires burning in hell.

Sasha, being slightly taller than her husband, which is to say slightly taller than myself, appears at once attainable and elegant in a low-cut blue black satin dress, she has a smart face, a resigned face. She's accepted middle age *and* gluttony, and it's that *cockiness* that beguiles... she's not a typically overcompensating hedonist, and I'd guess that what I've observed is just as clear to Cynthia. The problem, of course, is Cynthia's complete and utter *lack* of elegance, that and her unwillingness to *see* this. Sasha is not merely unrepentant, not merely resilient, not merely particular in that feline manner, but...tender? It's certainly there: have I provoked a shift? I always, *always* know, within 20 seconds.

Sasha is *druggy-luscious* and the alcoholic puffiness of her face kick-starts the machinery - old, old, old - installed in my soul by Lydia when I was so young that the problem grew to become one of an Oedipal nature, and to think that it's still about *mother*, to think that it remains an issue of a deliberate maternal re-assignation: or even a *mis-assignation*, to think of the notion that *one must go where one is led* and that I once believed I'd be led to *home*, a *new* home, to think that it's no longer even *about* sex because if I am now truly *infernal*, well...I can only hope that she stinks of cigarettes, when the time comes.

-200-

"There is no hurry," Rip says, tapping a blue glassine bag of yellowish methamphetamine into the long-stemmed glass pipe but within minutes we are standing in the grim sub-zero of Ludlow Street and I'm telling a story about having once run from Motor City to Mars Bar in an attempt to blah blah blah, "sssh," Cynthia tells me, because Rip and Sasha have their cell phones synchronized in the cold lining up a drug deal for the Face Hotel which Cynthia is unreasonably enamored of, and "you'll see" she keeps saying as Ben and Fiona drool into one another's necks and mouths causing little white puffs and George singing "Time Is On My Side" with all the words wrong, until a cab stops for us all, I say to Cynthia, "won't we get a parking ticket?" — she says, "SHHHHHHHHH."

-201-

In the cab, Rip and Cynthia shove dollar bills at the cabbie to change the radio station…we wind up with Modern English, "I Melt With You" and I'll be goddamned if we aren't all unified, if only for a moment, by that. Fiona releases meth smoke in tiny cream-colored puffs, we tell the driver it's…whatever.

-202-

The Face stretches 40 narrow stories into the light-polluted sky two blocks north of the Empire State Building, and the cabbie is demanding more money upon realizing that he will be required to navigate its underground parking garage. In the front sent, George has taken to unendurable snoring and this time he will *not* be moved. The backseat orgy is forced to untangle itself (Cynthia and Rip, Fiona and Rip, Rip and Ben, Ben and Cynthia, Cynthia and Fiona) (Sasha and I, at opposite ends, remains chaste although not without objections from the others) when the car is approached by two Middle Eastern security guards, grinning at us as Rip and Sasha give them their room and license plate numbers. "The man is a cripple," Rip says, and that is followed by one of Cynthia's insidious bursts of fake cheer in which she attempts to assuage her conscience by correcting Rip with some banal, self-conscious Jersey-ism or other. I am obsessed beyond guilt or consequence with getting Sasha all to myself immediately.

When we arrive at the couple's vehicle, a black BMW sedan, Rip is babbling ecstatically about possibly fucking Fiona and I'm most likely correct in predicting an entire litany of sexual psychosis but the cabbie wants us out of the car. Neither Rip nor Ben nor a combination of them will support the bearlike bulk of old George: Sasha and I get him to a standing position while the back seat is cleared, and then the rest is easy enough. Not even a small head-on-door collision is sufficient to rouse old George in the greenish fluorescent light. I'm caught by a notion of Sasha and I reminiscing about her blue black satin dress and the night we gave up our coats to the gone old man, in New York, at the rock 'n' roll hotel, the night we met, and I am stung by it.

-203-

A New Year's Eve party is roaring in the high ceilinged lobby of the Face and it's just well-lit enough for me to be embarrassed by my dirty jeans and all, but also late enough that no one is sober enough to care. I'm mad for excuses to extricate myself from the group, from *any* and *all* groups now that my world revolves around whatever's between Sasha's legs.

Ben and Fiona have become fairly conjoined as if in living advertisement for more sex partners, and it occurs to me that the dozens of others present are only too happy to welcome them to their celebrations; then dread returns. Without Fiona to distract Rip I may not get Sasha, and it's entirely possible – even probable – that we are all to some extent engineering degenerate designs upon Sasha, which absolutely *mortifies* me, *shatters* me, set to apocalyptic horrors and self-loathing and the dwarfing assurance that I'll be alone until the end, a night like this or even *this* night but a smile from Sasha and I forget all that nonsense, jolts of pervo-megawatt rattling my bones to the marrow when Rip drops a wad of what I'm sure are hundred dollar bills on his meth connect right at the bar and I lean into Sasha, say "I never once saw it when I lived here, I guess it's a big thing in New York now" and her classy pout dissipates with the disappointment at my having said something so trivial. "I love your dress," is my only consolation but at least she laughs. "You don't remember me," she says into my ear, melting my brain. "I met you in Denmark, forever ago. You don't remember."

"No."

"That's okay. You were with Lydia, it was very nice. You were nice."

Rip buys expensive whiskies for everyone and we nod our heads to the music; a strange pall settling despite the speed, if only a few minutes, until Sasha herself says the magic words: "Fuck these people, what a boring fucking party. Let's go to the room." She winks at me on the way to the elevator.

-204-

The Face is black-carpeted hallways, plain white walls lit by plain neon tubes and decorated with framed black and white portraits of Patti Smith, Joey Ramone, John Lennon, Jim Morrison, Iggy Stooge, David Bowie, Jonny Cash, Sid Vicious, Leonard Cohen, Bob Dylan, Bruce Springsteen, Jimi Hendrix, Keith Richards, Keith Moon, Alice Cooper, Debbie Harry, ad infini.

Every 20 feet we pass a black Ikea desk on which has been secured a Vaio laptop computer. Some of them also have typewriters, and I stop at one, hit a key. Non-functional.

At room 2129, we stop and Rip produces a leopard print "FACE NYC" keycard to open the lacquered black door.

-205-

The room is pure synthetic, not just rock but RAWK: more leopard print, mounted guitars (on wall and floor), black shag carpets, turntable (non-functional), glass coffee table, Union Jack-covered light switch panels, fluorescent pink lampshades, red vinyl chairs, and one *fully* functional black leather 4-seater directly in front of a 60-inch wall-mounted plasma television (also functional).

The ceiling is mirrored, and Fiona is the first to strip down. Amusingly, it's Rip she services first. Ben is frozen in the toxic thrall of the scene. Cynthia fiddles with the goddamn TV, looking for radio, for music, and I pull Sasha to me, my hands on her waist, my mouth on her neck, finding it disagreeable, the energy wrong, the scene having gone entirely to seed in my eyes, or maybe it's a ploy but when Cynthia's banal murmurs collide with the rest of it (framed record sleeves, framed newspaper articles, framed concert tickets, another typewriter) and Ben begins fellating Rip (Fiona: "That's so fucking hot."), patting myself down and say, "Shit, did I lose my cigarettes?"

Glancing at Rip, now fully enmeshed in Fiona *and* Ben, Sasha says, "It's a non-smoking room."

Having settled upon a glam-rock station playing only the most obvious glam-rock, Cynthia purses her lips for an imaginary photographer and approaches the floor-scene, a skirtless Fiona lowering herself upon Rip's huge, terrible erection as Ben fires up the pipe. On the coffee table, next to a copy of *Rolling Stone's Big Book of Rock*, lays a pink glassine bag about the size of a sugar packet, fairly bulging with high grade ice.

"I'll just go in the hall."

"It's a non-smoking *hotel*, Gene," Sasha says, disgusted.

"I'll right back."

-206-

In the hallway I wait five minutes, another five, I wait 15 minutes, for Sasha, sending out coded signals, for Sasha, the door clicks, I spin around: no one. I smell her, spin: no one. I feel her, spin: no one. Her fullness and heat now a physical presence in the hall, conjuring gory details: lipstick prints, swollen red lips, black heels, clouds of cigarette smoke and (funny to look back) sweat and dope and three, four, five kinds of musk, an ungroomed chubby cunt sopping, flooding me with *her* when we're midway through a weekend, and "is it okay?" I whisper, "Is there a center to us?"

The response is muffled, through the lacquered black door: "Can you hear us?"

(Right in the hall?)

(Yes.)

(Can you hear them?)

(It's a rock'n'roll hotel.)

(You're so beautiful. You...)

(My hair only curls this way only when we're fucking, is it, it must be your sweat, something in your sweat, speed maybe, or-)

(Kiss me. Can you come in me?)

(Your eyes are huge, your eyes are like-)
(Open your legs for me.)
(There's nothing out there, it's just-)
(On the floor?)
(Yes.)
(The chubby part, that section between the stocking and your panties-)
(Here?)
(Yes.)
(Can you feel me?)
(Yes.)
(Turn around.)
(Don't hide.)
(Turn around.)
(It's only squirrels, put the phone down, you're-)
(Can you hear us?)
(There's someone downstairs-)
(Can you hear us?)
(I don't know how to be separate.)
(We're *not*. We're-)
(What was THAT?)
(Is there a center to us?)
(Can you hear that?)
(I've got to check the doors.)
(I fucking love you, Gene)
(The chubby part, the-)
(Here?)
(Yes.)
(Do you hear-)
(-the nightbirds-)
(Yes.)
(Are you ready?)
(Yes.)
(Are you afraid?)
(I'm afraid.)
(Oh my baby...)
(Yes.)

-207-

I make it to the Face's rooftop, seeing flashes of things around corners, glimpses of boom mikes and smiling young men in black t-shirts not missing the tiniest eruption of sound, my footfalls spelling out my visions in full color diagrams, but there are fewer places to hide all the way up, with the Empire State Building in full control of the sky, its tapered pinnacle the real McCoy, its blinking antennae uncompromising and steady in the dread island smog, the light-polluted center of the world in its witching hour.

Lydia opens herself to me, our animal sounds rising against an electric dawn.

-208-

Atomic blast of clarity calling up shivers in that subzero void when I locate the black BMW, pulling my well-judged thermal top off my face and back onto my body, now exposed to the cameras saying "George?" but in that moment I am not certain I didn't somehow cross over into the tight frozen underground garage of *another* building because the lights are flickering and the smell reminds me of the Jersey City Marriott or was that the Radisson and what if we killed old George, if he's still in there will he call me a bastard or will he refuse to even look at me stiff and frozen terminal old George last seen undone and dancing like a sad old circus bear at a Lower East Side DESIGNER DIVE with high class Eurotrash, the goths that time forgot, OLD money and "it's just a couple of THRILL seekers, Captain" but maybe old George will believe that we just GOT here that he only *just* passed out – and all the while am I still standing there feeling MOORED to the fellatio and bestial grants the drug STINK of Room 2129 a TENSION drawing me back as if physically shoved or as if TETHERED TO IT on an electric strap still telling myself with a wad of bills in my back pocket "we'll get old George seen to" but the car's back seat is empty.

-209-

The concrete maze begins to spin and accelerates until I locate the control center with five six seven dark men in cop jackets with guns and radios with Pinkerton badges and I have to tell them, "*I'm* a Pinkerton," which is a FACT, "I've got a CLEAN record with you guys."

"Sir?"

"*I'm* a Pinkerton, I joined up in nineteen ninety-"

I *feel* the blood drops before I see them.

"Sir!"

The Pinkerton rushes into his booth for a tissue, and when I take it he says, "Oh, *now* I remember you guys, you're the *swingers*."

"Heh... heh..."

(Spinning *faster* now.)

"I don't to see an ambulance here today, you guys take it easy, ok?"

The Pinkerton takes me four rows over, as I'm bleeding through the clumped tissue, and points to a *different* black BMW, I thank the unfazed man, adding "I really *am* a Pinkerton" alone again to face the real scene, moment of truth in the gray light revealing an open passenger door bringing visions of George dead between the cars until crazy lonely old George materializes from behind a pillar in the next row in an auditory fog of alarm burps and door slaps, he's zipping himself up: "Oh GENE, I'm so happy to see you, my friend," but the pervo-overdose rages on and, "I'm so sorry, George, I'm so fucking sorry," I say, "give me five minutes," I say, "a bottle of whisky to put the fire out," I say, "go ahead and have a cigarette, my friend. I'm going to the deli."

"What the hell, Gene. You know?"

George takes a Marlboro from my pack.

"Would you get me...if they have it, could I have some coffee and pie?"

"What kind?"

"Oh, any kind. I like any kind of pie. Peach is good, if they have it."

-210-

The lobby is busy and no one pays us any mind.

George doesn't understand why I drink the pint of Jim Bean so quickly with six warm Heinekens, but he's as purely noble and loving as any man I've ever known when he taps my knee and tell me, "You guys drink too much. But you're young. That's alright, I guess. I had my day, you know, drinking too much."

He puts the fire out, like that. And the very *last* thing he says to me, the two of us sunk deep into that Italian leather sofa in the Face's lobby at checkout time is, "Meth? Hell, they gave that stuff to fighter pilots in World War II."

His cab pulling up to the curb through the enormous lobby windows is a bracing thing. He winks at me and is gone and I taste the tears before I feel them.

(FADE OUT)

I'm all the time aware it's reality and not literature I'm engaged in... at times I am living at the tips of my senses.

Alexander Trocchi
(Fiend)
(1925 – 1984)

"Get OUT! Get OUT of my CAR!"

That's what the voice says and I suspect has *been* saying for *some* time when I recognize the crate of *Odd Couple* memorabilia and the broken zippers and the drug packets, the ancient rowhomes above me, it is Cynthia's gray hatchback, and it is another day on Van Horn Street, and it is the beginning of 2013 in New Jersey.

"Get OUT or I swear to GOD I'll smash your fucking computer, Gene - GET! OUT!"

Her voice echoes up and down dirty Van Horn and I *see* her round old face gone mad, mad eyes, mad mouth, mad hair, mad woman, and that's when I know she has not slept, that I should not have slept either, the word flashes - "*blackout*" - just as the contents of Cynthia's arms become known to me.

It is the Monastrell brain.

I pull myself out of the little car and to my feet. The woman retreats into the middle of Van Horn. I follow with my palms up: "Don't do it."

My feet submerged in oily slush, I take steps, baby steps: "Don't do it."

"I didn't want to FUCK those people, I did it for *YOU*," the woman howls, almost knocking me over with the black metal box which I take in my arms like my own bastard child, as blue sparks explode through my optic nerves each time the woman slaps me, I hug my brain tightly standing in all that dirty water the woman's fingernails in my scalp and the open hand slaps growing harder the mad woman so mad she can't speak through her psychotic crying jag crying, primal crying, bestial grunting and "I probably have *AIDS* you rotten motherfucker, you awful, awful person and now I have no *FRIENDS*, I'm HOMELESS now and I'm BROKE, and *YOU* did this, this is YOU, everything they say about you, ALL of it, it's TRUE, it's TRUE, it's TRUE..."

"Cynthia, you have amphetamine psychosis, let me help you get to sleep."

"FUCK you, FUCK you, FUCK you! RAPIST! FAGGOT!"

"Cynthia-"

And then she's got the car key gripped like a shiv and *baps* me with it, the first one is a mild surprise, but then the 2nd 3rd 4th *bap*, she's *bapping* me how they say, what they called it in Detroit when you use your keys like that, to stab someone in the face, the thin tight skin of my forehead bursting apart against my skull, BAP! BAP! BAP!

I squeeze my own bastard child, tighter, tighter, thinking of the water, the water and the oil, the oil and the ice, the blood falling like shower spray off my nose my chin my lips, and the woman retreating behind her own ropes of snot and saliva, it's early afternoon and the neighbors are out, Dominicans and Salvadorans, Puerto Ricans and Mexicans, and I'm running, I've got my center and I'm running... through the bloody snow...

Exiting a nameless barroom I am weightless and not so much at a loss as several steps removed, I walk and walk allowing brief idle wonderment at the city after midnight, and before long it is Van Horn, and the darkness there, no Honda hatchback in sight, and I round the corner with panic creeping in at the edges: past the laundromat, the bodega, the Chinese takeout, all gated up like military strongholds, and the silence, not even a police siren in the cage-lined streets, the eerie change of the stoplight from green to red, without traffic, a shiver, a small warmth, a small face: I find my phone, dial.

"We're sleeping Gene."

"Is Sammy okay?"

"Sam's fine. When you coming home?"

"Soon."

And then I find myself trying its front doors, letting my fingers explore the rust-eaten searing-cold chain and padlock, the dirt-caked notices, the ancient hand-carved oak.

A shiver, then.

A pop, another shiver.

(Laughter?) (Night birds?)

"We go forth without mercy."

I rummage through my pockets, finding a cigarette, the last cigarette.

Toss the box.

I light my cigarette and place the Monastrell brain behind one of the NO TRESSPASSING signs.

I descend the half dozen stairs, hop the chain link fence, and stroll quietly beneath the cathedral's gaping stone arch side windows.

A fluttering, a tapping...

(Laughter?) (Night birds?)

I stare up at the backs of the houses opposite: families, mostly, sleeping off their own excesses, dump as apes.

And then I turn, standing, rigid obsessed, something brought back from hell, rigid, unreasoning, mechanical, at best a half-received prayer, my *own*, decades late, but I have patience, a sweetness, a hunger, and there it is again, weak, sick, but I wait for it, I stand and shiver and sweat until I see it, until I'm *sure* I see it, until it happens again – wait... wait... *wait for it...*

THERE.

(A flash of light.)

Paterra County Jail
Sex Predator Unit
January 2016

FADE IN (Written May 2015)
Teenage Fanclub - "Alcoholiday"
Neil Young - "I'm the Ocean"

SHIPWRECK (Written June-August 2015)
The Kills - "Future Starts Slow"
Alejandro Escovedo - "Bottom of the World"
The Dum Dum Girls - "I'm Coming Down"
The Brian Jonestown Massacre - "Hide and Seek"
Aerosmith - "What It Takes"
Guster - "On the Ocean"
Flamin' Groovies - "Absolutely Sweet Marie"
The Weirdos - "Life of Crime"
The Beach Boys - "Wouldn't It Be Nice"
Paul Westerberg - "My Daydream"
Rolling Stones - "Torn & Frayed"
Primal Scream - "Space Blues #2"

GIGOLO (written September - November 2015)
John Doe - "Garden State"
Black Angels - "Bloodhounds On My Trail"
Dream Syndicate - "Ain't Living Long Like This"
Alejandro Esovedo - "Anchor"
Big Star - "Kizzamee"
Morphine - "The Night"
Lou Reed - "Kill Yr Sons"
Big Star - "O Dana"
The Pogues - "White City"
The Records - "Starry Eyes"
Wyldlfe - "City of Inbreds"
Big Star - "Jesus Christ"
The Schramms - "In The Mirror"
Green On Red - "Time Ain't Nothing"

NECROPOLIS NOW / FADE OUT (written December 2015)
Rolling Stones - "Stealing My Heart"
Dream Syndicate - "Let It Rain"
Pere Ubu - "Final Solution"
Blondie - "X Offender"
Richard and Linda Thompson - "The Wall of Death"
X - "Sex & Dying in High Society"
The Germs - "Lion's Share"
Modern English - "I Melt With You"
GG Allin - "Eat You Out"

Oasis - "Helter Skelter"
Iggy Pop and James Williamson - "Beyond the Law"
Steve Wynn - "What Comes After"
Bruce Springsteen - "Radio Nowhere"

www.ingramcontent.com/pod-product-compliance
Lightning Source LLC
Chambersburg PA
CBHW020436030726
47495CB00006B/1830